I LEAVE IT UP TO YOU

I LEAVE IT UP TO YOU

A NOVEL

JINWOO CHONG

BALLANTINE BOOKS
NEW YORK

Published in the United States by Ballantine Books, an imprint of Random House, a division of Penguin Random House LLC, New York.

BALLANTINE BOOKS & colophon are registered trademarks of Penguin Random House LLC.

LIBRARY OF CONGRESS CATALOGING-IN-PUBLICATION DATA
Names: Chong, Jinwoo, author.
Title: I leave it up to you : a novel / Jinwoo Chong.
Description: First edition. | New York : Ballantine Books, 2025.
Identifiers: LCCN 2024039023 (print) | LCCN 2024039024 (ebook) |
ISBN 9780593727058 (hardcover ; acid-free paper) |
ISBN 9780593727065 (ebook)
Subjects: LCGFT: Novels.
Classification: LCC PS3603.H662 I33 2025 (print) |
LCC PS3603.H662 (ebook) | DDC 813/.6—dc23/eng/20240826
LC record available at https://lccn.loc.gov/2024039023
LC ebook record available at https://lccn.loc.gov/2024039024
International edition ISBN 978-0-593-98353-9

Printed in the United States of America on acid-free paper

randomhousebooks.com

9 8 7 6 5 4 3 2 1

First Edition

Book design by Susan Turner

For Bram

I LEAVE IT UP TO YOU

TWENTY-THREE MONTHS LATER

1

WHAT THE ACTUAL FUCK, MAN?

WAKING UP IS AN EASY THING TO DO. TO BE ASLEEP, THEN NOT. TO BE A mind out there in the dark with no ground underneath, no legs or arms, no chest, no blood pumping in rhythmic bursts up my neck, no body at all, no hands, no hair or eyes, no ass or dick. Yes, sir, just your eyeless, handless, assless, dickless self just hanging out there in space for forever until suddenly, you're not. Because *suddenly* is in fact the best word I can think of to describe it. Suddenly, SUD-DENLY, with all the absolute cosmic consequence in the universe, a strange and terrifying surprise takes place and a thing that was not ever supposed to happen—happens. So quietly that nothing about it feels extraordinary at all. You wake up. You being me. Me being somebody, just some guy who in a singular moment has found him-self all at once awake and sore in the neck. Clenching my fists shut, opening my eyes, two of them on my face exactly where I remembered them to be. Seeing another someone sitting there in front of me, composed of bold lines as though drawn on fresh white printer paper with a king-size Sharpie. Giant blue eyes—two of them—staring back at me. Like a tether, a spark from him to me, into my face, my neck, down my chest and arms, to the bottoms of my toes buried under warm, scratchy fibers. I hear a thought click slowly into place, my first thought in a very, very long time: that in the beginning, there was me, and also him.

"Ren?"

I didn't hear my own voice but felt my throat vibrate. His eyes were fixed on me and had been all this time. He didn't move. Maybe he hadn't heard me. I tried to arrange my perception of him; parts—the eyes, the shoulders, the chest—were swimming around, jagged and refracted as if underwater. I noticed then that he was covered, head to toe, in crisp blue fabric. A cap over his hair, a surgical mask over his face. There was a cord of neck muscle pushing against his skin. Ren looked upset. I tried to tell him everything was fine, to calm down, since I had a lot to ask him: Where was I? Why did my entire body feel like vibrating air? Like Jell-O? Like it was broken in every conceivable place and hastily put back together again by someone with only a loose understanding of the human body and which of its parts fit into each other? He looked really, really upset, more so by the second.

"Ren—" I tried to say again, opening my mouth, making the shape of his name with my lips. I said my husband's name a lot, punctuating my existence with it as though I had a nervous tic. I felt safe when I said his name. He always appeared, full and warm, when I said it, moved ever so slightly in his sleep when I whispered it to him in our bed. I was in the middle of saying it again when I felt my throat strain against something sharp and hard. It occurred to me that there were not—as I'd assumed—just us two things within this new universe I'd woken up in. Among the great many things that were now making their presence known—a harsh overhead light, a dull warmth gathered at the small of my back—was the grip end of a canoe oar or a golf club that, for reasons unknown, I'd been deep-throating in my sleep. I made a soft choking noise, testing it out again—"Ren?"—and felt the canoe oar strain against the right side of my esophagus, scraping soft tissue. I brought my hand up toward my neck, continuing to choke. I tried to stay calm. I didn't want to freak him out. But Ren's eyes had gone as wide as plates.

"Oh *fuck*—" he said loudly, in a rough and booming voice that took me a second—two—to realize I did not recognize. "Oh holy motherfucking *fuck!*"

A pause, while I continued to choke. Then, gathering his breath, the person sitting in front of me, who was not in fact my husband, said this: "This really isn't supposed to happen."

I tried to say something along the lines of "What a fucking weird thing to say" but gagged before my lips could form the words. Not-Ren's voice was deep and flat, clear like audio recorded on an expensive podcasting microphone and filtered straight into my ears through noise-canceling headphones. I'd never heard a voice so sharp and high-def in my entire life; his was a knife that had cut away all the fuzz around the world, making it new and whole. He had a wonderful voice. There was a lot to admire about a voice like that, despite its obvious distress, despite its not being my husband's and currently not trying very hard to tell me where my husband even was. The broomstick in my throat was starting to make me tear up. Weakly, I pointed at it, asking him for help.

"Jack—" He was suddenly a lot closer than before, one hand steady around my neck. I caught a glimpse of dark, curly hair poking up over the collar of his shirt while he reached for something above my head. "Just stay calm. Can you do that, Jack? It's a breathing tube. You've been intubated—"

I remembered that Jack was my name. Jack, plus a big, obnoxious *Jr.* that has been appended since birth, not only on my birth certificate, but also within normal conversation. Jack Jr., Jack Jr. Hey, look over there, it's Jack Jr. just fucking around minding his own business and being an exemplary citizen and shit. Hey, Jack Jr.!

Why's the sky blue, Jack Jr.? Oh, that's easy, it has something to do with the refractory properties of the atmosphere, which scatters blue wavelengths of light more than any other on the spectrum of visible radiation. Happy? Need anything else? Not a thing, Jack Jr., you're a real stand-up guy, Jack Jr.

The existence of a Jack Jr., naturally, implies the existence of a Jack Sr., himself the face that bloomed inside my head when my thoughts came to rest on my family, an act that itself was as infrequent an occurrence as humanly possible. Umma used to call me Jack Jr. for convenience, I could only assume. It seemed that between myself and Appa, there were simply too many variables, too many arcs of potent, chaos-making destructive interference she would be entertaining by calling either of us Just Jack. The solution, of course, was to label us Jack Jr. and Jack Sr. Which stuck at birth and would forevermore. So, it was cute. Every guy I'd ever dated had commented at some point or another on just how cute it was—Ren included—and I found myself agreeing at least half the time, depending on how well the relationship seemed to be going and just how much I was going to forgive said guy—Ren included—for mentioning my family. I didn't like when people mentioned my family. I hadn't thought of my parents in a long time.

"Jr.," I tried to say, but only managed to gag some more.

He was holding my head up at an angle, angling my face up at the ceiling while sticking his thick fingers into my mouth. He was telling me something, either to keep breathing or to stop breathing, and I couldn't completely tell so I tried to do both. After another few seconds, I felt a heaving, gurgling scrape in the back of my throat, far deeper than I've ever been aware of in my lifetime (even in college), then made a noise halfway between a burp and a cough as the offending probe exited my larynx. The flexible plastic tube, fixed at the end with a fun little yellow inflatable cuff that—I don't know—kept it secure inside me, trailed spit across my face while he pulled it out of my mouth. I was gasping for air, realizing now that I hadn't been breathing much this entire time. The room was coming into sharper view: a window spanning almost the entire wall, through which a black city was silhouetted faintly against orange and green moonlight. There was noise off to my right; he was ducking his head out the door and yelling. I tried to ignore him. I felt small. The universe, as it turned out, was a lot bigger than I'd been led to believe thus far, and it was stressing me out. I turned my head as far as it would go, trying to bury my face in something, a pillow maybe, but the light was too bright.

"Please, please just stop yelling," I said, a hoarse sound from the back of my throat, screwing my eyes shut.

He turned around, and I noticed for the first time that on top of the surgical mask over his face and skullcap over his head, he was wearing a plastic shield that looked like half of a dog cone pointed down over his forehead. His clothes were pale blue and looked like paper.

"What are you doing?"

"What am I doing?" I said. "I'm lying here trying to sleep. Not to mention almost choking to death on whatever it is you just pulled out of me. What the fuck even was that?"

"A tube, endotracheal tube, it's a breathing tube," he said, chopping his words up, staring at me, apparently terrified to find I could speak words.

"Okay. Well, thank you for that. Can you find my husband? Do you know where he is?"

"I'm trying to get you a doctor," he said, his big booming voice beginning to waver more as something—it couldn't have been me, since I was just existing here in front of him—continued to freak him the fuck out. "This . . . this is just—holy fuck. You're really—you're really not supposed to be—"

"Doctor," I repeated slowly. I sat up and saw that I was lying in one of those motor beds with plastic handles on all sides. It looked like the luxury kind that could curl into a ball with you in it. "Why are you looking for a doctor?"

I'd almost forgotten the questions I was waiting to ask him, since he seemed to need more help than me. I needed to speak to Ren. Ren would be able to tell me in no uncertain terms what exactly I was doing here, in this room I'd never seen before, in a luxury motor bed ball-curler with four humming metal boxes hooked into the wall and to various wires taped to my arms and chest. I moved, uncomfortable, and felt the taped wires strain against my skin. Did this guy know Ren? Or maybe just know where he was and why he wasn't here with me?

The hallway outside, for all his shouting, had remained quiet and dark. He turned back to me.

"Jack," not-Ren said, finally.

"Jr.," I said, "Jack Jr. It's Jack Jr."

He blinked, saying nothing. It wasn't getting any easier to take my social cues from the only part of his face I could see.

"How do you know my name?" I asked him. "What am I doing here?"

"Listen, Jack, if you'd just—"

He'd put his hand on my arm but I wrenched it away, upsetting some of my wires. One of the machines gave a loud beep in protest.

"I know what you can do," I started slowly. The temperature of my head had risen a few degrees and was making me shake. "You can get my husband, and tell him where I am, or better yet, tell me where he is."

Not-Ren's eyes kept darting into different corners of the room, around my head.

"Will you do that?"

He took a deep breath, abnormally patient. "I will do everything you want me to do, Jack, I just need to get your doctor in here first."

He was being nice at least. I felt bad for tearing my arm away from him. I tried to soften up. He still looked like he was having a cardiac episode.

"So, you're not a doctor."

"I'm your nurse," he said, speaking slowly, enunciating each word like he was reading from a book to a toddler. "Your—one of your nurses. I have you Tuesday, Friday, and Saturday nights."

"You're a male nurse? Is that real?"

"Of course it's—" He stopped himself. Again he turned around, searching the hallway behind us. "I—we—I really need to get your doctor in here. This—holy fuck."

It didn't matter much anymore, the words *holy fuck,* conveying enormous, unfathomable heights of surprise, since he'd said it ten times already. Was it a thing he just liked to say? A catchphrase? Did real living people have catchphrases? I thought that maybe they did. Joan Rivers used to carry the end of each punch line with a thrust of her fist and the words *it was JUST*—. All it took was a beat, something for her to say a split second before the laughs, the slim moment in which the audience absorbed the fact that she'd just finished a story that ended with the implication that Newt Gingrich had a tampon up his ass. Ren and I loved watching her stand-up. There were hours of it online, along with the documentaries and TV specials. We would've killed to see a show of hers live.

Meanwhile, I had a couple of concrete theories about the *holy fuck*s. Number one: I was, in fact, dead. And be it a shift change or improper training among the angels in heaven, or, more likely, the demons in hell, somebody—the guy standing in front of me, obviously—had supremely fucked the check-in process. Number two: I had become an X-File and woken up in somebody else's body. Somebody else named Jack who was not even a Jr., which would explain why he was getting my name wrong—somebody old and frail and confined to a motor bed in the hospital, which felt the most logical, seeing as I was, at this moment in time, lying in a motor bed in what I could only imagine was a hospital. I was only twenty-eight. I was nowhere near death. The picture of health. I exercised regularly, I ate vegetables, I didn't even smoke, not even as a teenager at a prom after-party or something. I didn't even go to my prom. Yes, my back hurt sometimes when I slept wrong, but it was because I never sat up straight.

It was my own fault. Bad posture alone didn't make a person feel as fucked as I currently felt, certainly not enough to land me in a motor bed in the hospital. I screwed my eyes shut, shaking my head. *Hospital.* Thinking coherent thoughts felt a little like trying to juggle a pack of angry puppies that didn't want to be anywhere near me, at which point the only way to keep my mind clear was to repeat what I knew, continuously. I was in a hospital. I was listing reasons why I was in a hospital. Theory number four—no, number three: I was tripping balls on the floor of a bathroom somewhere in the Village, in which case I should be mad at Ren for making me go out, because I knew myself enough to know that none of this was my idea. Ren liked going out. Ren and his wild public school teacher friends liked procuring drugs of an illicit nature and doing them in the bathroom because it made them feel alive, but didn't like to do it so often as to have no other choice but to consider it a genuine and integral part of their lives, which it wasn't. Somehow, he had roped me into his schemes last night and the glass powder his friend's cousin's dealer had cut into the coke had put me in the hospital, surely. Go figure! First time I ever do coke and I wind up in the hospital with a tube down my throat and an imperiled male nurse getting sweatier by the minute.

I pictured Ren's face, bobbing up and down in the blackness. Ren must have been so worried about me. If I was in the hospital, he wasn't far away. Looking for something comforting, I settled on a memory that made me happy, that autumn weekend we'd taken a trip, nothing big, rented a house up in the valley, followed the river all the way up in a rental car. I'd taken a week off work. He owed me for that one. School had let out for something inexplicable called Fall Break a week before Halloween and he'd stopped coaching the soccer team the last year because the away trips were starting to encroach upon his sanity. For the first time in his working life, he actually had time off that wasn't in the summer. It was the closest thing to camping either of us would ever do, and by the first night, I was already out of bug spray. No, it was nice. I wasn't trying to sound ungrateful. This happened all the time. Ren often mistook my meaning and I often mistook his. It was something that typically happened at least a few times throughout the day when two people found the opposite things funny, the single exception being the exquisite vintage comedy of seventies-era Joan Rivers on VHS. I wished I could watch some right now. How much longer was I going to be here?

My nurse had been saying something this whole time but had only just stopped, noticing I wasn't listening.

"I'm sorry," I said, "you were defending your nursehood to me and I wasn't listening. Ben Stiller was in a movie about this. About male nurses. It's called *Nurse Gaylord*."

"I know the movie, and no, it's not called that."

"Pretty sure." I shrugged. Then, a beat later, "Am I high?"

"Propofol. It was keeping you asleep."

He pointed blankly to the tube sticking out of my wrist, which snaked up my shoulder and joined a bushy mess of wires twined around a half-full baggie on wheels.

I was about to ask him what each wire did and where on my body it corresponded to when a woman nurse came through the door, stopping where my male nurse was standing halfway through the doorway. She was wearing the same insane plastic headgear. Was I contagious? Was I being operated on and just hadn't realized it? I lifted my head off the bed and saw my body, which looked eerie and sunken draped under white sheets, but certainly no part of it was bared to the lights and cut open. She stared, and I saw her eyes go wide at the sight of me.

"Oh my God—"

"Get his doctor. Somebody on call, right now."

"Oh my God—"

"*Get his fucking doctor*—" he shouted, scaring us both. She took one last terrified look at the both of us and sprinted out of the room. We listened to the pounding of her feet against the floor grow softer.

"That was—" He glanced down at himself hesitantly. "Sorry."

He seemed to want to say something else. He thought better of it, I suppose, and said only, again, "Sorry."

I laid my head back down against my pillow.

"This must be a really stressful job."

I was trying in my diminished capacity to stay friends with my male nurse, because he had the answers to my questions and was only just now getting over what appeared to be a nervous breakdown. Mine was a role that required some patience. I could do this. I could be understanding.

"What time is it?" I asked.

"One in the morning."

I felt around my body with my hands. I was wearing a bedsheet, or something that felt like it. My chin, angled onto my chest by the steep incline of the motor bed, scraped against prickly chest hairs. I noticed he—I needed to call him something; Nurse Gaylord?—was still holding the open end of the endotracheal tube he'd pulled out of my throat in his hands, and from the looks of it had crushed it into a curlicue.

I was losing hope in him. Maybe the other nurse would find Ren out there. I was aching to talk to somebody I knew. Nurse Gaylord made a final, hopeful glance out the doorway for somebody, anybody, to come into the room. Eventually he put his hands on the back of a chair pushed up against the wall and carried it right beside me, sitting down.

"Okay," he said, breathing in and out. "Okay, okay, let's try to talk. I can talk. This is fine."

He was talking to himself, not me. Waiting patiently was the only thing I could do for him. He blinked himself down to a lower tier of mania. He clenched his fingers around the tube, bending it farther in his hands. Finally, he spoke.

"Jack . . . Jr. Jack Jr., tell me: What do you remember?"

"Remember about what?"

"Well—" Nurse Gaylord knew exactly what he wanted to ask but was trying very hard to ask it in a way that didn't hurt my feelings. I knew the tone well. "What's your—I mean. This is really—" He was getting worked up again. "I'm really not the one you should be having this conversation with. You need a doctor."

"You're the only one here."

"More than a doctor," Nurse Gaylord hadn't heard me, "you need . . ."

He trailed off.

"Your parents," he said faintly, "Jesus Christ. We have to call your parents."

He was on his feet again, pacing, again losing his shit. I was starting to feel bad for the guy. He lived the rest of his life this way, I imagined. Just came home from being a male nurse and became a male person still racked with all this anxiety over things that didn't seem to matter very much. Painful, probably took up a lot of his time. He reached for the phone on the wall.

"What are you doing?"

"I'm calling your parents, what do you think I'm doing?"

"Can you . . ." I'd become tense over the sight of him dialing. "Not? I mean, do you have to?"

He screwed up his face at me, confused. "Yes, I have to—" He swore under his breath. "Jesus," he was saying, "I don't even know if they're—"

It was the very last moment of peace. By the time I'd registered that there was noise in the doorway, it was already too late. A swift, sharp punctuation of silence hung isolated in the air for just a second longer, then exploded. So much was happening all at once. Bodies had come pouring in, one by one, filling the room. Voices from every corner. Some were shouting at me, some were directed at Nurse Gaylord, others seemed to ping-pong between themselves, all arguing. I felt hands come up to my neck again, pressing on each side. At least eight pairs of eyes floating above blue surgical masks, plastic shields reflecting light in every direction, catching the bulbs overhead like strobes.

"He was intubated."

"He's confused."

"He's breathing!"

"Can you state your date of birth for me?"

Over undulating sets of shoulders, I saw Nurse Gaylord being shuffled out of the room.

"Tell us your date of birth, Jack. Do you remember it? Do you know where you are?"

"Your date of birth. When were you born? When were you born, Jack?"

"Jr.," I said weakly, fighting a bulging pressure that had started to build in my stomach and was creeping its way up my throat. "Jack Jr.—"

"Hold on." Somebody had grabbed my hand and was pressing their latex fingers hard into my wrist. The air seemed to move in front of me. I counted waves, like disturbed water in front of my eyes. "Hold on, something's up."

"His face. All the color's gone out of his face."

"Look at me," at least three different voices around me said within a hair's breadth of one another. The steady vibrations had grown into a hungry ring in my ears. After a moment—

The blue-scrubbed doctor who was most center field in my vision had bright red hair and a mess of freckles poking out from under her mask and plexiglass head shield. I didn't know why I was staring. Maybe it was just that I'd never seen a person with that many freckles before.

"Shock," she said matter-of-factly. "He wasn't like this a second ago. Get that RN back in here."

I had enough sense, then, to move my eyes. There were no hands on my body. There were swirls of blue mixed in with the light, growing faint as they backed away. I searched each face for Nurse Gaylord's eyes and found them easily. I let out my breath, relieved.

"Is he impaired?" Dr. Freckles asked Nurse Gaylord. "Did you notice anything?"

"No, no—" Nurse Gaylord edged himself back into the seat right in front of me, blocking a good portion of the blurry faces around him with the silhouette of his body. The noise had subsided to dull hums around us. "He's confused, but he was talking. He was asking questions."

"Ask him."

Nurse Gaylord looked around at the dark shapes that closed the two of us in. He reached for me, hesitating.

"Can I touch you, Jack Jr.?"

After a while, I nodded shakily. I felt his fingers, warm around my wrist. There was a tenderness to it, one of my only comforts in this moment in time. It was a softness in the way he touched me that made me want to trust him. That, or I had nobody else, which I didn't want to believe was true but was, currently. Dr. Freckles hovered over his shoulder, watching intently with the rest of them. I could sense the other bodies in the room. I could hear again but only barely.

"Are you okay?"

I tried to do something, either nod or shake my head, I hadn't yet decided, but found I could do neither. Nurse Gaylord glanced around him, at the other eyes. I appeared to have missed a beat of time in which it was decided that they would all leave us alone. Slowly, they filed out. It was just him and me.

"Can they not do that again?" I asked him in a voice that sounded a lot more pitiful than I felt. I hated sounding this soft, but there wasn't much to do about the fact that I'd been about five seconds from puking all over myself as well as all over the hundred pairs of hands that had just been skirting up and down my body. Either puke or pass out, maybe both. I knew one thing: I never wanted to feel that way again.

"We won't do that anymore," Nurse Gaylord assured me. "There's just . . . I don't know what to say. You haven't been awake in a while. A long time. We just called your parents. They'll be here soon."

"I told you I didn't want you to call them."

"The other nurse called them—we have to call them," Nurse Gaylord said. "They've been waiting to see you."

I wasn't ready for this. I hadn't seen my parents in—I didn't know how long, and I didn't think it was because I couldn't currently think straight that I didn't know exactly how long. There should have been conversational shorthand for the kind of passive, unrealized relationship I had with them. There was none that didn't make one of the parties involved look like the asshole.

"Can you please just . . . ," I said, "find my husband? Where's Ren? I'm just really—I don't want to do this without him."

I didn't want to say what exactly I was, as embarrassed as I found myself, then and there. Nurse Gaylord didn't answer me for a long time. I watched him try to decide what to say to me, going through any number of options and discarding them in a quick mental cycle that played out in his eyes.

"He's at home," he said finally. "I didn't know you were married."

"We're not," I said, faltering, "I mean, we were going—why isn't he here?"

"I'll tell you this, Jack Jr.," Nurse Gaylord said, "we get your doctor in here, and your parents, and make sure we're all on the same page, and then you can call him. Does that sound okay?"

It felt like the only terms he would agree to. My head had begun to throb. I missed Ren. I felt more alone than I had in a long time, looking at him. Slowly, I nodded, not wanting to but doing it anyway. He seemed to relax. For the next minute, I watched him shuffle around the room, organizing the machines gathered around my bed, tapping on screens and buttons. He traced each wire and tube down to its proper place on my body and made sure the seal was tight around each bandage.

"Does anything hurt?"

"My head."

"I can give you something for that. What else?"

"My . . . throat."

He reached for my neck, feeling around with a much softer touch than he'd used while de-tubing me.

"You're swollen," he said. "I'll get you some ice."

"You said 'in a while,'" I told him. "I haven't been awake in a while. What does that mean, 'in a while'?"

We had arrived at a point in time that he seemed to have known was coming, but I could see it was still scaring the shit out of him. Poor guy. I felt sorry for him. He stepped away from me, paused to rub his hands down the front of his shirt.

"I can get you the painkillers first. Some ice, too."

I didn't say anything at this. He understood. Pulling the chair he'd brought up to the side of my bed, he sat.

"Jack Jr.," Nurse Gaylord said slowly, "what year do you think it is?"

"Nineteen," I said, "two thousand nineteen—twenty nineteen."

Nurse Gaylord took in a little breath, then let it out. "Okay," he said, "so, what I need you to know right now is that . . . it *was* 2019. What I mean is—it was 2019 when you went to the hospital. End of October."

Each of us waited for the other to say something. It was an unnatural break in the healthy and comforting rhythm we seemed to have had up until now. He wanted to tell me something and at the same time didn't want anything to do with me. It was all there in the look he gave me.

"Okay," I said. "What happened to me?"

I knew that we used a question like this to take stock of a large number of things, a set of circumstances that lends something of an explanation for the extreme disappointment, trauma, general chaos of life. I was thinking, for example, of a boy in my eighth-grade homeroom who had given me at least a thousand erections that year—in bed, in the shower, on the bus, under my desk—who had ended up not only laughably straight but also in jail for beating some old guy outside the local pharmacy so badly that he died. For no apparent reason, mind you. It still confuses the hell out of me. He was going to be in jail for the next couple of decades. It was a situation like that in which you'd naturally ask something along the lines of "What happened to him?" This made sense to me. Answering this question about myself involved a lot of answers.

What happened to me? I'd lived in the same city for fifteen years and worked an advertising job writing emotive, persuasive, manipulative advertising content that corporations paid millions of dollars for other people to read. I'd met Ren, whom I liked enough to marry, and he'd decided the same. I was happy. I did things like go for runs and listen to podcasts and had, until tonight, found a level of comfort in a life entirely of my own making that most people would only dream of having. What else was there to know? Bad fall? Brain aneurysm, miraculously survived? I glanced down at my legs. I had both of them, didn't I? Not sepsis, not something flesh-eating that had taken an arm and a leg to fend off. What *had* happened to me?

The polite, funeral-friendly word for dying in Korean means literally "to go back." To the dust, to heaven, to the nebula in space where Earth formed billions of years ago. The meaning of this particular phrase behind the literal is flexible and not actually as religious as it appears; I am told this despite my people's shocking propensity for gathering in huge, gossipy worship groups that are known to overrun Fort Lee's bus systems right before noon on Sundays. It was a poetic and hopeful euphemism for the stoppage of one's heart that I heard Appa say for the first time when his father, my grandfather, died on my sixth birthday, while I shoveled the last of my ice cream cake into my mouth in the backseat of the car, on the way to the hospital.

"We have always come from somewhere," Appa told me while he drove us back home that night. He sounded too calm given what was happening, despite the fact that we'd just left my grandfather in the morgue and had been given back the wedding band he'd worn for fifty years in a Ziploc bag. I remembered this more than anything, the way he said: "One day, all of us will go back."

It was a strange feeling, to think about Appa again. He had meant it in the biological sense. As in, my grandfather would eventually be embalmed, entombed, and buried deep underground, where his body would succumb to the bugs and microbes in the soil, and in fifty years all that would be left was bones and dust. I didn't know what I believed, other than the fact that, obviously, I was dead. I'd gone back to where I'd come from. This didn't explain why I was, again, awake. So I was wondering, honestly: What does it mean to come back from coming back? The verbs would cancel each other out, wouldn't they? Meaning I have not come back or gone anywhere and instead have been here this whole time. It sounded too stupid to be true. I was asking my nurse, I guess. A lonely thought that meant that I had nobody else. At least not right now.

And so I sat there, with nothing else to do and nobody else to listen to, while Nurse Gaylord answered my question, speaking slow and soft.

"You drove your car into the north end of the Hudson River. You fractured your skull in nine places and almost completely severed your spine. In surgery, they reattached your left leg and replaced some of your vertebrae with pins. Since then, you've been in a medically induced coma for twenty-three months, and . . ." He checked his watch. "About eight minutes ago, you woke up."

So, almost right about the leg. That was pretty good. Nurse Gaylord was waiting for me to say something, maybe that I understood. And I did. I tried to lock in on the words: twenty-three months. Call it two years. October 2019 showed up like film trying to capture its subject in extreme motion. There was a car, though I couldn't be sure whether I was seeing it myself or because Nurse Gaylord had just mentioned one. There was Ren, whom I expected. The little cabin we'd rented for the weekend. Dead leaves from the previous fall on the ground, turning slowly to mulch. He was so excited when he saw it for the first time, telling me it looked so much better than the pictures. I was happy to have made him happy. It was one of the rare moments when a young person with limited life experience like me found a genuine reason to be thankful. Thankful that I had Ren, that he loved me and I loved him. I drew in my breath, harder to do this time around. I thought of something to say, and decided on:

"I have to take a shit."

Nurse Gaylord didn't know what to make of me right then. I could see it in his eyes.

"That's not really possible," he said. "You've been eating intravenously for two years. You have no shit."

He had alerted me to the tape around my wrist, on which a dangling plastic tube was sticking out of a black and blue spot just behind my middle-finger knuckle.

"Well," I said diplomatically, "something's in there, and I'd like to get out of this bed and over a toilet sooner rather than later."

We stared at each other a moment longer.

"Okay, then."

Nurse Gaylord shot a look over his shoulder at Dr. Freckles, whose head I noticed then was sticking out of the doorway behind him, flanked by what looked through the window like every doctor in the entire building watching through the half-closed blinds. Between them, silently, he received the go-ahead to move me. I could sense Nurse Gaylord's apprehension. He'd most likely expected to remove himself from the situation now that the doctors had arrived, and yet, he was still the only one here, and if I knew one thing, it was that I didn't want him to go.

The motor bed gave a tired whirr and pushed me farther into a sitting position. He helped me out of bed, swinging out my legs, feet covered in those rubber-grip psycho-ward socks, and placing each foot flat on the ground. I missed my slippers at home. I knew exactly where they were, half under the right side of the bed. Ren went barefoot around the apartment. We'd sacrificed central air for big, ridiculous windows that looked out onto the street. In the mornings, when only the e-bike couriers were zooming around, the entire world was blue.

"When can I go home?" I asked. He didn't answer me. Together, we got my gown off my shoulders. He unstuck some of the wires and unclipped a few others until I was free, save for the IV in my wrist, which he attached to a mobile coatrack and wheeled next to me.

"Slowly," he said, "your legs haven't been moved like this in a while."

With a few tries, we angled my upper body over the edge of the mattress and, inch by inch, slipped me off, bringing my weight onto my ankles. My knees buckled instantly, sending me crashing into Nurse Gaylord's waiting arms.

"Why isn't this working?" I said, my face smushed into his chest.

"Give yourself time," he told me. "Find your balance."

Working together, we brought my body upright. He reached behind me and unstuck something that had been Velcro-ed to the bed, a frosted plastic baggie filled with—

"That's not—"

"You're slipping again, Jack."

"Is that—"

"Just ignore it."

"That's attached to a tube on my dick, isn't it?"

"It's called a catheter, and don't think about it."

"How can I not think about it?"

Nurse Gaylord dragged me back to an upright position. Our chests were pressed together, my nose directly in the divot of his collarbone, which smelled like detergent and sweat.

"They'll take it out in the morning."

"Take it *out*? It's *in* there?"

He walked me to the toilet, an absolute torture-machine-looking thing with guardrails on every side and pulleys hoisting various saddles and buckles into the air. I sat down, easily, since I wasn't wearing any underwear. He kept his arms on my shoulders, as though afraid to let go. I sat there for a few minutes, forgetting and remembering and forgetting what it was I'd come here to do. I was too ashamed to speak up for another five minutes. Soon after that, the silence was too hard to ignore.

"I spoke too soon."

He looked me over carefully. "We knew this going in, did we not?"

He was making a joke. I might have even laughed if I weren't at that very moment staring at the silicone tube that was sticking straight out of my urethra and coiling around my right leg. It was a strange thing, to think of laughing. Not when I was, deep down, afraid of what I was not being told. It was all so stupid. I didn't want to laugh. I didn't want to do anything. I missed Ren. Again, always, I missed Ren.

Nurse Gaylord let my shoulders go and sat on a chair pushed up against the wall. The front of his plastic visor had fogged up to the point where I could barely see his eyes.

"Why are you wearing all of that?" I asked him.

He seemed to consider what I said for longer than necessary, and while I waited I had time to register movement outside the bathroom. Somebody had come in and was clearing up the motor bed where I'd been lying. Nurse Gaylord thought for a few more moments, then pulled the visor off his forehead along with the skullcap. His hair was sandy brown, longer than I thought it would be, and stuck to the sides of his head where the elastic had cut in.

"A lot's changed. We wear this all the time on shift now. Used to be much more."

"Black Death," I guessed.

He didn't laugh.

"Okay, another time," I said. "It's 2021 now, right? Hey, what happened to Trump?"

He didn't laugh at this either. I couldn't even tell if he'd smiled from what I could see of his eyes. Nurse Gaylord looked sad. He'd watched me talk as though sitting in front of something upsetting, like a dog death scene in an otherwise happy-go-lucky children's movie. We'd come a long way from fourteen minutes ago, when I'd thought him the only other thing in the universe. I missed it. This world was too complicated. I thought of my parents. It didn't feel good to think about them, the way they must have been speeding across the bridge—possibly in separate cars, possibly only one of them. I wasn't sure anymore. They'd been called, I assumed. Nurse Gaylord had said something to that effect, I just couldn't remember exactly what.

"This is weird."

"I know it is. We're going to answer every question you have. I want you to know that you're completely safe here. We're going to talk through the next steps together with your parents so that everybody's on the same page. We have physical therapists to help you move again, we have people who can help you figure out your insurance. It's going to be fine, Jack Jr."

"I was talking about trying to shit in front of you."

He stared at me.

"Oh."

"I guess that other stuff, too," I said, taking in the white-tiled room. We coexisted in here, silently, for the next minute or so. I could see my window through the open door.

"Are they really coming?"

"Who? Your parents? Yes."

"Where am I? NYU?"

Nurse Gaylord demonstrated some measure of confused disappointment, bringing his eyebrows just a little closer together.

"Mount Sinai?"

He blinked at me again.

"Where am I?"

"The hospital."

"I know that. What state?"

"Jersey."

What felt like a very long minute passed between us.

"New Jersey," he repeated.

I felt unsteady, reaching my hands out for the guardrails—useful after all. My head felt twice as heavy on my neck.

"I'm in New Jersey?"

"Yes," Nurse Gaylord answered me slowly. "What's the problem?"

"Why did you bring me back there?" I said, taking deeper breaths. "Did you? Did my—did they move me here? Why did they do that?"

"You've been here almost the entire time you've been asleep," Nurse Gaylord said. "You spent about three weeks in the ICU at Mount Sinai. When you were stabilized, they moved you here."

I was shaking my head, hearing it all and not wanting to. I was in New Jersey; I knew the hospital. The view out of the window had been nearly exactly the one I remembered from Harabeoji's room the day he died. We'd tied one of my birthday balloons to the end of his bed and he'd died with a big 6 floating above him like the angel of death.

"What . . . what happened to my apartment?" I asked. "What about . . . what about my job? What did I—"

"Easy, Jack Jr.," Nurse Gaylord said, "you're making yourself upset."

"I'm not upset, I'm—" I stammered, growing hot. "I'm in . . . New Jersey! I'm in fucking New Jersey and nobody told me! What the actual FUCK, man—"

"Why are you so upset about the fact that you're in New Jersey?"

"Oh, I'm sorry, Nurse Gaylord," I found myself shouting. "Maybe you aren't aware of the fact that New Jersey just happens to be the rectum of the United fucking States of America—" I was trying to do something, maybe fling myself off the toilet so that I could crawl out the door and across the river back home to the city. "It's where dreams die. It's where everything good turns to mountains and mountains of shit that you can smell for miles on the turnpike, which by the way is the only useful contribution this entire state has ever provided to the citizens of America. Do you know how *sad* that is? For the best, most useful thing an entire STATE has ever produced to be a ROAD? A ROAD! IT'S A ROAD, FOR GOD'S SAKE."

I had started to shout and only realized it halfway through. Twenty-three months. It had been twenty-three months.

Dr. Freckles and two more nurses stood flanking the bathroom door, as if they formed a tunnel guiding me back to bed. Nurse Gaylord made a motion of appeasement. A thousand thoughts flipped like Rolodex cards through my brain.

"What happened to Ren?" I said again pitifully. "Can you please just tell me where he is? Please—"

It was like watching somebody flick the lights on and off. I had enough time to see Nurse Gaylord spring out of his chair before I slipped off the toilet, just narrowly missing one of the guardrails with the side of my head. The lights were swimming. My ears rang. I put my hands up to my face, trying to cover it all, eyes, ears, nose, everything. I wanted the simple nothing from before. It was perfect, that nothing.

"This can't be happening," I said, feeling his hands on my shoulders. "This is so fucked, this is beyond fucked."

"Breathe, Jack Jr. Please, just breathe. Your family's on their way."

"I don't *want* to see my family," I said, strangled, "how many fucking times am I going to tell you—"

There was something off about the voice that came in through my ears, small and hollow, as though it were made of metal. The universe had shrunk to dime size around me, just a little platform of cold earth where I lay, shrunk down to the warm palms he put on either side of my neck. There wasn't space in my head for anything else. It, all of it, was gone so quickly.

I was thinking about that day in the hospital, this hospital, in which all of us, Appa, Umma, my brother James, and I, had spent the rest of the night pacing the same hallway, hanging our feet off the metal benches they kept pushed up against the walls. James and I weren't allowed near them when the doctor came out to talk. The question occurred to me years later, that if they didn't want us there—it felt pretty clear they didn't, out of fear, grief, or something else—why didn't they send us home? James was seven years older than me. He'd watched me at home before. I remembered annoyance. There was so much cool shit to do back home, games I'd just unwrapped, Legos and remote-control spy planes taking up space on the kitchen table. Up until Harabeoji had sunk to his knees on the lawn outside and tipped over to lie sprawled in the dirt, it had been the best day of my life. He kept saying he was okay while he was being wheeled into the waiting ambulance, telling Appa I could keep eating my cake and that nobody needed to go with him.

I didn't actually remember being told that he had died. When I tried to envision it, where I was sitting, maybe on one of those metal benches, probably holding Umma's hand, something like that, I came, always, across a blank. Surely, I'd been told then and there. There couldn't have been a way to hide it. The doctor was coming out every half hour with news, right there in front of the doors, in front of Umma and Appa. It was a scary inscrutable blankness that kept me awake every now and then, to the point where I'd begun to tell the story by filling it in with the most probable situation. It sounded believable enough. A doctor coming out, telling us there was nothing they could do. Us, driving home, with the ice cream cake I'd brought in its box melting into a pool of flavored sugar between James and me. An afternoon spent picking up the toys, dinner, then bed. I didn't know where the life ended and the fiction began.

I imagine that Appa cried. When he was alone, out of earshot. I'd spent the entire funeral service the next week staring at my shoes because I didn't want to see Harabeoji's face sticking out of the open casket. I'd convinced myself that his body had already begun to shrivel up and knew that I'd never forget it if I saw something like that. That's all I remembered: voices, hymns I didn't know, and the tops of my shoes.

I was crying now. I was crying for no reason, or rather, no reason I could think of, just hunched over on my knees, sideways on the floor, crying without knowing how to stop while Nurse Gaylord tried to pull me upright. Pathetic. I had nothing to cry about. I shouldn't have been crying and yet somehow I was. I was alone. Everyone else had gone and taken the sense with them, out of the world, and left me here. It was so, so fucked. It was a level of fuckage that scientists might be studying for the next hundred years, so much so that there was nothing else to do but laugh, loud and long, doubled up on the floor with Nurse Gaylord's hands on my shoulders trying to get me to sit back up. I felt somebody run into the room, put their hands on my body, angle my face upward to them. I saw that it was Appa, and that his hands were cold and wet from the rain, and that the lines in his face were so much deeper than I remembered, that his hair had turned all white in the time I'd been gone. And for the longest time, with my eyes fixated on his face, wondering how in the fuck he had gotten so much older without my noticing, I just kept laughing, tears streaming whole rivers down my face, thinking just two things: that all of it was the funniest shit in the world, and that I would never really figure out why.

2

HOW TO REMOVE A CATHETER

HERE'S THE VERY INTERESTING THING ABOUT NOT MOVING FOR TWO years: Anything and everything after waking up, even the slightest expenditure of energy by any muscle group in the body for longer than a moment, even two moments, can just knock the absolute shit out of you, just slam you straight out of the universe. Out cold, no memory. You're on, and then you move your arm for a bit or blink your eyes a few times, and like that, you're off. Such expenditures of energy—I was learning now from experience—included sitting up, opening your mouth, moving your head an inch to the right to try to locate the water they left for you beside your motor bed. Forget about speaking. There was certainly nothing I could think of that might have explained just how talkative I'd managed to be that first night however many nights ago. Nobody seemed to want to tell me exactly how long it had been. Which I could understand, even if it was annoying. I tended to forget most everything these days. Was it Wednesday? Night or day? I could never tell from the light outside. Was I alone in bed or was there someone in the room with me, either wiping my face or moving my arm or changing out my fluids, or just sitting there, off to the right, near the point in my vision where my eyeball ended? Knowing near nothing and being unable thus far to retain any new sets of information, no matter how small, hadn't been making for the easiest existence. Mostly, I found myself following orders. Blinking whenever I was told to, squeezing hands whenever I was asked to, kicking out with my feet, making muscles with my biceps and stomach. They kept asking me for the day I was born, which I thought I was getting right about half the time. Sometimes, everything hurt. Other times, there was peace enough to convince me that this really was the happiest plane of being I could ever achieve in my life, mostly born out of relief that the pain was gone or that my brain had emerged, however briefly, from the fog.

When I was awake, I could feel light on my skin, through my eyelids; I could feel the scratchy blankets on my legs and smell clean, filtered air coming in through the vents. And just as I decided to lift my head up or try to get someone's attention for some food or water, it was gone, quickly, the little asshole in my skull decided I'd had enough surface time and slammed me dark once again.

I liked going dark, honestly. It was a place that made far more sense than the one I kept visiting when I opened my eyes. Nobody touched me while I was in there, nobody talked to me or asked me for the dates of things. I'd gone so long without stimulation that new sensations felt like barbs on my skin. Being awake felt like holding my breath, like counting seconds, struggling against a discomfort that mounted, slowly, slowly, until I couldn't take it anymore and returned, very gratefully, to the calming wipe of sleep, refreshing as a cold towel pressed to my head. Sleep was the natural state of things. Why even bother waking up, at this point? It was terrible up there.

I was awake but with my eyes closed one morning or afternoon when it felt quiet enough to venture a little farther rather than wait for sleep again. I opened my eyes and saw Umma sitting at the edge of my bed. I blinked, once, then twice, waiting for her to notice. There was not much I could do to prepare myself for the sight of her, my first sight of her in almost four years, not even counting the coma. She looked so much smaller. It was not an uncommon thing, especially among Asian ummas, for women to transform suddenly into tiny, doting halmeonis, but I'd never imagined it happening to my own mother. Surely not so soon, though, I needed to remind myself, it was not particularly soon at all but entire years that stood between us. She was hunched over her phone, holding it just a few inches away from her face with her glasses hiked up on her forehead and a mask over her mouth and nose.

I tore my dry lips open. I needed to get it over with.

"Umma."

She made a sound I'd never heard her make before, falling away, clutching at her chest. Her phone clattered to the ground. She took a few seconds to realize I'd been the one to speak. She was already crying.

"Oh God," I whispered, "please don't—"

There was no stopping her. My mother crowded my face until her eyes, clenched shut and leaking, were the only things I could see. I felt her fingers through my hair.

"I'm here," she kept saying, "I'm here, I'm here."

I concentrated, focusing all of my mind on it, and squeezed her hand. She made a sound, a strangled noise halfway between a cry and a laugh, and laid her whole body on my arm, shaking. I wanted to put my arm around her but wasn't quite there yet, motor-wise, so I tried again and squeezed her hand a little tighter. Coming back was easier than before. I wanted to tell her I was okay.

"Jack," she said, muffled through my smock, and kept saying it, again and again.

"Jr."

It was one of those good days, in which I could move my lips to make sounds I could hear inside me and sometimes ended up put-ting enough breath behind them to be audible. It was easy today. I pulled my head up, off my searing-hot pillow. She saw that I was trying to sit up and found my remote, moving my bed into a higher angle. Over the hydraulic hum, I slowly rose high enough to see her whole face. We looked at each other for a while. I was close enough to her to smell the soft detergent on her clothes. Umma's tears had soaked almost entirely through the mask she wore; her nose had poked through like it was pressed up against wet tissue paper.

She took a long time to say: "I haven't seen your eyes in years."

I'd been having trouble finding the right response to things like this. Not for lack of caring, but really—what *do* you say after something like this? I swallowed, wincing; my throat was still sore. She tried to fidget with her mask and tore the papery fabric in her fingers.

"Damn it—" She darted around my bed and found a new one in the purse she'd left on her chair.

"Seriously," I said, croaking. My head was starting to hurt. "Why is everybody wearing those around me? Am I sick?"

"You're not sick."

"So, what?"

Umma secured another blue mask around her ears and didn't answer me.

"When did you come?"

Umma glanced at the clock on the wall to my left, and I followed her eyes, reading six, though morning or evening I couldn't be sure.

"Couple hours ago. James dropped me off."

"James was here?"

"Of course he was."

"Of course he was?" My voice had come through more forcefully than I'd meant it to. I saw her eyes narrow slightly. If I was going to get any lip for that, it wasn't today.

Umma only shook her head, just a half inch counter-then-clockwise. "You were sleeping. He says you've been asleep every time he's come. He tries but it's difficult, you know, with the baby."

"What baby?"

She seemed happy about this one, telling me that a baby boy had been born about six months ago, that he was plump and quiet and his skin was still pink. He looked just like the two of us, she told me. I remembered that I was an uncle. Jageun-abeoji. A word in Korean that meant "little father" and was reserved for the brothers of a child's father. It would do to bless any poor child assigned an uncle quite like me.

"Why would he come here," I said, sounding crueler than I meant but not entirely.

Umma didn't respond to this. It appeared, simply, that we were just not going to talk any further about James today, which had been most any day back when I lived at home, back when I stayed in New Jersey by choice. In her defense, it was a lot to get into. It was enough of a mouthful, an older brother who, after getting into a habit of drinking himself near-dead in his late teens and becoming a father at twenty, continued to drink, drive, and wreak havoc on both family and home until several unanticipated stays in rehab and jail had achieved the sort of uneasy sobriety that automatically became the elephant in any room. See what I mean?

We were quiet for a while. The TV was on above her head, *Frasier* rerun.

"How many times have you come here since I woke up?"

She really didn't want to tell me, I could see it.

"Few times a week," she said eventually. "You've moved your head and arms a couple of times. You haven't been awake like this since . . ."

We felt a hum in the air as the box vent rattled to life above my bed. The pain had arranged itself into steady pounding beats on the right side of my skull. The number of wires and tubes attached to me by sticky tape had either doubled or tripled since the last time I'd had enough mental faculties to check. I shook my head.

"I'm sorry."

She frowned. "For what?"

Staying conscious was taking its toll on me.

"That I'm this . . . fucking"—I shook my hand, trying to find words just out of reach—"baby, I don't know. That I don't remember anything, that my head hurts, that I can't stay awake for more than five minutes. I just . . ."

She had given me that look that I remembered, the one that had several meanings, interchangeable but otherwise inferable from context. An array of meanings ranging from "we'll talk about this at home," to "put the Nerf Longshot CS-6 Blue rifle back where you found it and help me bag these grapefruits," to "say another word to me about the Nerf Longshot CS-6 Blue rifle and your life as you know it will be over." Actually, I guess they all meant "shut the fuck up" in the most motherly way that she, in all her wrath—and there was wrath—could muster in places of public attention. I shut the fuck up. I felt like a teenager again. It wasn't exactly strange that Umma had decided to treat me like I'd just left the house for school that morning. It was exactly what I knew she'd do.

"You have always done this," Umma said, "mope and hem and haw and blame yourself for something you have absolutely no control over. Ever since you were a little boy. Did you know that? Do you remember what you used to do?"

"Well, I'm at about a fifty percent success rate on knowing my own birthday, so I would venture, no, not anymore."

Again, the Look. I avoided her eyes.

"Sorry," I said. Umma nodded, gathering herself up to sit more rigidly in her chair.

"It's not good for you to talk about those things right now. It upsets you. They said you need a few more weeks until you're ready to come home. You need to learn to relax again."

"I'm relaxed," I said, ignoring the mention she'd made of coming home, meaning back to the house I'd left when I was eighteen and hadn't been inside since then. "I'm relaxing right now."

She didn't bother responding to that.

"Can I have some food?"

She gestured to the plastic cloche on the table between us. "Salmon today."

"Do I like it?"

"It's been puréed."

I laid my head back against the soft heat of my bed. "Just leave me here. Go on with your life. Live, laugh, love."

I could tell Umma wanted to smile at that one, but her eyes remained sad. She understood my humor better than Appa. She spoke much better English; maybe that was why. Something that happened if you moved here and started learning the ABCs at five like she did instead of nineteen, like Appa did. She rubbed my hand with both of hers.

"Why are you still my same son, after all this time? You haven't changed, not one bit."

"Not one bit?" I repeated curiously.

"Well," she said, "you've never taken anything in your life very seriously, and even now, fresh out of a two-year coma, you don't. You are exactly who you are, Jack Jr."

There was quite a bit to unpack in the assertion that I *never* took anything seriously. There were many things I took seriously. My parents' divorce, for one. The full year during which Appa would retreat to the bedroom upstairs before Umma would come through the front door to take James and me to school. Weekends we spent with her in a carousel of revolving apartments all over Fort Lee while she tried to settle down in one, found she hated something about it, and packed up her few belongings and moved to another. Umma had grown up in the city, I remembered. She used to tell a story about taking the M11, at seven years old, down from Chelsea to her father's favorite cigar store to pick up his smokes and back. She was, and had always been, the most independent person I'd ever known, and had spent the vast majority of my childhood being the opposite. It was the divorce that had freed her. I liked this kind of restlessness. I'd inherited a constant need to rearrange my surroundings from her, no doubt. And still, both of them, Umma and Appa, looked so sad as we left each house for the other. It was the worst part of the whole thing. It didn't feel very good to think about this period of our lives. Umma didn't like to talk about it. I imagine she liked to think that she and Appa had always been divorced. Rather that they'd been lifelong friends who'd had children and never married in the first place, which was a narrative I'm sure they'd agree with.

She reached out and cupped my chin in her hand.

"This face," she said, nothing more.

"Umma," I said slowly, "maybe you can tell me a few things."

I could almost see the muscles in her shoulders tense themselves, armed for evasive maneuvers. "You're very tired."

"Who's paying for this room?"

"Insurance."

"For two years? This gigantic room and all the drugs and everything else? I made seventy grand a year, Umma."

"Insurance," Umma repeated.

"We don't have any money."

"The only person who knows about money is your brother, and he says it's fine. Checks come in and out and we never have a problem."

"But—"

"And if you're going to ask again," Umma said, cutting me off, "you're going to get the same answer."

I sat back, defeated for the time being. "What happened to my apartment?"

"Your landlord let you out of your lease. We put most of your things in storage. That reminds me, we're going to have to take you there to get all the things you want to keep."

She was thinking about the fact that I'd driven my car into the Hudson, wasn't she? It's what I was thinking. It was all I'd been thinking about, every little moment before sleep came and every little moment afterward.

What a strange, awful thing, to know what you've done.

"Umma," I said, "where's Ren?"

Hard to read her as it was through the mask, I saw it again: that she knew the answer to my question was much more trouble than it was worth.

"It's late," she said instead. "I'm going to stay until you sleep."

She pushed me backward into the bed when I didn't have anything to say about that. "Sleep."

I had half a mind to resist but was very quickly running out of stamina. It had been six years. I hadn't seen her face in six years. I redid the math, slowly. Two years I spent asleep. Another four before that in which I received her calls with varying interest and slowly but surely stopped returning them. I didn't know which was worse. The edges of the world had become hazy and were drawing shut like curtains over my vision. I had enough time to see her for just a few more seconds, to make out the shape of her in the dark, her hand holding mine. I slipped under.

HERE IS WHAT I SEE when I picture Ren. 1) The low slope of the arches on his feet that flattened every pair of shoes he owned. 2) Moles, everywhere, at least a hundred all over his body. Big ones, on the line of his jaw and on his inner left thigh. Small ones that came up like little dots, so light as to be mistaken for spots of the sun after a day at the beach. They say moles like that are expressly Korean; some believe them to be a sign of great future wealth. Judging from how many had cropped up on his body, he was going to either successfully short the housing market one day or, I don't know, marry David Geffen. 3) Hands whose fingers were so much longer and more elegantly shaped than mine were. He could've played piano if he wanted to, I always told him. Ren had anatomically perfect hands. I told him, do something with them, play music, write calligraphy, call Aveeno about any open spots on their billboards. Something. He never did. He thought it was the funniest thing in the world. Jealous, he called me, in his fuzzy little voice he used right before he fell asleep or right after he woke up.

I loved watching him in the mornings. You've never seen some-one so at peace, someone who shot it in all directions like rays of light, nourishing the space around him like water to dying grass.

This was a bad idea. I don't want to do this anymore.

BY THE WAY, A CATHETER is way farther up your junk than popular culture would have you believe. I don't know why I spent my entire life thus far thinking it more resembled something simple and easy, like a thick, noninvasive plastic condom with a drain, but I did, and on the day that a very nice Taiwanese nurse—thick black hair and a birthmark on her nose, we could have been cousins—came in and told me it was time for the whole thing to come out of my penis, I greeted the idea with far greater enthusiasm than I did what pro-ceeded to happen in the moments afterward. There are, in fact, a lot of things—a lot of horrific, complicated things—to say about what happens then: the draining of a balloon that kept the entire contrap-tion secured inside me, within my bladder; the momentary words of reassurance, seasoned and gentle, but firm and with a hint of dispas-sion; the pulling—so much pulling, in fact, that I thought I might have blacked out just watching it all come out of me, which they said not to do out of caution for squeamish patients but I did anyway. In case I wasn't clear: Do not watch a twelve-inch hose get pulled out of your dick under any circumstances.

She left with the tubes and baggies sealed away in a giant Zip-loc, along with my dignity, back out the door at the same time that Appa walked in from what looked like an especially cold fall morn-ing. He was wearing a jacket zipped up to his face and a plastic shield strapped to his forehead by elastic bands. He raised his arms, smiling.

"He is risen!" he said. "You're up earlier and earlier each day. Good sign, huh? They told me your catheter's out today. Was that what I just saw her taking out of here on my way in?"

I didn't know what to say about the fact that we—my parents

and I—had decided without speaking not to talk about all the time we'd gone without seeing one another. It had become easy to play along.

"I would like to steer clear of talking about anything that goes in or comes out of me for the next half hour, I beg of you," I said. Appa had taken to bringing me food that he consistently forgot to get cleared by hospital staff. This, coupled with the fact that the food was most often Korean and therefore typically unclassifiable under the checklist options of "protein," "vegetable," and "fruit," led most of the time to my putting a lot of faith and trust in my gut, which usually had the decency to wait until Appa had left for work, but not always. It was safe to say that my toilet shyness had effectively vanished over the course of the days I'd spent in bed since.

I could tell with better clarity that it had at least been a few weeks. Waking up wasn't the feat of strength it used to be, and neither was staying up, at least for a few hours. Time still managed to meld itself together when I wasn't paying attention. Often the date they'd say at the end of the newscasts they let me watch now would catch me by surprise. It was evening. Appa didn't usually come around then. The restaurant was open tonight, I assumed, though I couldn't imagine who was managing the kitchen if not him.

To know my father, one needed only to know the restaurant— a zany but harmonious hybrid of Korean-Japanese sushi and sashimi served in the traditions of both cultures—into which he'd put whatever hopes and dreams he had left over after the spiritual and bodily expenditure of raising two natural-born sons. He'd taken out a loan to buy the property, a bait and tackle store from which he'd retained only the walk-in freezer and the air-conditioning units on the roof. The rest—the signage, the netting hung over the walls and from the ceiling, the grimy countertops—had been laid out to rest on the curb outside while he made his amateur renovations. He did the floors himself, installing the tile plate by plate across eight hundred square feet of dining space. I knew this only because he took great care to tell me whenever anybody did so much as look at them. There was about a hundred pounds' worth of extra tile in the garage at home that had sat there since before I was born. The place's name, he said, was easy. The names of his two boys, John (nobody called me—or him—John) and James. John-James. Jo-Ja. Joja. A dream of his: that both of us would eventually find things to do that suited our individual talents and passions—just as long as it was at the restaurant. Front of house, back of house, he didn't mind. I spent cumulative years of my life behind that bar, beside him, knives in hand, in matching kitchen whites. In any case, the name Joja did not and continued not to make much sense. Better Jaja, right? Jack and James. I didn't even go by John in utero.

"Close your eyes and picture a place called Jaja," Appa used to say. "What do you see? You see nacho chips, pico de gallo. Tacos? Quesadillas. Over my dead body, a place called Ha-Ha-Ha."

"That's racist," I would say.

He'd raise an eyebrow at me. "Oh, and you think 'Joja' isn't? Joja, Choseon, Shogun. They all match. It's the right family of sounds. You hear that and you think: Fresh fish! Exotic Tastes of the East. You can practically hear the imperial gong. You need to make it simple for the white people. Complicate things and they won't buy."

"All of that is racist," I said. I was thirteen at the time. We had been talking while he ran prep for the dinner service, a task that began for him at eleven in the morning—that was, after a few hours' sleep following the fish run of the morning, in which he—and later I—haggled with grizzled import fishermen at the Fulton Fish Market for the freshest cuts of lean tuna and snapper. I was being generous, saying "morning." Appa liked to make the fish run seemingly before his competitors had even reached REM sleep the night before, which put us there anywhere between four and five A.M. each day.

I remembered that on the day I tried to tell my father that he was a racist—which he was—after I'd said it, he'd taken a great deal of time to process the back portion of a bluefin tuna and didn't acknowledge me until he was done.

"The *world* is racist," he told me, and I heard that his voice had gone flat and solemn. "The world *is* racist, Jack Jr."

He set down his knife, the silvery yanagi blade that he'd owned my entire life, that he sharpened against a black plate stone twice a year in the kitchen sink. He approached me slowly. He put a hand on either side of my face with all the solemnity of somebody telling their son that, actually, they weren't actually their son, or something just as absolutely devastating. Except what Appa said to me that day was this: "We are all just trying to stay alive."

Appa didn't like to be serious. He kept a resting, jovial altitude slightly above seriousness at all times but was known to come down to us, to me, with things like this. He could make me realize that nothing he ever said was as loose as he would have had any of us believe. He had apprenticed at a handful of restaurants in and around Kyoto through his twenties. Interesting to note: You did not in fact have to be Japanese to call yourself itamae, a Japanese word for "chef" that meant, literally, "in front of the board." He didn't call himself that anyway. He didn't really make sushi, he always said. Different fish, different cuts, techniques melded together with the methods of the Korean fishermen of Daegu, where he had been born and lived until his late teens. I could never describe it the way he could.

A writer wants to die face-first in their typewriter, at work on the next best thing. Appa would have gone the same way if he could: slumped over a deboned amberjack half-dried by the morning sun. Only he'd most definitely have had the foresight to clean his knife off first.

Not to say he had never thought of retiring. I remembered clearly the one and only time that he'd brought it up. I was not going to think about that today. Did he forgive me for it? I didn't know. Would it ever come up again, between us? I hoped not.

In my hospital room, at the foot of my motor bed, Appa sat in the chair in front of me and took hold of my left foot, grinding his knuckles hard against the heel. "Hungry?"

I didn't bother answering. He had already reached behind him for the damp plastic bag and had placed it gently in my lap. Dumplings today.

"I'm not supposed to have salt."

"You think I'd give you salt in the state you're in?" Appa shook his head, switching to my other foot. "Eat them bland, if you're so worried. You always drowned them."

I handed him the little cupful of soy sauce and ate with my fingers.

"Why aren't you working tonight?" I said. "It's almost six."

"Eat first, you're hungry."

"I'm eating, Appa, you can see me eating right now—"

"I was looking for the right time to tell you," Appa said, quickly and in an unbroken breath, as though reciting something from memory. Evidently somebody, maybe Umma, maybe the doctors, had reviewed and rehearsed this particular piece with him. "Well, *they* were. They say you're doing well. Your physical therapy's coming along, you're eating more."

I chewed, listening. The big beefy guy who came into my room twice a week, whose arms were bursting out of his sweat-wicking polo shirt, had remarked the last time that I was, in his words, a "grade-A fuckin' superstar." I'd touched my toes for the first time while standing up.

"They think . . . you can come home."

I swallowed. Appa was still holding my foot but had stopped grinding. He looked nervous.

"Okay?" I said.

"With me," Appa said. "Your mother and I, we talked and we think it's time. Especially since you've been doing so well."

He smiled at me.

"You must be excited. Getting out of here. Your own room. Well, you're sharing it now with the computer at home. Don't worry, I'm hardly there."

"Yes," I said softly, and nothing else. His arrival with the dumplings had made me forget the sickliness I'd felt in my stomach watching the nurse pull my catheter out. It was coming back now.

"Well, that's what we think, anyway," Appa said, trying to fill the space. "It happens when you want it to. They—we want you to be comfortable."

Somebody had edged into my room behind Appa, holding their head down. It took me a second to recognize Nurse Gaylord under all the protective gear. We didn't have many chances to talk anymore. He'd fulfilled a brief, pivotal role as my doctor, caregiver, parent, and therapist for the span of that single half hour after I'd woken up and was now back to being just my nurse, one of four on rotation each week: three women and then him. He caught my eye for a second, tapping his fingers at the monitor set in the corner of the room.

It had taken a bit of work to understand that what most people wanted from me right now was to receive credit for giving me a choice when I didn't actually have one. Doctors, nurses, Umma certainly, and more certainly, Appa. It was the exact thing I'd been hoping to avoid the entire time I'd been here, the very dreaded discussion of What Happened Next. To any impartial third party, the answer was simple: Go home. Not just with anybody, with Appa, back to the house where I'd grown up. A tragically ironic turn of events. There was nothing else I could say. Pushing back would lead, inevitably, down a path toward questions like "When can I go back to my job?" and "How long will I stay at home in Fort Lee?" I knew some of those answers. The apartment: long gone. The job, sick leave that expired eighteen months ago. The agency that employed me had since broken up and existed now as three separate firms, none of whom had hired back my old manager or any of my teammates. I still didn't know where Ren was. I tried not to think about him. I'd learned to stop asking.

There remained the question of who was paying for this room now, for the painkillers in a steady drip into my arm, and who had been paying for them the past two years. Umma was a determined enough person that I could ask her a hundred more times and still would get the same answer, which was nothing.

Eventually, I nodded.

"Yeah," I said, "okay. I want to go home. Let's go home."

Appa's face lightened a bit. I felt air leave his chest, as though he'd been holding it, waiting for me.

"I think he's ready, yeah?" He turned to Nurse Gaylord, who had come around to the same side of the bed.

"I'll get his doctor in," Nurse Gaylord said. "They'll check you over one more time"—the corners of his eyes wrinkled together, and I realized he was smiling—"and you'll be out of here."

"Unbelievable, really," Appa said, clapping him on the shoulder. "Together more than two years, you and me. You've been here with him the longest, haven't you?"

"Believe so," Nurse Gaylord said, sounding proud. He glanced at me, then at Appa. "I don't want to have to tell you this," he said, "but, if he's leaving now, you should know. . . ."

Appa frowned at him, briefly, coming to realize what he meant. "Oh, fucking hell."

He crossed the room to the window, peering outside.

"Cockroaches." He said it so venomously that I almost saw a different person standing there. I'd never heard Appa put so much contempt behind his voice.

"What are you talking about?"

"Reporters," Appa said. "They've been camped out every couple of nights trying to talk to you ever since you woke up."

There was silence as he and Nurse Gaylord waited anxiously for the reaction they expected me to have.

"There's people out there who want to interview me," I summarized quietly.

"It was a couple of them at first," Nurse Gaylord said. "A couple of the national guys. After a week they moved on. It's just New York One, most of the time."

"Are we going to talk to them?"

"*We* are leaving." Appa picked up his coat. "I have a baseball bat in the van."

"What exactly are you going to do to them with a baseball bat?"

"I'm not going to do anything if they keep their distance," Appa said, and it was not lost on me that he told me this in Korean while Nurse Gaylord looked passively over his shoulder at the waiting news vans. "We won't talk about this any further. This is a happy day. We had a feeling, the family, that today would be the day, so the restaurant's closed and we're throwing you a little homecoming—"

He was talking to nobody, halfway out of the doorway, when he mentioned he'd be back in a few minutes, leaving my nurse and me alone in the room.

"How do you feel?" he asked me.

"That's a complicated question," I said.

"I meant more like, are you in any pain," Nurse Gaylord said sheepishly.

"Oh, no."

He came over to the foot of my bed and lifted each of my feet gently. "How are the knees? You're going to be walking for the first time in a while."

I shrugged, watching him roll my ankles gently in clockwise circles. I didn't have anything on, other than a gown, and was probably giving him a straight-on view up my thighs the way he was lifting. I didn't mind. Nurse Gaylord had a way of making me comfortable, more than anybody else.

"A little stiff," he commented, about my ankles, I assumed. "Please just try to do your stretches. They really help."

"I will, thank you—" I said, pausing to look at him. "Um . . . Nurse Gaylord?"

He turned his head and laughed, loudly, and the sound rang in my ears long after he'd finished. I felt happier than I should've felt, having made him laugh. He set my feet down.

"Is that what you've been calling me in your head this whole time?"

He sat next to me and dug around the ring of keycards on his neck to show me the oldest-looking one. A grainy headshot, the first time I'd ever seen the lower half of his face, and above it, the name written in scratched-out letters: "E. Cuddy, RN."

"What's the E for?"

"Emil," he said. "Everybody calls me Cuddy. Except my family. We're all Cuddys. That would be weird."

We looked down at his ID for a while.

"Thank you," I said, "for taking care of me."

"Easy as pie," Emil Cuddy said softly. "You'd be surprised how many patients like to bite on this floor."

I had enough sense, then, to feel heavy at the fact that we would never see each other again. It was a moment that I expected he experienced many times over in a single day. People coming and going. Things would never be quite the same as this. He put his hand on my shoulder.

"Good luck, Jack Jr."

A team had filed into the room behind him, and he disappeared as I was coaxed out of bed and onto my feet. I craned my head as I was wheeled in a chair out into the hallway, looking for him.

3

UNCLE JJ GETS HIMSELF SOME BARBECUE

THE VAN, A '92 CHEVY G20, HAD SPROUTED MORE DENTS THAN I thought humanly possible when Appa finally wheeled me close enough to see it in the parking lot. True to his word, he'd made me wait in the lobby while he ran out and retrieved his weapon. He held the bat over his shoulder while we crossed the asphalt and passed the nearest dark blue van with a satellite dish on top of it. I watched, nervously, but the message had been received. The wheelchair, I'd been told, was mainly for liability reasons, though I'd be allowed to keep it the first six months. The sun had already fallen. I was dressed in spare clothes Appa had brought from home and was still getting used to the way they smelled. Everything had a smell now. I'd become used to the bleach back in the hospital. They'd put a surgical mask on me, which had soaked the bottom half of my face in sweat. I tugged it off once we were outside. The harsh floodlights around the parking lot were catching little particles of dust that sprayed back and forth in the sky.

I knew that Appa had been driving this van for the last twelve years, patching tears in the seats with duct tape and paying the bare minimum to resuscitate its engine when it gave out on a semiannual basis. The entire back area had been stripped to make room for pallets of ice and fish. In a happier time, James and I used to battle most fish-run mornings over who sat in the front with Appa and who rattled around with the dolly and the jumper cables in the back. Often, given the potholes they never bothered to patch on the Van Wyck Expressway, it was a matter of life and death. Appa helped me to my feet. I hesitated, standing in front of the old G20's scratched-to-hell front grill. I placed my hand flat on it, raising goosebumps up my arm at the feel of the metal under my fingertips. It almost seemed like I'd spent more mornings rattling around inside it than in my own bed. I knew every dent and scratch, cold under my hands.

"I haven't mentioned," Appa said, slapping the sliding door with his hand, "Juno's with me."

"What? Juno's here?"

The door slid open from inside before I could say another word. All of a sudden, my gangly nephew stepped out onto the asphalt, decked in sweats, socks, and a pair of the same rubber slides we all used to wear to take showers in college. He was about a foot taller than I remembered; his body looked like somebody had stretched it in every direction for fun. He blinked, trying to adjust his eyes, seeing me.

"Oh, fuck," he said.

"Juno," Appa warned.

"Yikes," Juno said. "Sorry, H-Man, definitely didn't say *fuck*. Never have. Don't know what came over me—"

"Juno," Appa groaned, "just say hi. Please. Let's get on with it."

He left us on our side of the van. We stared at each other. I didn't know what to do but spread my arms wide. "I should . . . yeah?"

"Oh, sure," Juno said in a way that made me feel both stupid for asking and entitled for assuming he wanted a hug in the first place. His baggy hoodie swallowed me, and I breathed a mixture of his deodorant and maybe weed for the briefest second before he pulled away. "Thanks for not dying, Uncle JJ. We missed you."

"Let's go, boys, they're waiting at the restaurant."

I was allowed the front seat. Juno closed himself into the back and settled into a pile of homeless-shelter blankets that he'd molded into the shape of a low-backed chair.

"I bet the masks freak you out, right?" Juno said as we pulled out of the spot and down the road. "We wore them everywhere. Even getting food delivered, you had to put it on for the guy that came to the door. Which doesn't actually make any sense when you had people come into the restaurant with their masks on and take them off once they got to their seats. And people wondered why the numbers spiked so many times on the East Coast. Of course it goes all the way back to the way the government waited until the last possible moment to—"

"We're not talking about that," Appa said. "Juno, I've told you a hundred times not to stress him out."

"I'm not—" I tried to say, drowned out immediately.

"You know, it doesn't happen every day you get to explain to somebody who doesn't know," Juno said, "like those reality TV stars that don't know who gets elected president because they're trapped naked on the island trying to build a fire and take a shit on the beach. Uncle JJ, do you feel like that?"

"Juno."

"H-Man," Juno said, imitating Appa's cadence in a scarily accurate impression of the gravel in his voice.

"We are trying to take things slow with your uncle," Appa said over the roar of the engine. He was basically shouting at this point. "I've told you what this means, haven't I? It means no covid, it means no Trump, no news, nothing."

"Understood," Juno said solemnly, "no news, no nothing. Let's talk weather, yeah? Is that on the table? It's very cold, Uncle JJ, which is good news, you'd think, because of climate change. Can I do climate change, H-Man?"

Appa didn't answer, maybe to keep himself clean and away from rage-induced-stroke territory. Silence, then. I was the only one who was grateful not to be speaking. The van choked and coughed up the ramp onto the freeway, from which we saw the dark face of the hospital in which I'd spent two years of my life fall away and reveal the city across the river. We heard laser noises from behind us. Juno had brought his Nintendo Switch.

"He does the runs with me most weeks," Appa told me. "Hard worker, when he wants. Kid doesn't play any sports, nothing. I keep telling James . . ."

I was watching the city fan out in front of us. It was my first real look at it in who knew how long. Lights on from tip to tip, extending far out into the dark water. I had always liked the way it looked from our side, from Jersey. It looked like a city that didn't have any problems, close enough to see every lit window but far enough not to make out anything inside them. Jostled around by the irregular asphalt on the road, I felt my head grow heavy, but it was manageable. It was ten minutes, tops, from here to the restaurant. Still unfamiliar. Trees whipped past, the sound of the wind egged on by our ancient engine.

"I want you to know," Appa said, "if it's ever too much, you just come tell me, right? I'll take you home. I know it's a lot. I know it's been a lot."

I smiled at him. "I'm okay."

It was true, for now.

I had started to acclimate to the engine noises, though I'd already promised myself, after at least a couple moments in which the brakes appeared not to work, to tell Appa to face the music and impound her. We pulled off the freeway, hitting a network of streets and little brick façades that looked far more familiar. Once we passed the Sunoco station, lights blazing, I'd situated myself. My first time seeing the neighborhood in close to ten years, and nothing—and I do mean nothing—had changed. Same ugly stamp stickers on all the bus stop windows. Same little pop boutique on the corner, just before the block where the restaurant stood, a spindly mannequin in a sleek green sweater dress. How many times had I driven this road in the passenger seat with Appa? In the early moments of the morning just as the dark had begun to fall away with the rising sun. I remembered so much of it.

It was around that time of the morning, on the fish run, that Appa used to tell me how happy it made him that I wanted to stay. That the restaurant would have a new and exciting life when I was finally working it alone. It was a day I imagine he had been looking forward to ever since I was born. Before that, even, since James was born, though James never took to the craft like I did. The two of us, Appa and I, were like artists for a time, sharing a love for the food, the knife work. And when it went away, it seemed Appa kept living it, trying to keep it alive. It was the worst part of the whole thing.

As fast as I'd had time to recognize the neighborhood, we'd slowed to a stop in front of the restaurant. I craned my neck against the window to look up at it. We'd convinced Appa to hire professionals to install the new signage around 2008. A stark white box with the restaurant's name perched right on the corner. Sleek and expensive looking, now with a couple of bits of dust and dead bugs behind the white plastic. Somebody was going to have to climb up there and clear it all out. The windows were bright and lit but frosted. I could see figures moving around back there. Juno stepped out onto the sidewalk and opened my door.

He traded a glance with Appa, then offered me a hand. It was happening really quickly, faster than I'd imagined.

"Remember what I said," Appa told me. I took Juno's hand and made my first step, foot hitting concrete. The rhythm was harder than ever to find. I realized my heart was beating faster as Juno led me to the door, dug into his pocket for a key, and let me inside. Buzzy conversation halted to silence. It stayed silent when I pushed the door open, flooded my eyes with light, and saw the restaurant for the first time in twelve years. The tables were empty, chairs balanced on top of them in increasingly convoluted figurations. The window to the kitchen was a light box near the back that threw everything into relief. I was struck first by how tiny it all was, how much we were able to make happen inside these little walls, earning just enough money to pay the bills but not enough to afford much more than a few new baubles and a box of candy canes at Christmas. I remembered that none of us minded very much. This place was where Appa made his life meaningful, and was to be mine as well, one day. Money was a difficult thing to hold up as one's reason for living. Still, I knew he and Umma had suffered. It was unimaginable, the kind of work Appa had probably done to keep Joja open while the country shut down. At the same time, there was nowhere else he could be but here.

They were gathered in front of the sushi bar, Appa's station. I saw Umma first, holding a little plate in her hands, eating with chopsticks. Behind her, my brother, James, who had grown a scraggly Asian beard fit for a backpacking nomad. We looked at each other. I felt the seconds pass. I could count the years more succinctly with James. More than three since we'd spoken on the phone, five since I'd seen his face. What do you say to a group of people that you spent years of your life trying very hard not to see, not to think about, not to talk to more than a couple times a year, anything, and are just now coming around to meeting as if for the first time? As if you hardly knew them to begin with? Umma put a hand on his shoulder.

"Hey," I said.

"Hey," James said quickly, repeating it more so than responding. He was quiet for a while, a moment that felt much longer than it really was. We came to our senses at the same time. He turned his head toward the kitchen, called: "N-Noa, Noa, he's here."

James's wife pushed through the kitchen doors, puncturing the silence.

"Did someone say he's—" She stopped, seeing me. "Oh . . ."

She crossed the room, moving faster than I'd ever seen her, and tackled me. I tried to breathe easy breaths with her arms around me, the two of us teetering on the spot. She was crying, "Oh God, I prayed for this, thank God, thank God." She held my face in her hands. "You look really good."

"Noa," I said, trying not to get her hair in my mouth when she wrapped her arms around me again, "Noa, you're crushing me—"

Appa and Juno had edged themselves in beside me.

"I just can't believe it," Noa said, wiping her eyes, letting me go. "There's so much to say, too much—"

She stopped herself. Over her shoulder, James had turned his back and was serving himself another plate from the trays set on the bar.

"Well," she said, "maybe I shouldn't—I mean, we definitely shouldn't be—we've been told not to—"

"Noa," I said, squeezing her hands, "it's really good to see you too."

She nodded, taking slow breaths. Umma had come around to us and had curled her arm around my waist. Noa had caught her breath. Shaking her head, she tried several times to speak.

"Breathe," Umma said, to all of us. "This is going to take some getting used to. How was the car ride?"

"Bumpy," I said. I was led farther in, closer to the bar. I could smell barbecue and ssamjang and wanted to figure out the easiest way to get to it before my legs gave out. "Appa needs to sell that van. It's a death trap."

"Why don't you tell him that and see what happens?"

"You make it sound like you already know what he'd say."

"Don't you?" Umma asked me, smiling.

"I really didn't make enough food," Noa was saying, "there was ten pounds of the short rib on sale at H Mart that I found myself saying—"

"Noa," I said, almost begging her, "please, just—it's great, Noa. It's all great."

She nodded again. "I'm sorry."

"I'm not trying to cause chaos around here," I said. "It kind of feels like I am."

"Don't say that," she told me, "how could it be anything else? I mean, God, the way you used to look when you were sleeping, I just—" She stopped herself again. "I'm really bad at this. Come here, eat something." She guided me to a chair and plunged my shoulders downward. I sat.

Noa had always been different. I knew exactly the last time we'd spoken. Juno's fourteenth birthday. She'd called after I left a message. She said something I could still remember, word for word, that Juno had been "begging tooth and nail" for a Nerf Accustrike Raptor-Strike rifle with the built-in clip extender. I'd told her, "fighting tooth and nail." People *fought* tooth and nail. She'd said, "My apologies, William Shakesqueer." Massively stupid. Low-hanging fruit to be honest. But for a straight woman? For Noa? Star caliber. Call the Apollo.

Noa had gone in the direction of the food to find a plate for me. Umma nudged me toward the bar. "Appa's been running around the house getting your room ready. He told you, didn't he? The computer's in there. James—James, come here."

A plate of the barbecue had been pushed into my hands along with a plastic fork. I ate quietly. James found his way to us. He'd put on weight, most of it around his gut. Gray hairs on the sides of his head. He shifted his weight on each foot, trading off every second or so. We were both eating, each aware acutely of the other's presence. It was worse than I'd imagined.

"Weird," he commented finally. I felt my balance tip and realized Umma had left us to talk alone. I tried to figure out whether he was saying that talking to me was weird, or looking at me was weird, or maybe just that I was weird. "How does it feel?"

I shrugged. "It's a lot to get used to."

He was doing that thing that had always gotten a rise out of me when we were younger. Observing the rest of the world beyond me, making veiled attempts to pay attention. It was his method of avoiding confrontation, which, elegantly and easily, led very swiftly to confrontation most of the time. He was drinking a tallboy of Diet Coke, which I didn't think they even made, but there it was, a mammoth of a drink with aspartame playing the role of alcohol.

"You've got a baby," I said.

"I've got a baby," he said, turning up the corners of his mouth in order to smile. "Can you believe another boy? We called him Sam."

I had no idea how to talk to him. I looked around, trying to attract another participant to our conversation.

"Is it different, this time?" I asked him.

"Sure it is, Jack Jr.," James said. "We have even less money this time around."

He smirked, as though having made a joke.

"He's—" I broke off. "Sleeping, I guess."

"We put him down in the kitchen."

There was nothing more to say about my new nephew, nothing James was going to tell me. We took turns looking around the crowded restaurant.

"It looks good."

My brother's eyes flitted in my direction for a brief moment. "Yeah, it does," he said. "Good enough to miss it, this time? Or no?"

I let the words rattle around inside me while a flush of realization came over James's face at what he'd said to me.

"What the fuck, James?"

He made something of a blustery roll of his shoulders, trying not to care. "So we're not joking about that. Got it."

"No, James, what the fuck did you say to me? I walked in here five minutes ago."

"It's really nice of you to come in here and tell me how good the place looks, Jack," James said. "Cracked tables, duct tape all over the pipes, you're being really generous. Thank you so much for that."

He was trying to hide something, more than likely the fact that talking to me was taking more of his mental faculties than he had ever been willing to give me. We were, at present, having the dumbest possible argument any two people could possibly have, and were managing to get as worked up about it as two cousins fighting over a dead grandparent's bequest. It was too late to tell him that I'd meant what I said instead of sniping at him the way he always seemed to delight in doing to me. I saw Umma out of the corner of my eye, watching us.

"This has been fun," I told him. "I'll go now. I'll go see my nephew."

"You shouldn't be walking."

"Don't tell me what to do."

"I'm just—" James fell quiet. We looked around us. Umma and Appa off by a corner of the dining room, consulting each other about the paint on the walls. Juno eating silently with Noa at a table with his Switch in his lap. James shook his head.

"I really, really don't want to do this with you today, Jack. You are getting upset over absolutely nothing. You need to know this."

"You're a fucking asshole," I said, barely listening, hoping that pronouncing the words themselves would make things make sense again, being wrong.

He appeared to shake it off, smiling again. "You know, Jack, we missed you. We missed this."

I stared at him. "What are you doing?"

James smiled again, and I saw more clearly how much it hurt him to do it. "Just . . . missed you. You still manage to be that person you were ten years ago. You are a person who cannot stand to live without everybody's attention. It kills you. It's impressive, honestly. We all—"

Space had closed around us for a moment. The sound had been my plate, which had fallen out of my hands and shattered in a sloppy mess around our feet. I saw Umma's eyes next, wide and hurt.

"Jack." Appa had come over to us and laid his hands on my shoulders. "Let's take a seat, huh?" I didn't remember standing up.

I was being steered away but didn't move. "I'm sorry," I said, blinking.

"He's upset," Noa said. "Somebody get him some water."

"Jack, we're going over to the chairs now—"

"Appa, I'm okay—"

"Just come here."

"No."

"Jack—"

"*No*—" I made them all jump. I hadn't meant to be as loud as I was. Whatever pressure lock I had over the boil of my emotions was, like everything else, massively atrophied and apparently unable to keep me from saying anything.

"Jack, please—"

"I am sick," I said, "of being treated like a vegetable. Do you see me standing here? Do you see me right now? I'm not asleep anymore. I've woken up. What I need is somebody to just answer my questions and stop pretending like I didn't just—"

"I know," Appa said calmly, "I understand you, Jack. I just think it would be better if—"

"Where is Ren?" I asked, my voice faltering. "Why won't anybody tell me what happened to Ren? Why isn't he here?"

Appa was trying hard to smile but I could tell it was breaking up inside him.

"What happened to me, Appa?" I asked him. "What happened? Please, just tell me what happened—"

The silence had become a roar in my ears, sapping energy, filling every part of my body with heavy liquid. James had fixed his eyes directly on the floor, at the food I'd let fall to the ground. Appa took a little breath in. I saw him turn Umma's way for a split second. When you think about it, there's very little parents are able to keep from you once you progress to adulthood. There is nobody you know better than a person who spent thirty-plus years baring their hopes, fears, everything to you, in the way they tied your shoelaces, made you lunch, paid for your college. It struck me that I could recognize every look Appa gave anybody. I'd seen them all. In this one I knew: He was going to tell me something that would hurt me. Theirs was a calm that might have seemed callous to people who didn't know them. But to me, I could tell. They were as afraid as I was.

"Please," I said.

"We shouldn't be talking like this."

"Oh, I'm sorry," I said, "we're going to pretend that it's normal, that I drove a car into the Hudson and crashed so badly that a piece of my brain is missing. I've got it now. Thank you, for letting me know. Thank you for all of this *fucking* patience."

I felt guilty as soon as I said it, as there had been a nicer way of saying it, especially to Appa, but whatever he might have done in my youth to curb me for speaking that way to him, he wasn't going to do it now. He took a while to speak.

"Jack," he said, "we don't know why you did that. The first six months you were asleep, the police went over every second. We had to tow your car out of the water. We don't know."

"That doesn't make any sense."

"We did everything we could. You were the only person there; you're the only one who would know."

"Why wasn't Ren with me?"

"He wonders why," James said quietly. "Really."

"*James*—"

"Fuck you—"

Somebody, I don't know who, was holding me back from getting within swinging range of my brother. I fought, momentarily, not yet ashamed, and was finding my legs starting to give out. I hung limp in—I turned my head slightly—Juno's arms.

Appa closed his mouth. James had forced his eyes downward farther. There wasn't a thing in the world I could do to make him look at me, no matter how bad I wanted it. Noa was standing between us, color drained from her face. She looked ready to cry, which made me feel worst of all.

"It's late," Appa said finally, "this was too much. Let's all just—just go home."

He raised his hand, putting his palm in front of my face when I opened my mouth.

"I will answer all the questions you have in the morning. Let's just go home, Jack. It's late, I've got a fish run in the morning."

My face burned. I felt his hands steer my shoulders toward the door. Again he pushed, and this time I let him guide me. I felt their eyes on us as we headed out to the van. Appa glanced back at the frosted glass; the amber light seemed without some of the color it'd had just a half hour ago.

"I'll be right back," he said, and was gone. I stood, beginning to shiver. Juno came through the doors, finding me.

"That was really emo of you," he said after a while.

I stared at him until he shrugged. He took out his Switch.

"I'm sorry, Uncle JJ. I know you're frustrated."

Sounds of clearing tables had come from inside the restaurant.

"Juno," I said, "I need to borrow your phone."

"Why?"

"Just give it to me."

He dug it out of his pocket, unlocked it, and placed it in my hand. I hobbled to the other side of the van, on the street. I knew the number. I'd memorized it around the time I'd started to put his name down as my emergency contact. I remembered it well. It was right after I'd bought the ring, right after he'd told me yes and we'd started looking for something to do, something private but cheap, something we could do to celebrate, before we told anybody. A cottage, some-where upstate. Nice thick woods, the smell we both loved. Long, winding roads that hugged the Hudson all the way up the river. How far north had they found the car? Was it the way I imagined it? The back fender sticking out through the water, the front a mangled mess of glass and crumpled metal? My fingers found the right buttons. I held the phone up to my ear, waited. Dialing, then rings. Then a click—"Hello?"

I felt my spine straighten, hearing his voice. I tried to think sim-ple, coherent thoughts.

"Hey," I said slowly, "it's me."

The voice on the other end didn't respond.

"I know," I said, "I know it's weird. I know you didn't know . . . or maybe you did. But I'm awake now. And I miss you. And I don't know why but my family doesn't want to tell me what happened and—"

I caught myself, feeling my eyes water.

"I just don't know what's happening anymore. I just need somebody to tell me something. Anything. Just tell me anything. Please."

I could still hear him, faint background noises on the line that sounded like television, or maybe a sensibly busy dinner out. It was all I wanted. To go back to how it had been, before the dark, before the sleep that seemed to have wiped everything I used to have clean off the face of the earth and replaced it with—this. With me, getting stopped from jumping my own brother like we were ten years old again by his teenage kid. With me, being cruel to my parents just for the sheer satisfaction of taking my anger out on someone I knew I could hurt. I didn't want this anymore. All I needed was Ren. If I had nothing else but him it would be all right, we would find a way. And he would tell me so. He was always better at calming me down, better than anybody. So I waited for it to happen. Waited for just about another second, enough time for me to register he was still there, before he hung up. I heard the click, then the whoosh of silence. I took the phone off my ear and saw the call screen change to rows of icons. Juno had come to me on the other side of the van.

"Uncle JJ?"

I heard it, a couple more times, or maybe not, before pain exploded in my knees where they'd hit the asphalt, cold and hard, sharp and gritty. I heard shouts, understanding nothing. I felt the cool rest of sleep coming, after all this time, and remembered thinking a word, just one word, *Finally*.

I OPENED MY EYES, ADJUSTING to bright light and familiar bleachy smells; waking up was almost easy now. I'd forgotten how far I'd come. I blinked, acclimating to the presence of several blurry shapes, sun coming in through the windows. A part of me just wanted to go back to sleep, but something spurred me on, farther out toward the surface. Beeps and ticks. The sun, high and shining white over me, was not the sun and had slimmed out, shimmying into the shape of rods along a white ceiling. Fluorescent bulbs. I blinked, and blinked again. Nighttime. I was in a warm, sterile bed with sheer curtains pulled across the dark view of the cityscape. In front of me: a blaring TV screen, a doorway into a busy hallway. And I was there, warm within the sheets, lying across from him, sitting in his chair like he always was, wrapped in plastic-looking clothes, a mask, a visor, covered from head to toe so that the only parts I could see of his face were his eyes.

"Oh." I turned my head away from him, shameful. "For fuck's sake."

Emil Cuddy laughed.

"You know," he said in a voice that heated me like bathwater, "I'm beginning to think you kind of just like being here."

4

FISH RUN

HE WASN'T WRONG. THERE WERE MANY UPSIDES TO INDEFINITE CON-
finement in a hospital suite. The most attractive part by far being my
best friend, my motor bed. A 2009 Invacare G-Series Full Electric
Bed. Top of the line. Plus, memory-fill pillows for increased lumbar
support. One button sits you up, props your feet, heats when you ask
it, cools when you've had too much heat. On top of that, people who
brought you water, food, juice in the mornings when you asked for it.
This was no secret, I realized: I *did* like being there. There was no
end to the pains outside the confines of my Invacare: aging parents,
alcoholic brother, hospital bills, stagnating economic climate for
small family-run businesses, Ren. Always Ren.

My blackout had been chalked up to dehydration. I was told that
I needed to be very careful, to drink at least six large glasses of room-

temperature water a day. This was said to me in a tone that suggested that a single cube of ice was going to burn a hole straight through my throat and kill me.

So it happened that I had spent seven more hours of my life completely unconscious despite not wanting to, during which time I was bathed once again, fitted for another breathing tube—and catheter—and placed in a fresh Invacare G-Series Full Electric Bed two doors down from the room I'd slept in for the last twenty-three months. There was no telling what kind of calamity would ensue this time, whether my stay would turn out to be a blip, a result of being discharged just a hair too soon, or I was coming back in for the long haul and would remain in this room for another two years. My heart rate, though normal, had been slow when they brought me back in from where I'd collapsed outside the van and sent Juno's cell phone scattering to the ground. They were taking precautions. It had been a long, disappointing evening. I was not only possibly confused but, from what I could gather, single again.

Cuddy held a water cup and attachable bendy straw to my lips. I drank. I had been blinking slowly and doing nothing else for a few minutes since and was, for now, happy to remain while nobody was there to ask anything of me.

"How long was I out?"

"Almost the whole night," he said, "exhaustion, they think. Not enough water, bit too much time on your feet than you were ready for. It happens. You're stable."

I wasn't, but he sounded like he knew what he was talking about.

"I felt somebody touching me."

"I needed to make sure we weren't dealing with something more serious," Cuddy said. "Plus, you were covered in dirt after you fell."

"You touched my balls."

"You know I've touched your balls, like, three hundred times, don't you? You got a sponge bath every other night."

"Gross."

Cuddy ignored me. "Your dad said there was some kind of disagreement. Something stress you out?"

I finished the water. He crumpled the paper cup in his hand and lobbed it into the trash can a few feet away.

"I don't have my life anymore."

"Categorically untrue," Cuddy said. "Unless you mean figuratively. In which case, I'm sorry. This must be frustrating for you."

"Happens," I told him, which didn't make any sense given that things like this probably never happened, hence the shock and awe I seemed to produce wherever I went. I wasn't in the mood to explain it all to him, even if it would've given me somebody to talk to.

"Oh my God," I said suddenly, "I'm thirty."

"There's nothing wrong with that."

"Nothing wrong, sure, but I'm still thirty. And without even realizing it," I said. "Are you thirty?"

"Two years ago."

"Just talk to me about something." I grabbed at my forehead with both hands, pressing down into my eye sockets. "I need to think about something else. What do you do on your shifts?"

Cuddy was nice enough to do what I asked, setting down a fresh bag of saline and taking up his spot in the nearest chair.

"It can be interesting some nights, other nights just a lot of walking around, checking vitals, flicking baggies. Quiet, really. This floor was an overflow ICU until recently. We wore a lot of hats while it was happening. I'm glad we're getting back to normal."

"For how long did you . . ." I didn't want to ask but didn't have anything else to say.

"About nine months," he told me. "Every bed in this building we used for the covid folks that needed to be intubated, minus a couple." He paused. "Yours, for one."

He'd looked away from me while he said it, glancing down at his hands. I was used to talking to him this way, through all the plastic and masks. I'd gotten used to it. I could tell so much about what he was thinking just from the little inch of his face that showed. He could telegraph whole monologues with those eyebrows. It felt nice, knowing someone as well as I knew him. Except I didn't really know him at all.

As for what he'd just told me, I knew more than Appa thought I knew. There wasn't much of a way around it when the TV stayed on all day. More than five million dead around the world, last I heard them say. It was a heavy number. It was hard to imagine watching a number like that pile up over the months like Cuddy had. Like they all had.

"I bet that was tough."

Cuddy raised and lowered his shoulders. "Look at us now. Hardly anybody in for that anymore. Changes in a second. It feels far away. But yes."

He sighed.

"I saw a lot of nursing friends quit this past year," he said. "It just kills you, in a way. People have a finite measure of energy. When it's gone, it's gone."

"That's good," I told him. "Good line. Get some documentarians to film you saying that."

I swallowed, wincing as my burning throat coiled up inside me.

"Did you want to? Work the ICU and see all those people die, I mean."

"I didn't have a choice," Cuddy said softly, and I couldn't tell whether he meant that he wasn't given one or he didn't let himself have one. I glimpsed his eyes under the plastic visor. "It's not good for you to talk about things like this," he said finally. "You're only just acclimating."

He stood.

"You've got a busy day ahead of you, Jack Jr. You're being discharged in an hour."

"What? What time is it?"

"Four-thirty."

"In the morning?"

"Your dad's on his way."

I sat up, feeling stronger. "And what do you imagine he thinks he's about to do with me at four-thirty in the morning?"

"Something that couldn't wait," Cuddy said, amused. "He mentioned something about a fish run? I'm not sure what that is. He was really excited on the phone telling me about it. Is that right?"

I waited for him to follow that up with something that was supposed to make me laugh. As though he knew. As though Appa weren't actually rocketing his way down the freeway in the van to come and get me and take me on my first fish run in twelve years. Which is, as it turned out, exactly what he was doing.

"You've got to be fucking kidding me."

CUDDY CAME WITH US THE second time they wheeled me out through the double doors, a scenario that, aside from the addition of him walking with us, was unbearably similar to the last time I'd been allowed to leave like this. Same nippy bite in the air, same psycho-ward socks on my feet, different spare clothes with Kirkland Signature labels. Juno climbed out of the back of the van and helped me to my feet.

"Uncle JJ, I'm helping you to the right side of the van," he announced slowly. "I'm doing it very slowly, and you don't need to be afraid or go crazy on us again."

"I can see what you're doing, Juno, you don't have to tell me."

"H-Man said I have to make sure you know what's happening to you at all times," Juno said. "And to talk to you so that you're always hearing somebody's voice. Here goes. Yesterday, I made my chem partner and me fail a lab because I screwed the beaker in backward and spilled one-point-eight-molar hydrochloric acid onto the floor. *Molar* means—"

"I know what *molar* means," I said, feeling my face burn, agitated by the cold air. "Just stop talking." Cuddy was trying very hard not to laugh, watching us. I slid onto the pleather seat and buckled myself in. Juno shut the door behind me.

Cuddy approached the window. We had arrived, again, at the very last time we would ever see each other for the rest of our lives. There wasn't much else to say that we hadn't already been through.

After a moment he pulled his mask to his chin. The edges of the beard I'd seen on his cheeks and neck thus far hadn't totally indicated its fullness, or the fact that with it, he looked a lot older than the picture ID he'd shown me. I'm not sure why he did it. Maybe he'd remembered he was outside. Or maybe he'd just wanted to show me.

"Thank you," I said. "Again."

"Good luck," Cuddy said. "Again."

Appa had packed away the wheelchair and started the engine.

"I can't believe I've got you on another fish run," he said, almost to himself. He sounded about ten years old. "How long has it been, Jack Jr.? Since the two of us went out there together?"

"Since before I knew how to use a toilet," Juno said from the back.

"Just so you know, they've changed up so much of it," Appa said, "commercial as hell now. Some people just walk in there like it's a grocery store now. They used to ban idiots like that, didn't they? Who's self-possessed enough to think they can just walk into a proper fish market like that? People like that don't even know what they're looking for. They're slowing it all down for the rest of us. They're wasting their time, and ours."

"Would you explain to me one more time why you're not driving me home?" I asked him. "Do you know I still haven't been home? Did you remember?"

"You've been asleep eight hours," Appa said, waving me off. "If you get any more sleep today, your brain's going to go soft. Humans aren't meant to sleep longer than eight hours. Is that right, Cuddy?"

He punched me hard in the arm.

"Ow."

"Two of my boys, just like it used to be." He grinned. "I think we're ready, Juno. We set?"

"Ready, H-Man." Juno had wrapped his head in the hood of his sweatshirt and had slumped up against the door.

"Emil, do me a favor, come to the restaurant sometime," Appa called over the engine. "Any time you like. You eat for free, always."

Cuddy waved his hand modestly. He seemed to read the desolate expression on my face and smiled in an apparent effort to cheer me up. What an image we must have struck for him.

"Please take care of yourself," he said to me. Then: "I don't want to see you come back here."

"Wishful thinking," I said.

"That you'll take care of yourself or that you won't come back?" Cuddy asked me.

Appa pulled out of our parking spot before I could answer.

WE MADE THEM EVERY SUNDAY and Thursday, always Sunday, always Thursday, before the best of the vendors sold out. Appa had come to know almost all of them by now and tended to court them in the fashion of a swing voter approaching largely inconsequential state elections: that is, trying to keep as many opportunities open as possible at the risk of absolute alienation, which is what might come from bartering an entire community of fishmongers down to bare insanity. Purchases depended on the season: sea bream, snapper, salmon (Pacific, not Atlantic, Appa insisted. He swore against farmed fish), mackerel, sweet shrimp, king crab, trout and flying fish roe, littleneck clams, razor clams, abalone when the crop was good. "Tuna, Jesus, the *tuna*," Appa used to say, to anybody who would listen, "fifty pounds of tuna a week, it's all people want to eat. Can't make it fast enough. Mashed up, mayo, chili pepper. Perverse, if you ask me. Only flavor you're getting is the mayo. These fucking people."

We tried not to mention spicy tuna around Appa.

Such was the rhythm of my childhood. As soon as I'd turned ten, it was across the river in the van to the salty-aired open market in the Financial District two days a week. Each morning, four-thirty in the morning. The shopping would take an hour, less in the colder months. Back across the river, to the restaurant. After James and I had gotten all the pallets off the van and into cold storage, Appa would drive us home. We'd get an hour, maybe ninety minutes, to scrub the fish guts out from under our fingernails and climb into bed for a few desperate chasings of sleep, after which the sun would rise and the world would wake alongside us. In 2005 the glorious Fulton Fish Market moved from Manhattan to sunny, barren Hunts Point, on a lot that included both a Budweiser brewery and a megasize Citarella. Almost twice as long to drive. Still, Appa went. I hauled fish every week until I graduated high school. Things had changed by then. Yelling and screaming and doors slammed shut. James in rehab, James in the hospital after breaking his teeth falling down the stairs in the dead of night. James in jail for a day and a half after driving his car into a telephone pole with two-year-old Juno in the backseat. It was the only time I'd ever seen Umma hit somebody, James, square across the face with her palm when Appa brought him home that afternoon. Nobody remembered James in those days like I did.

Still, after the fish runs ended, remnants leaked through. Ren once told me I still woke up some mornings and paced around the room, putting on imaginary gloves, picking up imaginary pallets, before I could be coaxed, drowsy and compliant, back to the blankets. I didn't believe him. He was absolutely fucking with me, given that I'd never remember doing any of it. He'd heard all the stories about the fish runs and had ample material. Still, one wondered.

After half an hour of dark roads, tires screaming as they hit new patches of asphalt, we had reached the parking lot, miles of it, out in the open overlooking the river. In the distance loomed the green-topped warehouse, serviced by slow-moving trucks pulling away from its industrial loading bays. It had come out at us faster than I had expected, revealing itself, sidling into shape between gaps in the morning fog: the New Fulton Fish Market, enrobed in moonlight, in

all its briny glory. Appa chose our spot in a sparser patch of the asphalt, then ordered me to sit tight; he and Juno opened up the van.
When he waved, I unbuckled and stepped onto frozen ground.

"You need a hat," Appa said. He jerked his head in Juno's direction. "Give him your hat, Juno."

"It's really ok—"

Juno pressed his hat into my hands. Both of them stared at me
until I put it on, getting a shock of Pantene conditioner and teen-boy
smell, and maybe more weed, as I did so. Appa put an arm around
my shoulder and walked me up, leaving Juno to lug the dolly up the
incline after us. We stamped our frozen feet against the ground. Our
breaths dispersed chains of fog around our heads, moving in unison.
If I was ever to imagine the crews of guys who actually went out on
the water to catch all this for us, the lucky customers, I imagined
them the same way: stoic, braced against the cold, looking forward
to hot soup and a cigarette when it was all over. Our job was easier,
much less deserving of soup. My ears rang, adjusting to the silence
from the roar of the van's engine. We weren't alone. I could count a
couple groups of guys, working in pairs or trios. Several were on their
way back, pulling their precious freights, dollies laid high with iceboxes wrapped in cellophane, back across the frozen ground.

James and I were each six years old when Appa took us to the
market for the first time. He'd explained the ungodly hour, the long,
bumpy drive, hours working in the cold. "You understand what we're
looking for? The Quality." He rubbed his pointer and thumb together in front of our faces as he said this, illustrating. "You wouldn't
believe how many scam artists buy frozen, boys. Five-star restaurants. Manhattan! All frozen. People say: Hey, it's good protection
against parasites, spoilage. I say to them if you want to cut corners,
don't you dare set foot in this business. Load of hacks, giving us all
a bad name. Supermarket sushi, for God's sake. If I ever catch one
of you eating supermarket sushi, I'll kill you."

I don't know about James. He wasn't cut out for the business,
but maybe he was more impressed by the theater of the market, the

push and pull of the vendors, the artistry of the butchers and fish-mongers, than he ever shared with any of us. I, for one, drank the fucking Kool-Aid. There was nothing more badass than my father among those fishmongers, using the curved ice pick he kept in the van to pick up those fish by their gills, hoisting them out of the ice, feeling along their bellies, lifting their spiny fins and splaying them out in the air. Watching the master labor away, his never-ending search for the Quality. I was lucky to be there.

There was a lot to say about when it all went to shit. I was finish-ing high school. I loved Appa and I loved the restaurant. I was better than anybody at the knife work, the sculptural skill required to form the perfect bite, the equal ratio of fish to rice. Taking over the restau-rant had been a moment I'd been waiting for, preparing for, my entire life. It was all I could do. All I was good at. What happened, then?

LET'S CHANGE THE SUBJECT.

The inside of the warehouse swelled into view as we passed through the doors, air colder than the chill outside. Down an open walkway in the middle lay hundreds of tables, stacked boxes packed with ice, tanks spilling water out onto the floor to swirl around the drains set into the concrete. The smell always hit you first, abso-lutely nothing like the supermarket: entrails, brine, chum. Appa had kept his hand around my shoulders as we walked. I took stock of it all. Scallops pulsing in saltwater vats. An octopus wholesaler laying each tangle of white and purple tentacles out like cabbages in the ice. I peered over the tables at the teams of guys on the edges, break-ing up the larger catches. Appa stopped us near one of the tables, out in front of a two-hundred-pound bluefin tuna hoisted into the air by chains. Juno handed him his ice pick, and, like a maestro, he was off, leaving us with the dolly. Juno was scrolling something on his phone, which I saw now was sporting a massive crack on its front.

"Hey, Juno," I said.

He glanced at me, hardly noticing.

"I wanted to say I'm sorry," I told him, "for last night. And for your phone."

"Sure," he said. A yawn rippled through his body and he stretched his arms high above his head. "I probably shouldn't have given it to you in the first place."

He kicked some more feeling into his feet. He was on thin ice to begin with, wearing socks and slides around so much free-flowing fish fluid.

"You didn't tell anybody what I did, did you?" I asked him.

He shook his head. "Sounded like you didn't want anybody to know."

Juno looked at me properly, an inquisitive expression crossing his face. I noticed, then, the dash above his left eye, the thinnest white line in his eyebrow that was all that remained of the scar he'd gotten when James had crashed his car almost fifteen years ago. Noa left him, taking Juno and disappearing for six months after that. Was there anything else she could have done? My own mother probably agreed. But as it was, something there was meant to stay whole. She'd come back, and James had been sober ever since.

"Do you ever think about how fast things change, Uncle JJ?"

"It feels a little too early for questions like that."

"No, really," Juno said. "Just a while ago you were hooked up to machines, so asleep that somebody could've come in and pulled all your teeth out and you wouldn't have noticed. Now you're out here, on a fish run again, talking to me. I was so little when you stopped working at the restaurant, and now you're back. It's crazy. What are we supposed to do with that? What does it mean?"

Appa waved at us from where he stood. I waved back.

"I think it means I don't belong here anymore."

"Nobody belongs here but H-Man," Juno said. "He's the only person in the entire world whose favorite part of the day happens before the sun is up."

Appa had made his selection, two portions of belly and back that were being packed with ice. He pointed to the carcass still on the table. "Clear eyes, Jack," he said. "Remember what I told you? Cloudy eyes means rotten fish. These boys are fresh killed, you can see the life still in them, can't you?"

"Can you tell me something?" I asked Juno. "'H-Man,' where the fuck did that come from? You've never called him that before."

"It beats Harabeoji, like, fuck, what a mouthful. And so *ethnic*." Juno bowed his head, miming prayer with his hands in front of his chest. "We serve at his pleasure, blessed and wise Grandfather."

We laughed at that.

"Your accent's gotten better," I said. "Who are you practicing Korean with?"

Juno seemed genuinely interested in me for the first time that morning. "Couple of dramas I've been watching. Maybe they're rubbing off on me."

"You're watching K-dramas," I said flatly.

Juno cleared his throat loudly. "Good plot. Complex characters. Really draws you in. I like the period stuff."

His voice hadn't even dropped the last time I'd seen him. I didn't know who this guy was, sometimes, when I looked at him. Some little clues, here and there. We had the same nose. Noa's rounded eyebrows. I had known only one thing about the twelve-year-old version of him: The bigger the truck, the greater his love. I sent him fire trucks, oil tankers, scale models of those land movers with wheels as tall as buildings. Every birthday and Christmas, he was the easiest to buy for. Sometimes, the phone call he gave me afterward was the only time we talked the whole year.

We watched Appa engage in hushed conversation with two guys by a carcass currently being divided up.

"You must be happy about the baby. It's special, having a brother."

Juno made a noise through his nose, a noise entirely identical to a noise I'd been hearing James make my entire life. He changed the subject just as fast as his father, too.

"Are you ever going to talk to my dad again?" he asked me.

"What do you mean? We talked last night."

"Yeah, you did, and you fucking died, like, two minutes after."

"That wasn't why I passed out—" I stopped myself. "Besides, how should I know? Why don't you ask him? He doesn't talk to me either."

"Easy. You make sense, Uncle JJ. He doesn't."

He said this harsher than anything I'd ever heard him say. What was clear: We had crossed into territory that didn't feel so comfortable anymore and I was gambling by pushing it any further.

"We used to talk," I said unconvincingly. "Just because things are complicated doesn't mean they're difficult."

"Uh-huh," Juno said. We didn't have anything else to say about it.

"You're being really good to him, coming out twice a week like this," I said, nodding my head toward Appa.

"Whatever. It makes him so happy," Juno said. Appa was on his way back, two guys behind him teaming up to carry the icebox over our way.

We stood and watched for a moment before Juno started.

"Crap—" he stammered, "I forgot my ice."

"Juno, where are you—"

He'd already taken off at a run toward the nearest vendor.

"My extra credit," he shouted. "I need ice. Hey, sir, sir—"

"Juno—"

"Like, clear ice, ice you can see out of," Juno was explaining, using mostly his hands, while the vendor crossed his tree-trunk forearms over his chest. "I get ten points added to my chemistry final if I can make an ice lens that refracts enough light to fill—"

I ran to catch up with him. "What are you doing?"

Juno hadn't yet given up with the bear in the overalls. "I don't know, man, maybe you pass glaciers out there in the water, are you sure? I'll take anything you have."

"Kid, it's five in the morning. Buy something or fuck off."

"I will *buy* the ice," Juno said, "I've got money—"

I steered him away. It was far too early in the morning for a fight like the kind Juno seemed to be itching to have.

"What's going on with you?"

"I need a B in chem."

We reached the doors to the parking lot. I stepped in front of him, blocking the vendors from view. "Explain."

Juno breathed a sigh as burdensome as though I'd asked him to give me one of his kidneys.

"Dr. Cappiano is a sadist," he said. "First of all, he makes us all call him 'Dr.' even though he went to SUNY New Paltz, and second of all, the only extra credit he's giving us is this impossible ice lens project. Who thought of this? Are we in Greenland? The Arctic Circle?"

"I don't think people are normally supposed to get points on their final exams for doing anything," I told him. "That's kind of the point of a final exam."

"I'm getting a C unless I get the credit."

"Just freeze a pot of water in the kitchen."

"I've frozen twenty pots," Juno said. "Every single one: cloudy and cracked. I might get a B if I had an extra ten points."

He got an idea, just then.

"You know chemistry."

"I absolutely do not. I worked in marketing."

"But you're gay."

"Where are you going with this?"

"I don't know, gay people pay attention in school."

"And you . . . don't?"

"If I did, I wouldn't have shattered one of H-Man's pots last weekend." He trudged ahead, taking the dolly from me. "It was ceramic. Show me where on the pot it said 'do not freeze full of water.' Fuckin' anarchists. I've had enough."

APPA SAID THE CATCH HAD been good this season for sea bream, so we'd doubled up on an order. It would shine on his omakase this week, he told us, with a little pickled radish, some shiso leaf. Perfection. Juno hauled the dolly back out onto the asphalt while we followed. The sky had cleared up a bit but still shone green and black over the water. More trucks had pulled into the parking lot. Our totals amounted to salmon, snapper, yellowtail, mackerel, sweet shrimp, scallops, squid, octopus. Appa held in a separate Styrofoam box three cases of tender urchin, Hokkaido strain. He handed this to me as we approached the van.

"What'd you think, Jack Jr.?" he asked me. "Good? Bad? Remember everything?"

"I'd love a good night's sleep, if that's what you're asking."

He patted me on the cheek in response. "Juno, easy with the last box there, the Styrofoam's cracking. . . ."

WE WERE FLYING DOWN THE freeway, headed home. Juno was asleep in the back, head lolling from one shoulder to the other while propped against the iceboxes, which had been strapped by bungee cables to the sides of the van.

"This was amazing," Appa said for about the fifth time, "I'm so glad we did this. It's so good to have you on the fish run, Jack. It's not the same without you."

He kept his hand on the gearshift, squinting out through the windshield. Behind the clouds, the sun had just barely started to surface.

"When you've got some more strength," he said after a while, "maybe you'd want to do some prep with me? Like old times?"

I shrugged.

"It'd be fun," Appa said, testing me out. "We've made a lot of changes to the menu. Couple of interesting takeout options from when we all had to shut down. When I tell you it's a whole different business, let me tell you—"

He laughed to himself, breaking off.

"I shouldn't talk so much," he said. "You look tired."

"I'm okay," I lied.

We drove another mile. The wheels whined under us, crossing newly paved sections of the freeway.

"Some day this week I'll take you to the storage unit in Edgewater," he told me. "It's where we put your things. We've got some clothes at home, in your room."

I nodded wordlessly.

"We've got that couch from your apartment too. I was wondering where you'd want it."

"It was Ren's," I said.

He didn't respond right away. I could see him out of the corner of my sight keeping his eyes on the road.

"Appa," I said.

Again no answer.

"How long do you expect to keep this up? You're lying to me."

"I'm not"—he stopped himself momentarily—"lying to you. I'm not lying, Jack Jr., I promise."

We had reached a new stretch of the road, where the van's tires didn't screech so much rolling over it. Appa glanced behind us at Juno, who was sleeping with his mouth open.

"Maybe your problem is that you only think you want to know," he said, "when actually, maybe you don't. Maybe it wouldn't do you any good to know and you're just not able to see it."

"You need to let me decide that."

"Why?"

"Why should you let me be a regular, normal person?" I said. "I don't know, Appa, because it's the right thing to do? Because I'm not a child?"

"I have taken care of you since the day you were born," Appa said. "You didn't blow your nose without me there. And then what? You just . . . go away after that? Never again? Just because you decide you've grown up?"

"Maybe I don't need to be taken care of anymore."

"Jack Jr."—Appa closed his eyes briefly—"think about where you are right now. You're a couple weeks out of a coma that you've been in for nearly two years. You didn't know who was in the room with you ten days ago. You'd freak out crying and hitting and wanting to go back to sleep. You're moving so fast. Do you know that? If you don't do this right, you're going to break down again. You're going to be in and out of the hospital. You're going to be taking all these steps back when you should be moving forward."

My head had started to throb. I turned away from him and closed my eyes, pressing my forehead against the icy window.

We listened to the road another half mile.

"What if I hurt you," he said, finally, "by telling you? Think of that?"

"He's not here, Appa," I said.

I said it again, wanting to be sure of it myself.

"He's not here."

I thought I would tell Appa later that I had called him. It was beginning to feel less and less right, keeping it from him. It didn't look much like justice, keeping secrets in reverse.

Here was something else I remembered about Ren: the way his hair got weird and wavy the longer it grew. You'd never guess how much hair changes a person's vibe. Ren was, in many ways, the most uptight person I knew, but that hair, when he missed a haircut every now and then. There was a person who was up for anything. To whom a world of experience could just rumble on by and who would sit there and look at it all and smile without a care to be had.

When I looked at him again, Appa had formed a fist with his hand on the steering wheel. We had crossed the river and let ourselves out by the off-ramp just fifteen minutes from home.

"We were engaged," I said.

He turned his head toward me. "When?"

"Couple of days before the accident, I don't know." I shrugged. "We were upstate because we were celebrating. We got a house up there for the weekend. It's where it happened, didn't it?"

He nodded slowly. I found myself shrugging. "I thought maybe we'd come down, see the restaurant after the weekend. He could finally meet all of you."

Appa made a noise with his lips, carefully.

"We did meet him," he said. "He never mentioned you were engaged, though."

"When?"

Appa took a long, slow look at me sitting there across from him. I remember the light at this intersection being so long. His hands were strong, still, but there was much in his face that had softened in the years between.

"When *wasn't* he there, those first few months," he said softly. "Every day. Sometimes more than your mother and I were coming. He brought you music, read books to you, rubbed your feet."

He seemed to linger there, perhaps remembering it himself. He pressed his lips together, hard.

"You know, Jack Jr.," he said, "it was the worst thing I'd ever seen in my entire life, the first time I saw you in that bed. Stitches all around your hip, bruises just . . . just covered in bruises. Your whole face: You were so swollen that I couldn't even recognize you. Every day I came in and saw you, I felt like I was dying, looking at you. But Ren . . ."

He smiled.

"He was good to you. He was good. Told us all sorts of things about your life together, the trips you'd taken. Showed us pictures of the apartment you had together. He lived there a whole year after, you know."

I swallowed, feeling him wanting to reach for me but stopping himself.

"What happened after the year?"

We had driven onto a quiet stretch of the road, lit with streetlights. We stopped at an intersection.

"We were all waiting," Appa said. "We'd done a year together like this, you know. Think about what that means. Every holiday, every special thing that passed, was reminding us you still hadn't woken up. I begged the doctors for something. I told them nothing was off the table, I wanted to try anything that might work. But they said your brain had taken hits that should've killed you. There was no telling when you'd come out of it. If you'd ever. They said the very best thing we could do for you was to keep you comfortable. We couldn't have moved you to Jersey without Ren. He took it all in stride, he made every arrangement, letting your job know, your finances, everything. He paid for half, the whole first year. It's the only reason the restaurant stayed open. That and takeout orders, that first covid summer."

He tried to make himself laugh.

"It was the craziest thing, watching you breathe. Just laid there and breathed all day. Even if the tube was there, even if your eyes were closed. You breathed for two years. How could we give up on you? It always seemed like when you wait for something, spend years and years waiting for it, sometimes you lose sight of what it means, what matters to you. We couldn't with you. Not with you lying there. It was killing him. It was starting to dawn on us that we were going to stay like this forever, waiting for you to wake up. Your mother and I, we had no price. If it was going to be forever, it would be forever. If we had to shut down the restaurant and sell our house, so be it. For us."

"And after that," I said slowly, "what happened after that?"

Appa didn't answer for a minute, searching the road. I could feel my lungs shrunken inside me, waiting, not able to give me full breaths.

"Appa," I said quietly. He looked at me.

"He was young. He had so much life left out there. He loved you. Can you blame him?"

Behind us, Juno made a noise; the both of us bolted around, seeing that he stayed asleep. I turned to face the road, breathing deeply.

"If you'd seen him go through it, come to the hospital, day after day, and realize you weren't ever going to wake up . . . ," Appa said. He pulled ahead, stopping a little farther down, in front of the restaurant. Our breaths were making fog around us, misting the glass. Behind us, Juno adjusted slightly and started to snore.

"Is—" I choked. I hadn't spoken in a while and whatever breath had come out was ragged and worn. "Where is he now?"

Appa sighed. The sun was just peeking up over the tops of the buildings down the road.

"Still in the city," he said. "I called him when you woke up. He didn't know what to say, like the rest of us. It'd been a long time since we'd spoken. He wanted to let us know . . ."

He trailed off.

"He wanted to let us know he'd gotten married."

I nodded shakily. It was an easy thing to do, now that I was doing it. Maybe in my little mind somewhere, I'd been ready for it, had already seen it come to pass and was just now seeing a vision fulfilled. There really was no other explanation, was there? That for days and days he sat at the corner of my bed, reading to me. It was exactly the kind of thing he would do, and not to win points with Appa or the doctors, not even to make himself feel like I was somehow still there, in some capacity, with him. That he was optimistic enough to believe that sleeping people still heard everything around them. And that somewhere, while I floated, I was at peace, hearing him read words.

I had already lost so much time. It was the saddest part of all of it, really, that something true and real had been made and broken all while I slept and I would never really understand how it had happened. I'd only hear the story told. I could've smiled at the thought of Appa telling Ren about the restaurant. Maybe he'd taken him on the fish run one morning. A morning in which I must've looked especially stable, which gradually became every morning. The two of them in the van together, Juno nestled between the pallets in the back. Appa telling him some crackpot story of when I was a kid, the kind of story he could've only gotten away with while I wasn't there with them. Maybe he'd taken him back to the restaurant, offloaded the produce, and cooked him something. Kimchi jjigae, dumpling soup. A recipe my mother had shown him. There they were, celebrating my twenty-ninth birthday together, calling one another, talking about new things the doctor had said, making plans, sharing insight about how I looked, the way my hand had twitched that one Tuesday and only when they were playing music on TV, saying they would have killed to be there to feel me move.

Cut to a car in the river. Me, with my leg torn off and reattached and in a motor bed with a tube down my throat and everybody, probably, wondering in the very backs of their minds whether or not I'd done it on purpose. It was the only thing I couldn't quite make myself believe, that I truly didn't remember. It seemed so improbable, like an answer that would have solved every problem I would ever have in my life, just so comfortably, unendingly out of reach. What does that feel like, you wonder? Like shit. Like I'm nothing.

Appa was still looking at me, turned away toward the window.

"I'm sorry," he said.

I waited, testing out my breath, trying to become level and not show him how bad I hurt, sitting there, shivering through my coat.

"It's done," I told him. "It's okay. Thank you for telling me."

He nodded. "I love you," he said.

I blinked a couple times, holding my hands clasped together in my lap.

"I love you too," I said quickly. "Let's do the fish, okay? It's getting hot in the van."

I had climbed down to the ground before he could respond and pulled the door open. Juno shook himself awake and stepped out, arching his back. We worked in silence. Appa and Juno brought the iceboxes into the kitchen while I unpacked and scrapped the Styrofoam. Juno and I handed him the cuts, wearing plastic gloves, and he placed them into storage. When he was done and the boxes had been cleared, Juno poured himself a mug of hot water.

"Everything good, H-Man?" he asked.

Appa was wary around me, still, and nodded his thanks to Juno. "Yeah, Juno. You're off tonight," he said. "Go do something with your friends."

"I didn't have plans," Juno said, picking his backpack up off one of the tables. "I can be here."

Appa waved him off. "Go. Have fun."

Juno shrugged. He raised his hand out toward me. "Take it easy, Uncle JJ."

I smiled. Then, seized with unearned confidence, I reached my fist out over the wood tabletop. He considered it, hesitantly, with what looked like amusement, and bumped his fist against mine. He pushed the door open, releasing a gust of wind, and was gone. We were left alone behind the bar. Appa leaned his hands against the smooth wood, hanging his head down.

"He's good, isn't he?" he asked me hesitantly. I nodded.

Appa had stepped a few inches closer to me. He dug into his jacket pocket and removed a wallet—my wallet, now that I could see it more clearly. He passed it across the bar to me. I opened it up, feeling with my fingers around its frayed rubber-edged leather. Fifty bucks off Amazon. Inside were my driver's license, some credit cards, my health insurance card from work. A receipt, crushed into the billfold, for an iced tea and a prepackaged salami-and-cheese plate from Starbucks, dated January 14, 2017, in the morning. I glanced his way.

"We sold your phone," he said. "We can get you a new one Monday."

I nodded.

"I know you might have some more questions," he said.

"I'm a little hungry," I said instead.

Appa breathed out slowly. "Yeah," he said, "okay. I'll make you something."

"It's okay," I said. "I'll do it."

He watched me move into the kitchen. We were silent for the

better part of the next twenty minutes, him standing by the sink while I worked. I took kimchi from the walk-in fridge, left it to boil in a pot over high heat, covered over with water, pork stock, sesame oil, sugar. Jjigae took some time to get right, but I had time to spare and it looked to me like Appa did too, content to stand there and watch me cook, so I went with it. There was pork belly in the freezer, which I cracked over my knee and sliced into slivers when it had thawed some. Next came garlic, soy sauce, a bit of rice vinegar. I left my bootleg jjigae to simmer on the stove and checked the rice cookers for any remnants, finding a few cups' worth in the last, still warm. I set two bowls up on the counter and, with a ladle, poured us equal servings of the soup over rice. Steam had enveloped the kitchen. Appa took the bowl from me, along with a spoon.

"What do you think you're doing," he asked, "making my jjigae for me? Think you've cracked the code?"

"You taught me well."

He sipped the steaming red soup, sighing as the heat filled him. "Good?"

"Better than mine," he said, sounding surprised. "You make this for yourself?"

"When I have the ingredients. Ren always liked it when he got sick."

Appa made a noise, lifting a spoonful of the wilted kimchi to his mouth.

"Appa."

"Mm."

I ventured around the kitchen, a space that had not changed since I was born, save for the extra rice cookers. My legs felt stronger here than outside, beginning to thaw up, the ground solid underneath me. My left leg, the one they'd reattached, never moved quite as smoothly, as though it were a joint missing some oil. It hurt most at the end of the day, in bed, after I'd taken my weight off of it. I was lucky it was only a bit of pain now, the physical therapists told me.

Luckier still to have kept it. I looked squarely at him, determined for the first time in a while.

"Can I work here?" I asked him.

Appa frowned. "What are you talking about?"

"Working here," I said quietly. "Really. Would you hire me?"

"You mean part-time?"

"I'll be full-time if you need," I said. "There's only going to be more people from now on. More orders, more fish to handle. Fewer and fewer people getting sick. I'm thinking . . . you might need the help. And I might like to be here."

Appa stared silently at me. He was thinking about that night, more than ten years ago. Which part? I wondered. The streamers and balloons, especially the ones losing their helium that had started to trail on the floor? The look we gave each other, right before I walked out through the door, leaving them all there? Was it James's laughter or Juno's screams? Or was it just everything at once, sounding off in every plane, on every cylinder, like it was for me?

Or maybe he was thinking about what it felt like to be needed. To have responsibility, a weight on your shoulders. And it came to pass that what I was feeling then was not just a purpose I hadn't been able to figure out before but clarity. That the restaurant, with its duct-taped pipes and piling bills, was going to close unless something changed. For once, I was awake, again in this very strange new world, this time with something to be awake for.

"You're not serious," he said.

I smiled at him. Smiled knowing that the first fish run we'd shared together in more than a decade had just about wrapped itself up and deposited me in a state of being that felt worlds away from the one I'd lived in before. A moment in which I found myself standing there with our hot breakfast, smiling at my dad, thinking of what was going to happen to me. Not much, admittedly. But for now—for me—enough.

ANOTHER MONTH LATER

5

THE TAO OF HOT WATER

TO SLICE FISH, ONE MUST SEE WITH THE FINGERS, FEEL WITH THE TIPS of the pads the tender flesh, capturing the lean meat at its ripest, the vertex point after capture and before spoilage where its flavor is forward but not overpowering. Fish without the sea, its essence independent of its medium. This is measured in a multitude of ways, but none more accurate than by touch. The most experienced itamae can assess any fish's worth with only his fingers, moving up and down each striated curve, the subtle conversion of bone to flesh to skin to scale—

What an asshole I am.

Here's the only thing you need to know: You need a sharp knife and a steady left hand to slice fish. That's about it. Believe what you want, but sushi happens to be nothing but the practice of simple and regimented knife work. The hacks may tell you different, that the food as well as the preparation of it is an art form on par with the great literature of the world, that eating good sushi is like seeing the perfect combination of exotic flavors dance in midair as you chew. Then they collect $350 for your meal and serve you a frozen white grape they say is from Kyoto but is really Dole, from the Food Emporium down the block, for dessert. Like every other commodified food form prevalent enough in this country to have trickled down to a version of it sold ready-made from your local bodega, sushi is only as difficult as you make it. Simple food, with minimal preparation. Let it speak for itself. Appa said once himself: There's a reason everything's raw. He said it to be funny, first and foremost, but also because he, like many men of his age, was locked in a never-ending tug-of-war with change. Motherfuckers in Manhattan were putting caviar and uni foam on Wagyu beef nigiri. You know, food that really lets you taste the money you spent on it. You'd imagine there was demand for that sort of thing in Fort Lee, just across the river, and there was. But Appa would be lying dead on his ceramic tiles before an ounce of fake Kobe beef crossed his bar. Thus Joja was and would always be: an original.

Did this translate to good business? Have I ever seen the restaurant full? Or the better question: Was there currently a second mortgage on the house to pay for the broken water heater, a leak in the kitchen stove? Was there in turn a mortgage on the restaurant to help pay off the house? There are questions and there are *questions,* and Appa did not answer either.

I asked myself a lot when I was a kid whether he actually liked what he did. Making food, slicing fish, serving customers by hand. Certainly, he hated running a business. In all respects, he was pretty mediocre at it and hadn't done so personally since James started managing the numbers for him. Money made him angry. But the slicing, the sculpting with his hands the perfect piece of nigiri laid delicately, a swipe of fresh-ground wasabi between the fish and the rice placed on each of the stone tablets set out in a line on the bar, he was supposed to like that, or had liked it, at some point in his life.

Did one ever wear out their passion? I'd never seen him smile doing it. He made it look like a chore. And it was, of course. He obsessed over quality, taste, watched faces anxiously when they took their first bite. Then I'd think to myself that there was more to loving something than smiling at it.

He never let me forget it: He'd been through the wringer in Kyoto, apprenticing, learning to speak the language at a time when plenty of self-respecting Koreans would've taken a swing at any of those guys in the kitchen just for being Japanese. Appa's father wasn't the punishing type but had, I've heard, expressed some measure of disappointment in his career choices. There was no talking Appa out of it. He wanted to learn the skills; acquiring them from the source was the only option. Come to think of it, I'd never heard him speak Japanese. I wondered if he remembered, still. He returned, twenty-five, to Queens, then Fort Lee, and had been here ever since. He was a line cook at a Korean-Japanese noodle house on Linden when the young woman who would become my mother, a pharmacy assistant named Ari, stopped in on her lunch break. As I've been told, he made her the spiciest jjamppong on the menu and she'd eaten the whole thing without taking a single sip of water, drinking the piping-hot broth down to its dregs. That had impressed him more than anything, more than her careful attention to laughing at each and every one of his jokes. It would take him eight years to marry her, lease his own restaurant, start a family, and serve her the very first omakase over the bar he'd built. It was a nice story. Thinking of them happy made me happier still.

I remembered why I was awake before my alarm. Juno needed to be brought to school today—within the hour. James had an appointment and was taking the car, I didn't remember exactly for what. Noa had asked nervously over the phone, and I'd told her I could. In bed now, I regretted it like I'd known I would.

It was Wednesday, one of my mornings off between fish runs. I stretched, opening and closing my eyes, training them on the little white ceiling fan above me, and rolled over onto my stomach. The mattress was the same exact one I'd slept on all my teens. It had mellowed in this room, my room, for the past twelve years I'd been gone and had just now taken up its old post under me, providing minimum comfort and maximum dust. My room, he had left almost exactly the same. It smelled like nothing, instead of sweat like it had while I underwent puberty. A solitary window, curtained over with sheer blinds, glowed with blue morning light. I angled my head sideways and saw the trees out the window, starting now to shed leaves. We had settled into the cold by now, no longer just a little nip on the nose but a full-blown ache in the joints. Today, thankfully, was not one of those days. Still, there was service tonight, prep to be done and wares to be washed after closing. The counters needed a solid wipe-down, along with the floors in the back kitchen. I spent at least an hour slicing cucumbers into thin, shoelace-like ribbons that we used for garnish and alongside most of the maki rolls. They were nice to look at more than they tasted like anything. On top of the food prep, the door had started to jam slightly, leaving itself open when customers pulled it just a hair too wide and letting in the brisk wind if nobody bothered to check it. My first task today, to be attended to after breakfast and drop-off duty.

I found my phone and shot a text to Juno: *Coming to get you in ten.* A little flag at the bottom of the screen let me know that he'd read it. I waited for a response but none came. I tapped idly on the screen, weighing a second text.

"Little shit . . ."

I stood, smelled under my arms. I was due for a change. I stripped and carried my bundle of dirty clothes across the hall to the laundry, piling them inside and cranking the machine. I caught a glimpse of myself in the mirror that Appa had hanging over the wooden chest that housed the extra blankets. I tried actively not to look at myself these days, as there were usually too many things that upset me. The deeper circles around my eyes. The ring of raised skin surrounding my left thigh that signified where the stitches had healed. There were no more bruises, thankfully, but a spot on my right eyebrow had gone bald with scar tissue; same with a line traveling down my head along the length of my right ear where they'd popped open my skull. I'd lost weight and hadn't managed to put it back on, not even while eating the way I had been for the past month. I looked away. I put on a set of clean Kirklands and made my way to the kitchen.

It was still a surprise, to see the house where I'd grown into a person, to remember a specific point on the wall, a scuff mark or a dent, that I could trace all the way back to an afternoon I'd accidentally launched a Hot Wheel off the track to clatter against the drywall. Little bald spots in the white carpet where Umma had used hair clippers to cut stains out of the fabric when bleach didn't work. Here was a kingdom of memory, more now a kingdom of receipts. Papers piled into corners of every room, old packing boxes flattened and stacked against the wall since, I assumed, there was no more room in the one-car garage. Among this wreckage were the finances involved in keeping me alive for the past two years. The place now had the look of a person in a state of transit, never here, whirling through like a tornado while life, and business, raged on. Appa never saw this house as his home, just like he never saw the restaurant and its bar as his place of work.

There was still-warm coffee in the machine on the counter, which I drained. The landline was beeping red, messages from the township about a few outstanding tickets Appa had earned parking the van too long in front of the restaurant after the fish runs, directly in the path of a fire hydrant. Out behind the kitchen was the backyard, mostly dead on account of the cold. We had shared the backyard all my life with an old Korean couple that James and I had guessed were in their eighties back when we were kids. Their daughter had moved back into the house and had been wheeling them both around the yard for an hour each afternoon the past few months. I craned my neck to see over the flower box into the yard, hoping to catch them. I was so often working whenever she took them out that I'd become a bit starved for their attention. The daughter, who was at least ten years older than Appa, liked to remind me that the grass in the yard we shared used to be green and there was obviously some kind of plant food we were forgetting to pick up from Home Depot. On days when I could spare a sit out on the back porch while she took turns ferrying her mother and father around the grass, I'd comment on the same old things and tell her that the spring would be kinder to the grass. Lou—her name was Lou—would tell me she would believe it when she saw it, while her father, mostly silent, came to life every few minutes to babble about the unsatisfactory way she was dragging his wheelchair over the dirt's rough knots. I brought her fish jeon from the shop we liked best in town. She liked the pork, she told me, but the chewing was difficult for her parents.

I liked Lou. She was a widow with two grown children who had uprooted an entire life—hers—to come back to Fort Lee. If I didn't think she'd drill her judgment straight into my eyes, we might have had a lot to talk about. Appa was not a conversationalist, and certainly not with anybody he was forced by law to share a backyard with. In all this time, the fact that my brain was floating dormant in a meat balloon for two years had never come up between them. I could tell she thought I'd been fired from my job, or perhaps convicted of some minor felony that didn't warrant jail time, and was now exercising the only option I had left in moving back home. Much like she was doing, I had always wanted to say to her, but that wouldn't have been very nice.

Lou was not out with either of her parents today, so I rinsed my mug, locked up the house, and left.

I shook myself a little further awake outside the van, which was parked precariously on the incline leading up to the house, one of a row of five duplexes that lined the block going all the way down to the well of the valley. If I stood on the van, I would've been able to see the city peeking up past the trees across the river. It was five minutes to James's house. I crawled onto the driver's seat from the road and switched her on. A slight rumble, old coughs (old girl), a roar as her engine woke. I'd made peace with the fact that I would never get used to driving this thing, its pedals and levers tuned intimately to Appa's hands and nobody else's. I was not technically clear to drive, I reminded myself, on my doctor's orders, but no mention had been made of a criminal offense when the question had been asked. I was doing fine, anyway. I had driven her once down the block and pulled into an empty space just before the intersection when I was twelve years old. I knew this van better than most. I pulled away from the curve and coasted down the incline. Was I sure I'd locked the door? I thought so. Had I left the coffeepot congealing its last sips in the sink or had I rinsed it out? Questions for fifteen hours from now, after the dinner service.

James's house was the right side of a two-level house on the corner of the next cluster over, under the bridge, on the other side of the valley. I stopped the van by the front yard and stepped out. The lights were on in the kitchen. James's old sedan was parked in front of the garage. It was a bigger moment than I've made it seem, wasn't it? James had bought this house ten years ago and I'd never come to see it until now. There were pictures, of course. Umma liked to send me pictures whenever she could, hoping my curiosity would get the better of me. I brought my phone out and thought of texting Juno to meet me outside. Certainly easier, but I feared what Umma would say about it if she ever found out. We had not managed to speak much since the fight we'd had in the restaurant a month earlier, and I'd found myself mostly glad for it. There was something to be said for the peace it gave us. I started off toward the front door, steadying myself on the iced pavement. I could hear Sam crying inside. I knocked.

A jagged blur came out from the lit hallway, magnifying the crying on the other side of the crystal-faceted glass set into the door, and opened it inward. Noa cocked her head sideways, a handful of her hair crunched in baby Sam's fist. He was screaming, evidently punishing his mother for evil by yanking on her hair, which she was in the middle of cajoling him to let go of. I stood there, like a spectator.

"Really sorry," Noa said, turning her head. "Sammie, that's not nice. Sammie, please let go of Umma's hair—"

"Do you need help?" I asked her blankly, answering my own question by taking Sam's wrist and gently pulling his fingers apart. My ears rang by the time I'd gotten her free. Noa laughed, angling her head away from Sam's hands.

"Thanks. You're really helping us out," she said, stepping inside. "Juno's ready, almost. I think. He'll be down. You want something to drink?"

"I'm okay."

She stopped midway through the hallway, turning around.

"Hold on a minute. You've never been here before, have you?"

I lifted my shoulders, not knowing what to do with my hands. My nephew had quieted in his mother's arms and was staring at me in utter confusion. I must've looked too much like his dad.

"Can that really be true?" Noa smiled at me. "I guess so. If I weren't about to change him I'd give the tour. Or maybe James would want to do that. Come on in here. James . . ."

I followed her into their kitchen, seeing first my brother's back at the counter; he held in one hand a mug of hot coffee.

"Coffee?"

"Had some already."

He turned his head slightly over his shoulder. "How've you been," he said, without inflecting his voice into a question.

"Good. Busy," I said.

James hid his face again. "I've got somebody coming in to look at the freezer tomorrow," he told me. "Can you let him know?"

I knew that Appa didn't think the freezer needed any work and had told me so just yesterday afternoon.

"Sure," I said.

After another moment or two, James got up, taking the paper he was reading with him. Our eyes made contact for the first time that morning.

"Appreciate you taking him to school," he said, patting my shoulder. He turned around and barked in a voice that made me jump: "JUNO!"

"It's not a problem," I said weakly. James kept his hand on my shoulder.

He glanced Noa's way. "I'll be back around noon."

"I need—"

"Potatoes, I know. Sesame oil?"

"I've got another bottle."

We heard footsteps above us, descending the stairs out in front. Juno stumbled sleepily into the kitchen. We all watched him retrieve a banana off the bunch on the counter and stow it in his hoodie pocket.

"Everybody sleep well?" he yawned.

"I need you down here sooner before school," James said, "your mother's been waiting for you."

"I'm sorry."

Juno said it without meaning even an ounce of it while packing up a stack of papers and textbooks he'd left at the table. He realized James was still watching him and cleared his throat.

"I'm sorry . . . Father?"

Something like that would've gotten me destroyed back home, most certainly by my own mother, but James didn't say anything. His hand was still on my shoulder. After another second, he slid past me out into the hallway. Noa, Sam, and I listened to the sounds of him putting on his boots and closing the front door behind him. I let out my breath. Juno was engrossed in something on his phone that I guessed was far more important than texting me back.

"That wasn't terrible," I said.

Noa smiled knowingly at me. "More words than I get some mornings. I'm glad you've put that silly fight behind you."

"Is that your impression?"

She got hopeful for a moment. "Have you held the baby yet?"

She brought Sam over to me. I opened my arms, accepting him, and buckled my knees a little to bounce him against my chest the way I'd seen her do. Sam watched his mother for a sign, permission to trust me. Losing interest after a few moments, he made a glossy bubble on his lips and wiped it against my shirt.

"How's work?"

"It's been good," I said. "Whatever fear's out there still, it's not here. More people coming in to eat than ordering takeout, some nights."

"You're wearing masks, aren't you?"

"I am. He's not."

"You'd think so." Noa rolled her eyes.

"What's that about?"

She shook her head. "Nothing. And thank you, by the way. I asked every one of Juno's friends' mothers to drive him. They're still not bringing the buses back on regular routes. It's been chaos."

"He's got a bike, doesn't he?"

"On that incline around the corner? He'd die. Feel some text come through on his phone and try to read it while steering. I know him."

Juno snorted. "Can we go, Uncle JJ? I'm going to be late."

In my arms, Sam had tipped his head back at me. I remembered that I was supposed to smile and say something nice, and did so: "You're a good boy, Sam." I looked dejectedly at Noa. "That was stupid. I don't know what I'm doing. I sound like I'm talking to a dog."

"I mean, he *is* a good boy," Noa said, "most of the time. You'll get the hang of it."

Juno had taken up his bag and gone out to the front door. Sam had changed hands and was nuzzling his face into Noa's neck, safe again.

"Did you bring your—"

The door slammed behind him.

Noa closed her mouth pensively. I hesitated.

"I can go and ask—"

"Oh, no, it's all right," she said, straightening up. "Wasn't important."

She always smiled, no matter what.

I STOPPED THE VAN TWO blocks down the road at a red light. Juno's feet were up on the dash with his head angled down at his phone.

He noticed me staring at him.

"What's the good word, Uncle JJ?"

"What's going on back there?"

He shrugged. "You're gonna have to be more specific."

I should have been minding my own business. Of course I knew what I should have been doing. That was never my issue. I tightened my fingers around the steering wheel.

"Just seemed a little tense, is all."

"You've noticed," Juno said. "My dad loves pretending he's okay with the fact that his liver's drying up inside him. That's what the appointment's for. Rehab didn't come soon enough, they said."

I tried not to react. It hadn't crossed my mind that Juno was probably old enough to know and had more than likely asked. It wasn't hard to guess. I was thirteen when they brought Juno home from the hospital. I don't know where I was the night they told Umma and Appa, certainly not in the house, as I would've remembered the screaming. The two of them, twenty years old, not a hope of college. They lived in the basement until Juno was five, after which James had saved enough for a house, the house we'd just left. Down payment, thirty-year mortgage. It was a lot to just dump out there in the open like that. But after all, there had always been two versions of my brother: the one I remembered when I was a kid, who played GameCube with me and had always let me tag along with his friends, and the one that didn't like anybody or anything except getting drunk. It had become hard to tell the difference.

"Relax," Juno said to me. Then: "Don't tell my mom I said that."

"Why not think before you speak, instead of trying to cut deals with me?"

We continued in silence for another minute, the kind we'd usually settled into by the end of the fish run twice a week. Appa was in the middle of choosing an oyster vendor and we'd spent the past few runs fighting our stomachs on the bumpy freeway after having volunteered to sample the wares. Not that the catch was bad, but even the freshest oysters, at four in the morning, two weeks in a row, could fuck you up once churned over the sweet rhythms of the road. I would think of asking him, each time, did all three of us need to be there? Surely there was an easier way. Then I'd imagine the face I knew he'd make, hearing that, and reconsider.

We pulled into the drop-off circle at the edge of the high school. From the dash, I saw a group of preschoolers from the day care across the street pointing animatedly at the van while two young counselors attempted to herd them together on the lawn.

"Honk the horn," Juno said.

"What?"

"Honk the horn," Juno repeated. I honked. The kids whooped and scattered, imitating the sound. The nearest counselor shot a heated look at us. Juno blew her a kiss.

He hitched his bag over his shoulder. "Thanks for the ride, Uncle JJ. Can I be off tonight? I've got homework."

I couldn't tell if I'd crossed a line with him. He treated everything and everybody with at least a percentage point or two of absolute disinterest. It was his fallback. But I might have pissed him off with the questions.

"Yeah, I'll talk to him."

"Love you."

He slid the door shut behind him before I could react. I watched him climb the little hill up to the doors and blend into a crowd of teenagers. I cranked the heat up.

"He loves me," I said to myself, smiling. "Not enough for a text back. Little shit."

AROUND NINE, I'D PARKED THE van at the curb two blocks from the restaurant and was walking the rest of the way, thinking of making something for breakfast, when I stopped myself from knocking over a burly guy who had stepped into my way from the road with a video camera on his shoulder.

"What the—"

"You're Coma Guy, aren't you?" The burly guy had already pointed the camera at my face. "Are you the right guy? You're Coma Guy."

"I'm not anything," I said, swiping at the lens he pointed at me. "You're supposed to ask before recording me. Now fuck off."

"Listen," he said, breathing hard. There were stains under his arms, probably from carrying his camera equipment up on his shoulder while waiting for me all morning. "You want to be on CBS? We're doing a thing. You give me ten minutes, I'll call the station and get a reporter down here."

They'd been popping up around the restaurant, only a block or two away now that Appa had taken to chasing them down the street.

"That's such an amazing offer to be in this thing you're doing. Thank you for thinking of me. For your thing."

"For CBS New York. You might get Gayle out here, you know? Random guy wakes up from two-year coma? Like, what the fuck, man? Who does that? I read most people die after, like, a month."

"Just"—I sidestepped him—"get away from me. There is absolutely no way fucking Gayle King sends one nasty guy with a two-ton camera to scout for a story. By the way, if my dad sees you, he'll kill you."

I didn't stick around to hear what he said next, jogging across the street to the restaurant past a white girl in a black jacket and combat boots.

"Hey."

I turned around. The girl, who didn't look much older than Juno, was wearing a hood pulled up over her head. All I could see was the black liner around her eyes, something I imagine she must have been proud of, there otherwise being no genuine way to justify the amount currently on her face.

"Do you work here?"

I glanced inside at Appa, running prep from behind the bar. Over the girl's head, the burly guy was hobbling across the road to a chunky gray van with the back doors open.

"Yes?"

The girl cocked her head to one side. "You don't sound sure."

"I work here," I said. "Can I help you?"

"I think you can, actually." She stood a little bit taller, bringing herself to her full height, just under my chin. "I'd like to know if you're hiring in the kitchen."

She was alone. I imagined briefly that there was somebody behind me trying to get their hand into my pocket without my realizing and took a small step backward.

"Really?"

"Joja's the best sushi in Fort Lee, everybody knows that."

"Use that line on everybody?"

"Absolutely not." She dug into the massacred white canvas tote bag around her shoulder and pulled out an envelope. "Seriously, anything you've got, I'll take. Dishwasher, waitress, anything. I have a letter of recommendation."

"From . . ."

"My aunt. She used to run the Lily? On Hillside? They closed last year."

"I remember," I said, not remembering, taking the letter from her. She lowered the blue mask around her face to her chin. "Good bar, there. What are you—I mean—"

I squinted inside at Appa again, hoping he'd noticed, but his head was still down.

"Do you really work here?" She'd become hesitant, for an instant, before hiding it well under a look of scrutiny.

"What? Yes. My dad's in there right now running prep."

"Your dad's itamae at Joja?" Her face had lit up. "What, so you're like, his apprentice?"

"I guess," I said, taking a step backward, which she matched with a step forward. "I mean I learned a lot from him when I was a teen-ager but it's been a bit of work to get myself back into the basics . . . no, wait, hold on. Just—"

I extended my hands. She'd come only a foot away from me.

"Oh, right." She took out her phone, scrolling. "I'm vaccinated, don't worry."

"That's not what I was talking about," I said, realizing I was still holding her letter gingerly in my hand. "You want to work here. Is that right?"

"That's right," she said. "I'm in high school and I've been cooking in my aunt's kitchen at the Lily since I was eight years old. I just turned sixteen. I know food, I know sushi, I've seen every documen-tary about sushi on YouTube and I can do it just as well. And I'm vaccinated, I think I told you that already—"

"Okay," I said quickly, "obviously, you're very impressive. But I don't think we have anything for you."

"I'll wash dishes," she said quickly, "I'll bag ice, I'll do anything. I just—"

She stopped herself, catching her breath.

"I want to learn. And I'd like a chance. Give me all the crap you don't like doing anymore. I'll do it. I'll work for ten bucks. Five bucks . . ."

I should've banged on the window to get Appa's attention. This girl got everything she wanted in her entire life, I could tell, and it wasn't because her parents were rich. I folded the letter in half and stuffed it in my back pocket.

"First of all," I told her, "I'm going to pretend you didn't just ne-gotiate your own salary against yourself. Second . . ."

The girl had opened her eyes wide, clearly unwilling to let herself believe any of the past five minutes had in fact been a fruitful endeavor like it was turning out to be, despite my best intentions. I scanned the road for the burly guy again and paled when I saw the gray van he'd disappeared into coming back around the block.

"Just come with me," I said. "Quickly."

I shouldered the door open, shuddering when the faulty hinge screeched right behind my head.

"What's your name?"

"Zeno."

I blinked at her. "Your parents know you're here?"

"I actually don't have to answer that," she said. "I'm legally independent. I have a learner's permit."

I waited for her to elaborate. She didn't.

"Okay then, Zeno. Come with me."

We stepped inside. Appa waved from the bar, frowning at her walking in behind me. I told her to sit by the window and joined him in the back.

"Friend of yours?"

"Not exactly. She wants a job."

Appa laughed, loud enough for her to hear. "A job doing what?"

"She said anything, washing dishes, cleaning the kitchen. She's a kid. Sixteen years old."

"And where did you meet said sixteen-year-old? You handing out flyers at Juno's school?"

"She was waiting out there. She's heard of you."

Zeno was still by the door, reading the Zagat "Best of Fort Lee" feature Appa had framed on the wall. He watched her for a moment.

"She was waiting out there for me?"

"I guess."

Appa smiled at me. "Don't you want some help back there?"

"What? I was hoping you'd help me get rid of her."

"So you don't want any help."

"Do you?"

Appa shrugged, picking up his knife. The belly of a silver mackerel lay in front of him, almost rid of its scales. "I had a lot of kids come work for me while you were gone. My old porter's a cook in this new place in Manhattan now. Flashy stuff. Uni pasta. Ninety-eight dollars a plate. Can you believe that? If I'd had to pay for it, I would've broken something."

He sliced a portion of the mackerel away on the scale-less side, digging into the ohitsu next to him for a portion of rice. He rolled them together in his hand, applying pressure with his first two fingers into his palm, pressing the fish against it into an oval. With steel chopsticks, he attached a little bunch of shredded radish soaked in ponzu over the top and handed it to me.

"What for?"

"New vendor. And I changed up the ponzu. I want to know what you think."

I ate it, chewing. "New vinegar?"

"Mm."

I swallowed. "It's nice."

"You think before the amberjack tonight? After?"

"Too strong and too early. Better after."

Appa snapped his fingers at me, nodding his head. He returned his attention to the fish.

"What about Zeno?"

Appa snorted. "That *cannot* be her real name."

"Just tell me what to do."

"I thought we were decided," he said, laughing. "What's the harm? You could use some help. Somebody to mop the floors, wipe the tables, wash dishes. She wants to learn, doesn't she?"

Zeno had taken a seat at one of the tables. I waited a moment, long enough for Appa to let me know if he was joking.

"Are you going to tell James?"

"James wants me to have help around here."

"Can we afford to?"

Appa smiled softly, ignoring me. "She look crazy to you?" he asked me.

"She's a teenager. They all look crazy."

"You think she's going to steal money out of the safe?"

"She brought a letter," I said. "Her aunt owned the Lily."

Appa took the envelope from me, skimming the letter inside. He smiled at something written near the bottom and turned it over, showing me. *Abigail is the hardest worker I know. Her dream since the age of five has been to cook. I have not begun to understand where this interest in Asian food came into play, but it's what she wants, and I will do my very best to help her find a path forward—*

He folded the note, stowing it in his pocket.

"Can I meet her?"

We walked over together. Appa shook Zeno's hand, and remained confused about the wide eyes she gave him until he realized he was still holding his knife in the other hand. He showed it to her.

"Do you know what this is?"

"That's a yanagi."

"Stainless, single-edged. Let me tell you a story. I was going to buy a one-way ticket to Kyoto to find some restaurants that needed help. My dad didn't want me in Japan. Said he wouldn't pay a single cent for it. I'd starve, and then I'd come home and realize I was wrong about this whole cooking thing. Especially Japanese. Do you know how much old Korean men hate the Japanese? Anyway, I went, and he didn't talk to me for three years. I came home, I opened this restaurant, and he bought me this knife, twenty years ago. Cost him two months' social security. He said if he ever found out I replaced it, he'd never speak to me again. A good sharpening every six months on the whetstone, and it's good as new."

He clapped me on the shoulder. He loved telling this story. I'd always noticed how happy it made him to tell it.

"My son's going to walk you through the kitchen. When you're done, you come out here and watch me. Good?"

He checked his watch.

"And if you ever skip school again to come here, I'm going to drive you straight home and tell your mother myself."

APPA MADE US DINNER HALF an hour before we opened that night. I'd spent the afternoon in the cold with a screwdriver, replacing the creaky hinge on the front door with one I'd run down to the Ace Hardware during lunchtime to buy. Zeno had been convinced to attend at least her afternoon classes after watching Appa break down a salmon and had committed to four nights a week without seeming to have consulted with her parents. I sat at a table to eat: a bowl of rice, chicken thighs, mayo, and chili oil. Appa placed a poached egg delicately over it all with a pair of tongs. I dug in, ravenous.

"Juno wanted the night off," I said. "Homework."

"He's got a C average in chemistry," Appa said. "I wouldn't bet those friends of his are going to be studying anything in a book tonight."

He took out his phone.

"He's still in the building. At least he's not skipping school."

"He lets you track him?" I asked, amused.

"I told him I'd never rat him out to James," Appa said. "Least I could do."

He settled into a seat across from me with his bowl. We'd eaten like this every afternoon before dinner service. Some days there was only enough time to scarf it down, sometimes the second half of it on our way back to the kitchen. But today, we'd left ourselves in a good place and had afforded ourselves the luxury of ten minutes. I liked to check our Grubhub around this time for preorders but was holding off for once.

"How did you do this alone, Appa?" I asked him.

He scoffed. "I've got, what, five tables? Ten seats at the bar? It's nothing we couldn't manage. We've only been getting people back in here a couple months ago."

He was telling me what I could probably never ask him and get away with: that the money was still not coming in, and would not for some time. He dug his spoon into his dinner, sticking it up so it stood like a shovel in soil.

"You're doing a good job."

"Sure."

"You really are," Appa said. "A month now, isn't it?"

"Something like that."

He smiled. "I don't know, Jack Jr., just something about looking over during dinner, seeing you there behind the bar with me. I would've killed to get James back there with me. He hated it, sure, but he didn't have your skill."

"This surprises you." I nodded. "That's disappointing."

The Pandora Muzak station I put on most nights wasn't coming through the speakers. Something had knocked the wire loose in the corner of the dining room, I'd figured out earlier today. Appa got up, retrieving two beers from the fridge. We tapped our drinks together. He checked his watch. In another hour we'd have to change. The crisp white shirts we wore were hanging in the closet from the dry cleaner. I liked this little slot of time we had to ourselves, enough time to eat, change, get off our feet.

"I can't believe you just hired her like that," I said.

"She's a good kid, I can tell." Appa shrugged. "Besides, the safe back there's been empty for two years."

There was a knock on the door. We raised our heads, saw through the frosted glass Umma's outline, her hand raised. Appa got up to let her inside. Umma showed us a paper Bloomingdale's bag with all of the tools she kept at her house.

"We had needle-nose pliers," Appa was telling her. "Didn't I leave those the last time I was over?"

"I tell you this is everything in my entire house and you don't believe me," Umma said, walking over and planting a kiss on the top of my head. "Nobody's got another speaker or something around here?"

"Jack Jr. needs music."

"Okay, no, I don't *need* music," I said, having finished my dinner. I surveyed the bag she'd left on the table. "It's about ambience. People don't like to hear other people chewing food all around them."

We took stock of the speaker hanging from the corner of the wall. "This isn't going to work," I said. "We're just going to have to unscrew the speaker off the wall and pull on the cable to see what's loose. I can do it tomorrow morning."

"Hire a guy," Umma said.

"I already hired a guy." Appa nudged me with his shoulder. "Where's my ladder? I can figure this out—"

He waved off any and all of our attempts to help and disappeared into the kitchen. Umma took our two empty bowls and walked them to the sink behind the bar.

"He said some girl's going to work with you in the kitchen," she said over the sound of running water.

"New porter. High school girl who says she wants to learn how to make sushi."

"A teenager," Umma said, raising the pitch of her voice. "A girl teenager. Does Juno know her?"

"Would you stop?"

"I didn't even say anything," Umma said. "Why care about these things at all? I certainly don't."

Something started buzzing faintly against a table. Umma rummaged around in her bag for her phone, answering it just before it went to voicemail.

"James? I'm sorry, I didn't hear you. Everything okay?"

James buzzed something unintelligible through the speaker.

"Meeting tonight," she mouthed. "Oh, the sound system's broken, by the way. We're looking into it. Your dad's looking into it, I mean. He said he wants needle-face pliers, whatever those are."

She listened to something he said. Appa knocked something over in the kitchen, echoing a bang on the floor.

"We'll figure it out. I love you."

She hung up, smiling at me.

"What?" I asked her.

"You remember the very last time you were in this restaurant, don't you?"

"Hardly."

"Don't lie, Jack Jr. How could any of us forget it? Talk about a spectacle. You running out of there, a big pillar of sweat from head to toe, never coming back."

"Thanks for that. I have so many good memories of that day."

She laughed, a little too loudly. "They come crawling back," she said. "They all do. Who was worried? Not me."

I knew my mother well enough to know she typically said things I was meant to take as the exact opposite, the very directness of her contradictions the clearest signal that she meant business and expected to be taken seriously. I remembered quite well the arguments she'd have with Appa back when they were married. Whole minutes-long altercations that I could hear through the floorboards while trying to fall asleep. If I were ever to ask them what had happened—and I never had—I'm not sure of the answer either of them would have given. That the restaurant work got to be too demanding? That they didn't have enough time for each other? That having kids together had made one or both of them realize they were slowly backing into a life that they were not completely committed to living? Maybe it was all of the above. She was talking about the night in the restaurant shortly after I'd graduated high school. The beginning of the end.

Another bang from the kitchen, louder this time, which broke my train of thought and made the two of us jump. We glanced at each other, hoping to hear at least some confirmation of life from Appa, though none came.

"Jack Sr.," Umma called over my head. "Shout if you're pinned to the floor by the fridge."

HERE'S A QUESTION. WHAT POSSESSES Derek of 497 Leonia Street to place an order—for delivery, mind you—of six avocado rolls and four sides of wakame salad? To each their own, whatever, but seriously? Do we think that Derek of 497 Leonia Street understands that I use only one avocado (67 cents) and about three cups of rice (a nickel) to produce his meal of eighty-nine dollars inclusive of delivery fee and tip? It really sounds like Derek of 497 Leonia Street is on a mission to make us the greatest possible profit for the least amount of effort. I thought this while packing his six avocado rolls in a platter-size tray. I guessed on the number in his party. Two pairs of chopsticks? Four? I imagined people living alone, splurging on some takeout sushi, being offended to find five pairs of chopsticks in with their meal.

I made the avocado rolls carefully, delicately. They were harder to handle than fish; at least fish had a bit of pushback, holding its shape when I pressed it all together inside a bamboo mat. There was a couple on a date seated in front of me, the man watching something intently on his phone, a sports game, while the woman watched me work.

"Is that going to come with the omakase?" she asked me. I told her no. She looked disappointed. I told her I could make her one and didn't quite hear her answer because at the other end of the bar, three guys in suits had just poured Appa a shot of the sake they'd ordered. Their voices rose up like a crowd's, turning heads. I laughed, watching Appa drink. I could tell he was feeling good, one of those nights he could connect with anybody who sat down in front of him, whoever it was. It was near nine. We had not managed to fix the speaker and were working with a louder-than-usual hum of conversation in the air with nothing else. Umma was by the door with the clipboard she kept for the night's reservations, waiting for the party nearest the windows to clear out.

The couple in front of me were eight courses into the omakase. Eel, mackerel, and toro left, along with the tamago we served at the end with a cold cup of sikhye. The eel was crisping in the toaster oven behind me. For such vanilla people they hadn't turned their noses up at any of the courses. We served raw squid soaked in red chilis near the beginning, which I would've bet anything they would have objected to, but they'd surprised me. I packed the last of Derek's avocado rolls into a plastic tray and placed it on the counter. Umma had at last vacated the table and came over with their bill, sliding it to me.

"Juno's not here tonight?" she asked me.

"He asked to take off. Homework."

Umma packed Derek's order away and stapled a receipt to the top. "I was beginning to worry. I hardly see him around any friends."

"He said 'homework,' Umma."

"And I said 'I'm not stupid,' Jack Jr." She smiled placatingly at the couple. "How's everything?"

The woman nodded, speaking too softly over Appa's frat bro trio behind us. Umma gestured to me. "My son. He's wonderful, isn't he?"

She agreed.

"He just woke up from a coma."

A silence settled over them both. I forced myself to laugh, shooting Umma a glare over their shoulders. She winked.

"She's joking." I turned around, looking for the eel. Umma poured me a glass of water and pushed it over the bar.

"Is that supposed to be a secret?" she whispered, out of earshot.

I drank, emptying the glass.

"You never know what white people might do with a little bit of guilt. Big tip, maybe."

"I'd really love for you not to weaponize my medical history against our customers."

"You are too dramatic for your own good," she said, and took the empty glass from me. "Guilt is a very important and healthy part of society. All mothers know this."

"I know all *mothers* know this," I said. "They're the reason it's true."

I'd pulled open the toaster drawer when the bell attached to the door rang, signaling another cold gust of wind from the outside.

"I have nothing else to say," Umma had said, the last thing I heard before I saw him. He hadn't even taken his mask off. It was a moment, unlike any other, that reminded me just how easily I could spot him out of any crowd, the speed of which might lead me to believe that I spent a great deal of time with my brain primed to look for him wherever I went. What did that mean, exactly? I wouldn't say. Emil Cuddy was wiping his shoes dry on the mat and hadn't noticed me yet.

"Fuck."

The couple had heard me. I bumbled an apology, plating their eel, wiping my hands dry on my apron. Umma had come to him by the door and had put her arms around his neck. He'd brought a bottle with him, which she took, and she led him to my end of the bar, setting him up two seats away from my couple. He was looking around, chatting about something, and saw me. With my arms straight at my sides as though I were swaddled in a giant blanket, I walked up to him stiffly.

"Emil Cuddy."

"Jack Jr."

He'd shaved tonight. He was dressed in normal-people clothes, which made him look weird. The bottle was a dry white. Umma brought over an ice bucket and placed it inside to chill.

"Dining alone?" she asked him.

"Didn't have anybody to eat with," Cuddy said. "A single's acceptable at the bar, no?"

"The best customers we have," Umma said. "Quick in-and-out, no fuss. Here to eat."

She smiled at me.

"He'll take good care of you."

She left us alone, sweeping away with impressive speed and through the door to the kitchen. Appa hadn't noticed us yet. Cuddy didn't seem to know what to do with his hands and so rubbed them up and down his thighs.

"Joja," he said, partly to himself, "John and James. Right?"

"How'd you know that?"

He shrugged. "I thought of your dad and what he might name a restaurant after."

"You know him pretty well, then."

I had said it, then realized that—yes—he probably did. Better than I knew him for the past two years and, more reasonably, even longer.

Appa had given himself a free moment and practically jogged over to us. His face glowed red from the sake. The next moment, he was talking loudly, having buried Cuddy's face in his chest with his arms wrapped around him.

"You won't be sorry!" he boomed. "This is such a treat for us, you've got no idea."

Cuddy patted Appa's back softly, asking politely to be let go, but Appa hadn't noticed. I asked for death, at this point more favorable than watching either of my parents interact with my former nurse for even one more moment of this lifetime. Appa finally let Cuddy go, wiping his face with his apron. He slapped a hand down on my shoulder.

"Great catch this week. Some of the best I've seen. Anything you don't eat? I'm kidding, you don't have a choice. Omakase only at the bar."

He ran over with the sake, scoffing at the dry white on ice, and poured us three shots.

"Appa, he brought wine—"

"Bullshit," Appa said, "you can't eat fish with wine. One drink before the meal, one after. That's tradition. That's how we do it in Korea."

"Nobody does that," I said. To him: "That's not a rule."

Appa had already downed his shot. I made eye contact with Cuddy, each of us waiting for the other. We drank. My ears popped. Appa gathered up our glasses: "Boys, I'll be back. You're out of mackerel, aren't you, Jack? I'll be back, I'll be back—"

He was gone in a thunderstorm of sound and movement. I took up my towel, drying a spot on the bar where he'd spilled.

"I'm sorry about that," I said.

Cuddy laughed. "He's been asking me to come by for two years. I suppose I deserve it."

He smiled.

"You look good. How's the PT?"

"I can touch my toes now," I told him.

"Extremely impressive." He smiled at me. "I'm just happy you're going. They get a lot of dropped appointments in that office. And suddenly they wonder why they can't get themselves out of bed after knee surgery."

"I'm the model patient, I make every appointment," I said. "Raise my arm when I'm told to, clench my butt cheek when I'm told to."

"You're a prodigy."

We laughed, on cue, and it wasn't as awkward as it should've been.

After a moment: "It's been a while. A month?"

I bowed my head slightly.

"I would've thought you'd be back in the city by now."

"It's . . ." I trailed off. My date-night couple had finished the eel and were trying to get my attention. "Temporary. Probably. No, it is."

I was not out of mackerel, despite what Appa thought, and threw two pieces together without speaking.

"You really can tell me if there's something you won't eat."

"Not a chance, I'm locked in." He sounded confident. "Full experience. You give me live sea leech in vodka and cream, I'll eat it."

"Will you?"

The corners of Cuddy's lips had turned up. I found myself noticing them for the first time, remembering that they were there. I'd grown accustomed to a solitary view of the inch-high gap through which I could see his eyes under his germ-proof equipment.

"I'd like to think so," he said.

"Squid?"

"Sure."

"Oysters?"

"Love them."

I took up my knife and started working. He watched me intently, taking sips of water. I set in front of him a wet finger towel and a plate of ginger, which he picked at. I set his first course on the flat marble plate between us.

"Amberjack," I said.

He ate it with his fingers. "Big or small fish?"

"They're big boys. Three to four feet, maybe?"

"Shit." Cuddy swallowed. "You want a letter grade after each one?"

"If you're feeling generous. Customer feedback keeps us genuine."

He thought to himself for a while.

"Fresh and clean, good jump-off point. If I'm grading the knife work, a B."

I wiped down the smudge that the rice had left. "Fuck. You."

"Did you know"—he ate another sliver of ginger—"I've never had sushi before."

I was genuinely curious, unable to think of a joke, which I knew he was expecting. I rushed my couple through the toro and tamago, placing the check in front of them while Cuddy waited.

"Is that really true?" I asked him.

He nodded.

"Why not?"

"My friends aren't big on food like this," Cuddy said. "They're sort of . . . a different class of people."

His second course was the soy-marinated belly of a king salmon. I fished for the portion of belly under the glass counter and paused, stooped over. Something had just begun, faintly, to smell. Not quite turned, but unmistakable. Cuddy was saying something about his friends. I reached inside, pulling the sliver of salmon belly from the back of the bar. I turned it over in my hands. A seam of the rosy flesh had turned slick and yellow. I glanced Appa's way. Cuddy had trailed off and was looking at me.

"Sorry," I said, tossing the whole thing in the bin at my waist. "What are your friends big on?"

"Ah"—he raised a finger—"what's the word. Trash? Dollar pizza? Wings? Pure filtered cans o' beer."

"You sound ashamed," I told him. "I could kill a dollar pizza."

Appa had never let a fish go bad in the bar. It was the worst thing anybody could do in front of a customer, short of serving the rotten fish to them anyway. I couldn't place where that belly had come from. Surely not from the last fish run. Appa would've seen it on ice at the market. The bar was subdivided, loosely, into three units: mine, Appa's, and a surplus we used for unforeseen circumstances. I took an extra cut of belly from there, watching Appa, who was bent over a carton of sea urchin, and brought Cuddy's second course back to his spot at the bar.

"Something wrong?" Cuddy asked me.

"All good," I said quickly, plating for him, "king salmon for you."

"Salmon, like smoked salmon?"

"No."

Cuddy shrugged, pausing to eat. He closed his eyes.

"Oh—what the fuck . . ."

"Good or bad?"

He nodded his head, eyes still closed. He held out his hands, chewing like some religious zealot.

"What's there to say anymore," he said. "Best two things I've ever eaten in my life."

"I thought you gave the amberjack a B."

"I was putting on a front for you," he said. "But you know what, I'm just a man. I have my limits. I can understand a masterwork when I see it."

I found myself smiling. "There's something my dad says about what a single cut of fish needs to accomplish. The most important is quality. Texture and taste, but also where and when it falls in the menu, one of the first bites or the last. It has to do with the rice, and the level of ferment, the vinegar. And it has to do with me, too, making it in front of you. The really special part of omakase. You trust me and I trust you, or at least that's how it's supposed to go. He does this thing to explain it—"

I rubbed my two fingers together, as though pinching a bolt of silk between my index and thumb. "Quality. You know? All of it comes together and makes something . . . different."

My head had started to swim a little from the shot. Cuddy smiled back.

"That sounded like poetry. You're a natural."

My face had heated to the temperature of a hot summer day. I wiped down his board, looking for something to do. The couple had gathered up their coats and left cash for me. In the half hour that had passed, the restaurant had become nearly empty. Cuddy was polite about the squid and the scallop, but I could tell his tastes by then. I angled away from the shellfish and gave him kanpachi, butterfish, and a belly cut of the hamachi. Most of the time he watched me work. Our words became less and less frequent. It was a comfortable rhythm I found I could establish with most customers pretty well if they were alone. Loners were a strange, amorphous demographic; you couldn't really tell a person by the way they acted alone at the bar. Groups, sure. Students, suits, old college friends, whatever. I tried to think of the person I'd assume Cuddy to be if he'd come in without my knowing him.

An hour later, he was the last one in the restaurant. Appa had cleaned up his side of the bar and was wrapping his leftovers in Saran wrap. We were running low. Another fish run tomorrow. I tried not to think about it.

Cuddy had just put the toro in his mouth, a leaner cut than I'd typically serve since he seemed to enjoy the protein better than the fat. He shook his head, chewing.

"Your dad taught you all of this?"

"Sure did." I'd wiped down my knife with my towel and was in the middle of slicing a portion of the tamago for him.

"When?"

"I was a teenager," I said. "Actually, right here, where I'm standing, for most of it. With this knife, come to think of it."

The knife, a wood-handled yanagi Appa had bought me in Queens when I was ten, had been lying in a drawer, evidently, from the time I'd left home to one month ago when I'd picked it up again. I had memorized every scratch on the handle. I'd cut myself exactly three times, twice on the left index finger, once on my foot when it slipped off the table and landed point down on my big toe. Story for another time.

I passed the knife to him, and he looked it over for a minute before handing it back.

"Beautiful," he said.

"She's a good one."

I'd never quite been looked at the way he looked at me. A mixture of fascination and fear, as though he was admitting he was at a complete loss about what I was going to do next. The way I'd imagine conservationists observed animals in the wild, the brief moment in which the thing they'd devoted their lives to had made itself known and they were in the middle of realizing that their training, all of their studying, had not prepared them for the sight of the real thing. He'd looked at me the same way the night I woke up and, it seemed, had yet to stop.

"I'm still training," I told him. "You should see my dad do this menu. He can talk, make jokes. It's why he gets all the tips. Being behind here is a social art. That's where I'm always coming up short."

"That's not true."

I smirked, setting the tamago lightly in front of him. "You're easy."

"Why's that? Because you know me?"

"It's more than knowing you," I said. "In Japan they don't talk at all. You could eat an omakase there in twenty minutes if you wanted to, and most of them do. Most people here want an experience. It's so much more than food here. It's . . . frustrating. I've never liked this part."

Cuddy drained his water. "You should give yourself more credit."

"That's not a strength of mine."

We had fallen silent. Umma was at a table, tallying checks. She saw me and winked.

"What's a day in the life?" he asked me. "Walk me through it."

"Wake up around six, make coffee, get to the restaurant, take the chairs down, clean the bar, slice cucumbers, make rice, slice more cucumbers, eat lunch, open at five, close at ten, go home, sleep."

"I think you're skipping some steps." He smirked.

"You wouldn't believe how often we run out of cucumbers," I said. "No matter what we do. It's the first to go. Couldn't tell you why, or how."

"I wanted to ask . . . ," Cuddy said, trailing off. "Have you . . . heard from your guy lately?"

I clenched my jaw tight, hearing him, but kept my head down, wiping away the water around my workstation. "No, I haven't."

Cuddy let out his breath. "That's pretty disappointing," he said. "I'm sorry."

I was too but didn't want to say it. We'd been closed for ten minutes. Appa had brought out his ladder and was tinkering with the speaker in the corner of the room. Cuddy ate his last course and wiped his mouth with a hot towel that I handed him.

"You ever . . . meet him?" I asked.

Cuddy's eyes widened slightly. "Uh, yeah, bunch of times," he said. "Practically camped out on the floor the first month after they moved you to Jersey."

He shot a glance Appa's way.

"Those were some hard times. You kept getting infections after the surgery. Your temp would spike and we'd have to call everybody. I remember so many nights I'd be watching traffic, hoping your dad or your mom would get here in time and I wouldn't have to tell them—well, you know."

And I nodded, without anything else left to do, because I did know.

Something I found myself imagining often: Ren's eyes, being a spectacularly fascinating shade of blue-gray that I have never and probably will never find a match for out in this world. Which is hyperbole but something I used to tell him. His eyes were so different from mine, so transparent. You could tell exactly what he was looking at, what he was focusing on. It had always felt like an invasion of privacy, something that didn't go both ways because my own eyes were dark brown, opaque. But we didn't have secrets. His was the easiest life to integrate. I knew what he thought, what he feared. What made him happy. I could see it all there whenever I wanted.

"Things were quieter after they put you in the coma."

I tried to laugh. "When am I going to get used to hearing that?"

He fell silent for a minute.

"They told you what happened," I said.

"Um, sort of. The big details."

He looked sorry to have brought it up.

"I can't imagine how it felt to hear," he said finally.

"Almost like somebody forgot to tell me it's all a joke," I said.

"I don't want to speak for someone else, ever," Cuddy said, after a while, "but I've seen a lot of things in long-term care. People a lot older than you, married for years. Some lady comes in with covid, she can't breathe, so we'll intubate her, keep her cool and rested for a couple days. Hope for the best. So many people died that way. And already, while they're still breathing, sometimes I can see in the guy's eyes that he's not there anymore. Something's changed. That's what kills me sometimes, how plain it is on their faces. It's like, when something that bad happens to somebody you say you love, you find out whether you've been telling the truth. Or not. You know, Ren stayed so long. A whole year."

He sat with me, tapping his finger on his empty glass. Silence expanded around us. Appa's sake had made my heart beat faster. I didn't know why I couldn't tell him that Ren was gone and was never going to come back. I was hearing the thumps of my blood up against my neck when a loud static hiss came over the speaker, making all of us jump. After another moment, I heard my Pandora station start filtering coolly through the air. Appa raised his arms in triumph, holding a screwdriver.

"Let there be jazz!"

I took the marble plate Cuddy had eaten off of from between us and wiped down his portion of the bar for the last time.

"Thanks for telling me that," I said, then after a moment: "Enjoy the meal?"

"The best food I've ever had in my life," he told me, smiling. "What do I owe you?"

I thought of the four meager tables we'd managed to fill tonight. Appa would kill me if I brought him a check.

"On the house, of course," I told him.

"Don't be so noble," he said. "Food that good deserves to be paid for."

"Be that as it may," I said, "you are always going to eat for free here. Always."

The door clattered open. Juno hauled a backpack thicker than his body behind him and set it gingerly down on a chair. He raised his hands when he saw Cuddy. "Watch out, ladies, Nurse Gaylord's here."

"Tell me you did not come here alone," Umma said, standing up. "Your mother's going to kill us."

"Not to worry, I know everybody here's wondering," Juno said, taking a seat next to Cuddy. "I got a ride. Paper's due tomorrow. Do you want to read it? It's about the SparkNotes article that was written about *Sula*."

"You're telling me you actually sat at somebody's house and did homework."

"We're a 'paper by committee' kind of crowd," Juno said.

"Promising." Appa had folded up his ladder and was carrying it back to the kitchen. "What are you doing here?"

"I wanted to show Uncle JJ something I made." Juno passed his phone over to me, tapping its screen. Cuddy and I watched along with him, a video he'd recorded of me working behind the bar. *My uncle JJ woke up from a two-year coma.* A sad pop song I didn't recognize was playing loudly over the video, which had switched to a close-up photo of my high school graduation photo. *He couldn't move much when he woke up, but slowly, he started getting better.* A clip played from the hospital of me rolling down the hall in a wheelchair.

"Juno, what the fuck is this—"

"Just watch it."

He's been making sushi to pass the time and get a better hold of his life. Another clip of me working in the restaurant, and a backward pan-out through the door to the sidewalk, where the restaurant's lit sign glowed softly against the sky. It looped and started playing again. I watched another five seconds before I realized. Juno lifted his arms triumphantly.

"Gonna ask the same question again."

"That's a TikTok, right?" Cuddy asked.

"It's a *draft*," Juno said, correcting him, "of a TikTok. And I want to know what you think before I post it."

Appa had gone through the doors into the kitchen, out of earshot. I watched the video again, picking up the phone to see it closer.

"What do you mean, post it?"

"It's just a fun thing," Juno said. "I made it this afternoon. Do you like it?"

"No? And what is this account called? Why is it called 'Fish Daddy'?"

"Oh come on." He waved me off. "It's funny. And endearing. And you *are* Fish Daddy. If I showed this video to anybody at school they'd say the same thing. Just be thankful the username wasn't taken."

"Juno, you can't post this."

"Why not?"

"You want to know why I don't want a video out there telling the entire world my personal business?"

Juno widened his eyes expectantly. "Are you embarrassed?"

"No—"

"Okay, so what's the problem?"

"I—" I stammered. "I don't even know what to—"

Umma had raised her head at us. I shoved Juno's phone back to him. "Do *not* show anybody this. Or post it. Do you understand me?"

Appa had come out of the kitchen with two bottles of Hwayo soju, which he set in front of the bar. Juno stepped aside, making way for him, and stowed his phone back in his pants.

"I've been waiting to bring these out, and there's no better moment than tonight," Appa said proudly, pouring out glasses. "Emil, we're so glad to have you here, finally. And I want to thank you for taking care of my son all this time. As you see, he's thriving—" He ran a hand through my hair. "Practically running the place. Isn't that a nice idea?"

"Jack Sr.," Umma said carefully.

"Whoops, didn't mean anything by it," Appa said. "Absolutely nothing. Let's drink."

We raised our glasses. Juno eyed us all. He'd have been an idiot to ask in front of Umma.

"And because we need something to toast to," Appa said, "I'm going with something very simple: To Jack Jr."

I had already gone a shade of red but could feel my face transcend to a new state of mortification as they drank. Appa wiped his mouth with his sleeve.

"We're all closed up here. Jack? Juno? When's the last time I took you to the baths?"

"I can't think of anything worse," Juno said, "or better. Let's do it."

They all started moving, pushing in chairs around us.

"Appa," I found myself saying, "Appa, what are you talking about? What baths?"

"Oh come on," Appa said, "the jjimjilbang I used to take you and James to when you were kids. It'll be fun."

"Are we really doing this?"

"Jack," Appa said, putting his hands on my shoulders. He was teetering on the spot and stopped to press his forehead into mine, partially for support, partially for the tender moment he seemed to want to share with me. "It's decided, it's done. We're leaving. Emil, you're coming with us, aren't you?"

Cuddy laughed. His eyes were lit just a bit brighter by the drink, which I took to mean he might be convinced to do anything if one made it sound fun enough, which is what Appa was banking on, and succeeding at.

"He really doesn't need to do that."

"You're going to love it," Appa said. "Nice hot water, steam saunas. The twenty-four-hour place is fifteen minutes from here. I'll drive us."

"Appa, he doesn't want to," I said. "*I* don't want to. Besides, I need to clean up. Fish run's tomorrow."

"Jack Jr.," Appa said in a way that I knew only preceded something both righteous and so, so stupid. "I did not pour everybody in this room a shot of my good soju so that we could all go home and go to bed."

"Umma . . ."

Umma seemed to be enjoying herself. She shrugged. "Let's make sure all parties are home before midnight, shall we? I'll lock up."

"Ari, come with us," Appa said. "It's just around the block."

"I've been around the block enough times with you," she said. "And you're going to have to call James and let him know where his son is. Now get out."

We filed out, hunching our shoulders against the cold. Cuddy had not yet made a dash for the street. A search had begun for the keys to the van, leaving the two of us on the pavement. I stood there, a bit dazed and jolted to be wasted and suddenly out here in the cold.

"You've got to have work tomorrow," I pleaded with him. "Doctor's appointment, jury duty, something."

"Sounds to me like you don't want me to come along," he said, swaying contentedly on the spot. Juno had climbed into the driver's seat of the van. I was being outnumbered and outmaneuvered.

"Jack Jr.'s embarrassed," Appa said, throwing open the van door. "White people don't do this sort of thing. Getting naked with each other, that sort. You'd be making great strides in the name of cultural diffusion."

He only sounded like this when he was drunk. Cuddy had already climbed into the back of the van. I sighed and followed.

WE FLOATED LIKE HEARTY-CUT VEGETABLES in a soup, the four of us, ass naked in a hot-water basin the size of a king bed. There was enough steam around to provide little more than a foot of visibility in any direction. After the ten minutes we'd spent freezing in the van, the hot water was like sunlight on my skin. I'd found my way in front of a jet that was pounding the bottom half of my back. We were making noise, echoing along the walls of the second-floor spa that were painted with green mountains and wintry sky. I closed my eyes. It had been a long day.

Cuddy paddled up to me from across the pool, situating himself at the next available jet. I could only see the dim outline of his head, a little closer, his collarbones and shoulders. He was hairier than I'd thought he'd be. The old guys in the locker room had stared when he walked in, passing judgmental looks Appa's way for bringing a white boy into their sacred space. We'd put our clothes into lockers and washed up while seated at a row of little plastic stools. The steam around us was scented, something like cucumbers.

"What's the matter?" Cuddy said. "Can't find anything to complain about?"

Juno had pushed himself out of the water and had made for the cold plunge pool. We heard a splash, then a screech that I suspected might have earned our party a demerit from the spa staff, accumulating points toward our immediate expulsion. Appa had doubled over laughing as Juno waddled back to us and tumbled into the water, sending frothy waves in all directions.

I had sobered up but was still in a state of loose calm, helped by the water. I closed my eyes.

"Why did you go into nursing?"

Cuddy laughed. "Why do I sense that you're waiting to see if I give you the answer you're looking for?"

"I could never be that conniving. I'm too drunk."

He stretched his arms up high above his head, bringing them down. "I was premed, like everybody else. And I realized the only thing I loved about it was the patient work. Giving care. That makes me kind of a putz, doesn't it?"

"How'd you end up here?"

"How *did* I end up here?" Cuddy gestured to the mist all around us. "I'm hammered and floating in a Jacuzzi tub with the people who just served me dinner. You tell me."

He peered down at his lap.

"You can see my dick, can't you?"

"Do you want me to see your dick?"

He snorted.

"Do you know what's weird?" I asked him.

"Everything about this is weird," Cuddy said.

"The fact that you might actually know them a lot better than I do," I said. He frowned at me. I jerked my head toward Appa.

"What makes you think that?"

"I'm thinking about what you said at dinner," I told him. "The way people show you who they are in a hospital. I can't imagine what they must've been like, the first few months."

Cuddy leaned his head back, finding the rim of the pool. "They're the kindest people I've ever met," he said, leveling his voice, as if trying to tell me something he thought I didn't know. "You're lucky."

"Lucky," I repeated. "That's me. Survive a car crash I don't even remember being in, come back home to family I've barely seen for twelve years."

He paused a moment, then moved himself closer to me.

"I know what you do," he said, poking me in the chest. "You don't let yourself be happy. About anything."

"Sure."

"I mean it," Cuddy said, pausing a moment to run his hands through his hair, "this is a thing that you're allowed for yourself, Jack Jr. Humans want to feel secure. And it's okay to be afraid, but you can't let it trap you the way that you let it."

I smiled. "Thank you. Same time next week? Do you take Cigna? Who am I kidding, I don't have health insurance."

He laughed and, repositioning himself, brushed my knee with his hand. "Sorry," he said softly, "I'm a mess. Your dad's an iron horse, drinking that stuff."

Off in the distance was another pool, shallower, with lukewarm water and sprinklers shooting streams in arcs across the surface. My head swam. I could only really think about the touch of his fingers on my leg just a few seconds ago.

"I'm . . ." I trailed off. "I think I need to cool down."

I wasn't lying. I climbed out, angling my hips away from him, and left him there, and waded around in the mist for a bit. When I was sure the others were occupied, I saw my way back through the doors to the showers. I stood under cold water for a minute, then toweled off and started to get dressed. I saw the doors slide open again: Cuddy wiping himself down with his scratchy yellow hand towel. He shot finger guns at me and faced his locker. I kept my eyes down until we had our clothes on again. He sat on the end of my bench and fumbled with his shoes.

"This may grow into a habit," he said. "I feel like a baby. Like I've just been born."

I had nothing else to say. He was smiling at me; his hair hung in front of his eyes, still damp.

"Thanks," he said. "For tonight. The food."

He'd stopped himself from saying more.

"Leave us a review on Yelp," I told him. "Couple more and I think we'll hit the full four and a half stars."

"Then it's my solemn duty," he said. "I'll stay up all night writing it. You'll never read another review as good. They'll quote it in all the top food-writing seminars. I'll be famous. You too, to a lesser extent, but mostly me."

We sat with each other, comfortable, for another moment. I felt his hand first, light and careful, another static shock on my thigh. Then his lips. I tasted alcohol, the tickle on my chin from the scruff around his mouth. It was, very soon, all I could feel while he kissed me, those pricks of his beard that I didn't mind, liked, even. I pulled away, opening my eyes. He was still leaned in, waiting, but I only smiled, then, after another second, stood up. The doors had opened for Appa and Juno. Whatever we said, sobering up in the cold after putting on our clothes, conjectures of how mad James was going to be that Juno was out past midnight, I didn't exactly hear. I didn't know if he did either, though conversation came so much easier to him than to me. He mentioned something about taking the bus, that he lived too far out of the way for us and didn't want to take up any more of our time.

And for however long it took for him to disappear down the street, and for us to drop Juno quietly off on his front lawn, and for the two of us to park the van in its place on the slope, for me to say good night and climb into bed, still damp, with my clothes on, I thought about the feel of that hand on my thigh, how good it felt. Thinking that nobody had really touched me like that for a distance of time that felt much longer than it actually was. That if he'd wanted more of me tonight I would have given it, readily, desperately, despite not knowing for sure how I'd feel about it in the morning. Thinking, and realizing it was hard to breathe and turning over and over, for an hour or more, trying to sleep, the thing I was already so good at but couldn't do tonight to save my life.

For the hundredth time that day, that hour, even, I missed Ren.

Missed his localized, endearing insanity around certain things like crumbs on the floor and shoes in any part of the apartment except for the three-foot radius in front of the door. Missed his stupid blue eyes in the most embarrassing, most saccharine way that I possibly could.

Something else I knew about Ren: He could never grow a beard.

My eyes opened. I sat up and saw moonlight filtering in through the curtains. My head hurt. I tried to make myself believe I hadn't really imagined what I could still see. Cuddy's hair, thick on his arms and curling up from where the pale blue collar of his scrubs met his neck. I felt desire. I shoved it down, deep inside, and threw my head back, hitting soft, forgiving coolness. It just kills, doesn't it? You ever wanted to know what it feels like to have absolutely no control? This was it.

MY PHONE WOKE ME UP three hours later. I could hear it buzzing somewhere around my waist and fished it out of my pocket. Juno was calling. Just five more minutes before Appa would be at my door. I picked up.

"What."

"I've got something to tell you."

"Are you hurt?"

"No."

"Then I'd better fall back asleep right now, for your own good. I have at least ninety seconds before we all need to meet my dad by the van."

"Do you remember that video I showed you?"

I tugged at my hair, trying somehow to ease the hangover ache out of my skull. "What about it?"

"So . . ."

I sat up, swearing as blood hit the backs of my eyes. "What about it, Juno?" I said slowly.

"So, you can't actually be mad at me anymore," Juno said, "because I already posted it."

"When."

"Yesterday afternoon, before I showed you. I thought you'd say yes, is why."

He waited.

"So I'm saying you can't be mad at me," he said, taking my silence as permission to keep talking, "because I have something to tell you about this video."

I fell back against my pillow, throwing my head a little too hard for comfort.

"I want you to take a deep breath and think about the fact that this morning, your video had thirty thousand likes on it. Oh, and about a million views. Cool, right? Cool! You're so happy. You're famous. There is a bright and shining career in content creation in the works for you and honestly you didn't even need me that much to achieve it."

He waited another moment, then another.

"Oop—" he said. "I just checked again. About a million point one. Good news? We're good with this, right? Uncle JJ? You there?"

6

THE PARADOX OF ACHILLES
AND THE TORTOISE

WHAT DID IT MEAN, EXACTLY? A MILLION VIEWS. THE NUMBER OF PEOPLE who had just watched a video set to sad-girl pop of the Fish Daddy slicing sashimi behind the bar. A circle that had expanded from six—one bound by Hippocratic confidentiality—to: however many. I almost didn't want to ask. Except I knew. A million people. A *million* people.

The three of us were shivering, and, in general, hating life and all existence, as the van plowed down the freeway toward Queens at five-fifteen in the morning, about an hour after Juno had called to wake me up. That was the thing about the fall: the most pleasant afternoons out of the entire year, but for several hours in the morning, death. You could stick your head out the window and think it was not only January but the absolute dead of night. Which it almost was. I shot glances over my shoulder toward Juno in the back. It was a late start. Appa was going to be antsy about the catch today. Mentally, I prepared myself.

After we parked, Appa jogged ahead to the market while I brought the dolly up behind him. Wheels clattered obnoxiously against the asphalt. I was unbelievably hungover. I could feel the pounding in my head clattering like shock waves down my thirty-year-old-actually-twenty-eight-year-old body. The impending sun had turned the sky as blue as the ocean. We trudged in silence, reaching the doors.

"He's kind of right about getting here early," Juno said, surveying the floor, significantly emptier than it might have been half an hour ago. "Shit's picked over. Who would've thought? Not me. Certainly. Definitely not me."

He'd kept himself talking, filling the empty silence between us, trying to get something out of me. I didn't answer, heaving the dolly over the rubber steps and onto the wet floor. Juno caught up with me. We walked the length of the warehouse, trailing behind Appa, pausing every now and then to help him load another icebox onto our haul.

"How mad are you?" he asked me finally. "Can I have a number?"

We walked another ten feet.

"Can I have a letter?"

"Juno—" I leaned my head against the dolly's handles. "Just . . . stop talking."

My nose caught an unmistakable whiff of raw chum, and my churning stomach gave another lurch. I dug my forehead farther into the steel.

"Just kill me," I whispered. "Just do it. Right now."

Juno made an exasperated noise. "Jesus, fine, I'll take it down." He pulled out his phone. "This could've really been a thing for us. People quit their jobs for the kind of views this got. I had to turn my notifications off; two point four million—"

I put a hand on his wrist. A moment crossed his face, one of pure elation, thinking I had changed my mind, until he saw the look I was giving him.

"We are not taking that video down."

He moved his head left to right, confused. "Okay?"

"Thanks to you," I said, "there are people who know about me, and about the restaurant, and more important, people so moved to action by this entire thing that they might even stop by the place and eat there, and tell their friends, and maybe even get their friends to come and eat there too."

"You know, there are better ways to make some money off of this kind of thing," Juno said, not looking at me. "Like, a GoFundMe page, something like that. Something we can set up so that any interested persons can just . . . send us whatever they want."

He smiled sheepishly at me.

"Wouldn't that be cool? We could solve all our problems. Solving problems is so . . . so cool, right, Uncle JJ?"

He shrank away from the look I gave him, still trying to smile but tensing so hard that it looked more like I'd just kicked him in the nuts. Which is what I wanted to do.

"That's not what you *did,* is it, Juno?"

Juno turned away, giving up. "I don't want that ice pick you're holding to enter my skull, so no, I didn't make a funding page without telling you. I'm just saying that it would be really easy to—"

"Enough," I said, "we're not talking about this anymore. Not about that stupid account or how many views it got or how much money we could make from a CashZapMe page or whatever—"

"A GoFundMe. You're thinking of Cash App, which is actually a completely different thing."

"I don't *give* a shit." I straightened up, making myself dizzy, and grasped the dolly for support. "A whatever. A Go-Fund-Your-Ass. Something that means that there's actual money out there that could help us."

"Which is . . . good."

"Juno, have you ever heard him even *say* the word *money?* Your dad ever say it?"

He looked at me blankly.

"If we ever took money from strangers and he found out, he'd die," I said. "This whole vision he has of having made it, having done all this on his own, goes away."

"Yeah, but . . . ," Juno said. "We need it."

I screwed my eyes shut. "Of course we need the money. Of *course* we do. You think we drive a van from the *nineties* for the aesthetic? The fucking thing's going to blow up on the freeway with us in it! Jesus Christ, all the things we could fix: The freezer, the broken toilet, the floors he installed falling apart right under us. My medical bills. Who do you think's paying for those? The government? We live in *America*. We are *Americans*. We are living pieces of shit floating on a giant, much bigger piece of shit where everybody laughs at us and everything costs too much money and nobody knows how to pay for anything—"

"Dude—"

"You think our prime destiny is to be five people in a single family working inside the same Korean-Japanese sushi spot for the rest of our lives? We were supposed to be something else. We were supposed to—"

I was breathing too hard. I wanted to throw up. Juno watched as I caught my breath. The warehouse had started spinning like a top and was just now coming to a relative pause.

"Sorry," I said.

He held up his hands. A backhoe was dispatching more pallets of ice behind us, making noise.

"Are you okay?" I asked him.

"Are *you*?"

Appa was waving us over. I braced my knees against the dolly's frame.

"Not sure."

We headed over slowly.

"H-Man's not going to find out about the account," Juno offered hesitantly.

I thought about this.

"Has he ever talked to the reporters?" I asked him. "You know, the ones that showed up outside the hospital. Have they been around the restaurant?"

"You saw what he did when he picked you up. They don't come within fifty feet of him or the restaurant. Unless they decide to run with the whole 'Old Man with Baseball Bat Terrorizes Local Journalistic Community' angle."

I walked a little ahead.

"You could've warned me before posting whatever that was. It's my face you're showing everybody."

"I thought you'd like it," Juno said. He saw that this hadn't convinced me. "Yeah. I know. I'm sorry."

He had done the one thing I didn't expect him to do, which was to apologize and mean it, and now I had nothing to stand on. I dug my fists into my eyes, holding them there, erupting brightly colored stars, which kind of felt good.

"I might have freaked out on you and I shouldn't have," I said.

"Might have?"

"Cuddy kissed me last night."

Juno stopped walking. Ahead of us, Appa had engrossed himself in another conversation and wasn't paying attention.

"Yikes," Juno said, keeping his face level.

"That a bad thing?"

"I thought doctors weren't supposed to have sex with their patients. That's some kind of law."

"He's not my doctor, we didn't have sex, and that's not a law, it's just a generally very frowned-upon violation of privacy and an abuse of power. Which he doesn't have. Because he's not my doctor."

"You sound like you already know what to do about it," Juno said, turning up the corners of his mouth. "Let me guess, you gave each other handies under the water? Seriously? Next to your own father?"

"Can you just . . ." I kept walking. "This was a terrible idea. Forget I said anything."

He jogged after me. "It really can't be my fault for being curious. You're the one telling me." He was at least ten times more excited than I was. "What'd you do? Did you kiss him back? I was serious about the underwater handies."

"Stop talking," I hissed, glancing around for Appa. "Please, Juno, a little decency about this."

"Yeah, because that's why you bring a good guy like that to a bathhouse." He beat his chest, turning up his nose. "In the name of *decency,* good sir."

We stopped halfway to Appa.

"How'd you know he was gay?"

"I didn't. He might not be. He was drunk."

"Did you do anything else?"

"No."

Juno blew a raspberry between his lips. "Weak sauce, Uncle JJ. I thought gay guys *thrived* in the bathhouse. That's like your home base. It's the gay equivalent of a meet cute at Trader Joe's."

"First of all, the gay equivalent of a meet cute at Trader Joe's *is* a meet cute at Trader Joe's. It's the gayest of the major chain groceries," I said. "Second of all, there's nothing wrong with what he did, or what I did—didn't do. I hardly know him. Plus . . ." I trailed off. "I kind of killed it. By accident."

"By accident," Juno repeated.

"On purpose," I said, correcting myself, "I don't know. I don't know anything. I've been dead for two years. What to do when somebody kisses you has progressed light-years beyond what I know."

"People may say that, but they're lying," Juno said. "It's chemistry, baby. Simple animal attraction."

"And you know."

"Fuck yeah I know," he said, "I've been around. I've slammed it once or twice."

We were laughing at this point. I pushed him backward. "Just get away from me."

We started walking.

"You gonna see him again?"

"I'm not saying anything anymore," I said. "This was a mistake. You're sixteen, I'm your uncle."

"That's pretty nasty, Uncle JJ. That's how all those Sean Cody videos start, isn't it?"

"Juno—"

He jogged ahead before I could kill him, and started hauling the pallets Appa had bought. We followed him around the floor like usual, talking less and less. We filled the dolly, but I could see from Appa's face that the catch this time had severely disappointed him. The slimy, turned salmon I'd found in the drawer last night swam up in my brain. It would have killed the restaurant if somebody had found a bit of that on their plate. I could imagine how quickly word would spread. Fort Lee could be a fortress, just the same three thousand Korean people day in and day out, talking among themselves in between worship services. I pushed it aside.

"H-Man," Juno said, "this is my fault. I wanted everybody to go out last night. We wouldn't have been so late today otherwise."

Appa ran a hand through his hair. "No harm done," he said, smiling wearily, "we'll figure it out."

Forgiveness of blockheaded teenagers appeared to run in the family. When we were packed away, we piled in and headed home. Appa cracked the window, letting in cold whips of air.

"Uncle JJ kissed Cuddy last night."

I wheeled around, finding him plugging his thumbs on his Switch, giving me a wink.

"Is that so?" Appa said.

"No, that's *not* so. Nothing happened."

"Ah," Appa said, confused. "So you didn't kiss him."

"He kissed me."

Appa glanced Juno's way. "Hear that? Makes a difference, apparently."

"It was supposed to be a secret."

"Never heard that before in my life, on my honor," Juno said. "We had to tell him something about yesterday."

Appa smiled at me. "What's he talking about?"

"Nothing," I said, sinking low into my seat, proving it was in fact impossible to die by sheer force of will. "Absolutely nothing."

"That's not particularly kosher," Appa thought out loud. "Well, I guess he doesn't see you clinically anymore. Is that why you invited him out to the jjimjilbang with us?"

"Jesus Christ," I said, "*you* invited him, Appa."

"Jury's out on who invited him, I'll give you that." Appa shrugged. "He's a good boy."

"That's what I said," Juno added.

"Let's just not talk anymore." I closed my eyes. "Nobody talk."

"We're being very excited for you, Jack Jr.," Appa said. "Nothing wrong with that, is there? You'd better get some details, though. How long's this been going on, you know? I'd hate to think he'd been getting handsy with you all this time in your sleep."

"Oh my fucking G—"

Appa ran over a rough patch of asphalt, rendering us airborne.

THE SUN WAS UP OVER our heads by the time we came back to the store. Appa went ahead, leaving us to unpack. Juno idled around the boxes, finishing a level, then shut his game off.

"I'm making miracles happen for you, Uncle JJ, I just know it." He stopped, taking out his phone. "Reminds me, I wanted to get some video of you unloading."

"For what?"

"The next video. I'm doing a whole 'fish run' kind of vlog. Like a day in the life. You know what they say. 'Hi welcome to a day in the life of a gay sushi chef who just woke up from a coma like and share for more.'"

I heaved two pallets onto the dolly and wheeled it onto the sidewalk.

"We'll need to keep interest high," I said after a while.

"You're talking like a goddamn star," Juno said, aiming his phone at me. "Don't notice me."

"How do I not notice you?"

"Don't hide your face. Make it natural."

"I'm trying."

He stopped, reviewing the footage.

"Good take," he said. "Okay take. All right, Fish Daddy, do another."

If he was trying to get out of hauling the pallets himself, it worked. I'd brought everything inside by the time he'd gotten what he needed. We broke down the bigger fish with Appa in the kitchen, me passing the right blades his way, Juno clearing the offal and disposing of it in plastic. When he was finished, he thawed us some soup from the freezer and set two steaming bowls in front of us. We ate out front, near the window, watching the earliest commuters start their cars on the road. Over the river, the little slice of the city that we could see from here had started to catch the light.

"I have a question, Uncle JJ," Juno said.

"If this is about anything Cuddy and I did not in any way do underwater—"

"How'd you get out of here?"

"Out of where?"

He gestured to the place around us. "Here," he said matter-of-factly. "The business. You went and lived in the city for how long? Ten years? How'd you do it? Why wasn't H-Man mad at you?"

"Why would he be mad at me for that? I wanted to go to college."

"Yeah . . ." Juno toyed with his spoon, scooping pockets of spicy oil from the top of his broth, saying nothing more. It dawned on me that he might have done something monumental and was only trying not to make it seem that way. For once, he looked genuinely uncomfortable. He seemed to be on the path of asking me what he really wanted to ask me, but before I could say so, he abandoned it and started eating again.

"What are we talking about?" I asked him.

"It's nothing."

"You're going to ask me a question like 'how did you get out of here?' and pretend it's nothing five seconds later?"

"Yep," Juno said, continuing to avoid me. "Sorry."

I drank the rest of my soup.

"You had a lot of guts, Uncle JJ," he said suddenly. "Getting out. Doing your own thing."

I shrugged. "I paid a lot for it. I didn't see you for years. Your dad, Appa, anybody."

I set my spoon down.

"I regret it."

"Is that the first time you've ever said that?" Juno asked me.

"What do you want to ask me, Juno?"

I saw him shoot a nervous glance through the kitchen window.

"Okay, then," I said, switching gears, "tell me what happens when Appa retires. Could be five years from now, ten years. Could be longer. What are you going to do then?"

"I—" Juno said, lifting his spoon dejectedly. "Am going to do whatever my dad tells me to do, most likely."

"But you don't want to."

He thought for a moment, then shook his head.

"I already know," Juno said. "It was happening while you were asleep. H-Man taking me aside, asking me to come with him to meet the vendors, run deliveries, go back behind the bar with him during dinner. Then you came along and now we're both here, doing it."

"That's what I wanted. I asked him for a job here."

"Yeah, but you're not going to stay," Juno said. "Someday you're going back across the river, aren't you? That's what you said at the market today. This isn't"—he waved his hand in the air—"what you want."

He wouldn't stop jerking his eyes over to where Appa was working. I'd never seen him look so afraid. I took a breath.

"I was being dramatic when I said that," I told him. "You know me. That happens a lot, doesn't it?"

He shrugged.

"So, you don't want to work here," I said. "You want to . . . what? Go to college?"

I measured in him a spark of relief, hearing me say it instead of having to come out with it himself.

"You can go to college, Juno, who's stopping you?"

Both of us knew the answer to that question. Juno had finished his breakfast and took a long swig of water.

"I don't know what I'm doing," he said. "And I'm not supposed to know, right? I'm supposed to be taking all this time to figure it out by the time I get out of high school. But he's making my decisions for me, I can feel it. So much fucking talk about me needing to learn responsibility, how we're all going to have to depend on me someday. It's driving me crazy and I don't know how to tell him."

We could go so long without talking about James, sometimes, despite the fact that he was the reason we knew each other. I balled my fist in my hand, then unclenched it.

"You have time," I said.

"Less and less," he said. It *was* true, there was no arguing that.

I made myself smile. "Okay," I said, aware of what I was about to suggest and doing it anyway for his sake. "So . . . what if I talked to him about it."

He eyed me quizzically. "You wouldn't."

"Who says I wouldn't?"

We fell silent again.

"I'll do whatever you want me to do," I told him. "Thanksgiving's next week, we're going to need things to talk about. I'll ask him what he thinks."

He didn't react for a while. I saw behind his eyes he was thinking hard, trying to make sense. I reached my hand out, making a fist.

"Promise."

He hesitated, then bumped his fist with mine. We were silent for a moment. I watched a little bit of the weight leave his shoulders. He looked like he wanted to smile. Then he smacked his palm to his forehead.

"My ice—"

He ran for the kitchen, rummaging, clanging pans together.

"FUCK!"

He emerged, holding a giant steel drum of a pot in his hands. The water inside had cracked and clouded as it froze.

"I did everything right," he groaned. "I read you're supposed to boil the whole thing, then add baking soda, and it's supposed to freeze totally clear."

We surveyed the pot between us.

"Salvageable?" he asked me.

"There's a little clear part right there. How big does this lens need to be?"

"Big enough to fit over a flashlight."

"Yeah, you're done."

The door opened behind us. Zeno hung up her coat alongside ours and lugged a tote bag filled with textbooks over one shoulder. She either didn't have a backpack or conscientiously objected to one on aesthetic or moral grounds. I guessed that moral grounds were more likely. She was glaring at something on her phone, clicked it off, and shoved it violently into her jacket pocket. Juno stopped, spotting her. A quick, quiet moment passed in which each was absolutely gutted to find the other there, standing in front of them. Juno came to his senses first.

"Abigail?"

She turned around, ducking her head.

"You know each other?" I asked.

"Chem partners," she said, turning around. "I didn't know you worked here too."

"I don't work here," Juno said defensively. "I mean, I work here, I just don't . . . I mean I'm not like . . . you."

"Elegant," Zeno said, rolling up her sleeves. "You should hear yourself."

I widened my eyes.

"Chem partners," I repeated. "You're the one who failed lab because he spilled one-point-eight-molar hydrochloric acid on the floor."

Juno jerked his head in my direction. "Who told you that?"

"You did, Juno, who else could have told me that?"

"Zeno," Appa said, waving her over, "there's an extra set of knives in the back for you. I want you to see something."

"Zeno," Juno repeated, watching her as she passed. "Who's Zeno?"

Zeno turned around, indignant. "It's my name now. I'm an artist, I'm a free spirit. I want to separate a persona of myself in this space to uncomplicate my headspace. It's like Deadmau5. Or Banksy."

"Okay, and Zeno's like . . . a cool character from an anime."

"Zeno of Elea was a Greek philosopher who lived from four ninety-five to four thirty B.C.," Zeno said, rapid-fire, as though she'd been practicing for this very moment every day for years—and I didn't need to know anything more about her to know that she absolutely had. "He invented the modern dialectic and *buttressed* the doctrine of Parmenides giving motion as an illusion both physical and—"

"Oh, I have it here." Juno had pulled out his phone. "That was easy. The paradox of Achilles and the tortoise. Achilles and a tortoise meet on a racing ground and engage in a footrace—"

"In a footrace," Zeno said impatiently, speaking loudly over him. "The tortoise, obviously, moves much slower than Achilles, and so in the name of sportsmanship gets a head start. However, in the time it takes Achilles to reach the position on the racing ground occupied by the tortoise, the tortoise has already moved ahead by a small amount. In the time it takes Achilles to overtake that small amount, the tortoise has moved ahead again. Again and again, into infinitesimal segments of distance, theoretically, Achilles will never overtake the tortoise for as long as they race. On the condition of an asymptotic curve, approaching a fixed point but never truly reaching it."

"That was, like, word-for-word," Juno said. "Sick, Abigail, how long did it take you to memorize that?"

We heard a knock on the window, three pounds of a palm on the glass. It took us, the three of us, a moment to put meaning to what we were seeing: A crew of people, one strapped to another camera setup, was waiting outside and peering through the glass right at us.

"Oh *fuck*—" I bolted for the door. "Juno, do not let Appa come out here. Juno? Juno—"

"I'm right here, Jesus," Juno said, "I'm coming with you—"

I grabbed the collar of his shirt and pushed him back inside through the doorway. "Distract him, do something. Don't let him see us."

The crew outside had elected a leader, a small woman in a Canada Goose puffer and holding a microphone, to parley with me.

"We're not talking to anybody." I felt myself straightening my spine, becoming an inch taller, as if that did anything. "Please, leave before my father sees you."

"Oh, I'm sorry," the woman said. "Is this the wrong place? We're looking for the Fish Daddy." She glanced back at her posse for a moment. "Uh, TikTok? Social—social network—"

"I'm speaking English," I said, fuming. "Do you see me speaking English? I speak English. You speak English too, don't you? I'm not talking to anybody about Fish Daddy. The account speaks for itself."

I looked over my shoulder. Appa was still in the kitchen.

"We're with CBS New—"

"Just—" I closed the door behind me. "Stop. Leave here."

"You know, for somebody who doesn't want to talk about the account, you sure do speak your mind in the comments."

"That's not me. My neph—" I stopped myself. "I've told you to go, now go."

I stayed in the doorway, stealing looks over my shoulder, until they disbanded, then stepped back inside. Zeno was wiping the glass partitions of the bar down with Windex. Juno stood up, angling his head in the window to get a look at the van as it drove away.

"Did they know about Fish Daddy?"

"Yes."

"And they saw the TikToks?"

"Yes."

Juno looked pretty proud of himself.

"That was way too close," I said, finding the jumble of keys in my pocket and locking the door behind me. "They said you're, like, constantly responding to comments."

"Uh, yeah?" Juno said. "I'm building a brand. It's important your followers see you as accessible."

"I—" I started. "You—"

After a bit more stuttering, I gave up. I steered myself away to the kitchen and stowed our used bowls in the sink along with the frozen pot. "Zeno, come look at this with me."

She followed me behind the bar, watching me arrange some of the fresh cuts in their refrigerated shelves under the wood countertop.

"When we close up on Wednesdays, before the fish runs, I want you to get all the wax paper out of these drawers and wipe it all down for the new stuff the next morning. They should be empty. If there's any fish left in here, just toss it."

"What was that just now?" she asked me quietly.

"What?"

"The reporters. Why didn't you want your dad seeing them?"

I turned my head to look at her and saw that she was asking in earnest. "You're not on TikTok, are you?"

"I love myself, so no."

"There's . . . something we're doing on there that's getting a few people, some people, talking about the restaurant. It's a publicity thing."

"You're commodifying your medical condition to engage in the grand capitalist exercise. Sympathy marketing."

"Well, when you say it like that . . ."

Zeno glanced down at her pocket, pulling her phone out. Her face grew tense, her eyes scanning a large gray text bubble that I couldn't read upside down. Except it wasn't a very tense look on her face anymore. More wounded. A boyfriend, maybe. Or maybe not a boyfriend anymore. An assumption I was sure she would chew me out for having. It didn't change the fact that something was wrong.

"You okay?"

"Fine," she said. After a while: "I know you're just helping your family, with whatever you're doing on TikTok. That was mean of me."

People her age were, in fact, capable of reflection, though you couldn't have convinced me of that at sixteen. I realized I was glad to have her.

"Do you want some soup?"

I gestured to the pot still simmering on the stove behind us.

She nodded. "I have to take care of the trash."

"You don't need to—"

She'd already gone through the doors to the kitchen.

Appa joined me behind the bar with a bag of ice from the freezer. We worked in silence for a minute or so.

"About last night," Appa said suddenly, "I know we were making fun, but I want you to know it makes me happy."

I nodded at him. "Good talk."

"I just can't help feeling like you spend a lot of your time alone. Which is fine, of course. But when I can't be there with you at home, and all your friends are back in the city . . ."

He thought I had friends. Or rather, friends that were mine and not Ren's to begin with. There was too much else to address at the moment.

"I'm just saying," he said, turning for the door.

"What do I do about the fact that I might have shut him down last night?"

He frowned at me. "I thought you liked him."

"I know. I do. I did. I don't know."

Appa glanced around the kitchen for a moment. "Did you say anything?"

"No."

"Did he?"

"No."

He paused, dug into his pocket, and tossed me the keys to the van. "Why don't you go find out what he's thinking?"

He noticed the perspiring pot in the sink, its dome of ice halfway melted out of it like a jellyfish carcass.

"Don't tell me he's ruined another one."

"He needs the extra credit."

IT WAS SIMPLE WHEN HE said it. It was simple when I was out there doing it too, climbing into the van, pulling away from the curb, driving out onto the freeway, cruising ten miles to the overpass, into the parking lot, through the swinging doors, past the freestanding hand sanitizer dispensers, to the reception desk. Simple until then, hearing them ask me what I was there for, and a few seconds later, after silence, if I needed emergency assistance or was suffering from an allergic reaction that prevented me from speaking. I moved my mouth, trying to breathe. My reattached leg was killing me. The girl at the desk knitted her eyebrows together.

"Are you having a medical emergency?"

"No, I'm not. It's not like that." I hadn't yet caught my breath. I could see her eyes flitting the way of the door. "I'm . . . I'm okay. I'm just—"

"Do you need medical assistance?"

"No," I said again, "I'm"—it occurred to me what I was trying to ask; I went for it—"wondering if you can tell me if Emil Cuddy is working right now. He's a nurse. Male nurse. Man-nurse. I don't know why I said that. He's a nurse."

She turned to her monitor, keeping her eyes on me, and flitted her fingers over the keyboard.

"He clocked out just a few minutes ago."

"So he'd be here, still," I said.

She stared at me blankly until I turned around and left. I wandered the lobby, checking the tops of faces above masks for a sign of his eyes. Nothing. I was going to miss him, or already had. I reached the turnstile doors again, craning my neck. Thinking this was good, that maybe if I didn't see him now I wouldn't have to say all the words I'd been going over in my head driving down the freeway in the van, when I saw him. The back of his head, boarding a shuttle bus with about ten other people dressed in scrubs. The bus pulling away from the curb, heading down the lane toward the freeway. I stood there, frozen, forcing myself to start moving.

"Cuddy! Fuck! Cuddy!"

I ran through the turnstiles, reaching the curb. The bus was a hundred yards away. I started to sprint, running down the sidewalk, flying past bodies in white coats, dodging two wheelchairs and their attending caregivers. This was to be my fate, I thought, chasing after this bus forever without ever being able to catch it, fighting against the illusion of motion until motion itself was no longer motion, until it was a bus slowing to a stop in front of the intersection just in time for me to crash straight into it, clip my legs on its fender, splay my arms against its rear windows, and hang there, starfished on the back of the bus, until at last I peeled myself off its white-painted chassis and came to a resting heap on the ground. Ah, the illusion of motion, the bus I'd just painted myself onto. I opened my eyes to the gray sky, in time for a man in a white shirt and tie, the driver, to drag me off the ground and onto the curb. I nodded and yessed my way through his questions and got to my feet, boarding the bus, searching the aisle for him.

"Cuddy?" I said. I could hardly tell the spinning heads apart. A blue blur stood up near the back.

"Jack Jr.?"

"Cuddy—" I took a step and fell onto the back of a seat. His face was coming into focus, still masked but easy to recognize. I realized he was holding me up. The entire bus was watching us.

"Hi," I said, breathing hard.

His eyes were wide with genuine fear. "You hit the bus."

"I hit the bus, yes. I'm okay. Maybe."

He reached up, almost as a reflex, to feel the top of my head. "Hurt anywhere?"

"Just my pride." I wobbled on the spot. "And maybe my skull. We'll find out."

"That's not good," Cuddy said. "Um, Jack Jr. Why did you hit the bus?"

"That's a complicated question," I said. "Really. What I'm trying to say is—my head hurts."

"It probably does. What are you doing?"

"I didn't know you wanted to kiss me, and I should've figured it out, and I didn't. So I'm sorry for that."

He blinked at me.

"You're sorry," he repeated.

"Yes."

"For . . . what again?"

"For getting weird. For being stupid. For . . . liking it."

Cuddy glanced nervously around the bus at that last one. He was still holding me up by my arms. The nurse sharing his aisle seat with him had occupied herself with her phone and was currently flicking through her open apps, trying to look like she wasn't listening to every word.

"I already knew that," he said finally.

I frowned. "How?"

He laughed. "You're not as tragic as you think you are," he said. "You're actually pretty endearing. I was going to ask your dad for your number today." He paused a moment. "Though it looks like I waited too long."

His eyes made wrinkles at their corners, evidence he was smiling at me.

"Satisfied?"

I had finally caught my breath but couldn't think of anything else to say. He patted me on the shoulder.

"I think you'd better let somebody here check you for a concussion."

7

WICKED SUNDAY

I HATED SUNDAYS. IT WAS A REMINDER MORE THAN ANYTHING THAT SO many pieces of the thirty-year-old life I was supposed to be living were missing. I woke, I worked, I ate, I worked, I bathed, and I slept. And yet, one thing had changed. For all of my talk of stasis, I now had Emil Cuddy's number saved in my phone. I'd crashed into the back of his shuttle bus three days ago and neither of us had texted the other. I didn't know what this meant. It had been so simple just two days ago. The steps forward seemed to have unfurled themselves with clarity. Next came a text, maybe a dinner. A kiss. A . . . something else. Sooner or later I'd be dating my nurse and nothing would even be weird about it, because he wouldn't be my nurse anymore. I fished my phone from under my pillow, found his contact page, and opened a new message. A simple *hey* would be okay, I thought. Easy and casual. *You don't mean very much to me, yet, but who's to say that wouldn't change? Would you like to find out with me? I wish you would.*

"Yikes," I said to myself, putting my phone away.

Appa was either tending to some home project outside or had left altogether. I took my towel to the bathroom we shared off the hallway and showered. There was nothing worse than a Sunday. Nothing worse than having to stop working and be a person, when there were so many things wrong with that faction of life! Take me back to simplicity, the good side, where things made sense.

On Sunday, when the restaurant was closed, Appa did things like weed the lawn outside, clear the gutters at his and James's places, and in general attempt to complete a gargantuan list of household, personal, and professional chores while at the same time forbidding my help. Forbidding me even to watch. I had tried this now for about six or seven weeks in a row, set alarms that he turned off without telling me, carried stacks of old cardboard boxes to the driveway that he would rip out of my hands, saying I worked too hard, I deserved some rest. It was near six in the morning. There was nothing I could do anymore about the fact that I had nothing to do, and had had nothing to do the past six or seven Sundays. My training had embedded itself into my veins. I was as awake as I would ever be when I pulled myself from bed and put on another layer of Kirkland sweats, because my breath was coming out in wisps. I stood still, listening for Appa somewhere in the house.

The room I'd been occupying for the past few months had been set up for two a few decades ago. James and I had shared it from the moment I was born to the day he'd moved in with Noa. The bed, still a twin XL, one of two that had survived over the years, was pushed up against the wall and dressed with sad green sheets. My shoes were where I'd stepped out of them, half under the bed frame.

That was when I remembered that I'd promised Juno I would liaise a very dreaded conversation about college between him and James. How, I didn't know. It started with talking, surely. Somebody making the first move, that somebody being me. It always had to be me. In the shower, I gargled hot water and let it spill out of my mouth. Appa and I shared a three-in-one bottle of hyper-volume Pantene Ice Shine that I was very certain he couldn't have bought himself. Most likely Umma had dropped it off after he'd let slip that he washed his face, hair, and body with Dawn. I lathered, rinsed, and shut the water off.

I would talk to James today, I'd decided. It would be fun. For exactly whom, I didn't know. But it was something to do, and I didn't have much to do between that and trying to find something to text Cuddy, which in truth was the less attractive option. I picked my phone back up off the sink and called James before I could regret it. A text would allow me to pussy out and convince myself this wasn't worth doing. He let me ring five and a half times before picking up. It took him a long time to say anything.

"Jack," he said.

"Um, do you want to do something today?" I said quickly. "Together? You and me? Today?"

For Juno, for Juno, for Juno.

"What?"

"Like, have breakfast? See a movie?"

"It's six in the morning."

"You're right, breakfast is better. Should we . . . do you . . ."

James let me sputter on like that for a few more moments that felt like years.

"He's not letting you do anything, is he?"

It was the most generous thing he could have done, in his limited capacity. I gave a sigh.

"He's not even here. I've asked to help him so many times that he just . . . runs away, I guess."

"That sounds right," James said emotionlessly. Then, in a move that surprised me: "Just come here."

"Really?"

"Unless you want to stay at the house."

"No, no, I'll come. What are you doing?"

He seemed to hesitate there.

"I do a morning AA meeting on Sundays. You can't be there, but you can wait outside for me. And when we're done . . ." I felt him pause a moment, as if trying to see if I would already opt out and tell him something like I was sorry for bothering and I'd just stay home. "We can get some breakfast."

"Um, okay."

He made a noise with his throat that communicated some measure of agitation. "That's what I've got, Jack. If you don't want to, there's other ways to spend your time."

"No, that's fine," I said quickly. "No offense meant. I said *um* as in 'so good.' 'Amazing.'"

James took that in for all it was, contemplating it, then told me he'd be there in five and hung up. I put my phone back on its ledge of the sink and glanced around. I cleared a space in the foggy mirror with my hand and got a brief glimpse of myself.

"That was good," I told myself. "A good job. A great job."

I hung my towel back up. I pulled open the door, buffeting myself with icy air that hit like needles.

IT WAS A PECULIAR SOCIOLOGICAL occurrence among Koreans like us. Two parents, both emphatically opposed to organized religion in all its shapes and forms, for their own reasons. Appa, who was no doubt rejecting some sort of forceful indoctrination from his own father that began when he was little, and Umma, who had taken it upon herself to disprove the existence of God. I'd gotten in trouble in the fourth grade one morning for telling the teacher what Umma had once said, that no person, not even a divine one, picks a two-year-old with an entire life ahead of them and decides to give them a malignant cancer that fills the entirety of their short little life with pain beyond measure. "And yet, it happens every day," I remembered Umma telling me while I tried to eat my Harry Potter lightning-bolt chicken nuggets from Burger King. "Kids just like you, younger than you, completely innocent in anything and everything. You'd like to tell me that God makes that happen? For what reason? Tell me."

"Please, I just want to eat my chicken nuggets," I probably said, too afraid to push further.

There was a discussion at some point that both Umma and Appa were requested to attend at the school shortly thereafter. From what I recall, it did not go well. The act had ostracized the two of them from the general churchgoing Korean folk of Fort Lee, and as a result, my parents did not have many friends.

I believed in God. At least, in somebody or something out there that made things happen, but was maybe not some guy who could see you cheat on your taxes or masturbate and punished you accordingly for it. I didn't imagine God was somebody who involved himself in much of anything. Just the very biggest things, like keeping the world spinning or making sure that the sun stayed hot. It was what I believed in order not to blame myself for every little thing, no matter how insignificant, that happened in my own life.

I was thinking about God, which I never did, because I was currently staring up at a statue of Christ that stood on top of the Fort Lee United Presbyterian Church, inside of which James was leading an AA meeting for what looked like at least twelve burly guys who had all filed in from their trucks and vans parked haphazardly in the lot around us. I could see them through a window to the basement rec room where they were all sitting, just the tops of their heads, some of which nodded along to something someone was saying. All this to say: I could have gone in and found somewhere to hide so that I could listen to it all. The doors weren't even locked. But something in me was afraid of what James would do in the not-small chance that he found out. So I was here, waiting in the passenger seat of his beaten-up Honda CR-V, and having to do something really exhausting like contemplate the existence of God in a way that I hadn't done since Umma had lectured me over those chicken nuggets two decades ago.

It was a strange thing, to see the world begin to wake around me.

I imagined the reason for the early meeting was that most of these guys worked demanding, physical jobs on construction lots all day and this, in the pitch-black of fish-run-level early morning, was the time slot that made the most sense. They had all stood up inside and were milling around a large to-go box of coffee that James had bought at the Dunkin' down the street. The sky had started to turn, slowly, into the regular icy blue of the morning.

I checked my phone. Nothing. I knew Cuddy worked the night shift, which only meant a text that I needed to be ready for might come at any time, which didn't make me feel much better.

When I thought about it, about the kiss, and the way I'd backed away from him, I remembered only a slim sort of guilt that cut deeply. I had forgotten what it was like to desire someone like that, other than Ren. I didn't like what it was doing to my judgment. More than that, I didn't like what it was doing to the Ren that I was trying, still, to hold full and precious in my mind. It was a hard thing to do. I closed my eyes, I saw dark, curly hair, covering the whole of Cuddy's chest, felt the weight of his hand on my thigh. When I opened them, James was walking toward me with the empty coffee box. A click as he unlocked the doors and slid into his seat next to me. It was easier not to look at him; I was grateful.

"So you lead a group for construction guys?"

"What? They're not all—"

James glanced around him at the six pickup trucks that were pulling out onto the street around us.

"Huh."

He said no more, driving us back into town.

"Are they nice?" I asked him when we were back on Broad Ave.

"They're a good group," James said. "Some are there more than others."

Maybe he was wondering what exactly we were doing here, sharing space, having conversations. It wasn't something we usually did.

"Do you talk, too?"

"I'm not really supposed to share details," James said. "'Anony-mous,' you know."

"Oh," I said, "sure."

I racked my brain for things to talk about with him. The restau-rant? The weather? The pandemic? I imagined James opened up quite a bit at his meetings. It was impossible for a human being not to have some kind of valve. If it wasn't his family, and it most defi-nitely wasn't his family, it was going to have to be the Construction Workers Union of Fort Lee United Presbyterian Church. I wondered if he talked about us. I wondered if he'd ever talked about me.

My phone buzzed in my pocket. I saw a text from Appa: *Costo what.*

He pinged again. *Costco. What need.*

I typed back, *Nothing.* A second later: *Toothpaste.*

A little thumbs-up appeared over my text. Appa had surprised me there with his tech savvy.

"Where are we going?"

James had asked me. I looked up, at the passing road. We were near the restaurant.

"I thought you knew a place for breakfast."

"I don't eat breakfast."

"Then why—"

James jolted us to a stop as a guy on a bike crossed the intersec-tion on red. Our seatbelts cut into our shoulders on opposite sides.

"You should eat breakfast," I said. "I should know. Coffee sends me to the bathroom for at least a half hour every morning. It's dehy-drating. Terrible for you."

James pushed air through his nostrils. He'd found my vacuous banter at least a little bit amusing. The city was waking. We sped on.

When I was in the first grade, James took me to the houses on Boulevard East, a stretch of old properties that overlooked the city with a sharp cliff down to the waterfront towns. We sat on the frozen ground while he put something together, a paper glider he folded up using poster board, sturdy and lightweight. The finished product had roughly the same wingspan as me. I watched, wide-eyed, while he took it, made a running start, and hurled it over the edge of the walkway with a graceful arc of his arm. I screamed. If I'd had the vocabulary, I would have said something like *Holy fucking shit!* because the glider had made it in a near free fall down to the road below before it swooped upward like a bird, soaring high, out over the choppy river water, coming to rest, drowned finally almost a third of the way between New Jersey and New York. DO IT AGAIN, I had shouted, rabid with joy at my aeronaut brother, who said after he saw it land that he wanted to try to get it all the way over the water to the city docks. I wondered if James remembered that day. There was a way to find out, a small voice reminded me. I opened my mouth but saw that we had turned the corner and ended up in front of the restaurant.

"What are we doing here? It's Sunday."

"You never picked what you wanted for breakfast," James said, unbuckling his seatbelt. "I need to get the old radiator out of the broom closet before it starts growing mold."

"Yeah, but—"

I stopped talking, tapering to silence, because I had at that moment seen something over James's shoulder that I definitely wasn't supposed to see. Zeno, closing the door of the side entrance, through which we took out all of our trash each night, with a rolled-up sleeping bag under one arm. She turned her head; I saw it all happening just moments before it hit us both. Our eyes met.

She stood there, looking at me for a while with her hand on the doorknob. I couldn't be sure exactly what kind of look I was giving back. It was almost eight in the morning. The sky was still dark. As if I were watching it happen through molasses, James frowned at me, turned his head, and saw her.

"Is that the girl?"

"Zeno."

"The girl you hired?"

"James, it's—"

He was already out of the car. I jumped up and immediately gar-roted myself with my seatbelt. "James!"

"What the fuck are you doing here?"

Zeno, admirably, hadn't budged from her spot and had taken her hand off the doorknob, letting it shut behind her. I ran around the side of the car, reaching them.

"Let's calm down. She's fine."

"Fine?" James repeated. "She's been sleeping in the restaurant."

"I sleep there all the time. In the kitchen on top of all the rice. It's a thing."

"Jack, shut the fuck up, enough with the jokes."

"Not jokes," I said quickly, my face growing hot. Zeno's eyes were darting back and forth between us. "Definitely not jokes. I'm just saying, this is not something we need to blow up over. So Zeno sleeps in the restaurant sometimes. I'm sure she's got a good reason."

I wondered, for the thousandth time, watching James level dag-ger eyes at me, what I could possibly be thinking. I edged around him, looking at her.

"Does my dad know?"

For the first time, Zeno aimed her eyes at the ground. After a while, she shook her head.

"This is fucking ridiculous," James said. "She could be robbing us. She could be inviting friends over. She's not even supposed to have a fucking key."

"I don't have a key," Zeno said quietly. She raised her head, find-ing both of us looking at her. "And I'm not doing any of that. I've been putting a stick in this door to get back in after you all leave and I've been sleeping here. Sometimes."

"Okay," I said, breathless. My head was swimming. I just wanted some breakfast. This was supposed to be the most wonderful Sun-day there ever was and now I was an unwilling accessory to some sort of runaway situation. Not to mention, James still looked like he was going to kill her. I stepped between them. "So, for how long?"

She shrugged.

For the longest time, nobody said a word. James was glaring at me, erasing as we spoke the little baby steps of progress I thought we might have been making in the car.

"Jack," he said, "we are letting her go. We might even be calling the police. I haven't decided. Maybe you can tell me you agree with me, and we can sort this out without telling Appa."

"Yes, okay," I said carefully. "That does seem like one reaction you could have to a situation like this."

"Jack—"

"Can you . . ." I faltered, second-guessing, recommitting, powering through. "Let us talk? For five minutes. I promise. Please."

Zeno still had her eyes fixed on the tops of her shoes. I stared him down, pleading silently with him, telegraphing, *I will do anything, literally anything, for you to do what I asked.*

He was staring at me, then at her, then turning away, then walking back to the car before I realized it had worked. I watched him dig a can of seltzer out of the door compartment on the driver's side and crack it open. I let out my breath.

"Okay, that's better," I said, looking at her. "Easy."

She didn't answer me. I thought of ways to build trust. I leaned against the wall, letting my shoulder go numb.

"So."

"I always watched from down the block," she said quickly, "after I propped the door. I was really careful. I watched it until everybody left."

"I guess I'm just wondering how none of us ever noticed that," I said.

"Small stick," she said, "twig, really. It doesn't take much."

I dug my fists into my eyes, rubbing, trying to find relief. "Zeno . . . what are you doing?"

"I'm—" She seemed to have had a better idea of what to say before she'd started. She gave up. "I don't want to be home sometimes. Is all."

It had the air of something she had been waiting to tell me for a while. I knew this much about teenagers, having been one. When they decided to tell you something, you listened.

"Something to do with your parents?"

"My mom." She said, "It's just my mom. And me. And she's an asshole."

"I would guess that she's not."

"Well, maybe you can talk to her about being less of an asshole, because that's been my life," she said, turning away, kicking a loose pebble across the sidewalk and into the gutter. "She doesn't get it. She thinks I'm an idiot. She thinks I'm not preparing for my future in a way that she approves of. She doesn't understand food, or making it, or eating it. She thinks it's a waste of time."

I had opened a floodgate, which I'd been ready for, in my defense. I had never seen Zeno look sad before. I approached her slowly. She'd turned her face away but was wiping her eyes, leaving black streaks on her fingers.

"That sounds heavy," I said. She didn't answer. I shot a look over my shoulder, at James, who was watching us like someone who had just called the manager over to get a couple of delinquents kicked out of the Walmart.

"I can understand some of that," I said. "Speaking a different language than your parents. Not literally, of course. Although we do speak different languages. My family and I. Korean and Eng—you get the point."

I shrugged.

"I don't want to tell you it's going to get better right away. It probably won't. You've got a while before you can leave here and make your own decisions. But you'll come to an understanding. Sooner or later."

"You don't know that."

"Well, I know you," I said, "and you happen to be a responsible, caring person. And if you don't find it happening on its own, you're a caring enough person to make it happen."

She smiled at that. I dug my hands into my pockets, feeling the cold.

"But you're going to have to stop sleeping here," I said. "It's dangerous, and I know she's worried about you."

Zeno didn't object. She hitched her sleeping bag more securely under her arm.

"Why didn't you just ask?"

"Like you would've said yes?"

"I would've done something to help you, I'm pretty sure," I said, frowning. "Something like going to talk to your mother myself."

Her face paled, slightly, exactly the way I wanted. "Oh, that's really not necessary."

"It's kind of a good idea, isn't it?"

"No, it's really not. That's not a good idea."

"I'm very glad you agree." I smiled. "James will drive us."

I raised an arm at him, which she grabbed and pulled back down.

"Not necessary," she repeated. "I'm just going to go home. You're not firing me, you've done enough."

"I don't know that I said *that,* but it does seem like the best thing to do. It puts me in the best possible light."

I stuck out a hand.

"Promise me something."

She took it uneasily. I'll be honest, it was a joy to keep her on her toes. "What."

"Promise me that if you do something dumb again, please, just let me be the only one who finds out."

She took another look over at James, and we shook on it. We went our separate ways, her farther down the street, to the crosswalk, and me back to James.

"Problem solved," I told him.

"That didn't sound like a problem solved."

"What do you know? You didn't hear."

"You were five feet away. I'm not a naked mole rat, Jack."

"Well, she's never going to do it again and I can't afford to lose the labor, so this is what we're going to do."

James raised his eyebrows at me.

"Surprised?" I asked him.

"You're an idiot."

"No, I don't think I am. There is nothing that girl hates more than sentimentality. Would you imagine me coming to their house, having some drawn-out conversation with her mother about how she's doing a great job and that they might even come to learn something by meeting each other halfway? Who am I, Dr. Phil? I'm not set up for that. I'm barely holding myself together. This way, she does it herself. I call that Scared Straight."

I almost got into the car, then stood up again.

"And if we did fire her, we'd for sure have to tell Appa. And if you need reminding, we don't want that."

I'd said my piece. I got back into James's car and waited for him to join me. What a weird Sunday this had turned out to be. Here I was, wanting only some rest and relaxation, instead of whatever any of this was. James closed the door behind him and started the car.

"What do you want for breakfast?"

"Easy," I said. "Pancakes."

We pulled away from the curb. There was one last thing I needed to do. It was Sunday after all. I pulled out my phone and opened a new message.

Do you want to hang out?

I pressed send. If was correct about where James was going to take us for pancakes, I'd be ordering a short stack and a plate of the potato latkes with sour cream and applesauce. Good Sunday. Getting better.

8

UNCLE JJ SEES A PLAY

UNCLE JJ READS A PLAY

UNCLE JJ READS PART OF A PLAY

UNCLE JJ LISTENS TO SOMEONE READ PART OF A PLAY

YES. JUST LIKE THAT. PROPER CAPITALIZATION AND A PERIOD LIKE HE always did. Except that now we had a date, a date on which Emil Cuddy and I would do something, maybe have a meal, watch a movie, just sit together, kiss mouths, kiss other things, some, all, or none of the above. Who was to say, really, what would happen now?

It had been churning my stomach up ever since I'd woken up on Monday morning and seen it.

Lou was wheeling her father around the yard when I made my coffee. I had a spare minute, so I brought my drink outside, shaking frost from the picnic chair we kept on the little porch, and took my seat. Cold, and a little bit of water, had already started to seep through my pants. In the way of mornings to be found in the North Jersey area, it was nothing special, maybe some snow in the afternoon, which I was looking forward to. It took Lou another tour of the backyard to notice me.

"You're up, are you?" She moved her head and pointed it at the hose coiled on itself in the grass. "Move this out of our way."

Lou's father gave a roar that made us both jump: "You're going too fast over the rocks I'm going to fall out do you want me to fall out do you are you even seeing where—"

I stood, jogging over to her, stooping into a short little bow. "Morning, Lou ajumma, how are you?"

She waited for me to gather up the hose. I watched her apologize to her father, rounding the corner of his chair and rubbing his hand softly in hers.

"You're so careless," her father said, drawing the throw blanket pulled tight over his legs farther up his chest. I watched Lou take this with some genuine introspection, as she wondered for the briefest moment if she really was.

"Your accent is an embarrassment," she said to me eventually. "Nobody speaks Korean in the city, do they?"

"Actually they do," I said cheerfully. "On the one street with all the good barbecue in Manhattan, and then for miles and miles out in Queens. Flushing. You'd love it there."

"Stop making fun. What's going on with you?"

I lugged the hose over to the hand-pulled wheel and started winding it back in. "Nothing."

Lou watched me suspiciously, then after a while continued pushing the wheelchair over the grass. Her father had noticed the single cloud hanging in the sky right above us and was peering up at it with suspicion.

"Those bushes don't need watering," she told me. "Your father's going to freeze their roots so they can't grow in the spring."

"I'll let him know. Many apologies."

"I know those bushes. They need dry soil."

"Yes, yes."

"Are you listening to me?"

"Yes, Lou ajumma."

She narrowed her eyes. "What's going on? Something's going on with you."

I took my seat up on the porch, downing a third of my coffee. "Thanksgiving next week." I shrugged. "The restaurant's closed for two days. Just means more opportunities to spend more time with each other."

"It's not that. It's something else."

I smirked. "I told you, nothing."

She scoffed. "Appa"—she patted her father on the shoulder—"I'm taking you back inside."

She took him around the yard, slower than before, and wheeled him back inside. I heard her setting the TV to blast KBS World. When she came back out, she raised her shoulders, hands open, expectantly. "Well?"

"I have a date tonight," I said quietly.

"Ah." She smiled. "Pretty girl. You've got a good face. I bet she's beautiful."

"She is," I said, pausing for a moment. Lou had either never learned that I was gay or been told and had forgotten. "Maybe I'll bring her here afterward. If I'm so lucky."

"That's what you're so happy about."

"Am I happy? I'm nervous."

My mug was empty. I swirled the last drops around its bottom. There were very few mornings as bright as today's was; hardly any clouds. Lou liked when I talked to her about the weather, as if she hadn't noticed it herself.

"Do you think it will get any colder today?"

"Getting colder and colder." Lou hugged her arms to her chest. "You're young. You can stand it."

"I may stand it but I still don't like it."

She liked this best out of all the things I'd said to her this morning, apparently, judging from the smile. "You let me know when you bring that pretty girl home. I'll make soup for her."

"That's so nice, Lou ajumma, thank you."

"It's about time you got married like your brother."

"That was an accident."

She shushed me, and from across the yard I could still hear the cut it made. "Don't speak like that about your hyeong. I know all about it."

I dipped my head an inch lower. The sun was making us both squint. A car had pulled up outside, the sound curling around the house to reach us in a half echo. "Can I get you anything else today, Lou ajumma?"

She waved her hand dismissively at me, like I'd said something stupid. Gravel crunched along the side of the house. Umma was carrying a jumble of plastic bags in her arms. She said hello to Lou and climbed the steps to the porch. She pushed one of the packages over to me. "For you. Did you eat breakfast?"

"I had coffee."

"Disgusting." She unwrapped the pork jeon, still steaming, and fed me one whole.

"Ow—Umma, it's still hot."

"I wanted to get them over to you as soon as I could. Just made, they told me."

"I was going to go tonight and pick some up."

"Isn't that convenient"—she winked—"for you. Here's the fish."

She took it and held it up for Lou, smiling.

"Did Appa ask you to come here?"

"I need an invitation?" she asked me. "I lived here too."

Umma lived in a second-floor walk-up condo in the middle of town and was dating a man nobody had met but whom she insisted was much too young for her (two years). She swore it was nothing serious, which was why we'd never met him. She'd refused continually to say whether they were living together, which raised more questions in addition to the ones she was trying to avoid. It's weird, right? Like, we can all agree that it's weird. I thought this as if I'd say anything to her about it, which I never would. Umma was and continued to be the scariest person in the family.

I took another jeon and split it in half with my fingers.

"You know about my date?"

"Of course I know about your date," Umma said, "it's all anybody's talking about. You are the center of my universe, blessed son, and when I birthed you, my life became yours."

"Ouch."

"I think he's a very handsome young man."

"Sure."

"You're not letting yourself be excited, and it's *your* date," Umma said, sitting down and pulling the steaming Styrofoam tray toward her. "What are you doing with him?"

"He didn't tell me. Just that he wants to meet me at the restaurant and go from there."

She chewed thoughtfully. "Doesn't sound like he's got much of a plan. Oddly honest, would you say?"

"Simple."

"Simple," Umma repeated, breathing hot fog into the air. "I don't actually know anything about him. What kind of white is he?"

"Gee, Umma, I forgot to ask him."

"You don't think he's talking on the phone with a friend of his clarifying what kind of Asian you are?"

"Irish. I think he's Irish."

"What are his parents' names?"

"I don't know."

"Siblings?"

"I swear to you, Umma, I will find all of this out from him to-night, and when I do, you'll be the first to know."

She smirked. "He always took very good care of you. He was certainly the nicest one there. How was the jjimjilbang? I'd assume well."

"He deserves some time with me without my entire family there," I said. "Let's just say that."

We sat contented for a while. The rest of the banchan, wrapped tight in plastic, would make for a promising lunch. I reminded my-self to bring it over to the restaurant and packed them all tighter to-gether in their plastic shopping bag. In my pocket, my phone gave an angry buzz. A text from Zeno: *Where does the mop go.*

Back closet next to the paper towels.

She read it and didn't respond. I held my phone up to Umma.

"Is this, like, a thing? Do people just read texts and not answer?"

"You're complaining to me about young people barely making an effort to speak to you," Umma said, "think about that. 'Happy birth-day, Jack Jr., I love you, what are your plans today? Are you eating well?' 'Thanks. Busy.'"

I smirked. "I deserved that."

"How is that girl working out?" Umma said.

We had managed to keep the secret. And by "we," I meant James had decided telling Appa was more trouble than it was worth and begrudgingly done nothing about the nights Zeno had been spending in our kitchen. The rest of my wicked Sunday had passed without much incidence, and Zeno had come back to work and never spoken to me about it again. I thought about telling Umma.

"She wants to learn anything and everything," I said instead. "And I'm pretty sure she's not doing any of her homework because she's always here."

"There are worse things. She's not my daughter. If she were, I'd have more of a problem."

We ate another jeon each.

"Are you working too hard?" she asked me. "Is he making you?"

"No and no."

More silence, enough to convince me that the important Thing she'd come over to talk to me about really was just a simple two-part yes-or-no, which I'd passed with flying colors. She pulled her hood tighter around her face.

"Your father has mentioned some things to me," she said.

"Can you be more specific?"

"About the restaurant, and him getting older, and thinking he might want to take some more time for himself."

"That really doesn't sound like him."

"Doesn't it?" she asked. "So much changed, Jack Jr., like you'd never believe. Both of us. Since the day the hospital called." She began to smile. "Do you know how they told us? You'll like this story. We were in the restaurant with James and we'd just closed up. Appa picked up his phone, I saw his face when they were talking to him, and I knew. Do you know how it feels to wait for something for two years straight? When you know, you know. He didn't even really tell us. One minute we were talking about something, the fridge, something like that; the next, the phone had fallen on the ground and all three of us were out the door without our coats, running to get into the van. He drove like a maniac that night. I thought he was going to crash that van."

"He drives like that all the time."

She reached out and touched my face with the cold tips of her fingers. "Anyway, he's tired."

"I know."

"What am I supposed to do with him? And with you? Why are men so much trouble? I ask him all the time what he wants to do and he waves me off. Like a burning building waving off the firefighters' hoses, 'It's fine, come back later, I don't know what you're talking about.'"

"Pride," I said.

"No, not pride." Umma rolled her eyes. "It's you. He isn't smart like you. The second you ran off, he decided the only use he was to this family was his arms and legs. Sixty-year-old arms and legs. He's doing all of this, still, because he's afraid you won't take over for him when the time is right."

I frowned. She was waiting to see something in my face.

"Who says?"

"Jack Jr.," Umma sighed, "you work there every day. You make all the takeout orders, you serve the omakase, you've even got regulars. You're teaching that girl all the same things Appa taught you when you were a teenager."

"I help him out around the place." I shrugged. "So what? He'd never just hand the restaurant over to anybody else. It's a child to him. His firstborn."

"He was going to," Umma said. "Don't you remember?"

"That," I said, "was a long time ago. And a very dumb idea."

"Well, things change," Umma said, standing up. "And I don't know exactly when, so don't ask me. But one day he's going to realize he can't just keep sprinting through his life the way he's doing now."

"He has Juno now," I said. "Let it skip a generation."

"You don't really seem to be letting it skip, Jack Jr. You seem to be here."

She was right. Why was I here? What justification could I give? Nothing that came to mind. I just was, even though there were some other places I could be. Back across the river, for one. It had been long enough. A choice, then. I had made a choice. Umma knew what she'd done by asking me this, so she didn't wait for an answer.

"Don't run from your problems. You're thirty," Umma said. She pulled open the sliding door, about to retreat inside to the warmth. Lou was in the right-hand corner of the yard with her mother now, guiding her hands to graze over the tops of a thicket of tall grass. Lou's mother was a lot less of an asshole than Lou's father was. It seemed from the minute she woke up to the minute she slept, she spent the day with a smile on her face. Umma would not live to be that old, she had always said. *I lived my good years. If I live that much longer, I'll be bored.*

"I didn't know he was in trouble," I said.

"No," Umma said quietly. "You couldn't have. You weren't here."

I looked away. She gestured to the very tips of the skyscrapers we could see over the green edge of the valley.

"You were over there, living life. And it made me so . . . happy. To think of you over there, working, being with friends, in love with somebody special. But that's where you were—over there, and not here."

It really was too cold out here for our own good. I thought of spring.

CUDDY HAD ASKED TO PICK me up from the restaurant, partially because I was already going to be there running prep and partially because it was on the way. On the way to what, he wouldn't tell me. I was only just getting used to him, honestly. He texted me full sentences and most often explained the jokes he made right after, afraid somehow that their meaning was not transmitting correctly through cyberspace. I didn't know exactly how it had been decided that he'd be the one taking me places, but I could take a hint. I'd been eating celery from the pantry all morning and afternoon and had gone home for a lengthy shower before showing up at the restaurant.

Zeno was collecting slivered cucumbers from Appa in a hotel pan by the bar. There was soup base to replenish and the sides and belly of bluefin from the previous fish run to break down in the freezer. All in all, we'd seen worse. They raised their eyes momentarily at me as I washed my hands in the sink.

"What are you doing here, Jack Jr.?" Appa said, confused.

"He's being picked up here," Zeno said, smiling slightly to herself.

"Oh," Appa said knowingly, which was funny because he didn't know anything. "Chivalrous. Keeps the mystery alive."

"Why don't we all just get back to work." I felt my face getting red. "There's nothing to talk about."

"What are you wearing?" Zeno asked me.

"What? What do you mean?"

"You need to wear something like you have a real, actual life outside of work, which I'm not so sure you do," she said.

"She's right," Appa said.

I'd already begun to sweat. I opened my jacket for her.

"Good enough?"

"Good," she said, pausing, "enough."

"I like what I'm wearing."

"Did I say I didn't?"

"Go ruin another one of our pots."

"I don't need extra credit on my final," Zeno said, smirking. She wiped her hands dry on the apron around her waist and took the filled hotel pan back into the kitchen. I took the last apron left from the pegs by the bar.

"I can do the tuna back there."

"Already done," Appa said, "don't touch the fish. You'll smell."

He saw the look on my face.

"What?"

"I'm getting the sense that everybody's a little too invested in me tonight."

"There's nothing you can do about that," Appa said.

I spent a minute watching Appa clean off his work surface, running a damp towel repeatedly over the wood. Him standing there, with his knife, the ohitsu on a stool at his side, was the only place I'd ever seen him that looked entirely right, everything in place. It had been his place for thirty years.

"Appa."

He looked at me. I had already waited too long. "You need something?"

I shook my head. The door chimed open. I was getting used to the feeling of turning my head to see him in the doorway, fidgeting his mask off his ears, kicking his boots dry on the floor. I met him by the door.

"Let's go."

"Uh, hi," Cuddy said, smiling, "what's the hurry?"

"I'm being attacked. Quickly."

"Emil," Appa said, "can you have him back before his curfew?"

"We're going, goodbye, everybody."

"Is he here?" Zeno poked her head out of the kitchen doors.

"Now, right now. Move—"

I pushed him outside, where the wind hit us. It was colder than I'd thought it would be. We were standing a foot apart. He glanced over my shoulder, through the window.

"They're cute," he said.

"They're starved for attention."

Our eyes met.

"You're cute," he told me.

And I, with absolutely nothing to say that I could think of as all the blood rushed out of my head, hearing that, said back: "Thanks."

He raised his eyebrows at me. "So you *can* take a compliment. Good to know."

"You're hinting at something. Something you really want to say."

Cuddy watched me for a few more seconds. We had traded less than twenty words between us since I'd texted him and asked to meet. He'd written back and apologized for not getting in touch first, blaming a weekend of late-night shifts. I'd said he was forgiven, and he'd asked to pick me up. We stood now on the precipice of what was going to be either a good night or a very big mistake, with no middle ground in between. He looked confident.

"Up for a walk?"

"Long walk?"

He tipped his head to the right, then to the left. "Give or take a mile."

"A mile," I repeated. "You put a lot of faith in me."

"It's a second date." He shrugged. "I'll give you a chance."

———————

AND IT WAS A MILE, with no give and all take, a mile going entirely up the street, under an overpass, another few blocks past the gas station where I habitually filled the van's tank, past the turnoff to the freeway, to a stretch of the road I had never been on that moved with the south-flowing river. Wind whipped the hair I'd spent an hour on into a cowlicked mess. Our fingers were frozen, stuffed inside the cuffs of our jackets to stay warm. He turned his head toward me, facing the wind.

"Ever been here before?"

"If I had, I would've come in the summer."

He laughed and shrank his shoulders slightly in toward his chest. Behind him, the city rose up like jewels catching all the light. We'd made it to the peak of a little hill, where a few benches waited. Every now and then a stranger walking their dog passed briskly by the two of us standing there. An empty flagpole stuck out of a brick and plaster pedestal in front of us. On its front was a plaque commemorating a Revolutionary-era fort whose corner made up the little landing we were now standing on.

"It's beautiful during the day, too," he said, "but I wanted to show you at night. People don't usually see it at night, this view."

We were standing in front of Manhattan at an almost-perfect perpendicular angle, showing it at its very longest, stretching from one end of the river to the other. I stepped closer to the stone ledge, counting the piers. A cruise ship had docked around Fiftieth Street, dwarfing the rest of the city.

We were on a cliff ledge a few hundred feet above sea level. Behind us: a row of quaint town houses with luxury SUVs parked in front of their garage doors and signs that read PRIVATE PROPERTY. I held out my hands, trying to frame it.

"It looks weird," I said finally.

"The city does?"

"From up this high. I've only ever been right on the river looking at it. Imagine getting up in the morning and seeing a view like this every day. Scary."

"Windy," he added.

We actually hadn't talked much on the way here beyond making light of the cold, the wind that had started to pick up the closer we got to the water. I was seeing him again and yet had gotten the same exact feeling as the first time, that he was a different person in his normal clothes and that I almost wanted the scrubs back.

"I walk around here almost every morning," he said, "every chance I get. I'm . . ." He swiveled around, searching. "Five blocks that way. I pass by here on my way to the bus stop."

"So you *do* wake up to a view like this every morning. Have you been hiding a trust fund? Did your great-grandfather own one of those town houses?"

"I rent the basement of one, if that's what you mean," Cuddy said. "Concrete floors. My view is shoes passing on the sidewalk. A dog if I'm lucky."

He stretched his arms high over his head, yawning.

"If I had a million dollars, that's where I'd live," he said, "even though I'm pretty sure I'd hate it after a while. So much noise. All that life going on over there. Just walk out your door and take your pick of twenty bars down the street, a show, a concert, whatever. I bet I'd like it, for some time. Isn't that the way it goes?"

He'd stepped a little closer to the ledge and I followed, finding my place beside him. I hesitated, then extended my arm.

"Right there," I said.

"What's that?"

"Where I used to live."

He angled his head, moving his eyes right behind my hand. "Really?"

"Riverside Park. Seventy-ninth Street."

"How close to the water?"

"Right up against it. If I were there and stood in front of my window, I could probably see where we're standing now."

He looked impressed, which wasn't what I wanted, but I lowered my hand, glad I'd shown him anyway.

"Do you miss it?"

"Not really anything to miss, to be honest," I said. "There's nobody there for me."

He frowned. "No friends?"

"I'm sure," I said, shrugging, "couple of acquaintances. I don't know. I lost touch. After I woke up I wanted to reach out, but nobody called either, so . . ."

"Jack Jr.," he said, incredulous, "you don't have any friends."

"It's not a big deal."

"It isn't?"

"I didn't need friends," I said, "I had Ren."

I stamped my feet on the pavement, trying to work feeling back into my toes.

"I'm sorry."

"For what?"

"I brought up my ex on a date and that's annoying. I'd hate if someone did that to me."

He blinked at me for a moment. "You love apologizing."

"I guess I do."

He stamped his feet the same way I did, smiling at me. "We can go now," he said, "I just wanted to show you the park."

He reached forward and tucked two fingers on the inside of my wrist.

"Strong pulse," he commented, "that's good. No hypothermia. You've got some very efficient arteries."

His fingers were cold and soft, a little rub on the underside of my hand when he let my wrist go. For another moment we stared down between our feet, just a couple inches apart.

"So . . ." He trailed off.

"Pizza?"

He smiled. "We've got pizza here. Good place right around the block."

"Takeout?"

"We can do takeout."

We each waited, for the other to speak first.

"Sausage and peppers," we said at the same time. He laughed and put his hand through my hair, seeming to remember halfway through what he was doing, and retracted his arm. He took out his phone, scrolling through his apps once, then put it away.

"You're nervous," I said.

"So are you."

He reached down and took my hand in a way that let me know he'd been thinking of doing it ever since he'd given himself an excuse to check my pulse. For a moment I thought he wanted to stay there longer. I could tell what that view meant to him. I imagined passing a view like that every morning, on the way to a job, reminding yourself what it was you were really after. It isn't often we are confronted so head-on with the next thing that we're hoping will make us happy. He looked like he wanted to talk about it but didn't. Instead, he tugged me toward the direction of the street and I followed.

THE HEAT WAS BECAUSE THE basement had two coils instead of one, he told me when we found ourselves inside with dinner. He said he was thankful for it most of the time, as a draft usually found its way through cracks in the window frames even on temperate days. He didn't mention what he did in the summers, since there was no vent I could see and the window looking out onto the street probably couldn't have fit an AC anyway. It was a sauna, all except the concrete floor, which felt to my feet like I was padding across an ice rink. He'd been here for three years, paying a rent that fell under his means, along with some plans—hardly concrete, but plans, anyway—to move in the next few years. He said this as though making an excuse for the space, which was the size of my room back home and had only the one sink by the hot plate where he made dinner most nights. The floors creaked overhead, footsteps traveling across the ceiling. The old guy living upstairs didn't bother him much but almost never slept. The creaking, he told me, he'd gotten used to. He'd shown me inside through a door under the stoop leading up to the main house. He hung up our coats. The pizza in my hands was letting off steam.

"It's a piece of shit," he said.

"It's perfect," I said. "I love your coffee table. And that lamp." I jerked my head toward it, so he could see. "It's a good lamp."

"Excellent lamp."

"Thrifted?"

"Aunt's."

We stood there another minute. He took the pizza from me and made us two spaces at the table he had in front of the couch. When we sat, we could see the sky out of the little grated window above our heads. He brought me a beer without asking. We ate, quickly.

"Where's your family?" I asked him.

"Minnesota." He smiled. "I don't see them very often."

"Kicked you out for being gay, I suppose."

"You'd be surprised, no," he said. "I talk to my mom and sisters almost every day. Air travel's just expensive, you know."

"I did know, just not in the way that you know," I said, "which I know now. I'm sorry."

"I have no idea what you just said, so . . ." He perked up his shoulders in a shrug. "All good?"

We kept eating.

"This is good," I said.

"They're the only pizza for ten miles," Cuddy said, taking another slice. "They've monopolized the community. Good garlic knots too."

"We have any of those?"

"In the bag."

I found the paper bag on the floor, lifting it off a stack of little paper booklets that he'd arranged neatly in a corner. The first one read: "TAKE ME OUT."

"Take me out," I said.

"What?"

I pointed at the little book. "Take me out."

"Oh." Cuddy got to his feet. "It's a play. Richard Greenberg."

"You read plays," I said.

He pointed at the IKEA bookshelf he'd set up behind his bed, showing me hundreds of little booklets that were stacked from end to end. "I've read every single one. I pick them up at thrift sales and on eBay. You can get most of them for five bucks or less if you know where to look. The library's pretty well stocked, too, but I like owning."

"You don't strike me as someone with much free time to read."

"You have a lot of it, actually, when you don't sleep very well," Cuddy said, standing, licking a spot of tomato sauce off his thumb. The light had slipped over his shoulders and illuminated him from the bulb right above his head, the shaggy gray sweater that dipped low around his neck and hung off his wrists. "By the way, are you cold?"

"It's a sauna in here."

He took the little booklet from me, opening to its first page. He cleared his throat and, in a gruff, aggressively heterosexual Brooklyn dynamo voice that shook me slightly when I first heard it, started to read something about some guy named Darren Lemming, and also locker rooms. I half-listened, taken aback by the way he threw himself into it with more energy than I'd ever seen him possess in my entire waking life.

He peered over the top of the page at me.

"Striking you at all?"

"The acting's really selling it for me."

"Not saying it's required," Cuddy said, "but if you don't do at least something to reference the character, it's just reading words. It's not *drama*. You might as well read a novel."

"Because we hate novels, obviously."

He mimed puking into the open book. "They're too long."

He gave me back the booklet. I wiped my hands dry and flipped through its eighty pages.

"What's it about?"

"A gay baseball player. And masculinity. And the poison of rumor-making."

"Is it your favorite?"

"I couldn't ever pick a favorite," he said. "It's just the one I was reading last night. You know, they do a ton of the scenes completely naked onstage. The last off-Broadway version had real showerheads and hot water in the locker room set."

"Did you go see it?"

He smiled sheepishly. "I've never seen a play in the city. From here it's a bus-ferry-bus-subway kind of commute. It never works out. Or hasn't, ever, for me. Have you?"

"I've seen a few musicals." I caught the quiver of his lip. "Oh right, 'musicals are not real theatre. Theatre with an 'r-e' instead of an 'e-r.'"

"Musicals are wonderful," Cuddy said, "to other people. Not to me. Most all of them put the flattest, most uninspired dialogue in between all those big blockbuster songs. It's hard to watch."

He sat down next to me. We'd eaten half the pie and were out of garlic knots.

"Do you write any of your own? Plays, I mean."

He didn't answer.

"No?"

"I try," he said finally.

"That's good. It's an industry that generally encourages trying." I saw his face properly in the light. "What? Did I say something?"

I felt him think about it for a while, weighing his answer. It seemed, to him, a pivotal moment that I couldn't quite understand. He reached out and put a hand through my hair again.

"You talked about it and made it real," he said. "I don't really like for it to be real."

"For what to be real?"

"The fact that deep down in a place I don't want to believe exists, I want to write plays and put them onstage and talk about tension and scene and other things with like-minded people and do all of that instead of be a nurse," he said, "which is what I am."

"Why can't you be both?" I asked him.

"I could never be both."

"Bullshit."

"Bullshit?"

"I bet there's a hundred theaters right across the river holding fellowships or open calls or whatever they're called. And you could apply. You said you write them, why not submit them?"

He smiled lightly. "Why are you so interested?"

I took in a breath, let it build in my chest, and let it out slowly through my nose. "Chalk it up to the fact that I've lost two years of my life that I'm never getting back. Speeds things up in ways you can't imagine."

He was shaking his head, saying nothing.

"Too soon?" I asked him. He encircled my ear with his fingers, touching lightly.

"Scary," he said.

"I know it is," I said, "I just think—"

I didn't get the other words out, as he'd put his lips on my face.

"I wasn't finished with my pizza."

"It's not going anywhere."

I brought my leg over his lap and pressed him farther into the couch cushions. He tasted like olive oil and oregano. I stopped myself from doing what I wanted to do, which was to take all of his clothes off and then mine. I pulled away from him.

"I made you uncomfortable," I said finally. "I'm sorry."

"It's okay," he told me. He bent his head low and buried his nose in my shirt. His hands brought my hips level with his. I saw him, close up, counted the brown moles on his skin, one above his lip, two on his chin, another right around the corner of his left eye.

"You make me nervous," he said, his voice muffled in my chest.

"Why is that?" I was trying to stay serious, despite the fact that he'd pressed our dicks together through our pants.

"Isn't this how it goes?" he asked me. "I watch you sleep for two years. I sponge you dry, change out your fluids, wipe spit off your face. And now you're just . . . here. Right in front of me. I don't know how to act around you. That's why you make me nervous."

"I'm just a person," I said.

From where I sat, straddling him, I could trace the wires of the lightbulb leading away into the wall, plastered to the drywall and painted over with primer.

"Why don't you sleep well?" I asked him. He turned his head and raised an eyebrow at me. "You said you have all this time to read plays because you don't sleep well."

He was silent for a little while. I felt each of his breaths depress his back farther against the cushions.

"What if I told you something you're definitely not supposed to talk about on a first date?" he said.

"This is our second date. The first was at the bathhouse with my father and nephew."

"I don't sleep well . . . because for a while, when I'd fall asleep, I'd dream about all the patients I lost. I stopped counting early on, a couple months after the virus was making all the news. The ones with no family, no friends, nobody we could even pull in for a video call, just to say goodbye. We didn't have any information to begin with. We didn't know what we were doing that was killing some of them faster than others. The best they could do was ask one of the nurses to go in and hold their hand until their pulse stopped. Then what? Bed's finally clear, somebody else can finally get a tube. We clean it all up, take the body to the morgue, bring in the next one. Again and again."

He had said it all so quietly, as though he were afraid to be saying it out loud.

"I can't afford therapy, so I just . . . don't sleep."

He smiled sadly.

"You really want me now, don't you?"

He closed his eyes when I brought my hand up to his face, cupping the angle of his jaw. I kissed him, slowly, and felt stings on my lips and cheeks where his beard rubbed against my cold-flashed skin.

"You're a person too," I told him. "A nice person."

"I've heard it before," he said. "Too nice. Usually from guys that always say they want nice to begin with."

"You *are* too nice," I said. "They're telling you the truth."

"What do you think about that?"

"I could use some nice," I said. "You said something deeply vulnerable and real, and you did it in front of me because maybe some part of you trusts me with that kind of information. My turn, now?"

"You don't have to take a turn."

This, of all things—be it the way he said it or the way that I knew now that the simplest version of events was true, that he'd really just wanted somebody to talk to and had chosen me—made me hard. Which wasn't a bad thing, by any means, but wasn't the effect I'd had in mind. I angled my hips farther away from him.

"I've missed my family," I said. "I love being around them, which hasn't been the truth in a long time. But still, if there was a chance for me to go back to the way it was, with my old job and my old life, my old apartment, I'd still probably take it. And I hate it, and myself. But I would. And I probably wouldn't even have to think very hard about it."

I dipped my head slightly, touching his forehead with my chin.

"There," I said, "we're even."

"I don't think you're telling me the entire truth."

"How so?"

"How many times have you actually thought about your old job in the past month?" he asked me. "How about your apartment? You already told me you don't have any friends left in the city. I think you just want Ren back."

His eyes were blue, a lot like Ren's, I realized. I stared, until I couldn't get away with it any longer.

"Yes."

He paused for a moment, then another.

"It doesn't matter," I said finally. "He's gone. He wants nothing to do with me. We're all moving on the best we can. We are all just trying to—"

I was thinking about the time I'd heard Appa say the same thing to me while he sliced fish.

"Stay alive," I finished. It hadn't sounded so hard, the way it did now, back then. Cuddy was quiet for a long time.

"Do you know what happened? Do you know why they found you in the river?"

I couldn't find it in myself to do something dismissive like turn away. I just sat there, looking at him looking back at me. There was a memory—I hope a memory—in which it all came together. In which I'm holding Ren in my arms; we've walked in and seen the view of the trees from that living room, its fireplace already stocked with wood; and we're turning, slowly, on the spot, thinking about it all. A memory in which I love him and he loves me. It was always going to be this way, I thought. It was always going to hurt to think about him from now on.

"I'm in the cabin with him," I said, "I'm . . . so glad, to be out of the city for a little bit. I'm going to marry him. I can't wait to marry him. And then—"

He'd placed my hand delicately into his, lacing our fingers together.

"I don't even remember getting in a car," I said. It sounded so unfair, hearing it. My eyes were wet. I swiped at my face with my hands, quickly and shamefully. I felt his hand on my shoulder.

"I didn't mean to make you sad."

I breathed, in and out, for a minute. My nose was starting to run. I slid off him and stood up.

"This wasn't supposed to happen."

"It wasn't your fault."

"I mean tonight," I said in a hollow, fragile voice that I hadn't thought I could ever sound like. "Things were supposed to . . . happen. It was going well, wasn't it? It was really getting somewhere and I just went and fucked everything with my feelings and then you made me eat all that pizza and I can't even bottom anymore unless you have a douche or maybe even just good water pressure in your shower but I couldn't possibly ask you to let me do that in your bathroom and what if you don't even have one of those showerhead attachments that can shoot the water out like a jet and then what would I do—"

I ran out of breath. Cuddy got to his feet, facing me. I had enough time to imagine what he was going to tell me, that this had been nice and all but it seemed like I was a bit too much of a mess for him to have much interest left in me. I wouldn't have blamed him for it.

"You think way too much. That must be exhausting."

"I've been told."

"We can do whatever you want," he said. "Besides, you think I'd care about a little mess? You want to guess how much shit I've wiped off myself in my lifetime? My old rotation was on our geriatric floor."

He put his hands on either side of my neck, rubbing his thumbs gently into the stiff cords.

"Feel better?"

"Depends on whether you really do have that showerhead attachment."

He laughed, bringing his forehead closer, touching it against mine. "You know what?" he said. "I am fascinated by you, Jack Jr."

He ran warm, from his head to the tips of his fingers. Like being with a hot water bottle. I closed my eyes briefly, drawing my hands nearer to his waist.

"Can I . . ." I was having trouble saying the words out loud. "Sleep here?"

He nodded. I let out my breath, lifted the front of his sweater, and felt with my fingertips the furry patch of his belly.

"You're tickling me."

"Sorry," I said, not stopping. I got his sweater up to his armpits and guided his arms out of the sleeves. We took our clothes off, stopping every now and then to help each other, and had gotten down to our socks, which he told me to keep wearing on account of the frozen floor. He brought me to his bed and took them off himself, tucking them into each other and tossing them onto the pile of our clothes. The sheets were cool, a relief. I saw down his chest and the length of his leg to his feet spread out comfortably, making divots with his heels in his paisley top sheet. I raised my head, pushing him down onto his back. He didn't resist when I inched myself closer, touching my forehead to the little cavity of his collarbone.

"How does it feel?"

"What?"

I pressed my chin into him softly. "To touch me."

His fingers had traveled down the length of my stomach to my hip, to the raised line where the stitches had healed. He placed a thumb, an index, and a middle finger on the three little moles to the right of my belly button, counting off as he did: "One, two, three."

Cuddy placed his mouth next to my ear, grazing it with his lips.

"These have always been my favorites. Just these three. They're perfect."

I didn't want to tell him exactly how it felt to hear him say that. We lay there, lights still on, pizza growing cold, not caring. Listening to the creaks in the ceiling continue, back and forth, for the longest time, before either of us finally drifted off to sleep. Grateful for the rest, however it came.

9

THANKSGIVING

WE WERE CLOSING THE RESTAURANT FOR THANKSGIVING AND THE DAY after, when the very last dregs of the fall would come swirling down like the leaves. I was up early that Thursday morning out of habit and turned over a few times in bed before finally getting up and digging my toes into the carpet. My phone showed me a text from Cuddy, which had arrived an hour before. *Morning.*

Beneath it was a picture of him on the bus, masked, on his way home. His eyes were heavy lidded and dark, begging for sleep. *Lights out,* I texted back, and set him aside, hunting the ground around my bed for my shoes. We hadn't seen each other since he'd gotten me on the bus the morning after our second date. He'd taken extra shifts around the holiday to be able to spend the night with me, I was sure, but he wouldn't say or accept my apologies. I dressed quickly and found my way to the kitchen. Appa was on the porch, speaking with

Lou's father wrapped up like a burrito in a wheelchair, their breaths gathering fog around their heads. He turned around, peering through the screen door at me, and waved. Lukewarm coffee in the pot. I poured it and, checking to see if he was looking, set it up in the microwave for a minute. My phone gave another buzz against my hip.

Plans tonight?

My coffee beeped. I used the bottom of my T-shirt to pick the irradiated mug off its glass plate and set it down in front of me. *Family dinner, nothing special.*

He typed back, *What does a sushi family eat for Thanksgiving dinner? Sushi?*

Aren't you supposed to be sleeping? Huevos rancheros, obviously. Side of cumin-rubbed lamb shank.

A picture came through of his face and bare shoulders lit by his phone. *I'm already in bed.*

He put a period at the end of every sentence, existing in perfect tandem with the autocorrect on his phone. Reminding me that he was in fact two years and what seemed like an entire generation older than me. *Show more.*

He showed more, stopping right around his belly button. There was the dark shadow of his chest hair, gathered in a neat little line down to his waist.

More.

I heard the screen door open. Appa had come inside and was shaking feeling back into his arms. A picture came through, I didn't see of what. I stuffed my phone back into my pocket just in time for Appa to notice.

"What's up with you?" he asked me.

I drank my coffee. Appa rounded the corner into the kitchen.

"Nothing?"

"Nothing," I repeated.

He doubled back, about to say something, then reconsidered. "You're up early."

"So are you."

"I'm headed in."

"To the restaurant?"

"James says we need to stay open," Appa said, rooting around in the fridge. "Something about our ledger this month. We could stand to bring in a bit more, and we have the inventory."

I frowned at him when he resurfaced, carrying eggs. "What are you saying? We're working tonight?"

"And tomorrow," Appa said. "Not you. Me."

He picked a can of Spam from the pantry, noticing me.

"Don't start."

"Why are we working just because James says we have to? Why doesn't he come and work for once?"

"Your brother fixes every problem we have," Appa said. "He pays our bills, he fixes our equipment, I haven't signed a paper or met with banks or paid the property taxes on the restaurant or the house you're sitting in right now in ten years. And again, *I'm* working, you're not," Appa said. "Put some rice in the microwave for me."

He was making breakfast for me, I realized, and before I could say anything had already gotten the lid off the Spam.

"When did you decide all this?"

"This morning," Appa said, turning around. "Enough, Jack Jr. It's done. We're making the best of the situation. James is coming in to help me with the takeout orders, you're all still having dinner here, we'll join you when we close up."

He raised a pair of chopsticks he was using to stir-fry the eggs and pointed them at me.

"Here's what you can do. You can do the fish run tomorrow."

He turned around, humming something while the oil sizzled. I stood up, downing the rest of my coffee.

"What, like alone?"

"Juno's going with you, of course," Appa said over his shoulder.

"Yeah, but . . ." I joined him in front of the stove. "Without you."

"Why not?"

"I've never done that before."

"Of course you have."

"No." I lowered the flame on the stove for him. "I haven't."

Appa shrugged. "What's there to know that you haven't seen me do? You know all the guys, you know what to look for. You can make everything on the menu."

He tipped the eggs and Spam onto a plate and handed them to me with his burned-up chopsticks. It was a meal he'd been making for me for as long as I could remember. I brought them to the table and took a seat. Lou's father was still out there, watching the sky with a puzzled look on his face. Appa sat next to me.

"She'd better get out there before he goes blind," he said.

As if he'd willed it to happen, Lou tottered up the lawn, finding him. We watched them engage in a mostly silent argument through the porch door glass that culminated in Lou taking her father back inside while he tried to launch himself out of his seat and onto the ground. They made excruciating progress across the lawn while we watched.

"Tell you what," Appa said, "this first time, I'll write you a list for the fish run. You'll have it memorized by next week."

I ate silently. It was happening exactly the way Juno had said it would happen, and I was still surprised. Sooner than I'd expected, too. Way too soon.

"I can't do the fish run by myself," I said finally. "Appa, I can't. I don't know anything. I don't have any real training."

"I've taught you everything I know," Appa said. "That's not the difficult part. You know what it means to make sushi. It's practice. You go out and *do* it. That's what you need. And you need it without me so that you can figure out how it is you actually want to be doing it. Put your own spin on the method. You know how lucky you are to have no formal training? Anything you want to do, you can just do. It's not like that for me." He put his hands on either side of my head. "You look stressed out. Why are you stressed out?"

I couldn't answer this. He let me go.

"You don't have rice," he observed. "I thought I told you to micro-wave one."

"I don't need it."

He waved me off, unconvinced, and put on his jacket. "What's Emil up to?"

I took out my phone, lighting it, and saw he'd sent me a photo of his toes peeking out from the bottom of his blanket. I swiped it away quickly.

"I don't think he's doing anything. His family's not around here."

"He's not going to visit them?"

I shook my head tentatively, knowing already what he was going to say. He seemed to know too, since he was already picking up the landline.

"Appa, he's sleeping."

"This'll be quick."

"Why do you have his number?"

He waved me down. I took out my phone. *Dad's calling you.*
?
My father is calling you to invite you to Thanksgiving with us.
Did he see my toes?

"Emil," Appa said, putting on the jolliest voice I'd ever heard him use, "you okay? How's work? You're not sleeping, are you? Look, I'm with Jack Jr. right now, he says you're not going anywhere for Thanksgiving, which means you're going to have to come here and have dinner with us. Well, with him, and his mother, and James's family. We're working in the restaurant tonight. Yes, it's all done with. You'll come, okay? Okay. Jack Jr. especially, he's so excited."

"Appa—"

He hung up, looking extremely proud of himself. "James will be at the restaurant now. I'd better get going."

"Appa, can we just—"

"I'm incredibly late, Jack Jr., I have to go."

"I just want to set some ground rules."

"Rules," he repeated, taking his coat off the hanger, "in my own house? From my own son? You know, I've known Emil a lot longer than you have." He pulled the door open. "Have a good day."

"Appa—"

The door shut behind him. Another text came through. *Huevos rancheros, huh?*

That was not my idea.

Seemed like it. Where, I wonder, did he hear that I'm not visiting any family this year?

I ate the rest of my breakfast at the table. Lou's father's spot on the corner of the lawn felt especially empty. I took my plate to the sink and stepped outside, sinking my feet into the ice-cold house slippers Appa kept on the mat in front. There were, finally, icicles that had started to drip down over the awning, glassy white and blue. Unsuitable for lens making. Juno's idiotic project had bled into my life so severely that I found myself actively upset over his failure thus far. I'd spent the night before googling how to make clear ice and hadn't found much support. Boiling the water, which rid the resulting ice of at least a little bit of whiteness, still hadn't solved the question of how exactly one was to carve a block of it into a convex lens capable of refracting a beam of light. Juno would be disappointed. He was running out of time before the end of December.

I stayed awhile in the sun, hands in my pockets, squinting around at the yard, the hose we now kept coiled tightly in a bundle pushed up against the fence. I'd brought my phone with me and sent Cuddy a picture of the yard.

Pretty.

I figured I'd let him sleep after that, which he typed a quick note to let me know he was about to do.

I was thinking, then, of Zeno. I'd started showing her some of the knife work. She'd dressed a belly cut of tuna by herself the other day. She'd made a habit of leaning in, dangerously close to the fish, while slicing. Like an old casino-goer staring down their favorite slot machine as the wheels turned and the lights flashed. I opened a text to her.

I hope you're not working today either.

Her read-receipt flag went up almost as soon as I'd sent it. A gray bubble hovered momentarily before she responded.

No. But I asked if I could.

I snorted. I wondered what Zeno and her mother had planned for Thanksgiving, if anything. I wondered if Zeno's mother had started calling her Zeno yet, or if that was something that was just never going to catch on at home. I didn't imagine the same woman who had driven her daughter out of the house some nights would take kindly to an at-will name change. But then again, Zeno probably hadn't asked politely.

Hope you have a good holiday. You're doing a great job. If you want to talk about anything, I'm here.

I lingered over the last sentence, worried she wouldn't get what I was trying to say, but I sent it anyway. I was prepared when the read flag came up again, as usual, and was about to put my phone down without even bothering to see if she'd respond—her habit was not to, almost always—when a gray bubble grew and shrank several times in the corner.

Thank you, JJ. You're a good fiend.

Then, later, **friend.*

I read the message a few times. Juno was the only person who called me Uncle JJ. That he'd maybe taught her what to call me made me smile. I liked JJ. With Zeno around, I was more in the mood for rebranding as something radical. I put my phone away.

From where I stood, the city loomed over the top of the valley, still gray but beginning to shine gold as the sun climbed higher over it. I had an obsession with this view. Wanting always to see it before I went about any given day. Which was nothing out of the ordinary, even if I didn't know what was ordinary anymore. I could go back to sleep, I thought. Or try to find something to watch on TV. Today was worse than Sunday. Sunday came and went with reliable consistency. This was PTO. *Vacation.* A day I was to spend not working while others worked at the restaurant, which today remained very much open. I could take a walk, read a book. Sad. Was this really it? Because Juno was still asleep and the only other person who might have occupied my time had just knocked himself out for the next couple of hours? It was. Really.

I REMEMBER A DAY, SHORTLY after Umma and Appa told us their marriage was over—these words, exactly, decidedly more theatrical than I think either of them was intending—when Appa brought James and me into the restaurant in the morning. There was light all around, big beams of it catching dust swirling in the air that came in through the windows. Appa hung up our coats, then his; sat the two of us down; and stirred day-old dak juk over a flame in the kitchen. He brought it out to us and sat facing us at the table. For a long while he watched us eat. I opened and shut my mouth on the burning porridge, breathing dragon breaths. Appa pushed a glass of water my way, which I ignored. James hadn't said a thing all morning. In another hour, Appa was going to take us to school and start his prep for the day. Umma would be back in the evening for dinner. She would still be working here, bringing menus and taking orders, pouring water and smiling, engaging in the easy push and pull that existed between the server and the itamae. She had been at Appa's side all my life, for years before, ever since he'd made her that noodle soup for lunch two decades ago. In the restaurant, at least, nothing had changed. I never did find out how exactly they'd had the discussion that resulted in Umma packing up her things and moving across town, and not the other way around. A court would award us to the father because he was the father, maybe, or the father with a steady income, ownership of a business. Or maybe he'd just asked her and she had said yes. I didn't know which I felt better about.

At the table, Appa put his hands together in front of him, linking his fingers. It was unlike him to be so still. He stayed alive by staying in motion, a hyperextension of his being, which, if never allowed to rest, never had to feel its own weight. He'd brought his knife over and gazed at it, on its side between us.

"Do you remember what I told you about this knife?" he asked us. James was still staring straight into his empty bowl.

I nodded. He smiled at me. "Tell me the story, Jack Jr."

"You wanted to go to Japan to learn sushi," I said, "and Harabeoji said he wouldn't let you, and that if you went he would never speak to you again. And then you went anyway, and he was mad at you for a long time. But then you opened the restaurant, and he came by to see it right before, and saw that your knife was the same one you brought back from Japan, and it was old and broken. So the next day he went out and bought you a new one, and he never told you out loud, but you thought he was trying to say that he was proud of you, and that he liked that you were a sushi chef even though you're Korean and we're not supposed to like the Japanese."

Appa had listened to this quietly, surveying the flat blade of the knife in front of him. He picked it up, holding it in one hand, and ran a finger along it.

"You should know," he said, "that I lied to you. About the entire thing."

He glanced at us over the top of the blade, to see if we were still listening. I remember stealing a look at James, searching for a hint of how to react. But James had tipped his head upward slightly and said nothing, and neither did I. Appa laid the knife back down between us.

"Your harabeoji never bought me this knife. I bought it right after I opened this place, when your mother told me I looked like an amateur holding the old one. You should've seen it, all scratched up, dented. The steel was starting to chip. It used to take me more than an hour every month to sharpen it. So I went and bought this in the city."

He put his hands back together again.

"He never understood what I wanted. He told me every week until he died to give it up, close up the restaurant and do something worthwhile while I still had strength, and while you two were still babies. But I didn't. This didn't stop him from saying it, I know, but even for him, it had lost its meaning."

He wouldn't look at us, saying it.

"Why did you lie, Appa?" I asked him.

He moved his lips back and forth, thinking about something.

"I think, after all this time, I was embarrassed. I wanted you to think I was doing something worthwhile. And maybe if you thought your harabeoji felt this way, you would too."

He almost laughed.

"Do you want to know what's funny? Sometimes, I catch myself thinking about the memory I told you, the way I said it happened, as if it was real. And I have to remind myself that it's not. Anyway, he isn't here anymore to remind me. It's been getting harder and harder to remember the truth."

He put his hand out, touching my face.

"I didn't mean to lie," he said. "I've felt guilty about it for your whole lives."

I would remember the way he said this, almost too easily, the way somebody's voice got when they finally said the thing they had been rehearsing in their heads, over and over. And it had always captured me, the way his shoulders had fallen after he said it. It was an understanding between us that he would probably never talk about this with us ever again, that he would repeat the same lie to others and expect us to keep the secret. I wasn't thinking about any of this at the time. Mostly I'd been sad to know Appa had lied to me, for the first and only time in my entire life. It hadn't seemed like something he was capable of, not to me, not while looking at me with his hand cupping my chin like he'd been doing. To my left, James hadn't made a single movement. His eyes had been fixed securely on the knife the entire time and he didn't react when Appa put his other hand on his shoulder. He hadn't said anything for several days, at least not to me, not since that conversation the four of us had had in the kitchen of the house that was now Appa's house and not Umma's anymore. Was it then? I wonder. The moment he decided he wouldn't ever talk about anything for the rest of his life? And when I decided I'd play along and do the same? It made sense. It was when our paths diverged, after which I could count on a hand the number of conversations we had about anything where more than a minute elapsed.

Time moved in crisscrosses sometimes, patterns that didn't make much sense while awake. Sometimes, I missed being asleep.

SO NO, APPA HAD NEVER lied to me again, not that I knew of. But lying was not the same as a purposeful withholding. For example, he had not, in fact, shown me everything he knew. He still made the tamago himself, whipping the eggs into a lather, measuring out equal parts oil and fish paste, and folding each in with extra-long chopsticks on a battered and masterfully seasoned cast-iron kera-nabe hovering over a barely lit flame. He made it look easy, despite the fact that even he threw out batches on rough days, claiming they lacked balance. I didn't even like tamago. The kind he made was too sweet and too bready for my taste, and far too much more trouble than what it was worth. He was going to teach me, I guessed. He'd never look at me the same way if I ever asked him to take it off the omakase.

There were hardly any cars that passed the house that morning as the time crept past eight. Most would have finished their shopping by now and were spending their mornings getting down the basics of their dinners, to be served just after noon in the traditional American fashion. Potatoes laid to boil, turkeys buttered and prepped for the oven. I knew who was cooking our dinner tonight, if Appa wasn't going to be. The H Mart in town was ransacked by the time Noa and I got there and parked the van, all the cakes in the bakery display picked over, hardly any of the good banchan left. We patrolled the aisles, pushing a sad, empty cart, pausing every now and then to peruse. Sam was thankfully asleep, strapped to my chest and drooling slowly into my shirt.

"What's Juno's favorite?" I asked her.

"He'll eat anything," Noa told me. Her eyes had been pink when I met her outside the house that morning, and I'd thought of nothing to do for her except hold the baby. We found japchae noodles and vegetable mix-ins, and picked up a recipe's worth in quadruplicate. She wasn't normally so quiet.

"Everything okay?"

"Hm?" She seemed to notice me there for the first time. "Oh, yes. All fine. Thanks for asking."

We walked a bit more. She put a few vacuum-sealed packages of rice cake into the cart.

"I'll tell you what he loves, actually," she said, searching the aisles. "Tteokbokki with that nasty American cheese on top. Couldn't tell you why."

"What are the odds they sell Kraft in H Mart?" I asked her.

She laughed at that, which made me feel better.

"Noa," I said, glancing at her. "Your eyes are still red."

Her hands went to her face, unthinkingly, wiping her eyes dry. "Everything's okay," she said.

Sam kicked a leg out into my stomach, cutting my breath off, and dug his face deeper into my chest.

"He really did a number on himself crying this morning," she said. "Not to say I'm upset. I'm not upset."

"You don't look upset."

"I'm not."

She continued down the aisle with the cart.

"It's been a long time since we've dealt with a baby. Is all."

I caught up to her. "You're doing a great job. I know James is thankful for another chance."

She nodded. I couldn't quite see the expression she made through her mask but it seemed more reassured than before.

"Sometimes I think it was stupid of me. Of us."

"Why?"

We'd come to the butcher's counter, where a manager was getting a picket sign marking two dollars off the marinated pork to stay up while skewered into the meat. Noa gestured to it, and I nodded. We asked for five pounds. Appa had an electric grill.

"We're not so young anymore, I don't know," Noa said. "It was so much easier back then. Little things, you know. Diaper changes. Bending over to pick up toys, food he drops on the ground. Just waking up every day. Of course, we didn't sleep the first year either. But we weren't sleeping anyway. Not with school and work."

Noa was the only person in my family that I'd ever introduced Ren to—though, I was still trying to regularly remind myself, they'd all met him, just without me. She'd always been warm, the warmest of all of us, a safe bet. She'd come to the city one morning; she'd had to be back home to pick Juno up from school. We'd taken her to lunch. Ren had peppered her with questions, wanting to know about the family I'd never talked about. I'd spent the entire time watching her nervously, afraid of nothing, really, but still afraid, and still she'd managed every minute, telling me later that she'd liked Ren and wanted my permission to tell James and Umma and Appa about him.

I reached over and took her hand.

"You're doing a great job," I told her again.

Her fingers, loose in mine, squeezed together. She looked down at our hands, then at the baby on my chest.

"We'd make a good little family, wouldn't we?"

"Yeah, but who's going to be the girl?"

We'd assembled a jigsaw of meats, fish, and soups, which they bagged in mountains of ocean-killing plastic and packed back into the cart. It seemed we were missing dessert but we figured enough alcohol would fill the gap. Noa's trunk was full, and Sam was transferred, still sleeping, back into his car seat. Noa pulled us out of the parking lot and down the road.

"Cuddy's coming," I told her. "Tonight. Appa invited him."

She smiled, keeping her eyes on the road. "Which is to say, you wouldn't have invited him yourself?"

"Seems a little early, don't you think? Thanksgiving with my entire family?"

"I forget all the time that you weren't there." She caught my eye for a second. "Well, you were there, I suppose. I think he's very sweet. And he's always been good to you."

"If only I remembered."

"You know, I always thought you were at least a little bit there. When you were asleep. I've read that people can still hear what's going on. You'd move your head if you heard us talking. The absolute weirdest thing. I guess you didn't, if you can't remember."

We were quiet for a while. There was enough cooking for the both of us ahead, and we were still missing drinks.

"Do you love him?"

I was having trouble seeing her face while a tidal wave rushed through my ears. I waited for it to die down and for my heart to slow.

"That's inappropriate," I finally managed to say.

"It's just a question." She leaned over and patted my knee. "Very healthy question. We've all got a vested interest. He might even keep you here."

"Keep me where?"

"Fort Lee," she said, "Jersey. Better than having you disappear over the river again."

"I never—" I stopped myself from saying *disappeared,* since it was mostly true and I was trying not to lie so much anymore.

"He's really nice to me," I said instead.

"He should be."

"That's all I'm saying."

I turned around, checking on Sam, who was still asleep.

"Keep your cards close, Sammie. They won't ever stop bothering you."

Umma was coming for dinner, she texted to remind me as we unpacked in Appa's kitchen. Other than a shortage of plates, we were making progress. I made us sandwiches for lunch and watched Noa change a diaper, telling myself I'd do it for her whenever I could. We took turns chopping a bound bunch of green onions, retreating to the sink to wash our eyes out. She'd always been fun. I hadn't spent this much time with her since high school. She'd come to the restaurant with Juno after his day care let out and hang around the kitchen. The third and most recent time I'd cut myself, with my knife point down on my big toe, I'd been laughing so hard at something she'd said that tears were coming out of my eyes. She'd driven me to the hospital with my foot—shoe and all—wrapped in a washcloth and Juno in the car seat behind us. We had a rhythm you couldn't replicate.

We were sitting at the table with tea, Sam's baby monitor between us.

"Does everybody really think I'm about to get up and leave at any moment?" I asked her.

"Hard to say," Noa said, "this family doesn't talk. I think we all might've assumed it was a matter of time."

I might have agreed with her a few weeks ago, though I didn't tell her this.

"There's so much work to do."

"We're almost done with dinner."

"No, I mean around here. The restaurant. I couldn't leave. I only just got here."

"I want you to do whatever it is that you want to do," she said. "We all do. I just thought, for all this time you've been here, at some point you'd be thinking about going back to your life, your job, everything."

"My job," I said wistfully. I hadn't thought about my old job in three months. I'd once been on a media panel at *Adweek,* during which I told a room of two hundred people that branded content was my life's passion, which not only earned applause but was recapped, photo and all, in the highlights newsletter the next morning. If there was anything advertising people knew, it was how to put a newsletter together with the precision and synchronicity of an Olympic opening ceremony. I took another sip from my mug.

"I'm a mess."

"Life's messy."

"A person can be messy without being a mess," I said. "I'm a mess. I'm in my thirties and sleeping in the bedroom I used to share with James when I was eight. I'm a cook with no training and I think I'm being set up to run an entire restaurant by myself. And I'm dating my nurse."

"Don't be dramatic," she said. "You're thirty. You're not *in your thirties*."

Over the monitor, Sam made a noise that we stopped in order to hear, then quieted down again.

"He wants all attention on him, at all times," Noa said. "A youngest child by sixteen years. Exponentially needy."

"He's beautiful," I told her.

"He is," she said quietly. We finished our tea.

"I'm not dramatic, you know. Everybody says that. It's homophobic."

"I don't even know what to say to that," Noa said, "except: You're dramatic."

She took our empty mugs and laid them out in the dishwasher.

"What did you say about running the restaurant by yourself? Who told you that?"

"Appa did," I said, "basically. He asked me to do the fish run by myself tomorrow. I'm reading the signs."

"That doesn't mean he's just going to hand it all over to you, does it?"

"I've never done a fish run by myself."

"He could just be asking you to take a more active role in the business," she said, shrugging. "Besides, why don't you just ask him?"

"Ask him what?"

"For the truth, idiot," she sighed. "Ask the king if he's abdicating. Save yourself all of this stress. You make your life harder than it needs to be."

I remembered the promise I'd made to Juno about today. I wondered if he'd told Noa anything about wanting to go to college and which side she'd find herself on if not James's. It had been keeping me up for the past few nights, despite the fact that it seemed so in-consequential back when I said it that I'd barely realized I'd said it. Only now it felt like a setup for untimely disaster. Who was I to make demands like that anyway? Juno wanted to be like me, which any sane person might take to mean he, too, was going to opt out of his own family for the permanent—if not for a coma—future.

"Noa," I said. "What do you think Juno wants to do after high school?"

"That's easy, he wants to go to college."

I frowned at her. "He told you?"

"I infer," she said. "He's never said anything to me about it. He doesn't trust me. Or James."

She smiled.

"He trusts you."

I was silent for a moment.

"He asked me to talk to you and James about it. He acts like he needs permission."

"Not permission. He just wants to know he's doing the right thing. There are schools out there that won't have a problem with his grades. If we had money to send him, I would."

"So, why even ask me?"

She looked at me knowingly. "Here's something you should know about Juno. He is, in every way, exactly the same as his dad. Minus the rehab. One of the many surprises in my life, that he turned out this way. They—the both of them—need to know that this family depends on them. And we do. Of course we do. I'd guess that Juno wants you to ask for him because he can't stand the idea that he'd be doing something for himself instead of for everybody else. And be-cause he's a man and also an idiot, he won't talk to me, or anybody else, about it. Sound like someone you know?"

I made a noise, leaning forward to rest my elbows on my knees.

"They are so alike, but they don't listen to each other. It's ex-hausting."

"He's afraid of what James will say," I said.

"James will tell him not to go," Noa said, nodding. "Not that it's his decision, but Juno thinks if you talk to him, he won't have to. He loves his dad. He doesn't want to upset him."

She waved her hand, as though trying to summon a word she was missing.

"James is getting so tired," she said. "It took so much out of him. Having a kid so young. Rehab, five times, was it? I lost count: bender, car totaled, arrested, rehab, sober, repeat."

It was so easy to lie to family. I wasn't talking about the little fibs, the inconsequential cover-ups—yes, I took the garbage out, I don't know why it's still blocking the garage door; yes, I did my homework, it's in my bag. No, I was talking about the ugly things one could just pretend didn't exist, the painful things, the embarrassing things that people could just collectively agree never to bring up. We'll say it was to keep the family together. Some secrets were worth keeping.

And that's the funny thing, isn't it? They'll say never telling you is not the same as lying to you. How long did Appa have left? How long did James?

She sighed. "I know it's hard for you to have sympathy for him."

I didn't have anything to say. Noa pulled her hair up into a knot at the back of her neck, tying it around with a band from her wrist.

"If it helps," she said, "we have no idea what we're doing."

"Is that scary?" I asked her.

"Not anymore," she said. "I have Juno, and your parents."

She paused.

"You know, James came to see you every week. Every single week for two years. When I'd come with him, he'd just sit in a chair next to you and look at you, sometimes five minutes, ten minutes, however long. You know what I'm forgetting? I also have you."

The front door opened behind us. I could hear the slap of Juno's shoes on the floor as he took off his coat and ambled toward us in the kitchen, reading the room for the obvious, but, to our surprise, saying nothing about it and heading to the fridge. Umma followed, stowing away her keys.

"What's for dinner?" He took out his phone, frowning down at it. "Lunch. Dinner-lunch."

"Japchae, pork, and takeout," Noa said. She sat up. "Soondubu, Jack Jr.? Maybe?"

"I'll call the good place." I got up. "Juno, make some rice. The bag's in the pantry."

THROUGH THE COMBINED EFFECTS OF the electric grill, the oven, and the work wattage of three adults and a teenager making dinner, the kitchen had heated itself to seventy-nine on the old thermostat, which in my recent memory had started lowballing the ambient room temperature around 2011. We were working with what was probably a core heat of over eighty by the time Cuddy came to the door with wine. I could feel him surveying the sight of us, sweaty, half changed out of our clothes. He'd worn a tight little sweater that hugged his arms and made me horny for him in the most frustrating way imaginable. He was just in time, Noa let us all know, leading him farther into the kitchen and toward the table we'd already set up with jeon and banchan. I was ordered to sit and make conversation. He smiled when he saw me, standing up. We stopped inches from each other, and he moved his head forward, stalling, then kissed me on the cheek.

"You're sweating," he said.

"I've been flambéing."

"Cognac?"

"No." I peered around him at the bottle he'd set on the table. "Is that what you brought us to drink?"

"You flambé with cognac, Jack Jr.," he said, "it's French."

"I was talking about my face, not the food," I said. "It's a wonder I haven't burned off my eyelashes. It's like being back in your living room. What do you know about French food?"

"Only how to flambé." He shrugged. "I watched someone do it on *MasterChef*."

There was noise in the kitchen, Umma supervising Juno's changeover of the pork from grill to serving dish.

"This is a great house," he said, "you've got so much space in the yard."

"Would you like a tour?"

He picked up the wine and uncorked it, then poured me a glass. "Offer accepted. Drink up."

Juno took a seat on his other side, holding up a glass.

"Do it quickly," he whispered, "before they see."

"Just pour him some," I said, "I'll say it was me if they find out."

"What are we talking about?" Umma brought over the barbecue, lancing the top with a serving fork and sitting down opposite us. "Wine? Are we partaking in this house tonight? That's not allowed."

"Busted," I whispered, clearing my throat. "Umma, Juno wants to drink. I think we should let him."

We all turned our heads to Noa holding a pan with oven mitts to place it gently between us on the table. She shot Juno a glance, a longer one than felt necessary. "He's not going anywhere tonight."

Cuddy poured the resulting glass and handed it over. It took Umma a minute to convince Noa to stop fidgeting in the kitchen and sit down. We raised glasses, mine already empty.

"We've never done this before," Umma said. "I don't know why we're toasting. But if we are, even if this family is not entirely together tonight, let it be to two people in this room. My son Jack Jr. And Emil Cuddy."

"I don't deserve that." Cuddy's face had blushed a shade of pink, and he nudged me in the arm. "Please, toast something else."

"Already said it," I told him, "can't take it back. That's a good one, Umma."

"Amazing one." Juno had drained his glass. "I'm starving."

"Emil," Umma said, "give your plate here. I'll handle it."

"Speaking of being together," Noa said to Umma, "you've come alone. Again."

"Hush."

"So, we're never going to meet the guy you live with," I said. "Are we okay with that? I don't think we're okay with that."

"I'm giving you another minute, that's all you get." Umma handed Cuddy's plate, piled high with food, back to him. "In the spirit of the holiday. I'll answer any question you want."

"What's his name?"

"His name's Jo, she told me," I said.

"Okay," Noa said, "what does he do?"

"He teaches. Next question."

"Are you going to marry him?"

"No."

"Do you think he's going to ask you?"

"If I did, he'd already be gone."

"Has Appa met him?"

"Of course." Umma took a sip of wine. "That was exciting, wasn't it? Let's have somebody else. Emil."

"That's mean," I laughed, "that's so mean. He doesn't want to answer your questions."

"Doesn't he?" Umma said. "How else are we supposed to get to know him? One minute, Emil. It's easy."

Cuddy made a show, draining his glass, earning laughs. He gave a thumbs-up.

"How old are you?"

"Thirty-two."

"Siblings?"

"Four brothers, three sisters."

"Why nursing?" Umma asked.

He pressed his lips together. "I feel useful when I'm taking care of people."

"You must be the oldest," Umma said, smiling.

"The very oldest," Cuddy said.

"I've got one," Juno said. "Did you honestly think Uncle JJ was going to wake up?"

He ducked when Umma aimed a slap at the back of his head.

"You don't have to answer that."

Regardless, I could see Cuddy was thinking about it. They quieted.

"It wasn't my place to guess," he said finally, looking at me. "So I tried not to. I'm being completely honest. Do you remember waking up, Jack Jr.?"

"I remember falling off the toilet."

"He remembers," Cuddy said to the rest of them, "I know he does. I'll never forget it. Looking at him and realizing his eyes were open and he was choking on his breathing tube. Like any random somebody coming out of surgery. I was trying to call for a doctor but my fingers kept missing the buttons."

He smiled down into his lap.

"Maybe that answers the question."

"You're very sweet. And *you*," Umma said, shoving Juno hard in the shoulder, "better count your blessings tonight. How's the pork?"

We murmured our approval. Appa had texted an hour ago, letting us know that the dinner shift was going slow but well enough and that they'd be able to close around nine. Noa lifted another helping of japchae onto each of our plates with tongs. The baby monitor caught some static, Sam moving around in his sleep upstairs.

"Okay," Umma said, ignoring the fact that we'd gone well over a minute, "so, nursing. What do you do for fun, Emil? How are you spending a Saturday?"

"I work Saturdays," Cuddy said, earning laughs. "But . . . I read."

"Plays," I said. "He's a playwright. He's read every play ever written."

"Not true."

"Close to," I said, "what's the difference? He's a great writer."

"You've never read a single thing I've written."

"You won't let me," I told him. "Naturally, I assume the best."

"Tell me something," Umma said, "how does a person get into plays, and only plays? No musicals? Why not write books?"

"I've never been asked that before," Cuddy said, thinking about it. "Dialogue, maybe? I could never write fiction. You're responsible for too much. Theater is so much of a collaboration between actors, the director, the crew. It's a community, that way."

"You're smart," Umma said, "I knew it. What's your favorite play?"

"He doesn't have one," I said, turning his way. "You've got some favorite playwrights, don't you?"

"Yasmina Reza, Donald Margulies, Neil LaBute," he said.

"I feel dumb," Juno said. "What about Shakespeare?"

"Boring," Cuddy said. "I'm sorry, maybe that's not the nicest thing. Old plays bore me."

"Stirring trouble," Umma said. "In any case, I know you have what it takes. You notice everything. You remember every detail. In Korean we call it noon-chi. You can pull anything into what you write, I bet it's so easy for you."

We settled.

"It's not the most ideal," Umma said, "being apart like this. On a regular year we would've eaten in the restaurant."

"What did you do last year?" I asked.

"It was takeout," Noa said.

"Definitely takeout," Umma said. "Did we eat at yours?"

Noa snapped her fingers. "We didn't eat together at all. They were saying it wasn't safe."

They all nodded. Umma finished off the wine.

"How was your family back home, Emil? We've never talked about what it was like for them."

Cuddy was mid-mouthful. He swallowed, wiping his lips. "I lost both of my grandmothers, actually," he said after a while. He caught my eye. "It's okay. It was quick. They didn't suffer."

Umma was gazing at him, expressionless.

"It's okay," Cuddy said. "It was early. They showed them both to me on an iPad just before they passed, maybe three weeks apart. My parents couldn't even come into the room with them. My mother, she hasn't really recovered."

He smiled sadly.

"We've moved out of the worst of it, haven't we? So much has changed. They were wonderful women."

He was extraordinarily strong, I saw, saying it, and for the hour afterward that we spent around the table, I found myself listening only to him, watching the subtle movements in his face as he observed the conversation and took bites of his food. It was the funniest thing, to watch him go from passivity to turning himself on when somebody aimed something his way. He seemed like one of those people who hated making conversation but was good at it anyway. When we were finished and our glasses were empty, a battle ensued over the dishes that I, with Cuddy's help, won. We stood next to each other, him washing, me drying, while Umma ran a mop over the kitchen floor. We hadn't spoken much. He handed me each wineglass in succession, gently. The sink ran loud down the drain.

"This was really nice," he said. "I would've eaten something out of my microwave tonight if it wasn't for you, and them."

He tilted his head, resting it for a minute on my shoulder. I dipped a finger into one of the bowls he hadn't gotten to yet and placed a dot made of suds on his nose.

"My mom's right. You really are sweet."

"This surprises you," he murmured. He'd shaved around the rough patch of his beard, tidying up around his neck and his cheeks.

"Maybe."

I felt his eyes on me.

"A very, very happy, happy Thanksgiving."

We finished and rinsed our hands. Juno was on the porch with his Switch. I showed Cuddy the rest of the house, leading him down the hall and through the rightmost door. He placed his feet carefully on the carpet, pausing at the creaks his steps made in the floor. I turned on the lights for him.

"This is the place," he said, breathing out.

"The real deal." I raised my arms. "A lot of angst played itself out inside these walls. Makes me nostalgic just to think about it."

"You shared this room with James?"

"There used to be bunk beds," I said, pointing out the corner where they'd stood. "Two desks. Hell. Until he moved out."

"You might be joking," he said, moving closer to me. "You also might not be. You really don't get along with him."

"I've never."

"Why?"

"James is . . . James. What else can I say," I sighed. "We don't have anything in common."

"You're related to him, not dating him," Cuddy said. "I hate my brothers and I still cried this year when I didn't have enough saved up to go see them for the holidays. All night. It was a disaster. You wouldn't have wanted to see me like that."

He made his way to my bed and sat.

"What is it between you two? I get it, remember. I've met him a hundred times."

"There's nothing to say," I said, "we don't connect. He was too old to be my friend when we were kids. While he was drinking, I was barely old enough to understand. He doesn't trust me. He pretends I'm not gay. When I blew up on everybody and left home, he acted like it was his dream come true, like I'd proven him right somehow. Like he'd been waiting for it to happen. He—"

Cuddy had taken both of my hands, pulling me onto his lap.

"You know"—I ran a hand through his hair—"you're really going to have to start charging my insurance for the sessions. Seems like a lot of missed income."

We lay down, side to side, and watched the ceiling. Cars passed below.

"Is it weird? Being in this room."

I shrugged. "Not any weirder than anything else in my life."

We were quiet for another few minutes. I started to laugh. He raised himself up on his elbows.

"What?"

I smiled at him. "I used to lie down exactly this way to . . . you know, fifteen years ago." I slid a little farther off the bed. "Right here. No, here. Exactly like this. With my pants around my ankles and my shirt on, in case somebody walked in."

He assumed the same position, testing it out.

"Lying down?"

"I had to be comfortable, didn't I?"

We laughed, turning inward to face each other.

"I have something for you."

"I know," he said, "I can feel it."

"No, seriously." I sat up. "Do you know what you should be doing? You should be working at a theater in the city. I was looking it up, all of them have part-time readers that go through drama submissions for original things the company can put on throughout the season. Think about it, you'd be reading plays, you might even get to pick something that gets produced. It's like the first step, everybody's saying that's how a lot of playwrights get started." I sat up and found my phone. "There's tons of them, I saw. Somebody will take you. You'd get so much experience, mentorship, everything."

He was staring at me with the same sad little look in his eyes as when I'd made him talk about writing plays the first time. I showed him my phone, the list I'd found online. He scrolled quietly.

"These places take people with actual credits," he said finally. "They do workshops, fellowships, they've had things produced already."

"Who says? You? You're only saying that because you don't have anything. Yet. This is how you get it."

"I work."

"These people work too," I said. "It's part-time. You can do all your reading on a weekend if you want."

He groaned, falling back onto my mattress.

"Cuddy, please, just think about it."

"Is thinking about it all I have to do?"

"Think about it"—I lay down next to him—"and apply to one.

Most of them want a résumé and ten pages of writing. Anything. It doesn't even have to be a script. Just apply to one. See what happens."

He turned over, onto his stomach, and buried his face in my sheets. "I knew I had to do more than just think about it."

It took me another minute, without his help, to turn him over and uncover his face.

"Just one. Please."

He put his hands over his eyes, saying nothing, then made a noise through his nose. "They'll never pick me."

"Keep thinking that," I told him, "you'll be pleasantly surprised if they do. How's that?"

Three knocks echoed on the door.

"Uncle JJ," Juno said, muffled, "I need you to drive me to the restaurant so I can check on my ice."

"Ice," Cuddy repeated.

"Extra credit, chem final, long story." I got up and opened the door. "Why can't you walk there?"

"It's freezing," Juno said. "They won't take me. Please? I need a lens by Monday."

He glanced over my shoulder at Cuddy, who was sitting up on the bed.

"It'll be quick. You'll be back doing whatever it was you two were doing in here in no time. No judgment, by the way."

"Is it your goal to say the absolute wrong thing in every situation you find yourself in?" I said, getting my coat on. "Half an hour. You promised."

"Ice lens, right?" Cuddy said, standing up. "They did that at my high school. How many points?"

"Ten."

"How big?"

"Big enough to refract light from a flashlight." Juno shook his head. "It's fucking pointless. Even if I could make clear ice, I'd still need something to cut it into shape, or melt it, or do whatever the fuck—"

"You've been freezing water, haven't you?"

"He's used every single one of our freezers and broken most of our good pots."

"I put baking soda in the last one," Juno said, "I've read if you add it to boiling water—"

"You can do all of those things," Cuddy said, "but you can also just . . . drive down to the river and break off some of the ice along the bank."

He looked between us hesitantly.

"Can't you?"

We all stared at one another.

"Oh. My. Fucking. God."

WE BROUGHT THE VAN DOWN the hill to Edgewater and parked it next to the football field where the river water was the stillest. The three of us, guided along by a flashlight Juno pointed at the rocks, hopped the railing along the walkway and climbed over the boulders. Our knees were singing hellfire by the time we reached the water, our fingers burned to their cores by the cold. We made Juno wait on the nearest rock while I lowered Cuddy down toward the water, over a patch of snowed-over ice between boulders.

"Are you there?" I asked him.

"Give me another six inches. I need my foot to touch."

"There's a police car," Juno said. "It's coming right here. No, wait, it's not. It's turning around."

"Juno, shut up," I said. "Are you good?"

"I'm good." Cuddy aimed with his foot and stomped down with his heel. The ice sounded solid but hollow. He stomped again, then a third time, and his hand nearly slipped out of mine when his foot went through, splashing water all around. He let go of my hand and slid his foot, inch by inch, onto the ice. We watched as he pressed it, lightly at first, until more portions of the ice gave way. Several floated into the black pool he'd made in the center. Cuddy reached up and got ahold of my ankle, stretching his arm over the water, and pulled the floating pieces toward him, choosing a large, hexagonal plate of ice that he lifted from the water with one hand. His knuckles were red. We held our breaths. Juno pointed the flashlight at it in his hands. He turned it over. Our eyes fell on the other side, smooth, thick, and, save for a few bubbles, perfectly clear. We saw through to the snow collected on the rough edge.

"Holy fuck," Juno said.

"Holy *fuck*," I repeated.

Cuddy climbed back up, away from the ice, and placed our crown jewel into Juno's arms. Juno stared down at it, his eyes wide, and lifted it over his head.

"HOLY FUUUUUUUUUUCK!"

I'd never screamed so loud in my life. We were cavemen, roaring and rolling around the archaeological find of the century, the ice that Juno was pumping up and down in the air, so vigorously that I thought for a second that if he dropped it, I'd throw him into the water myself. We ran back to the van, shutting ourselves inside and blasting the heat. Juno had already started chipping away the frost.

"FUCK YOU, DR. CAPPIANO! I'm going to get a B. I'm getting a *fucking* B!"

He got up, putting his arms around Cuddy's head.

"I love you, Nurse Gaylord. More than Uncle JJ does. I swear to God. I love you."

We were electrified driving back up the hill, toward the riverside park, where Cuddy let himself out and only let me accompany him as far as his front door, citing the melting ice inside the van.

"Why do I feel like I've run a marathon?" he said, laughing, holding out his hands. "My fingers hurt."

"That was really nice of you."

He smiled, shy again. "High school chemistry. It's a killer. What a dick teacher, by the way. Light refraction is pure physics. Nothing chemical about it."

We calmed down. He dug into his pocket for his keys.

"Thanks," he said, "for tonight."

"Will you come back soon?"

He laughed. "I will come back very soon."

He kissed me, pausing for a second to loop his hands around the small of my back.

"Pick a theater on the list," I told him. "Just one."

"Jack . . ."

"Please? Just do it tonight."

He hadn't yet pulled himself away from me, resting his forehead in the curve of my neck.

"Is there any harm?" I asked him. "Really?"

He thought about it, then shook his head with his hands still around my waist.

"Just do it. Don't be afraid. I'm going to call you tomorrow to make sure."

"Yeah, yeah," he sighed, "I know. Thank you."

Then he opened his door and stepped inside.

"He said you love me."

"Who?"

"Juno." Cuddy smiled.

"That's—" I broke off. "I don't have anything to say to that."

He nodded, letting it be. "Goodnight, itamae-san."

"I'm not Japanese."

"Oh, that's right. Better be . . . Fish Daddy."

He closed his door before I could respond. I waited until his lights went on, then climbed the steps up to the street, to the van waiting down the road.

THE HOUSE WAS QUIET WHEN I parked, its lights out front still on. Juno and the prizewinning slab of river ice had been delivered home to Noa. I went inside, trying to rub feeling back into my fingers, and saw my mother at the kitchen table with a fresh glass of wine.

"Your dad's on his way."

"And you're . . . too drunk to drive yourself home."

She ignored me. I didn't know how a person could do what she was doing, just sit alone in a kitchen, without a phone or a television or a screen or something, and just drink a glass of wine and look out at the darkened line of the city and not have a nervous breakdown like I probably would have.

"I want to make sure he has something hot to eat tonight. It's like he's never heard of a microwave. Much less a stove. Cold rice, cold mandu, cold juk. Who the hell eats cold juk? Like eating sludge."

I sat down next to her. She gestured to the wine and I shook my head.

"Umma."

"Yes."

I slid my phone out of my pants pocket, turning it over on the tabletop. Cuddy had sent me a picture and three unread messages.

"I wanted to talk to you about something."

"That doesn't sound very good," she said.

"It's good," I said hesitantly. "Well, it's not bad. Well—"

"Again, that doesn't sound very good."

"If I told you that Juno made a bunch of little videos of me and put them on the internet and now millions of people have seen them . . ."

Umma waited a moment before speaking.

"Is there an end to that question?"

"I don't know," I said, "what are you thinking?"

She was still smiling slightly. "What am I thinking about what?"

"About the account."

"The account is not what you're trying to ask me about," Umma said, "I can tell. You're trying to ask me about something else."

I stood, without realizing what I was doing. With both hands, I rubbed the tender parts of my scalp on each side of my head.

"I guess I'm asking if you think it's a good idea to set up a dona-tion page. For the restaurant. For us." I looked to her for a signal, receiving none. "To help us pay my hospital bills and also maybe the mortgage on the house and the repairs to the kitchen, and it might also let us hire some actual staff so that we as a family don't need to keep working fifteen-hour shifts until we die."

She blinked at me, then again. I'd made it sound like I had a lot more to say but had run out of steam.

"I don't know why anybody would do something like that. Any of that."

"It wasn't my idea."

"And you suppose Juno thought of all that himself."

"It could really turn things around. There's people already asking all over the account in the comments about where they could go to donate money to us. You wouldn't believe how many—"

"I *don't* believe it," Umma said. She turned around, shooting a glance toward the doorway, opening and closing her mouth. "How many people see these videos of yours?"

"Thousands, Umma," I said. "And more every day."

"He will never take money from strangers."

"That's the interesting part," I said, speaking quickly, "we thought if you might be able to—"

"No."

"Umma, you haven't even—"

"No." She raised her eyebrows at me. "I'm not good at keeping secrets. You'd better tell him about the account. When he gets home. Right now."

"Okay, so . . . ," I said. "Why does he have to know?"

"Because you are meddling in his life behind his back," Umma said. "Not to mention all the work James does for us. You can't keep a secret like this from either of them."

"What if we need help?" I asked her.

"We have help."

"I mean real help," I said. "I know what's going on. All the money James is moving around trying to pay off bills with other bills. How much longer before we have to start thinking about closing the place? We could use all this attention for something good."

"They're not worrying, and neither should you."

"Maybe they don't see what's going on," I said. "Fully. Maybe they're in too deep."

She blinked at me, saying nothing.

"I didn't want any of this out there," I said. "These videos, they're about the fact that I skipped two years of my life, that I woke up and there was a different world here. But they've got people talking. We haven't even asked for money and they're flooding our comments wanting to give it to us. And . . . it's amazing, isn't it? Isn't it amazing that people care this much?"

She focused her eyes on a spot between my feet.

"But I guess you're going to tell him about it, anyway," I said.

Umma sighed, seeming to blow all of the air out of her chest while she did it. She looked tired. "No," she said, "I'm not. It's not my place. Anymore."

She gestured for the wine, and I poured her another glass.

"Your dad is a more complicated person than you give him credit for. He's not some stereotype. He's not some prideful monkey who isn't going to accept money because he needs to prove to himself that he can make his own way."

"So he wants to give the world the middle finger for being racist and unfair and everything else he says it is. Why, Umma? Why is that so important?"

"Not the world," Umma said, "not any of that. He wants to prove himself to you. To James. So that you can look at him and see the person you thought he was when you were little. If you ever have kids, you'll understand what that feels like. You'll understand the way it hurts, to be treated like an old thing on its way out."

"I've never—"

"You've never done it on purpose," Umma said. "But you've done it. You have, Jack Jr. That's what children do."

She sighed.

"This doesn't have anything to do with me. That's why I'm not going to tell him. It's also why you need to talk to him yourself. But I will say: I don't like this at all."

"I never said I liked it either."

She took a prolonged sip. "So I'm supposed to share in this ugly secret now, with you? Forever?"

"I'm trying to figure it out," I said. "I just needed someone to tell."

She softened, hearing me, and reached out to put her hand on top of mine—"You're freezing." She rubbed my hand between her two palms, working sensation back into my fingers. We were quiet for a while, for a few minutes, I wasn't sure.

"You have always done what you wanted," Umma said finally.

She almost laughed, catching my eye.

"You don't agree?"

"I guess I just don't like hearing it."

We were silent for another few minutes, quiet enough to hear the cars passing on the street beyond.

"It's true, anyway," I said. "I left, and I stopped talking to everybody and taking their calls. Your calls."

She stopped me from saying something along the lines of "I'm sorry."

"What you've done," she said quietly, "you've paid for, so many times over. You've lost—"

She pressed her lips hard for a moment.

"You don't need to apologize anymore."

Then our heads turned; the frosted front door was pried open. Appa shook snow off his boots and stepped inside, still dressed in his whites.

"My beautiful family," he said with a theatrical bow of his head. "When I'm home with you, the world is right."

"Somebody bought you a couple shots tonight, didn't they." Umma got to her feet, setting about the containers of leftovers we'd gathered up on the kitchen counter.

"How was dinner?" I asked him.

"Good, good," Appa said, "James is happy."

He sat and poured himself some wine. Umma brought him a plate. The two of us watched him eat, pondering the way he used a pair of chopsticks to gather together a combined bite of the pork belly, kimchi, rice, spinach, and bean sprouts all in one.

I saw for a moment how comfortable it had been, to sit between them, in this house. I'd missed this house. It was easy to forget how much I'd missed it, and the sight of them together.

"Are you retiring?"

They each widened their eyes a slight fraction, turning around, looking at me.

"I'm sorry," I said, "I know I shouldn't ask, and maybe you were going to tell me in your own time, but I just need to know. Because I feel like that's what you've been saying this whole time. Doing the fish run by myself, and what you said about me not needing to learn much more, which everybody here knows is completely false, and I just need—"

"Jack Jr.," Appa said slowly. I quieted.

"I'm sorry," I said. I got up. I turned around and had reached the archway door to the kitchen when I heard him.

"Yes."

I turned around.

Appa shared one last glance with Umma. He looked tired. He held one shoulder, the shoulder he used to power his butchering knife, at a lower height than the other. And when he smiled, I could read on his face the troubling sort of relief that I was very sorry to admit I had never truly seen there before. Like I'd lifted an immeasurable weight from his back and his knees and was allowing him, at last, to do what he wanted to do. I'd always wondered why Appa never smiled behind the bar, slicing fish. And I mean genuinely, not like when he faked it for the customers. It was hard work, demanding and precise, usually at the pleasure of people who didn't and wouldn't truly understand what it took to make sushi like he did. Appa never smiled at his work. He smiled like this for me, and only me.

"Yes?" I asked.

"Yes," he said.

SUPER-FAST FLASHBACK INTERLUDE CONCERNING—AMONG OTHER TOPICS—THE YOKE OF FILIAL PIETY INADVERTENTLY ENACTING DAMNING AND IRREVERSIBLE CONSEQUENCES FOR ALL PARTIES INVOLVED

JACK JR. IS EIGHTEEN YEARS OLD. JACK JR. IS ALMOST SIX FEET TALL, A quarter inch away that he has not yet given up hope will eventually bestow upon him the sound and rightful laurels of Grown Man, after which life will be easy. After which life will unfurl before him like an expertly laundered tablecloth being thrown across the wooden surface of an expensive dining table. Jack Jr. still has time. Jack Jr. has a high school diploma. Jack Jr.'s brain has not finished developing and will not fully do so for another seven years according to Reddit. Jack Jr. can score the back of a salmon with his knife, just deep enough to allow an even sear on the skin but not deep enough to pierce the tender orange flesh that so many customers come into the restaurant each night hoping to find laid delicately atop the most perfectly portioned slug of room-temperature vinegared rice. Jack Jr. can tourné-cut a potato, any potato. Jack Jr. knows, among many other things, that a proficient tourné cut can allow each and every potato or analogous sustainably produced root vegetable to turn quickly and efficiently in a frying pan. Jack Jr. is a fiercely loyal, unwaveringly dutiful, prodigiously talented would-be itamae who does not know what he would do in his life if he were—say—no longer allowed to make sushi anymore. If he were—say—not to see his father each evening after school and before the dinner service, the two of them side by side at the wooden bar in their whites with the infinite possibility of the clientele—endless permutations of conversations and tastes—walking in through the doors. Jack Jr. still has time. Jack Jr. is just about to experience the most formative evening of his young and impressionable life and he does not in the slightest bit know it. In fact, the future prescribed to Jack Jr. that early hour at which he woke in bed that morning—the future he in this moment believes to be the one true and inexorable path forward along the x-axis of time—feels so certain to him that even a thought of a digression, a divergence, is a nonentity in the folds of his mind. He has smelled the gummy brine of fish under his fingernails every night for as long as he can remember. His knife is a slim and supple length of steel that feels often like a sixth, very long, very sharp finger extending from his palm. His whites are more comfortable than pajamas. He has been thinking it for weeks. Service begins in one hour. Today is going to be the best of day of Jack Jr.'s life.

Jack Jr.'s father is outside on the street, visible when Jack Jr. rounds the corner of the curb, headed for the restaurant. He is wiping the windows down with a rag and some soapy water. And it does not at the moment unnerve Jack Jr. to know that his father, currently wiping a bead of sweat from his forehead with the front of his white sleeve, will no longer be working at the bar beside him. Though they have done it for years. Though the rhythm of their knives across their boards, the punch of the tickets on the spike after they have been filled, the sliding door of the refrigerated raw bar stocked with sliced portions of fish, have filled Jack Jr.'s every waking day for as long as he can remember. There is a lot to say about the youth of a cook. Brute strength and stamina that have not yet been traded in for wisdom. Jack Jr. has them in spades. He cannot remember ever being tired of fish. Tired of the runs, yes, tired of the hauling of pallets into the van and across the river, tired of the wiping and the washing and the locking and the trudging home only to shower, weakly, and collapse into bed. But the fish? Never. Jack Jr. will be slicing fish for the rest of his life. If he could only be so lucky. If he could only keep his mind and his skill sharp enough to earn and keep earning the privilege, the approval from his father. Jack Jr.'s father entertains a great many regulars who have come to know his casual and easygoing service, his ease with banter while slicing, chopping, and wiping at high speeds across the wooden counter where he works.

Jack Jr.'s father turns his head, spotting him, opening his arms wide. He tells Jack Jr. happily, with the wearied grit of a man looking forward to a gentle halt to the restlessness of his days, that there is something that he has not been altogether truthful about. Jack Jr. does not understand. In his private eighteen-year-old mind there is nothing that his father has ever admitted to lying about. Save for just one thing, something inconsequential. Jack Jr. asks what his father means. The sun is low over the tops of the street behind them, bathing them in dull orange light. Jack Jr.'s father means to say more but thinks better of it, and instead shows Jack Jr. inside through the door.

Jack Jr. feels a waft of warm, humid air hit his face, condensation on his skin. He finds, to his surprise, a tight little group of people gathered in the restaurant, holding among other things trays of tteok, glasses of champagne, and, in the instance of his brother, James— standing off to the side and making a concerted effort to erase the habitual scowl on his face—a fully asleep little boy hanging from his neck with his head resting on one shoulder. Their voices are loud, Jack Jr. has time to register, before hands fall on his shoulders, squeezing, patting his head. Jack Jr.'s mother puts her arms around his neck. In a great and genuine display of emotion, she explains to the rest of the gathered guests that of all of the futures she might have imagined for her son, following in his father's footsteps was one she did not completely expect. Jack Jr. is listening to her in a daze, choosing to count instead the rhythms her hands make while she speaks. It does not escape him that something has shifted his thoughts into a different order than they were in before he entered the restaurant this evening and found such a generous and loving group of people inside, congratulating him, toasting to his success. There is something he is not understanding about why they are all here. Why can't he—Jack Jr.—figure out what it is? What is there to say about the love of one's family? Indisputable. Unconditional. These are things he has been taught to believe all his life and given no reason, no reason at all, to shadow with even an ounce of doubt. This is the result of some overactive nerves, Jack Jr. is telling himself. He reminds himself that he did not sleep very well last night, despite having gone to bed a full hour earlier than he might have found himself doing on any other night but the night before he was set to take over his father's restaurant. It is the most logical reason for the change in the air, for the mute buzz that has begun to sound in Jack Jr.'s ears and is growing steadily louder. Jack Jr.'s father has found his way inside, setting down his soapy bucket. He places his hands on Jack Jr.'s shoulders, laughing along at a story Jack Jr.'s mother is telling about the first time Jack Jr. tasted wasabi. Jack Jr. has enough time to catch his brother James's eye. It is easy in this moment between them to find commonality, shared embarrassment at their mother's grandstanding. It is not lost on Jack Jr. that it is one of the first times in recent memory that James has even attempted to look happy while in his company. James is nearing the sixth month of his probation for driving his car through the back-end fence of the Linwood Plaza H Mart's parking lot. It remains unclear when—if ever—the state will return his license. It has never made sense to Jack Jr. that James did not enjoy working in the restaurant. It was the place in which they spent most of their time, from the very tender ages at which they first began to talk, to name things, to be able to grasp things in their little hands. It is perceived in this moment that Jack Jr. feels sorry for James in many ways apart from the most important: the fact that James does not enjoy making sushi. No, it is in fact much more apparent as the seconds continue to tick on that James just does not fit into their family as well as he does. It is perhaps the reason why he tries so hard to break from it and is compelled, whether by dependence, fear, or the apparent inability to stomach the burden of existence without a bellyful of liquor, always, to return. If James would only see that one's own family is the greatest gift of all, that to be with one's family is the only reason a person should be able to give as to why any of this life is worth living. This, Jack Jr. needs to believe with his whole heart, or else none of it will be worth it and none of it will work and all the great joys of his life will be empty.

Jack Jr.'s father is explaining that Jack Jr. thought something was terribly, tragically wrong just minutes earlier when outside the restaurant, which elicits laughs. The implication being that nothing could possibly go wrong for service tonight or beyond, that Jack Jr., with all of his training and his unshakable sense of duty to his family, to the restaurant, is more than equipped to continue a legacy that supersedes any one person. That the dinner service tonight represents not only the first passing of the torch but the symbolic and predestined passing of torches for generations to come, and by extension the prosperity of the family beyond anything that any living person in this room at this very moment can in fact comprehend. That Jack Jr. will be serving pieces of nigiri and boxing takeout for decades and decades until he himself will be standing here with his hands on the shoulders of a son, a Jack Jr. Jr., that successive generations of Jacks Jr. and Jr. and Jr. are flowing from this point in time, working diligently, heads down, behind the bar. It is exactly what Jack Jr. wants. It is all Jack Jr. has ever wanted. It is Jack Jr.'s true and only purpose. It feels very good to know one's purpose with such certainty, doesn't it? Doesn't it, Jack Jr.? Just very good. Just wonderful. So wonderful in fact that while Jack Jr.'s father has continued on with the story, conjecturing with bemusement about what kind of hypothetical apocalypse Jack Jr. might have been envisioning just minutes ago when he—Jack Jr.'s father—had mentioned he was not altogether being truthful about something, he—Jack Jr.—has started to shake.

And it is not just the shaking that compels Jack Jr.'s mother to raise a hand in Jack Jr.'s father's face to quiet him, but the look she is watching take shape on her son's face as he continues to shudder. Someone, Jack Jr. is not sure who, asks what's wrong, and Jack Jr. has the sense, even then, to smile and say with all the dignity he can muster that nothing is wrong. Because it really is wonderful that everyone has come in and taken time out of their busy lives to congratulate him on this most special of nights. Because there is so much left to do in the kitchen before the start of service. Because of all of the futures that are sure to exist along the x-axis of time, Jack Jr. has perceived one, just one, the one in which he fulfills an absolutely successful dinner service for the first time on his own, signaling to his father that yes, there are other people in the family who can be depended on for support, that it is the right and good choice to retire and begin to enjoy the days again. Because Harabeoji, dead twelve years but whose face Jack Jr. can still see framed with Technicolor balloons at his sixth birthday, knew that a life in America was hard work and would often be egregiously unfair but was in fact the price of the glorious opportunities sown in the ground, in the soil, in the air. And it's great, Jack Jr. says with a defiant intake of air into his lungs. It's so, so, so great, isn't it?

Jack Jr.'s mother is staring at him. Jack Jr.'s father still has his hands on his shoulders, standing behind.

What is wrong with you? Jack Jr.'s mother asks, not meaning to be so blunt but admittedly concerned after having listened to what she might only describe as one of the strangest trains of thought she has ever heard somebody pronounce in words.

Jack Jr. tries to speak. His lips are dry, and his throat is raw. He has stopped shaking but is afraid of what his body is trying to signal to him comes next.

Jack Jr.?

So, Jack Jr. says, quietly, just barely above the level of a whisper. Maybe. I. Was wrong.

Jack Jr.'s mother stares at him. Jack Jr. feels his father, at last, slide his hands off his shoulders.

Wrong about what?

About, Jack Jr. says, repeating the word. He notices that James's face has gone tight, as though the muscles there are constricted under the skin.

I think I was wrong, Jack Jr. says again. I don't think I want this.

A long moment of silence follows, during which Jack Jr. is unable to do anything but stare back at his mother, cannot begin to fathom what he might find if he turns around and looks at his father. He locks his feet in place, not daring to find out. It is excruciating to see all of them staring back at him. And just as Jack Jr. thinks it may end, it does, but not in the way he has been hoping. Not in the slightest, though it does relieve him to watch every face turn away, toward the source of a bolt of laughter that ricochets around the room. Jack Jr.'s brother, James, is doubled over, laughing, unable to keep himself still. In Noa's arms, Juno stirs himself awake, frightened by the sound of his father.

Oh, Jesus, James says, wiping his eyes with one hand, having either chosen to ignore Noa glaring intently at him over his shoulder or simply not noticed at all. This is just fucking hilarious.

For another minute, they all watch James laugh, contain himself, slowly, until the only sounds are Juno's as he squirms against Noa's arm, the makings of a tantrum building up in his lungs. They know this sound Juno makes. It is the surest way in which a four-year-old might tell anyone who is listening around them that something very loud and very anguished is about to transpire, for which there is no remedy.

So, Jack Jr. repeats himself. I think I'll go. Jack Jr.'s face has grown so hot that he can barely feel it move anymore. For a bit. For a second. I think I just need a second. And then I'll come back and we can do this over again. We definitely can. I'll make sure of it.

IT IS HERE, AT LAST, that he makes the mistake, and turns his head, over his shoulder, looks back at them. Jack Jr. spots his mother. His eyes meet those of his father.

There is very little in Jack Jr.'s mind that might prepare him for the way it makes him feel to look into his father's face like this, unable to explain himself. It is not lost on him, and most assuredly them, that he will not be back. That it will take him almost twenty-four hours to talk to his mother again, and in that conversation he will tell her that his wish is to move away from home and go to college. That another week after that, he will have a conversation with his father that will end with the two of them smiling but saying and having said absolutely nothing. That another five days after that, he will pack his things and rent a room in a six-person apartment across the river, and leave behind the yanagi knife that his father bought for him. That for an entire year afterward, he will work as a line cook at a bustling Greek restaurant in a quiet corner of the East Village, until the next spring he will find that he has been accepted to the business program at City College. That he will attend, and finish, a three-year program, and start a job copywriting for upcoming digital advertising campaigns, and meet a teacher on a dating app and find that life has never been sweeter than when he is curled in bed together with him. That he will not speak to his brother, James, for five years. That his mother will call, at first weekly, then monthly, and eventually so seldom that every time they hang up, she'll tell him that another year has passed, that his nephew, Juno, has grown another couple of inches. That Fort Lee, New Jersey, will grow ever farther away until he can find himself looking at it, out the window of a rooftop bar or through a gap in the skyline while biking down Tenth Avenue, without even thinking of the restaurant or his family. Jack Jr. is trying to find something to say to his family, something that might fix what he has done. Something that might, at the very least, help him understand why. He will remember the way his father is looking at him for the rest of his life.

He is thinking, and coming up with nothing. So instead he says, Also I'm gay. He opens the door to the cold air, steps outside, and lets it shut behind him at the exact moment that Juno, still struggling in his mother's arms, begins at last to scream.

11

THE FIFTEEN MOST CONSEQUENTIAL HOURS OF ONE'S SHORT, IRREVERENT LIFE

IT STARTED WITH ME TAKING OFF ALL MY CLOTHES. "IT" BEING THE fifteen most consequential hours of my short, irreverent life thus far, and the locale being Exam Room 4 of the in-network, Zocdoc-rated Neurology Consultants of Hackensack, New Jersey. I was shown inside an exam room and told to change into the hospital gown they'd hung over the back of the sterile chair in the center of the room. My appointment's purpose: to discern, after approximately three months of waking life, whether I was going to do one of two things: keep living with virtually zero post-vegetative symptoms such as blood clots, pressure sores, brain hemorrhage, nervous failure; or just fucking die in an hour with fewer explanations for it than for why I might have woken up in the first place. Either was possible, they'd seemed to imply back at the hospital, while letting me know that the checkups were likely to continue for the next few years and that I should get used to them. I did as I was told. It was four in the afternoon, their only open slot of the day. I hitched off my pants, stepping out of them, and folded them on the nearby chair. My shirt, crumpled under the extra-large Costco hoodie I wore over it, came next. I couldn't remember if the nurse had said specifically to take my underwear off. It seemed a bit invasive. These were brain doctors, after all. Then, there might have been something I was missing. The axial anal nerve, which provided a direct and clear line from the hypothalamus to a point just north of the butthole. Very important in the study of neurology; some would say pivotal. My guess was as good as anyone else's.

I covered myself with the gown and sat just as the door opened and my hotshot lady doctor stepped into the room.

She crinkled her eyes above the mask that she had practically suctioned to her face with tight rubber bands, showing me that she was smiling. "Jack."

"Jr.," I said. "Jack Jr."

She glanced down at the notes in her hand.

"I don't know why I always say that. I'm sorry."

"Nothing wrong with that at all, Jack *Jr.* Names are important. You okay?"

"As okay as I can be," I said.

"Pain?"

"Like, anywhere?"

"Head, neck, back?"

"Not really."

"Working?"

"Yes. My family's business. I'm up early almost every day and I get home around midnight."

"Those are some long hours."

"I'm used to it."

She went to the cabinets and pulled a big dog-cone face shield over her head, coming closer to me.

"I'm sorry, it's a bit cold in here," she said. "We don't see many like you. We want to give you a full exam, just to be sure."

I moved each of my limbs in various circles and shapes at her direction, clenching different muscles, looking around at all of the corners of the room. I was made to walk, to hop, to swing my arms, to roll my head clockwise and counterclockwise in succession. After ten minutes of this, she sat me down.

"You look great," she said, "nothing out of the ordinary. You ever get headaches? Migraine?"

"When I don't sleep right on my neck, sometimes."

"Longer than a day?"

"No."

She wrote all of this down, swiping back and forth on an iPad she brought out from under a desk. "What do you do for work?"

"I'm a . . . cook. Yeah, a cook, I guess."

She raised her eyebrows. "What kind of food?"

"Korean food. Also Japanese food. Sushi, other things. It's actually, well—it's my first dinner tonight, leading the kitchen. Which is not impressive, since the kitchen is two people. But I'm taking over for my dad and . . . yeah. Nervous."

"Your blood pressure's high."

She took a seat on a swiveling stool set up near a computer monitor.

"I'm going to advise you set yourself a bedtime, drink plenty of water, and stay away from alcohol."

"Secret to living forever?"

"Think of it as shortening the array of possibilities. You did a number on yourself two years ago. The hospital sent me your records. You're doing really well, Jack Jr., better than most people would consider medically possible. But unhealthy habits can expose gaps in your health. And in the case of your health, it's just a bit too much of a risk. Which leg did you have surgery on?"

"Left."

"Trouble walking?"

"No."

The answer to all of her questions had, thus far, been no, and it was stressing me out. We didn't ever talk like this when the butch physical therapist on the ground floor of the hospital pumped my legs back and forth once a week. Surely there was something wrong with me, maybe something that didn't show up on an EKG or in the way I moved my arm above my head. I wanted her to ask me to do more things, as though any number of exercises, once wide and varied enough, would isolate any problem in the human body.

She pulled off her gloves and stowed away the blast shield for her face.

"Good luck tonight," she told me. "I love sushi, by the way. Where is it?"

"It's a little place in Fort Lee. Joja? You might know it?"

She paused. "You're the Fish Daddy."

"Um—"

"From TikTok," she said, "my daughter's shown me your videos. I can't imagine how I didn't put two and two together. Looks like amazing food. You should be proud of yourself."

"Thank you, it's my nephew. He makes all of the videos and it wasn't my idea. It's important to me that you know it wasn't my idea."

She put out her sterile and distanced elbow, which I met with my own, in such a way that I couldn't tell if she'd either heard or believed me.

"See you in three months."

EMIL STOOD WHEN I MET him in the waiting room with my clothes back on. He put his thumbs up, down, up again. I answered him, checked out up front, and followed him outside to the parking lot, where we pulled off our masks and breathed frozen air.

"She recognized me," I said.

He frowned at me.

"From Juno's videos."

He snorted, setting off with me toward the van. "Don't forget what happened to the man who suddenly got everything he wanted."

"What happened?"

"He lived"—he tugged on my arm and pulled me closer to him—"happily ever after. Gene Wilder. Willy Wonka."

"Thank you, sir," I said. "All my problems are now solved. Good day."

We warmed our hands inside. The night had come fast and hard over the tops of the houses, the last of the sunlight shooting through the windshield and straight into our eyes. I started the engine and pulled away, toward the street.

"Did she at least like the videos?"

"I didn't ask."

"That's valuable market research."

He put his hand over my thigh, which he liked to do when we ate, or drove, or did anything.

"You feel okay?"

"I guess I feel weird, being so completely fine."

"You're thinking too much about it," he said. "Learn to relax. Try yoga. Go to sleep earlier."

"She told me something exactly like that. Is that a script you all learn?"

I took him to the janchi shop near Leonia and passed through aisles of tables laid out with neat Styrofoam packages. A great many restaurants had survived this way in the pandemic, by switching to a takeout-only banchan model. The dishes were easy to prepare in advance, packaged nicely, and made good use of the floor space they hadn't been able to use for sit-down guests. There was an overload of them around town, but over time we'd learned which were our favorites. They'd just laid out a pack of pan-fried mackerel, which I picked up. The cashier and the ladies working in the kitchen out back were staring at Emil as usual.

"Dumplings?" I asked him. "They're pork. You'd like them."

"Lay it on me." He bent over a package of pickled radish and lotus root, inspecting it.

"Nice friend," the lady up front, who was Umma's age, said. She had taken the mackerel from me. "Where'd you get him?"

"He likes the jangjorim you have," I said, speaking so he couldn't hear. "Is there any left?"

She retreated to the kitchen and returned with a fresh pack. "For the white boy."

"Thank you."

"Your accent really isn't very good at all."

"I know, I'm sorry."

"You don't speak Korean at home, do you?"

"Jack Jr." Emil held up some tofu. "Yes? No?"

"My mom likes that kind. Bring it over."

Emil padded up behind me and handed it over. "I love everything here," he said, smiling, though only I could tell he was doing it under his mask. "He's made me try all of it. Really good."

Our cashier nodded and said, "Good, good," putting on a grand-mother's face for him. She took my cash and made change. "He's a nice boy. You've got a nice friend. Looks like he could eat a lot."

"He's very nice, yes." I turned red, despite the fact that he couldn't understand us. "Thank you, we'll be back."

"Tell your mother we'll have more jeon this weekend. Beef jeon."

Outside, he carried our bags in one hand with his jacket sleeve pulled over his fingers.

"You've got such a different voice when you speak Korean," he said.

"If you knew, you'd tell me my accent was terrible."

We started the van. Broad Avenue around this time was bustling with Korean mothers, grandmothers, aunts, and gay sons like me ducking into the janchi shops, preparing their dinners while the men napped. They'd begun to hang lights over some of the windows. We passed a kitschy young curry tonkotsu spot that I'd wanted to try for the past few months but hadn't been able to find the time for yet.

"I want to tell you something," he said as we neared the block. I glanced sideways at him gazing contentedly out of the window at the passing street.

"Yes?"

"One of the theaters I applied to wrote back to me," he said, turning his head briefly to face me, then hiding himself again, "this morning. They want to talk to me. They want me to come into the city and meet their executive director." He said it as though reading it off a card, like he'd been practicing it all day. "It's tiny. A really small community theater in the West Village. But . . ."

He glanced down at his hands.

"Yeah," he breathed out.

I waited for him to say more and, when he didn't, slowed the van to a stop along the side of the road.

"And . . . how do you feel about that?" I asked cautiously.

He moved his head from left to right, with his eyes fixed on his hands.

"Emil," I said.

He took in a breath. "Good news, right?" he said.

"Are you fucking"—I didn't know what to do other than shove him into the window—"*serious?* Emil! EMIL—" Needing somehow to expel energy, I slapped the steering wheel with my palms. "Holy shit. Holy motherfucking shit—"

"They said it's an interview." Emil was laughing, trying to get ahold of my wrists. "Calm down, you're freaking me out. It's nothing. They get drama students to do this kind of thing. It's not even paid."

"You said theaters," I said, "Theaters, you said theaters. You applied to *multiple* theaters—"

"I should've told you," Emil said, "I know. I was freaking out. I'm still freaking out."

"I can't believe this." I was breathing far harder than he was. "I—you—when is it? When do they want to meet you?"

"Another thing," he said quietly. "I was thinking of telling them I can't."

The sun had firmly set and turned the sky purple. Ahead, the restaurant's signage was starting to glow brighter. I had half an hour.

"What are you talking about?"

"I have work." He shrugged. "I can't get myself all the way to the city by nine just for something like this. They don't pay, they're so small there's no telling when they might just close out of the blue, I don't know—"

He sounded ashamed, saying it.

"I was trying not to tell you today," he said. "I know today's important for you, and I know you're stressed. And I was going to tell them I'd changed my mind and just not say anything about it at all. But that felt wrong. You would've—"

"I would've killed you," I said. "I'll still kill you, if you don't email them right now and tell them you'll come at nine tomorrow."

"My shift's over at eight. I don't have any time."

"An hour's plenty."

"And . . . ," he sighed, "what if they say no?"

"Fuck them and move on."

"You say it like it's easy," he said. His shoulders shrank as he said it. "I didn't even . . . I don't even know if—"

"Emil."

It had flashed through my head within a split second, what I was going to say to him there. I'd opened my mouth, even, but stopped myself. He'd gone so pale just talking about it. I knew what I wanted him to do. Different approach. I took his hand.

"I know this is scary," I told him, "I know you've never done anything like this before, and changing your life up like this and putting your energy into something creative is a really scary thing. But you're right there. You sent in some of your own work, they read it, and they liked it enough that they want to talk to you about working for them. You are good enough to take this out of your basement apartment and into the world. They believe that. They just want to talk to you. Whatever happens next, we don't care."

He'd listened to me intently, swiping his thumb back and forth over the back of my hand. I had an idea.

"I know what I can do for you," I said. "I'll go with you. I'll meet you outside the theater, I'll bring coffee, cigarettes, antidepressants, whatever you need, I'll wait while you go in, I'll take you home, I'll tuck you into bed. I'll wake you up six hours later with soup."

He was moving his head, slowly, an ambiguous nod that I couldn't read.

"I don't want you to worry like this," he said finally. "This is such an important day for you. I'm already missing it for work."

"I'm not the only person allowed to be important," I said.

He hadn't given me much of a signal, so I backed off, sitting with my head against the seat. Cars passed us on their way down the street.

"Did you write something new to send them?" I asked.

He nodded. "Ten-minute script," he said. "Guy comes into a . . . sushi restaurant. Talks with the chef. At the end of it, they decide it was a date."

I nodded, fighting the urge to smile.

"I wrote it the night I met you," he said, "met you as in, you could hear me when I talked, and you could talk back."

"Thanks for clarifying."

He picked at a dried stain on his pants.

"Will you really . . ." He trailed off. "No, it's stupid. I'll go myself after work."

"I'm with you," I told him, "whatever you want. Do you want me there?"

He seemed, genuinely, to ponder the question. Then he nodded.

"Okay," I said. After a while I started the engine. "Okay, then. Done."

We parked, and he followed me into the restaurant. Lights flooded our faces from above. Jazzy piano filtered in from the speaker overhead. Zeno was at the bar, wiping down a stack of hotel pans. Umma, Noa, and Juno were gathered in the center of the dining room with their backs turned, fiddling with something making a lot of rubbery noise between them. Zeno cleared her throat. Noa turned her head, swearing—"He's back. Guys, he's back."

They turned the thing in their hands around, showing me. "SURPRISE!"

A gold and tinsel chain of letters, GRAND RE-OPENING, unfolded between them. There was suddenly so much shouting that I couldn't even hear myself telling everybody to calm down.

"Is he here?" The doors to the kitchen flew open and Appa nearly hip-checked himself on the bar running out. "He's here! Surprise!"

Emil pushed me in the direction of the banner. Somebody placed a glass of champagne in my hands.

"It's no big deal," Umma said, kissing me on each side of my face. "Just a little special thing for you. My son, the head chef. Itamae."

"Itamae." The others raised their glasses.

"Really, really nice," I said about ten times, "thank you, everybody, thank you. No, I can't drink anymore. I really can't—"

"Okay, everybody, fifteen minutes," Appa shouted over the noise. "Couple Grubhub orders already coming in. . . ."

James, whose head I could see in the window to the kitchen, had stepped out to join us. The others had descended on the banchan Emil and I had brought in. He had a glass of red Gatorade, which he raised in my direction.

"Congrats."

"Thanks," I said.

"Feel okay?"

I felt Emil's hands on my shoulders; he massaged his thumbs into the back of my neck.

"Everybody's been asking me that today," I said. "But thanks. We'll see how it goes."

They noticed each other. Emil put a hand out. "Sorry, man, we haven't talked in a while. How are you?"

They shook hands. James's eyes flitted back and forth between us and the others.

"How's the baby?"

"The baby," James repeated slowly, as though remembering, blinking Emil's way, "yeah, we're doing okay. Thank you." He drained his glass. "Excuse me. We've got dinner in the kitchen if you're hungry."

He left us there, finding Umma near the back of the dining room.

"Don't ask me," I said, turning to the rest of them. "Everybody, Emil's leaving for work now. Can we save the jangjorim for him?"

"There's enough," Juno said, his mouth full. "We'll miss you, Nurse Gaylord."

I cleared a path for him to get outside to the curb. Emil looked at my family inside with a happy grin on his face.

"You're going to be amazing," he told me.

"It's slicing fish, I'll be fine."

We were a foot apart, beginning to shiver.

"See you tomorrow?" I asked him.

He took his hands out of his pockets and ran his fingers once through my hair. "Since when do you call me Emil?"

I frowned at him. "When? I don't know, today, maybe? Yesterday?"

He nodded as though he liked the sound of it. "Just noticed," he said. "Thought I'd ask."

"What do you want me to call you?"

He didn't have an answer for this. I pushed him lightly. "Go, you'll be late."

I watched him shrink down the sidewalk until I couldn't see him anymore.

Ten minutes later, my stomach was full, hastily stuffed with fried rice and leftover dumplings. I'd changed into my shirt and the rubber clog shoes I wore in the kitchen. I gave my apron a secure and steady knot. The doors opened. Appa eased himself into our cramped quarters with Zeno behind him. He put his hand on my shoulder, smoothing my shirt at the seams.

"You look good," he said. "You look just like me."

"What a kind and thoughtful compliment to yourself," I said. "Anybody out there?"

"Not yet," Appa said. "Five minutes to five. You know how it goes."

He inspected me, top to bottom.

"You don't seem nervous."

I shrugged. Appa pressed his lips together. There was no time for whatever he'd wanted to say, both of us knew, so he only took his hand off me and passed me the yanagi, freshly sharpened, its polish like a clear sliver of glass along the edge of the blade. He went out through the doors and left us there. Zeno was working back of house tonight, coming out behind the bar depending on demand. It was a Friday, we knew the drill: couple parties bound to come in later than usual, mostly duos and singles at the bar.

"You good?" I asked her.

She moved her head absently.

"Zeno?"

"Mm." She rubbed her lips together. "Um, yes, I think so."

"Tickets come in through the machine over there, right?" I said. "Don't stress if things pile up in the sink. It's Friday, remember?"

"Yeah." She nodded, more to herself than me. I was nearly ready to get out there but stopped myself.

"Been a long two months, Zeno," I said. "I'm proud of you."

She nodded again, more forcefully. I remembered what I'd texted her on Thanksgiving, an honest little string of messages that had since been buried under things like *Where is the toilet plunger* and *Do you need more yams*.

"Okay," I said. I peeked out the window, where I saw Umma showing a couple to the bar. Juno, Noa, James, and Sam would be back when we closed. Appa, having claimed he'd stick around in the event of an emergency, was currently securing the balloons in my honor to the outside of the window. "We're on. I'm supposed to say something. Something inspiring."

"If you have to think about how to feel, it won't work," Zeno said.

"How do you know?"

"A feeling isn't something you *know*. A feeling is something you *feel*. That's why it's called a feeling."

"Zeno," I said, "what'd your Greek philosopher guy say about getting out there and doing something you're not nearly qualified or trained well enough to do?"

"He said, go out there and just fuck 'em up," Zeno said.

"I'll take your word for it. Let's fuck 'em up."

I held out my fist. We bumped, like rock stars, and I pushed through the doors.

AS IT TURNS OUT, THERE is not much consumer influence to be ascribed to new signage in gold and tinsel outside a restaurant, even on a Friday night. It was no matter. The nine Grubhub orders might not have noticed, but let me tell you, for the nineteen patrons—three singles, six couples, and one absolute train wreck of a white girl introducing her boyfriend to her parents—that came in from five to nine-thirty and took their seats at my bar, the air was fucking fire. I was comfortable. I was hitting every note, moving fast, making little mistakes and correcting them for good. Did I suppose I had the night some cooks dream of? Did I dare? Time would anthologize the kind of game I played, or some kind of stupid straight-man *Survivor* phrase like that, but I felt good. We were nearing the end.

The girl was brokering a conversation between the boyfriend and her father about whiskey, which was going better than any of the conversation of the past hour had gone. I'd set up a row of the king salmon on my table and was using a torch to blister the edges. The girl's mother stopped everybody talking and pointed me out.

"That's just so interesting," she was saying, "and beautiful. I bet that makes the flavor stronger." She nodded at me, speaking more slowly. "Is that right?"

"'Course," I said, enunciating, though this didn't seem to convince her, "we do it for the look, obviously, but the flame gets into the fish itself. You'll taste it."

"It's just marvelous," the mother said. "We're so lucky tonight. We were having trouble finding a nice place in this area."

I served them, narrating, "King salmon, pickled daikon."

The boyfriend, despite being a fucking dummy, was the only one thus far to say thank you all night, and did so now, while presumably resisting the urge to ask me for a fork. Appa was watching us from the other end and winked at me.

"How has business been?" the girl's mother asked us, while the others resumed their whiskey symposium. "I'm sure difficult, but I see people going out to eat all the time now in our neighborhood."

"We're doing what we can," I said. "Better than a year ago."

I'd decided to jump ahead and plate the uni for them, hoping the sight of me working diligently might inspire this woman to some extended silence.

"This was an interesting mix of ingredients," she told me. "Stan and I, we've had some omakase in the city. But this is almost . . . something else. Not Japanese. That crab claw with the . . . with the sauce on it."

"Ssamjang," I said. "It's Korean. I'm Korean."

"Are you *really*," she said, widening her eyes. "Would you say this is even sushi, then?"

"I'd say it's sushi," I said, glancing over at Appa, who was trying not to laugh. "The techniques are Japanese. The ingredients, some of them, are Korean."

She was staring at me with a mixture of awe and—I didn't know. Sympathy? She'd tell the mothers at school about a Korean sushi place in Fort Lee that she thought was *marvelous*. But the chef, my God, what a sourpuss. I don't think he spoke English very well.

They ate the uni, the boyfriend turning a shade of green when it passed his throat the first time. I'd been wondering this entire time why this girl hadn't told him not to bite the fucking things in half.

Maybe she hadn't noticed. Tamago next, made by Appa this morning, along with the check. The girl's father tipped 12 percent and hurried out the door, flanked by his wife. The boyfriend remained, draining his water. I cleaned up his plate first.

"You guys have a good night." I smiled.

"Thank you for talking to us," he said quietly, glancing over his shoulder at his girlfriend. "It's my first time eating any of this stuff."

"Oh. I didn't notice," I told him solemnly. "Seemed like it went well."

"I don't know, man," he said, getting his jacket, "I took a job in Minneapolis the other day. She won't leave the East Coast." He shrugged, making his eyes wide. "Want to make us dinner while we have that discussion?"

"Good luck to you," I said. The door closed behind them. Umma almost fell off her chair.

"The way that boy bit everything in half," she said, gasping for breath, "Jesus, I could barely hear the others talking, I couldn't take my eyes off him."

I took their check, pausing to confirm that the girl's dad had in fact cheaped out on as grand a scale as I thought he had. I passed the note to Zeno, who logged it into the register. She showed everybody the receipt and, with a flourish of her hand, spiked it with the others on the counter. Appa threw his arms up.

"Closed." He beamed. "You're done. Ari, turn that sign over on the door."

"I know what you should have done with that white lady," Umma said, getting to her feet. "You should've said halfway through, 'I'm just so sorry, I have no idea what you're saying. I think it's your accent.'"

I sat at a table, winded. My knife-hand wrist was cramping slightly, and my shoulder had started to hurt again, but I was otherwise no different. I laid my head against the table, pressing my forehead to the cool wood. The others would be in soon with drinks. Appa sat across from me. I picked my head up off the wood.

"Give it to me straight," I said.

"Nothing to give, Jack Jr.," he said, smiling, "you were perfect. All of it. I knew you would be, of course. Zeno, Zeno, come here—"

He took one of each of our hands and squeezed them.

"Perfect," he repeated. "It was perfect."

The door opened, as if on cue. Juno hauled a shopping bag of wine bottles onto the table.

I stood.

"Appa, what is this?"

"We're celebrating, aren't we? First dinner solo, we drink. That's the deal."

Juno had hooked his phone to the speakers and was playing loud, drummy music over our voices. I was poured a glass of wine, then another. James had taken a seat at the bar with a stack of papers that he was matching with today's receipts.

"Boooo," Umma said loudly in his direction, "booooo. Come on, everybody, say it with me. . . ."

I checked my phone. Emil had texted me an hour ago: *Going ok? Just finished. Went well :)*

For the first time that night, there was a knock on the glass outside; the sound rapped the air above the noise of the music. A man none of us had ever seen before was waiting at the door. Noa, closest to him and cradling Sam in her arm, opened her mouth.

"Who's that?"

"Who?"

"Him," Noa said, "he's just—"

She stopped herself.

"There's no way."

"What?" I came forward for another glass of wine. "What are you talking about?"

"There's no way," Noa said again, blushing red. A chair had moved aside; I'd heard the sound of its legs scraping the floor. Umma had gotten to her feet. She waved him in. Appa turned around, spotting him. He ran up, shaking his hand.

"Jo," he said, "thank you for coming, right in here, this way."

Umma had reached them, taking the paper bag from his hands.

"Okay, so—" she stammered. "Family. This is Jo."

"Hi, Jo," Juno said. "Or are you Grandpa?"

"JUNO—"

He made the tour around all of us, saying hello, answering the same few questions that I could hear shouted over the noise and the music while I ate. I was sharing some cake with Noa when Umma brought him around.

"My son," she said, "younger son. Jack Jr."

Jo, a very tall, very nice-smelling Asian man still with all-black hair, shook my hand. "You're the chef, aren't you? I've heard so much about you."

"I really hope that's not true," I said, louder than I thought. The wine had zipped straight up to my head when I stood and was currently heating my face as though I were sitting in front of a fire. "And I'm absolutely not a chef. Yet."

"Dinner was perfect," Umma said, beaming, "Jack Sr. said so. He did a great job." She pointed to James, sitting at the bar. "My other son. He's running up our receipts tonight. Very important."

She took him away. I sat down, buzzing. Noa had put a blanket over Sam's head and was in the process of getting a pair of socks onto his feet.

"Jo," I said quietly, "Jo, like, Joseph?"

"He's Korean," Noa said.

"Where are you getting your information?"

She shrugged. "Don't believe me, then."

Zeno was behind the bar, stacking the last of the dishes. I got up finding her.

"You've had enough tonight," I told her, "come out here, eat something with us."

"I'll let you have your fun," she said, "your whole family's out there."

"What, so you don't think you're family?"

She rolled her eyes so far, hearing me, that I thought she might turn them upside down.

"You were amazing out there," I told her. "You should be proud of yourself." I opened my arms. "Give me a hug, please."

She performed her bit of not wanting to, of being embarrassed by me, but she gave me one, miraculously, and surprised both of us.

"Let's get you out at the bar, starting next week for the dinner service," I said. "I think you can do it."

She didn't seem to want to believe me. "You're not serious."

"I am," I told her. "It's my rule. Wash a thousand dishes, get a promotion."

A pair of headlights flooded the windows for a moment, a mini-SUV making a U-turn and sliding into one of the spots in front of the restaurant. Appa had already run out, speaking animatedly through the car window. He turned away and knocked on the glass, a hollow sound that, for the second time, caught everybody's attention. Appa beckoned Zeno outside.

"My mom," Zeno said. "She's not going to wait for long."

She seemed on the fence about something, fidgeting back and forth.

"Um," she tried, stopping herself. Then she knocked the wind out of my chest, putting her arms around me. "Thanks," she said into my ear, and made for the door.

James had filed away the last of the receipts and was sitting with a glass of water, swirling it around in his hand and gazing up at the lights behind the bar. I wandered up to him.

"How'd we do?"

He noticed me there, rifling through the papers. "Same," he said. "We'll see about this month, but . . . looking good."

"That's a surprise," I said. "Genuinely. Better than last month?"

"It'll be hard," he said. "It's early. We get an uptick over the holidays but with covid, who knows."

He gazed at me pensively.

"You like this stuff, don't you? The cooking, working in the kitchen."

I was surprised by the question. I did my best to shrug. "I've known how to do it since I was a kid, same as you."

"I don't think so." He shook his head, smiling for the first time. "I've been behind the bar for dinner. Insanity. I don't know how Appa does it. Or you."

"You get used to it."

"Maybe you would," he said. "You're . . . something else. Special."

He picked up his water, gazing down at the little space between us for a moment.

"About what I did earlier. When you were talking to me with Cuddy—"

It happened, the third knock. We all turned our heads, a brief lull in the buzz of voices around the cramped little dining room whose windows were beginning to fog up. I squinted out into the dark and saw my last customer, the boyfriend, blond kid with his knuckles against the glass. He shouted something we couldn't hear.

"Juno," I said, "let him in."

The door was unbolted. The blond kid stepped inside, shaking himself.

"I'm really sorry," he said, unnerved by the amount of people staring at him. He spotted me. "Hey, man, I think I left my wallet somewhere in here."

Everybody watched me round the end of the bar, meeting him. "I'm really sorry," he kept saying, me telling him just how okay it was each time. His wallet we found in a shadowed part of the floor under the counter, hidden partially by the legs of the chairs.

"I got all the way home before I realized," he was telling me. "It fell out of my pocket."

"Not a big deal," I said, bringing him to the door. "Get home safe."

"Oh, by the way." He stopped me. "I wanted to tell you: My buddies and I, we love your TikTok. It's actually the reason we picked this place tonight."

He glanced around the room over my shoulder, something I couldn't do at the moment as my blood had gone cold inside me.

"I'm sorry, about what happened to you," he said. "The guys in our apartment, we just put some money into the page you set up."

He stepped out to the curb and was gone. Slowly, I turned around, finding, one by one, the rest of them looking back at me. Juno, pale in the face, was standing behind the bar. Appa was the first to laugh.

"What a weird thing to say," he said. "What's that all about?"

"He said TikTok," Noa said. "Juno, you're on TikTok. What'd he say?"

I'd forgotten how to speak. Umma was watching me, expressionless. The soft smile Appa had tried was half-faded from his face, noticing me.

"Jack Jr.?" he asked. "What is he talking about? What page?"

My lips had gone dry in the time it had taken for their eyes, all of them, to fall on me.

The playlist playing over the complete silence had continued on, echoing loudly around us.

Appa was still waiting for me, frowning.

"He said money." James spoke, turning our heads. He got up from his chair and approached us. "What money is he talking about?"

I was staring, frozen, at Juno, who wouldn't look me in the eye anymore.

"You can't be serious," I told him.

He shook his head, eyes fixed on his shoes.

"Juno—" I choked. "You said you didn't."

"I said . . . ," Juno tried. "I said I *hadn't* made one."

"No," I told him. "You said you would *never* make one."

"What are you two talking about?" Appa said.

"Okay," Juno said quickly, breathing hard. He clawed the air with his hands, trying to make sense. "Okay, it's—I can explain."

He stepped into the center of our little circle, taking a breath.

"We made a"—his voice caught in his throat—"a social media account for the restaurant, a while back. We've been posting videos of the food, and of Uncle JJ cooking, the fish runs, stuff like that. That's what that guy's talking about. He's seen those videos on Tik-Tok, a social media platform."

Nobody moved, not a muscle among us.

"I'm . . ." Appa shook his head quietly. "I'm still confused. What exactly was he talking about? He said he sent money to a page. On the internet."

"Well," Juno said, "there's a page out there, a public one, where anybody who's interested could . . . donate money to us. We could use this for, I don't know, renovations, or maybe to hire some more kitchen staff."

Somewhere, while he spoke, I regained control of my mouth.

"We talked about it," I said, to all of them, quickly. "Juno and I. We were always . . . thinking about it. Making a page. The people who like the videos kept asking how they could show their support."

"But you didn't know he made one." Appa said, and I read from his face that he understood now. "You just said so, right now. Do I have this right? Juno asked a bunch of people on the internet for money to help us? To help the restaurant."

I swallowed a lump in my throat, forcing it down. "We need help."

"You're not the one in this family who's responsible for that."

"Aren't I?" I said. "Didn't I walk out on you twelve years ago? Didn't I eat up all your savings in the hospital sleeping for two years? Do you genuinely think I believe you or I or any of us had good enough insurance to pay for me all this time? Are you ever going to give that story up?"

"That wasn't your fault, Jack Jr."

"I know it wasn't," I said, "I'm just trying to do something to fix things. I'm trying to give something back from everything I took from you. I just—" My voice grew smaller. A buzz had started up in my ears and was beating to the rhythm of my pulse. "I just thought we could help. That's all."

Appa had tightened his jaw but hadn't said anything for a while. James took out his phone.

"Show me."

I didn't move fast enough for him, evidently, since he turned around. "Juno. Show me the page."

"It's just a TikTok thing," Juno said, "it wasn't even anything—"

"Juno," Appa said calmly, "show us the page."

I stood silently, unable to move. The last video, a run-through of the fish market set to an EDM song Juno said was going big this past month, echoed around the room. Appa and James watched it carefully, lights dancing on their faces. James took the phone, swiping through. "Okay, it is, it's little videos of Jack Jr. cooking and the fish market and stuff."

Finally, his eyes went wide.

"Seventy-seven thousand dollars," he said, "there's seventy-seven thousand two hundred eighty-four dollars in here."

Appa took the phone from him. He swiped through, looking it over, keeping his face entirely still and completely unreadable. There passed a moment in which every possible scenario played itself out in my mind, moving so quickly and yet so slowly that it seemed we'd be waiting for him forever. Then, suddenly, he passed the phone back to Juno.

"Delete it," he said, to both of us. "Send all of that money back."

"Appa," I said, "I didn't know it was going to be so much. When I made it—"

"Okay, Jack, enough." He put out his hand, pain stretched across his face for a minute. "There is no reason here for you to keep lying. I know Juno made this for you. I know you're trying to protect him. And now that we all know, I want you to delete it. I'm not accepting money from strangers."

"Jack," Umma said, getting to her feet, "let's talk about this. We all deserve—we all need to talk about this."

He stared at her. "You knew?"

She took a breath. Jo stood awkwardly behind her, holding both of their glasses.

"Yes, I knew," she said. "And I wanted to tell you about it. But I also thought we might be able to talk about this as a family. Which is why I'm asking—"

"As a family," Appa repeated. "Tell me why this doesn't feel like a discussion, Ari. The only reason I know about this now is because some kid walked in and gave away your secret."

"So he did," Umma said. "So it came to be that tonight we're all finding out. What is the problem here, Jack Sr.? This happened in a month. The boys have millions of views on these videos in a *month*. We should've told you, I know. But we're telling you now."

Appa walked a short length toward her, rubbing the back of his neck with one hand. He shook his head. "We're not talking about this anymore. The page is going down. Juno, take it down."

"Jack—"

"I *know* how much money it is," Appa said loudly, "I know, Ari. You think I can't see what we could do with that kind of money? Do you think I'm doing what I *want* to do here?" He snatched the phone out of Juno's hands. "These videos, they're about the fact that Jack Jr. was in the hospital for two years. There are thousands of comments in here, 'get well soon,' 'praying for you.' They think we're charity, Ari. This restaurant is not a charity. Our lives are not a charity."

"We understand that," Umma said.

"When did—" Appa lost track of himself momentarily. "I—when did we start keeping things from each other like this? You and James are partners in this business now, Jack Jr. This is your restaurant. How are we supposed to get anywhere if you go around keeping things like this from us?"

"You mean a secret," Umma said, staring at him. "Are you talking about a secret?"

Appa's face lost a little color when he looked at her. He raised a hand. "Don't put this on me."

"This is your burden," Umma said. "You don't want to keep secrets? Tell him."

He was breathing hard, appearing, then, to notice it himself. He set James's phone down on the table beside him and sat. James picked up the phone and handed it back to Juno.

"Delete it. Now."

Juno moved his tongue, trying to wet his mouth. "I . . . I want to—I mean, H-Man—"

"Juno," James said forcefully, "get rid of this fucking nonsense, right now."

Juno turned his head, facing him. I could read it on his face, what he was about to do.

"Juno—" James began again.

"Fucking nonsense." Juno nodded, repeating him. "That's what I am to you, fucking nonsense, Dad. How about I say it again. This is just some FUCKING nonsense."

James brought his hand down like a clamp on Juno's shoulder, but he threw it off. Sam, in Noa's arms, gave a fretful cry, reacting to the noise.

"You don't understand anything," he said, his voice shaking. "You don't care about me."

"Juno." Noa was trying to stand, lopsided, with the baby in her arms. "Juno, please, calm down."

"He doesn't care about me, Mom!" Juno shouted. "I don't exist to him! He's decided my life for me and doesn't hear when I tell him that I want control over my own fucking life—"

"We are trying to talk to you," Noa said, "we are here, and listening, and we need you to take some breaths and calm down."

"I have an idea," Juno said, talking over her, "since we're getting some things off our chest tonight."

He stepped within a foot of James's face.

"I'm not working at the restaurant anymore. I'm going to college.

I'm going to take out loans and pay for it myself and go wherever I want to go and study whatever I want to study, and if you say anything to me about it, I will never come home again."

James set his face like stone as Noa and Umma started speaking at the same time. Appa was still sitting between them, staring down at his feet. Noise circled us like birds. Juno had taken up his phone and gotten his coat off the back of a chair. Umma was in the middle, trying to stop him. James was staring at the spot where Juno had just been. After a while, he turned his eyes to me. He didn't speak for a while, over the noise. Then, at last, he opened his mouth.

"Was this you?"

"What?" I said, anchored in place by the look he gave me. "What do you mean, was this me?"

"Did you tell him to say this to us?" James stepped closer to me. Everybody had quieted around us. Umma got between us, tugging at James's arm.

"James, enough."

"Never mind," James said, nodding his head. "Who else could it be? You're with him every day, you talk to him about all the things you did the second you left here and all of us behind. Of course it was you."

"You don't know what you're talking about."

"Don't I?" James said. "Don't I know that the second you come back here he wants nothing to do with any of us, the restaurant, anything?"

"Did you listen to a word he said to you just now?" I said, stepping closer. "He's wanted to go to college this whole time. You just didn't hear him."

"Sure," James said, "I don't hear him, not like you."

I tried to laugh, turning away. "Tell me more about that. Vent for me. You deserve it. You look like you need it."

"You think you know what goes on in this family?" James had rounded on me. "You think you have any idea the kinds of things we've been through ever since you left? I'm not talking about your coma. I'm talking about the day you moved out of town. I'm talking about the way Appa and I broke our fucking fingers building this place up for ten years. You think you know what he wants just because you make a handful of stupid fucking videos on his phone—"

"James," Appa said, standing.

"I'm not going to hear you telling me what to do with my own family," James said. "He spends too much fucking time with you, anyway. You're going to turn him into something he's not."

Appa had placed his hands on each of our chests, and with Umma's help, he forced us apart. He was breathing hard. Finally, he spoke.

"Enough," he said, "I've had enough."

He backed away. James was staring at the floor. I realized, then, that my fists were clenched. On account of the adrenaline, maybe. Or the prospect of finding James close enough to my face to spit into my shirt when he talked. Or maybe it was what he'd said before Appa had pulled us apart. I knew what he meant. The same thing I knew he meant when I told him the first time almost fifteen years ago. The realization on his part that I had, overnight, changed into something he couldn't understand, and while he would never tell me to my face, he would spend the rest of our lives trying and failing to see me as anything but.

I didn't say anything when James turned away from me and picked up his coat. Nor when I heard the slam of his chair to the floor, the intake of air around me, and realized I'd shoved him with my arms out and sent him crashing forward. Nor when his chest bounded over the counter and his shoulder slammed, with the force of a cannonball, into the glass partition of the sushi bar that housed the day's cuts. Nor when the glass shattered, sending shards in all directions around us and over him as he slumped to the ground, a cut opening on his forehead, and raised his eyes up to stare, for the first time in our entire lives, frightened of me. Nor when it dawned on my conscious brain that I had just shoved James headfirst into the sushi bar that our father had built with his bare hands thirty years ago, and that no amount of money, or time, or conversation, was going to change the fact that I'd shoved him, not just to retaliate for something stupid he'd done, but to hurt him, and to hurt him badly.

We were like this for the longest time, each of us looking at the other, until Sam started to cry. His gulps of air were heavy and panicked, sounding louder and louder, growing. I blinked, slightly, becoming aware. I turned around. Umma was crying, her hands up at her mouth. All of the color had fallen away from Juno's face. I saw Appa last, hands fallen limp at his sides.

There was nothing I could do. Nothing came to my mind, no words, barely any thoughts. I could only wait for Appa to do something.

Which he did. Which I saw, when he bent down and picked his coat up off the ground.

"Appa," I said. He didn't answer me. I stepped closer. "Appa."

"Do"—Appa turned around, a flare of anger like I'd never seen in my life coloring his face—"*not.*"

He looked around at them all. I noticed now there were tears in his eyes.

"I'm so tired," he said, breathless, then again, "I'm so tired."

He walked out of the restaurant and into the cold outside. Umma, watching it all, lowered her hands from her mouth. Then she, too, got her coat; met Jo, who looked how somebody wrapping things up with a group of people they'll never meet again would look, near the door; and left. Noa, holding Sam with one arm, followed. The whole group of them, filing out of the restaurant, leaving us there, disappearing down the curb of the street, starting their cars. James and I listened to the sounds of the engines faltering, coming to life, the crunch of the wheels on the asphalt as they pulled away and down the street, making no more sound as they passed over the hill and out.

I could only watch blurry shapes in the frosted window, listening.

I turned around and saw him, lying there with glass all over his chest. I felt a second pass, then another. I stepped over the shards on the ground and put out my hand. James considered me, a red rivulet working its way into his eyebrow, and took my hand. I pulled him up, standing clear of the glass that fell off him. For the longest time, we turned our heads, surveying the mess. Then, like things had come to a natural end, feeling that we had finished whatever we were doing, he went into the kitchen and brought out the dustpan and broom, and I cleared the nearest tables and chairs from the floor. The produce left under the glass wasn't much, things I hadn't yet gotten to packing away. I put on rubber gloves and gathered the biggest pieces of glass while he swept, clearing the wooden board and throwing the remains into the trash. We worked deliberately, carefully, hearing each other and the uncommon passing of a single car down the street, on its way home. When we were done, James took the trash out back and helped me move the tables back into place. We kicked up our feet, searching for anything we might have missed on the soles of our shoes. It had taken a half hour. Without anything left to clean, we'd come back to the difficult silence. The cut on his forehead was shallow and had already stopped bleeding. He found an old cloth in the kitchen, wet it under the sink, and dabbed at his head until the wound was clean. I watched him do it, facing the little window to the kitchen, where he could spot a reflection of his face. He was finished. He put his head down, resting his chin on his chest.

"James."

"I—"

We spoke at the same time.

"I shouldn't have said that."

"I shouldn't have—" I hesitated. "Assaulted you? I guess?"

We could agree on something, for once. He moved his head up and down in a loose nod. There were bottles of wine left on the bar. He picked one up, motioning for me. I brought over a glass, and he poured. I was about to drink when I stopped myself.

"Is that hard for you?" I asked him.

"What?"

"Watching us drink," I said.

He didn't seem to know how to answer a question like that. "I guess not," he said after a while. "Staying sober's not so hard anymore, with the baby. The doctor says I'm doing all the right things."

"We could stop drinking around you, if it was hard for you."

He seemed to consider it. It was like he'd never even thought of something like that before.

"No," he said shortly. I waited a moment, then drained my glass. He took it from me, placing it far down the bar, and he hitched himself up on one of the bar stools. I climbed up next to him, losing my balance, and he steadied my arm with one hand. We saw the mess of the open glass hood; the frost that typically grew over it as the night progressed had melted to droplets in the time it had taken for us to clean around it.

"He's so angry," James said suddenly. "Juno."

"You heard him. He thinks you don't listen to him."

"He doesn't know anything, why should I listen to him?"

"Doesn't mean he can't still teach you something," I said.

"You sound like Umma," James said.

"Maybe I do."

"He acts like I'll chain him up in the basement for trying to leave," James said. "I can't stop him. He knows he can do whatever he wants to do."

"You've told him this?"

James opened and closed his hands out in front of him. "All I did was hope he would stay," he said. "There's so much out there, he's young. There's time for everything he wants to do. . . . I just hoped."

"He can read a lot more into you than you think," I said. "He's practically an adult. A smart one. He wants to leave but he also doesn't want to disappoint you."

James made a noise with his mouth, a kind of pop between his lips. It was a sound you made when you didn't have anything else to defend the fact that you were wrong and someone else was right. I'd never seen him do that before, and especially not to me.

"That wasn't fair," James said. "When I said you put those thoughts in him. I know you didn't. He looks up to you. He wants to be like you. It's not your fault."

It felt nice, hearing it, but not in the way I'd expected it to. It was strange. I didn't like James being so honest. He put his hands through his hair, closing his eyes.

"I'm trying, and trying, and trying. It feels like I've failed every step of the way. I can't stop fucking him up."

"You were twenty. Barely."

"That too," James said. "My fault, completely. I couldn't have told you where I even thought I was that night. Worst of all, it makes me sad, knowing I think like this. What kind of fucking person says they regret having their own kid?"

He tapped his fingers on a nearby wineglass.

"I used to drink whenever I started thinking like this."

Perhaps the worst thing, I'd say, was seeing the side of his head from this angle and noticing so many gray hairs climbing their way up. My brother, with gray hair. It was coming for me next, if it had come for him so quickly.

"Why don't you talk to anybody?" I asked him.

"Like you?"

I was quiet for a second.

"Yeah," I said, "like me. I'm here now. I can listen."

"I did talk to you," James said. I thought I saw him smile for the briefest second. "In the hospital. Did you hear any of that?"

"Not a word."

"I suppose you could be lying," James said, "and I'd never know."

He leaned back in his chair.

"I started coming a few months in, just to be with you, watch you sleep. First six months, you looked like shit. Hair shaved off, stitches, bruises from the stitches, scars from the bruises from the stitches, everything. But it'd be nice, talking to you like that. I'd think about what you'd say, if you were awake, and I'd respond. Whole hours. It's stupid."

It was, and it wasn't. He'd put his hand out on the bar, and I wondered briefly if he wanted me to hold it and was asking in his own way. He was staring at it, like he was talking to the space between us.

"I was never close with you," he said, "I know. But you left, and it was like you'd gone in the middle of the night and hadn't said goodbye. And you were living this life out there, over the river, and you didn't want us, any of us, to be a part of it."

I was nodding slowly. He coughed into his elbow.

"I talked to you about that, too," he said.

"What did I say?"

"You said," James began quietly, "that I felt that way because it was true. And that nobody in this family is ready to have that conversation." He glanced at me. "Somewhere in the right area?"

I propped myself up on my elbows, hanging my head, massaging the back of my neck. "I might have been a little more polite to you, in person," I said.

"Would you have, really?" James smirked at me.

"I would've," I said.

"Bullshit."

We sat there another minute, blinking our tired eyes. It was near midnight now.

"Why didn't you tell us about the videos he was posting?" he asked me.

"Hadn't quite gotten to the whole 'reason' part yet," I said. "Maybe I thought something would come along and answer that question for me. And all I had to do was keep quiet."

"We're certainly going to need it now." He gestured to the broken bar.

"I'll fix it. It's my place now, right?"

"You're going to fire me? Is that it? Do you even know where our bills are?"

"Sure I do, they're with you."

He laughed, a sound that cut the air between us. It was honestly the first time I'd heard him laugh in ten years, and I don't know which was sadder, the idea that he hadn't laughed in all that time or that I just wasn't around to hear it.

"Ren," I said carefully. "Did you like him?"

James popped his lips a couple times, thinking. "Weird circumstances, meeting him," he said, "but I thought he loved you. He cared about you. What else is there?"

He gestured to the wine, and I shook my head. The thought had only just arrived, fully formed, into my mind, and I was speaking before it could become any more real and scare me too badly to ask.

"I need you to do something for me," I said.

I KNOCKED.

My last thought, before I heard footsteps, followed by the tinkle of the chain lock, and the whoosh of air as the door swung inward, was that he had moved all of his stuff out of the apartment we shared at some point, after his hope had been lost, maybe even after he'd realized that I wasn't going to wake up. I tried to imagine doing a thing like that, combing over memories, little items we'd bought together, fishing his clothes out of the closet that had slowly congealed over the years and had become just one closet of clothes for two people instead of the other way around. I saw his face.

He held the door open just six inches, shielding the rest of the darkened hallway beyond from me. He'd cut his hair short, which I'd never liked but admitted, now that he was in his thirties, looked good on him. His eyes, I remembered.

"Um—" My throat caught on the words I'd prepared, crushing them inside me. I had intended to eviscerate him. Take some of the anger that had been boiling inside me this entire night and pass it on to him just so that I might get some rest. But it had taken one look at his face for the words to melt away like sugar in the rain. I went with my backup: "Hi."

Ren opened the door farther, revealing the rest of the hallway and a slice of a living room with a view of some lights, maybe even trees. He looked tired, unrelated to the fact that it was after midnight. He took in his breath, slowly, and let it out.

"Hey, Jack Jr."

He glanced behind him briefly.

"I'm sorry it's late," I found myself saying, being too polite. There was a voice in my head screaming about all that had gone wrong before I'd gotten to his door but I wasn't able to listen very hard anymore.

"No, no." He widened his eyes. "No, it's fine. Please, come in."

He stepped aside. I made my way into the hall, taking off my shoes, and stacked them by a neat little rack of boots and loafers and a pair of umbrellas leaned against the wall. He led me into his living room, which was wide and open, stacked with books on one wall, a TV. He went about turning on the lights, throwing more shadows across the wall. He wore a pair of shorts that I recognized, green ones that were fraying at the seams, their waistband torn out after he'd started to gain some weight. The moles that covered his arms, crept up his back and neck, dotted his face. There was a time when I knew every single one. I still probably did.

"Something to drink?"

"I'm okay."

He took stock of the room, evidently trying to find something else to do rather than sit down, and, finding nothing, finally sat. I followed suit. A stretched view of the sky expanded behind him, underneath it the park.

"It's a really nice place," I said.

"Thank you," he told me. "It's been in David's family for fifty years. His grandmother's. The rent's controlled, so we just . . ."

"David." I nodded. "Your . . ."

I broke off.

"He's away," Ren told me. "He works on the road this time of the year."

I let out my breath. "Okay."

This view of the city was so different from that of the third-floor walkup we'd lived in on Seventy-second. Not of water, of New Jersey, but of tall buildings, metropolitan lives.

"What do you . . . ," Ren started. "I mean, what are you . . ."

He frowned, scratching the back of his head. He loosened his shoulders.

"What can I do for you?"

I dug my hands into my lap, trying to find somewhere to put them. It was probably what killed me the most, realizing how uncomfortable he'd gotten around me. Which was fair, I could have reminded myself. We hadn't seen each other in two years, not literally. Somewhere, inside me, I just wanted to feel like shit about it, which is what I did, and couldn't stop myself anymore.

"I called," I said. "A couple months ago."

He opened, then closed, his mouth.

"I know," he said. After another moment, he took in a shaky breath. "I know. I'm sorry. I—"

He gave up for a moment.

"I know what you want me to say," he said. "That I was telling you I didn't want to hear from you anymore."

My face had grown hot while he was speaking. "Weren't you? Telling me to fuck off, get lost, et cetera. That's what I got from you, because you didn't tell me anything else."

I felt better, saying that, though the look of hurt that registered on his face, cut me up almost as badly as if I'd punched him in the gut.

"I panicked," he said. "Your mom called that morning and left a message. I thought all day that I'd call, or come see you. And then I heard your voice and I just . . ."

Ren had never been good at fighting. It was one of the things I enjoyed the least about being with him, constantly feeling like a bully for making him cry, when more often than not he was only crying because he couldn't figure out how to organize his thoughts into words.

"I didn't know what I was doing," he said, "I wasn't ready. I know you're mad."

"I'm not," I said. I caught myself. "No, I am. Beyond words. I'm angrier than I thought possible, looking at you, and at the same time I'm . . . sorry, and hurt, and afraid. Maybe the more accurate thing to say is, I don't know what I am. Or I didn't know until now."

"So . . . ," he started. "What are you, then?"

I thought about it for a long time, thinking I'd come here with an answer, finding that I hadn't.

"I guess I missed you," I said, "I guess I just wanted to see your face. Know how you're doing."

Ren, who'd been pale from the moment he'd opened the door to me, smiled a little to himself. "I'm okay," he said, "teaching, still. David . . . he works in banking."

"Is he nice?" I asked him.

"He is," Ren said slowly. "I've been watching your videos, you know. The Fish Daddy stuff."

"You have," I sighed. "That's not great."

"They're really good," Ren told me, "I didn't know you could cook like that."

"I didn't either," I said. "Muscle memory, you know, that kind of thing. Stuff my dad taught me when I was a kid."

"You work at Joja full-time now."

I lowered my head. "Yeah, my dad retired recently. Tonight. You're looking at the new big guy."

Ren smiled. "Impressive."

He glanced down at his hands.

"I know what you think of me," he said. "You know, leaving. You were asleep. You were stable. And I left."

I didn't like the blame he was putting on himself.

"You stayed longer than anybody could have hoped for," I said.

He turned his head away, pinpointing his focus on a corner of the room. I sat for a long time, across the room from him.

"I'm not here to do that to you," I told him, finally. "I'm not blaming you, I'm not saying you should've done anything different. I can't. If I think that way, I'm going to die."

I shrugged.

"I don't know why time has to be such a mindfuck like this," I said. "I see you, I look at you, and it feels like—"

I stopped talking. He nodded again.

"What are we supposed to do now?" he asked, barely above a whisper. He opened his palm, facing up on his lap; I wondered what he had done with the ring I'd bought him, knowing that I'd never ask him.

"I guess I came here," I said slowly, "to see if you knew something I didn't, about the day it happened."

He frowned at me.

"The cottage," he finished for me.

He wiped his eyes with his sleeve.

"I've been over it a thousand times," he said. "I've thought it all over, trying to see what I missed."

"Do you know what happened?"

He took in a breath.

"It was the second day," he said. "The owners hadn't put any milk in the fridge. You said you'd go down and get some for us, down the freeway to the town a couple miles south. You—"

He stopped.

"You don't remember?"

I shook my head.

"You just got your keys, you said you'd be back. I heard you in the car, driving down to the road over the gravel. It made that sound, you know, the tires over it. It was an hour. I called you, you didn't answer. I was just thinking of calling again when the police showed up."

He closed his eyes.

"Three or four cars all in the driveway, the lights coming through the windows. I remembered thinking, why are there so many of them? They asked me where I saw you last. I said you'd gone down the freeway, along the river, that was the only way back into town. They already knew."

He shrugged, the saddest thing I'd ever seen him do, not wanting to remember it but remembering it anyway because I'd asked him to.

"They said somebody saw your car in the river, they'd towed it out. You were being put in a helicopter, they were telling me, you were injured so bad that the EMTs thought you were already dead."

He looked down at his hands. We both saw that he'd clenched them shut on the seat cushion.

"You know, those minutes where you're connecting the dots, and it seems so improbable that you want to laugh, and then punish yourself for even thinking something so horrible," he said. "And you're telling yourself the whole time, it's not what you think. It's not what you think. They have the wrong guy. You're stopped in traffic somewhere and this will just be a funny and morbid joke we tell ourselves years from now. Stop being an idiot."

He sighed.

"I don't know what happened," he said. "I've been over it with cops, the doctors, your family. They couldn't find anything, no other cars or marks on the road, no rocks coming off the cliff face, no animals. You just went over. I just . . . I don't know."

He was nervous, saying it. There was nothing I could do. We were both seated, leaned forward, backs hurting. What do you do when you hear something like that?

"So I just . . ." I trailed off. "You mean I just—"

"Do you remember anything?"

"No," I said, "I . . . I've tried, I've thought it over every night for the past three months. I . . . I've never—"

I'd run out of breath. We were quiet for the longest time, hearing each other breathe. Somewhere, out in the distance, a car horn sounded angrily over the hushed quiet. We had come to the realization, almost at the same exact time, that whatever we said would never fill the gap the way we wanted it to. He pressed his lips together, blinking, and I saw that his eyes were wet. I didn't know if I would have wanted to see him, while it happened. If I wanted to know the person he'd become when it was finally clear that what we had was gone, that I wasn't going to wake up. I didn't want to imagine the kind of agony that must have been, drawn out over days and days, weeks turning into months. His was not a tight, quick wound that hurt the most in the first few seconds. I bet it was slow. I bet it was like putting your hand in a pot of cold water and turning on the stove.

"I wish I had more to tell you," Ren said finally. He leaned back, exhausted, against the cushions. He wiped his face again, his breath coming in short little bursts.

And it was a moment in which it hit me, finally, that the thing I was looking for was something I didn't actually want to find. What was it? I saw some boulders falling down the rock face and swerved to miss them? My shoe jammed the accelerator to the floor mat? Or worse, that I had meant to do it all along and wasn't letting myself remember. And still, what was the point? It wouldn't change what happened. Regardless of how, I'd still be here, watching somebody I loved for nearly ten years bring himself to tears just by thinking about me. The brief, flightless anger that had flared inside me was gone when my eyes settled on his face. Ren loved me. I loved him. We happened to be two people for whom time had sped too far ahead for either of us to catch up. Which was to say, there was nothing left for either of us, and what's more, we were going to have to be okay without each other. Things change. They really do.

He looked uneasily at me, afraid.

"Are you mad?"

I found myself standing up, coming over to him, and, without thinking about it, getting on my knees to look at him squarely.

"No," I said. "I've been trying something out where I care a little bit less about how I feel and a little more about how other people feel. It's hard. But it feels right."

I tried to think of something to say. Ren made little sniffing sounds, his head bowed. I glanced over his shoulder and caught sight of the shoe rack again, arranged neatly by the door. I'd noticed it on my way in. I could see the missing screw on its left side. The little bag of screws had been one piece short when we'd built it. I said it without thinking.

"That's my shoe rack."

He looked up at me.

I nodded my head toward it. "The one we built. Right?"

He turned to look at it, wiping his nose with his sleeve, quiet. Then he laughed. Small and subtle, but unmistakable; I'd made Ren laugh.

"I think it is," he managed to choke out.

"That is . . . fucked up," I told him. "You took my shoe rack? You have, like, two pairs of shoes, what on earth do you need a shoe rack for? What's the big idea here?"

He was shaking his head while heavy tears rolled down his face and soaked the collar of his shirt.

"I really don't know," he said, smiling, then again, "I just don't know."

"Well I just want you to know," I said, hearing my voice break, "that's what I really came here for. I want my stuff back. What else are you hiding from me?"

We said more, other dumb things, while our eyes watered, trying to fill the space. There would be many more nights like this, feeling lost, like nothing I had ever done really mattered, I was sure. Even if I'd already had my fair share. But it felt good to make him laugh. It felt good to do that for him, standing in place of what we were really saying, that he was sorry and that I was too. It was a beautiful, lucky place to be, to know someone as well as you possibly could, to know what to do to make them better. And for now, in the universe of things we had left to say, this would have to be enough.

I TAPPED MY KNUCKLES AGAINST the window on James's side of the van, shaking him awake. He unlocked the doors and I crossed to my side, climbing in. We didn't speak for a while. He'd been silent, driving me into the city, to the front of this old little building on the East Side just because I'd asked him to. I was grateful and hoping that he knew I was without my needing to tell him.

"Do you want to talk about it?" he asked me quietly.

"No," I said after a while, meaning it. James didn't argue with me, sitting back against his seat.

"James," I said after a while.

"Yeah."

"When we were all in the restaurant," I said, "and Umma said that thing to Appa about keeping secrets. She told him to tell me something."

James kept his eyes on the windshield. I turned my head, facing him.

"What was she talking about?"

He didn't answer for the longest time. So long, and after so much that had happened already, that I would've probably appreciated his telling me not to think about it anymore. Then he sighed.

"Appa didn't tell you that he got covid, a few months after your accident," he said softly. "It was early, February something. Nobody knew what it was, and nobody knew how to treat it. The restaurant was closed for a month, before everything else locked down. That's why we lost so much business. And the hospital bills. It's why we're scrambling, almost a year and a half later. Fall behind once, and you just . . . you know. He was . . ."

He swallowed uncomfortably.

"He was intubated," he breathed out. "For two weeks. They told us less than five percent were surviving at that stage. They told us to say goodbye to him. We had to do it through FaceTime."

My blood was beating fast through to my fingertips. James found enough energy to smile sadly.

"He was actually in the same hospital as you, that month," he said. "One floor down. From the parking lot, you could see his room and yours, right next to each other."

I blinked, unable to move my mouth. The words were coming in slow motion to me, unfurling themselves.

"Why didn't anybody tell me?"

"He asked us not to," James said, "he begged us. He said you had enough to worry about. He said it was done, he was fine—"

"James."

He turned his head slowly to me.

"He is. Fine," he repeated himself.

"That's lying," I told him. "You understand that's lying, don't you? All of you?"

It was too dark and too late in the night to do much more. A siren had sounded down the street. James took in a breath and released it.

"Yeah."

I thought of a hundred things I could say, each fizzling out as soon as it came up in my mind. Instead, I lay back against the seat. Thinking, among other things, about the rotten cut of salmon I'd found in the bar that day, the day Cuddy and I had kissed for the first time. The smell that hit me. People were losing their sense of taste and smell, weren't they? I'd read that so many times. The mackerel and ponzu that Appa had made me taste for him. How much more had he tried to hide from me? I didn't say anything else, just reclined there, tugging at the levers under my seat to bring myself back farther. After a while, James did the same. We closed our eyes.

MY BREATH UNFURLED AS VAPOR in front of me when I woke. I raised myself into a sitting position, rubbing my face. There was frost on the windshield, illuminating blue light all around us from the morning. James was snoring next to me. I nudged him awake. He made a noise, choking, and raised his head up.

"I meant to drive us back after a minute," he said.

"It's not a big deal."

We knocked some feeling into our feet. James started the engine. A line of cars had passed us, back to back, sounding horns. It was rush hour, evidently. Ahead, the intersection swarmed with lights.

"We're going to be here forever," James said. "Did Appa call you?"

"No . . ." I dug into my pants for my phone. With a single-digit battery charge, it crackled to life. I saw it. Six missed calls. The name at the top: Emil. I blinked at it, clicking through them: eight in the morning, eight-fifteen, eight-seventeen. I went cold.

"Oh my God."

"What?"

"Oh my fucking—" I scrambled with my seatbelt, freeing myself. "Oh shit, shit, shit *shit*—"

"Tell me what's going on—"

"Emil has an interview"—I threw open my door—"at the playhouse. The theater. The thing. I told him I'd be there. I need to get down there."

"I'll drive you—"

"It's packed, it's going to be packed all the way down, I have to run—"

I didn't have time to say more. My phone started chiming an alarm. *Nine a.m. West Village.* I'd set it the night before. I was forty blocks away. I skidded to a stop on the sidewalk, my pulse pumping hard into my neck, bolted over the crosswalk and down Broadway. I was heaving breaths within a block or two, weaving in and out of crowds, losing my step on icy parts of the pavement. Streetlights passed above me as I ran. I found a bike lane on Tenth and continued down, pumping my arms and legs.

"Fuck fuck fuck fuck—"

It had become agony, the cold, the passing street signs, skimming down from the sixties to the fifties and farther down. He'd given me the address, which I was pinpointing generally, based on how far south I was. I ran, not stopping, feeling my lungs tearing apart inside me. Down to the twenties, the teens. I found the river on the west side and kept going down. Twenty minutes, twenty-five minutes. I was close. I took out my phone, finding the block. I ran farther, stopping when my head started to swim, gasping for breath on the sidewalk, continuing.

I came across the block, tucked away past Jane Street. A narrow path down the street to the building, the only one there that looked like a theater, signage up on the walls. I whirled around, wheezing, searching for his face. I took out my phone. Was he inside? I swore, turning around, spotting the bus stop on the edge of the street, just before the intersection. I squinted, stepping closer. Emil was sitting on the end of the bench, staring at his folder crumpled in his hands. He barely noticed when I called his name, flitting his eyes. He only saw me when I put my hand on his shoulder.

"Emil." I was gasping. "Emil, I'm sorry, I'm here, I'm so sorry. You finished it already? How'd it go?"

He considered me, shivering slightly, then got to his feet. I didn't like the look on his face, the look he was giving me.

"I didn't go in," he said.

"What? Why?"

He was shaking his head, and I saw how pale he was.

"You were right here," I said. "Were you late? They wouldn't have cared."

"I came an hour early, Jack Jr.," he said. "I sat here, I called you ten times . . ."

He trailed off. I searched him, trying to understand.

"Why didn't you go in?"

"*I freaked out,*" Emil said loudly, turning heads, "I freaked out, okay? Are you happy? I came all the way here and I fucking froze. I couldn't breathe, so I called you, and you wouldn't pick up. I didn't know where you were."

"I know," I said, "I'm sorry. There was—we just—"

"I didn't want to do this." He crushed his folder tighter in his fist, turning around. "I didn't want to do this, I wasn't ready and you made me, you forced me to apply to this thing and that and you wouldn't let me say no—"

"Emil, I'm sorry—"

"I wasn't fucking ready for this," Emil said, breathing hard, "I wasn't ready and you made me do it anyway—"

He caught his breath. Sweat had bloomed under the arms of the suit jacket he wore. He'd been shivering.

"I know you're mad," I said shakily. "I shouldn't have done this to you. I just—we had this huge fight in the restaurant and I couldn't call you because—"

"What are you even doing here?" Emil said. "Why did you run?"

"I ran here from—" I paused. "Ren's apartment."

Emil stared at me. "Ren's apartment," he repeated.

"James drove me to go see him last night after we closed," I panted, needing to tell him more but unable to while my lungs were still catching up, "and we fell asleep in the van. James and I. And I woke up and realized what time it was, so I ran. Here."

And I saw on his face, just then, how badly I'd hurt him. He opened his mouth several times, closing it each time.

"You went to see Ren," he said slowly.

"I can explain all of this if you just—"

He pulled his arm away from my hand when I reached for it. He was staring at me with a hardness in his eyes that I'd never seen before.

"Emil, it was nothing," I said.

He didn't respond, shaking his head silently.

"Emil—"

"Just—" He put up his hand, never taking his eyes off me.

After a while, he straightened up.

"I'm going home," he said quietly.

"Emil—" I jumped around the curb, stepping in front of him. "Please, just listen to me."

"I can't."

"I can explain—"

"Jack." His voice broke, a noise that sounded like a yelp, like I'd punched him in the gut. "*Stop.*"

He stepped away from me, rubbing his hands in his hair, raking his fingers across. The cold had turned his cheeks red. He tried several times to say something, unable to come up with the right words. Finally, he spoke.

"I'm not ready for this," he said. "You're not ready."

I felt the inside of me turn to churning water. Not only because he had said something I had thought many times would make me crumble away if I heard it, but also because I knew that he was right.

"What do you mean?"

"This . . . ," Emil said. "This was too soon. I confused you. I didn't mean to. I—"

He forced himself to take another breath. He turned his face away from me, stepping off the curb. "I can't anymore. I'm sorry."

He passed me, continuing down the block toward the intersection.

"Emil."

I found myself running after him, finding his arm.

"Emil," I said, hating myself, hating the wetness in my eyes, hating everything about the way I was holding on to him, the way he couldn't even look at me anymore. "Please don't. Please. I can't lose any more time."

I don't remember if I saw his face when he pulled away from me and stumbled over to the curb, where a growling city bus opened its doors and let him on, smoothly, perfectly, as though it had been waiting for him the entire time. Carrying him away, leaving frozen smoke on the air. I don't even remember if he said anything else to me. Maybe I just didn't hear it over the noise.

THE HOUSE LOOKED QUIET WHEN I let myself in through the backyard fence. My feet were aching, and my fingers had frozen themselves inside the sleeves of my coat, which I had pulled down over my hands. It was near noon, the amount of time it had taken for me to walk the length of Manhattan and over the bridge into Fort Lee, and finally down the familiar street and up the hill to the house. The sliding door to Lou's side of the duplex was closed. It seemed too cold for her parents today, too much wind. I was proven wrong when a figure appeared there, behind the glass. Lou slid open the doors and stepped outside in her slippers, seeing me.

"What happened to you?"

I'd stopped shivering suspended somewhere above the Hudson. I shrugged. "Went out for a walk."

"You look terrible."

"Didn't notice. No mirrors out there."

She batted her hand at me, perching herself on one of her lawn chairs.

"What are you doing out here, Lou ajummah?"

"I like cold days," she said, "clears the lungs."

I stepped closer, coming to a halt just next to the second lawn chair. She nodded toward it, and I sat.

"Could I ask you a question, Lou ajummah?"

"Ask me anything you want."

I pulled my arms close into my chest. "Are you afraid to lose your parents?"

She squinted at me quizzically. "What kind of question is that?"

"Just wondering," I said. "I've always been afraid of it. I'm worried I'll never get over it."

She had narrowed her eyes at me but hadn't yet told me to fuck off, which was good. I hoped she could understand what I was really asking, which was, will it ever be easier to forgive family for the things they do? Do the lines become clear between the black and the white? And if so, on what side do we come up in the end? Then again, I didn't have a father like Lou's. Maybe I was being silly.

"You're young," she said. "You're worried you don't have enough time. Trust me. You have enough time. Get to my age, or their age."

"So, you're not?"

"Oh, no." She looked out over the bright day in front of us. "I am still afraid. It's a different kind of fear. I think: Have I done all I can? Is there more I could have given? Family is give and take: When you're born, you take, and when you get older, you give, more and more, to everybody that gave to you. To them."

She wanted me to tell Umma how much she liked the fish jeon, which I told her I'd relay. I climbed the stairs to the porch, slid the door open. Without the glare, I saw Appa clearly in the kitchen, sleeping with his head down on the kitchen table. He jumped at the noise the door made against the rails, seeing me. I stopped in the doorway, unsure for a moment, then continued inside. The warm air felt like needles on my face. I took a long time to sit, willing my frozen knees to bend.

There had been choppy water under the bridge while I walked across, some sheets of ice floating near the top, a few birds. There shouldn't have been birds, surely, not this late in the fall. I'd found myself watching them the entire way across the water. Appa had noticed, I was sure, that my ears were blue and that a crust of frost had carried over onto my clothes from where it had blown off the bridge in big swarms of flurries.

Finally he said, "You're going to get sick."

I licked my lips slowly, rubbing the underside of my tongue over the cracked skin. I just put my hand up, making an "okay" sign with my thumb and finger.

We sat, apart from each other, saying nothing for the longest time. Eventually I thought to empty out my pockets, stacking my phone, wallet, and keys on the table between us.

"I've been up all night," Appa said.

"I'm sorry," I said, "I took a trip with James."

He frowned at me. I glanced at the clock, now reading noon.

"Long story."

Appa got up, retreating to the kitchen. I heard him put on a pot of water and waited, along with him, for it to boil. A while later, he handed me a mug, steeping an herbal tea inside. I drank half of it without flinching. We watched each other.

"I know you got sick," I said. "I know they said you were going to die."

Appa didn't do anything but nod slightly.

"Were you afraid?" I asked him.

"Of what?"

"Of dying," I said. "When they came in and told you they were going to put a tube in. Were you afraid to die?"

Appa had poured himself a tea along with mine. He turned the cup around in his hands, once, then again.

"Yes."

He sighed.

"I was afraid you'd never see me again."

We drank.

"Are you . . . ," I tried. "I mean . . . are you feeling—"

He smiled at me. "Sometimes you look at me like you expect me to live forever," he said. "I hate letting you down."

He stretched his arms above him, grimacing.

"It's gone, mostly," Appa said. "What's there to say? When I came back to work from the hospital, I couldn't lift a box without my head swimming. I could barely taste anything. It started coming back this year, slowly, but not fast enough. I was going to close the restaurant, you know. Before you woke up. How funny, right? Like the stars aligned, you come back right when I'm about to do it. You asked me to work here just a couple days before I was going to tell your mother and James."

I didn't have anything to say to this, or about the way he was watching me. My cup was burning the tips of my fingers. I took my hands off it.

"You should know," Appa said, "when you came in here and asked me if I was retiring, I was afraid you'd figured it out and were planning to tell me you wouldn't do it. That you'd decided enough was enough and you were going back to the city tomorrow. And I hoped, just like I did the first time you left, that maybe I'd done enough to make you miss us, miss the restaurant, and Fort Lee, and everything we have here. Just hoped, without thinking about anything or trying to come up with ways to stop you. Just hoped."

He nodded to himself, with a sadness to it that made my chest sink.

"I want you to know that I need you, Jack Jr.," he said. "No matter where you might be or how old you get. I'm always going to need you."

I'd finished my cup. "That's . . . ," I tried again. "Well, that's . . ."

I sank into my chair, and when my head was too heavy for my neck I put it down on the table and folded my arms around it, trying to shut out the noise. It started heavy and slow in the pit of my stomach, bubbling out. Ugly animal cries that shook my entire body. I felt the scrape of Appa's chair as he got up, the warmth of his hands on the back of my neck. I collapsed into him, putting my head against his stomach. I hadn't cried like this since I was a kid, so hard that I could barely breathe, aware somehow that the fifteen most consequential hours of my short, irreverent life thus far had finally, grindingly, come to a close and that nothing would ever be the same again. I didn't know how long I stayed there in his arms. Time was such a stupid fucking scam. I had wasted so much of it. There wasn't enough anymore to tell myself that I'd done it well, any of it. What's one guy against all of that? What's one guy to try to make sense of all of the things that don't?

12

UNCLE JJ LEARNS TO LET GO

THEY CAME SOLEMNLY, ONE BY ONE, THROUGH THE DOOR, WRAPPED IN coats, shaking snow from their boots. Umma, Appa, Juno, Noa lugging Sam's car seat in one hand. James took the car seat, placing it gently on the floor. We'd put together two tables in the center of the room and gathered the remaining chairs around it. I saw Appa's eyes flick to the bar, which we'd laid a split garbage bag over. The afternoon, less than twenty-four hours since we'd all been in here, was cold and getting colder. Christmas was coming. There would be salt on the roads soon, Santas ringing bells outside the Fort Lee municipal complex down the street. I checked my phone. Two hours to open. I saw in front of me that they were all sitting. James and I pulled out our chairs and joined them.

"Capitán," Juno said, bowing his head low, and was smacked on the back of his neck by his mother.

"Thank you," I said, "for coming."

"We all work here," Umma said.

"Thank you anyway," I told her. "For coming early. We have some things to talk about."

I could feel James's eyes on me from the side of my head.

"Or maybe, to start, I have some things to apologize for."

The table felt awfully empty without anything on it. I could sense the way they fidgeted with their hands, needing something to do. I was going to have to make this quick.

"I was being stupid last night," I said. "I embarrassed myself in front of Jo."

Umma had straightened her back, hearing me.

"Who is very nice," I said, "and who I hope can understand that I was, and still am, kind of crazy. Which is fine, because I know about it, and that's . . . that's better than nothing, right?"

She pressed her lips close together.

"I also completely screwed up the conversation you"—I looked at Juno—"wanted to have about school. I should've stuck up for you, and I didn't."

Juno hunched over his knees, looking at the ground.

"Lastly, I wrecked the bar," I said, "which . . . you know. I hurt the business. More importantly, I hurt the family. And I'm very, very sorry."

Appa kept his eyes down, on the center of the table. He raised a mittened hand to scratch at his nose.

"We're good," he said finally.

"Well, that's good news," I said, "this was going to be awkward if we weren't."

"H-Man's right," Juno said, "you still get a crazy pass for at least nine more months. A clean year."

"I'm sorry too," James said, catching everybody's attention.

"For . . . ," Noa said.

"For . . ." James looked at me. "What he said. As well. I'm sharing the blame."

Juno was watching him with a blank look on his face. I cleared my throat.

"Okay," I said, "so, we're both sorry, we're all in the open now. There are some things we have to talk about. The first being the TikTok stuff."

"So these videos," Umma said, "they're on your phone."

"They're on everybody's phone."

"They're on my phone?" Umma frowned. "Nobody sent them to me."

"What I mean is," I said, "they're on the internet. So if you wanted to find them, you could."

"I don't get it," Appa said.

"I know, and you can probably see why it was so easy to hide them from you, considering."

"Whatever," James said, "the videos are coming down. They made good marketing but we're not going to talk about what happened to Jack Jr. to get business. We have loyal customers. We have a presence in the neighborhood otherwise."

"So, Juno," I said, "do whatever that is. I don't know what you call it. Just get rid of the videos."

"Can I keep the account?"

"What do you mean?"

"I mean"—Juno took out his phone—"we've got a hundred thousand followers. It's not nothing. What if I did a video about how we're not posting about the restaurant anymore and just used the account for my own stuff?"

"What kind of stuff do you think we're going to let you post on there?" Noa said.

"You know," Juno said, "dances, memes, that kind of thing. You know how many people at my school would kill for a hundred thousand followers?"

"I don't care what happens after the videos come down," I said. "Just don't post about me anymore. And change the name."

"You know, somebody actually DM'd me last week asking if he

could pay me to take the name," Juno said, taking out his phone. "I've got it here somewhere. They're like a gay aquarium store in Fort Lauderdale. Literal fish daddies—"

"We're going to move on," I said. "Next, James and I talked, and we're going to hire some actual staff. Real staff. I'm not comfortable depending on all of you for that kind of thing anymore."

"We can't afford that," Appa said.

"We won't be able to afford it for about two months," James said, "but during that time we're raising prices, getting some more word out there, we'll do a proper reopening, invite a couple newspapers. We'll come around to it."

The table was silent.

"Good?" I asked. "Next thing. About hiring a staff, we can get going on steam for a while, but we can't do anything with the broken bar. So, I'm cashing out my old 401(k) to get it fixed."

I stood when the noise came from all ends of the table.

"It's my fault," I said, putting up my hands. "It needs to be fixed. I'm doing this for us."

"Jack Jr."—Appa had gotten to his feet—"you're going to need that money."

"I need it right now," I said. "I made it working a dumb job in the city that I only realized after the fact made me miserable. I'm putting it toward something I have a stake in."

"But—"

"Appa," I said, smiling, "I know what I'm doing. I've been looking all this time for a way to step up to do what you're asking me to do."

"And what's that?"

"You're asking me to take this over for you, to own a business. But you know what that means, right? You know that means you need to let us do it our way, don't you? That's what you meant to do by retiring, isn't it?"

Appa opened his mouth but caught Umma's eye. She raised her shoulders.

"What's your big brilliant response to that, Jack Sr.?" she asked him.

"Besides," I said, "we don't have another option."

"Well . . ." Juno trailed off. "There's eighty thousand dollars earmarked on the internet exactly for this kind of thing."

James and I traded a glance. Slowly, he nodded.

"That money's already spoken for," I said. "And it's not going to the restaurant. Not a cent of it, actually."

Umma's eyes darted between the three of us. James folded his hands together on the tabletop.

"We're putting it away to earn some interest. And in a year's time," he said, "we're going to give it to you."

Everyone turned in the direction he faced, looking at Juno, who was leaning down to scroll through something on his phone. He glanced up.

"What?"

"To you, Juno." Umma sighed. "They're giving it to you."

Juno frowned. "To me?"

James looked at him for a long time, and I saw, glancing down, that his hands were holding tight to each other.

"We're giving it to you so that you can pay for college," James said.

Juno shook his head slightly. His lips moved against each other in exactly the same way James's did.

"That's not funny," he said solemnly.

"I'll tell you what's not funny," James said. "The fact that you've been asking me to hear you, all this time, and I wouldn't. And I let it go so far that you've given up on me."

Juno's face was blank. I realized that he couldn't think of something to say. We were silent a full minute.

"Squared away," I said, looking around at them. "Right? Anything we missed?"

James cleared his throat, standing up. "We've got to open soon. Appa, there's something in the fridge we didn't know—"

"Everybody." Juno raised his voice over the whine of our chair legs being pushed backward. He rubbed his hands together.

"I want to say," Juno said, "that this is really nice, but I don't need all of that money. I'm—if I get in—going to a state school. That's if I'm lucky."

"We have time to figure that out," Noa said, "they want to leave you options."

"That doesn't matter," Juno said, "I'm not letting you use all of that money on me. It's too much. I wouldn't feel right."

"It's for you, Juno," James said.

"Well, can it not be *totally* for me?" Juno said. "I mean, fuck, that's a lot of pressure. On top of now going to college, I have to work as hard as I can to get into the best possible school?"

"That's generally what people do, yes."

"I won't do it," Juno said, trying to stand straighter, though he towered over everybody there except Appa and James. "You're going to have to think of something else to do with . . . half. I'm saying half. Fix the sushi bar. Get a new fridge. Or better yet, hire the staff you want right now and not dig yourself into the ground—"

"Juno."

"I'm only saying it because I might not even go. We're not even decided on whether it would be the best option and I don't like being put in the position of—"

"Just"—I raised my hand—"shut up. Say thank you."

Juno looked around at the rest of us. The rest of us, each one of us, stared back, knowing exactly how to do it without even realizing. Another few moments passed. His shoulders, once firm, sank an inch.

"Thank you," he said numbly.

I breathed a sigh of relief.

"That was nice. I feel good. I have nothing left to say."

Umma put her arm around Juno, looking at me. And I realized, looking back, that I'd been waiting a long time to see her smile.

WE WERE A FOOT ONTO the Bruckner Expressway when a boro taxi barreled past us, going sixty, maybe sixty-five. I'm only guessing since I'd braked so hard to avoid it that my head hit the front curve of my steering wheel with a smack like fireworks behind my eyes. I wasn't much for thought afterward. Juno, who was sitting to my right holding a Styrofoam pallet of oysters we couldn't get secure with tape in the back, let out a bark of a laugh that cracked the air. I swore, guiding us out and onto the shoulder. "Oh my God," I sighed, breathing, clutching at my head, "oh my God, it hurts. What the fuck was that?"

"That was cold," Juno said, rolling down his window, putting his head out. "MOTHERFUCKER! WE'LL KILL YOU!"

I yanked him back inside, holding my head. I was trying at the present moment not to puke. I took deep breaths, bringing myself back down. A welt had raised itself horizontally on my forehead. I brought the dash mirror down, peering at it. It was not yet five in the morning and we had just acclimated to the blasting heat coming through the vents. The market today had been as busy as we'd ever seen it. Even early, we'd fought a truck for space near the end of the parking lot.

"I'm okay," I said, nodding as though trying to convince myself, "I'm okay."

"Do you want me to drive?"

"Don't. You'll kill us."

"I've been in this van since I was a baby," Juno said. "I was birthed in this van. I can drive this van same as you."

"You absolutely weren't. Just stop talking."

Christmas was a week away. We'd be open every day of the week except Christmas Eve, through to the end of the year. I wasn't complaining. There wasn't actually much James let me do, apart from being there to cut the fish, and meeting and training the new kitchen porter and hostess we'd hired so that Zeno could work at the bar with me. Three weeks in, we weren't drowning in cash, but we weren't drowning either. James had told me it might even serve us to close one day a week. I didn't actually know how much he put through a filter before telling me, wondering if he did the same for Appa, but it didn't mean I didn't appreciate it, whatever it was.

My head had stopped spinning. I'd come out earlier than usual this morning to try some hot options in the kitchen before anybody got there. A hot menu was going to make better use of the kitchen in the back. I'd thought of the kimchi jjigae Appa had taught me to make, maybe japchae, something we could habitually throw surplus produce into.

Juno had become engrossed in something on his phone.

"I'm okay," I said, "thanks for checking on me."

"You scared me there, Uncle JJ," Juno said. "I'd be stranded out here with two hundred pounds of raw fish flesh on the highway if you died."

"I thought you said you could drive."

"Oh, I can," Juno said. "But I'd be *paralyzed* with grief. Can't imagine it, actually."

I eased us back onto the expressway, headed for home.

"Would you eat ramen if we served it?" I asked him.

"Surprisingly Japanese thing to do, Uncle JJ," he said. "Sushi and ramen's kind of their territory, no?"

"It doesn't have to be Japanese," I said. "I could make tteokbokki, budae jjigae, something like that."

"I know what you should do," Juno said, "you should put a TV in there and play K-pop videos all night long. I've seen barbecue places that do that kind of thing. It's fucking deafening. But it makes you hungrier."

"Explain to me how that makes you hungrier."

"I don't know, just jump-starts your adrenaline or something," Juno said. "Think about it. Make the place a little cooler, hipper."

"We have no space for a TV except above the bar. It'd be like a frat dive."

"Explain that word to me: *frat dive*."

Half an hour later, we loaded the last of the pallets into the fridge. He stretched his arms above his head, yawning, and climbed onto the nearest bar seat to rest his head on his jacket.

"I can drive you home to get some more sleep," I told him.

"I'm okay," he mumbled. "We're not doing anything in class."

He had, in fact, earned the extra points on his chemistry final for a lens that Dr. Cappiano said had proved itself the best in the class. He'd been talking about it for the past week and had resigned himself, along with the rest of his classmates and, evidently, his teachers, to a full downhill coast to the end of December.

"Breakfast?" I asked.

"Make me something you wanted to put on the hot menu," he said.

"What do you want?"

He pursed his lips, turning his head to be able to see me. "Kimchi jjigae."

I dried my hands on the front of my shirt. He'd closed his eyes and was fighting to stay with me, clearly. I smiled.

"Come to the back with me," I said, "I'll show you."

I expected him to complain, but he pulled himself up and followed me through the doors. I set him up a cutting board with the jarred kimchi Umma had dropped off and started with a pot of water. I talked him through it while steam filled the air, warming our faces and fingers.

"Sugar," he repeated after me, frowning.

"Every jjigae contains sugar," I said. "Otherwise it's a mess of vinegar and salt. A spoonful. Tablespoon. That one."

He stirred, observing the simmering crimson liquid.

"Can I ask you something, Uncle JJ?"

I was packing away the mess he'd made at the cutting board. "Yes."

He hesitated.

"He hasn't . . . talked to you lately, has he?"

I turned around, facing the wall. "Why do you always ask about him, Juno?"

Juno took a while to answer, humming something over the hiss of the steam.

"I like him," he said. "I want to know when he's going to forgive you."

I joined him at the stove, taking the spoon from him. Just about done. I killed the heat and continued stirring.

"I left him ten messages," I said, "he won't answer."

"You could go to his house," Juno said.

"Am I a serial killer?"

"I'm just saying, there are ways."

The soup had stopped bubbling and was giving off sheets of steam. I brought out two bowls, splitting it equally.

"He doesn't want me, Juno. There's nothing I can do about that."

"But—"

"Let me propose something to you." I gave him his bowl. "If he ever changes his mind, you'll be the first to know. Until then . . ."

Juno held his breakfast in both hands. "Sorry," he said.

I didn't say anything, leading him out of the kitchen to a table, where we sat. We dug in, burning our mouths. I brought over leftover rice from the night before.

"Good?" I asked him.

"Really good."

"What would you pay for jjigae like this?"

"Ten."

"There's at least four dollars' worth of pork belly in there."

"Twelve?"

I considered it for a moment, realizing I didn't know what I was talking about.

"I'll ask your dad. His job, anyway."

We watched the snow fall through the glass in the door, cars trailing black behind them on the road.

"I . . . um—added another school yesterday," Juno said.

"Where?"

"SUNY," Juno said, "New Paltz. Up the river."

He looked cautiously at me for a reaction.

"How far up the river?"

"An hour, two hours."

"Juno."

"It's far," Juno said, "almost too far."

"You've got to be joking," I said. "You're going to run out of schools in the tri-state area one day. What will you do then?"

"Massachusetts," Juno said, "one state over."

"You should be looking farther."

"I'm looking far enough," he said, draining his bowl. "Why are you so mad at me?"

"You're only doing this to stay close," I told him. "I've told you, your parents have told you, everybody's told you to go wherever you want to go and we'll make it work for you."

He stared down at his empty bowl. "We'll talk about it later," he said. "You're weird."

"You need a life outside of us," I said. "You're going to regret staying around here. You do so much growing out there, Juno, you become the person you want to be."

"So . . . what?" He hadn't taken his eyes off the table, refusing to meet mine. "What if I have everything I want?"

"You don't know what you want."

He opened his mouth to argue but met my eyes, finally. He made several attempts at something he was trying to stump me with but couldn't do it. It reminded me of the way James had looked at me that night, afraid of me, somehow. Afraid of how I made him feel. Afraid to just be a fucking person. Was it so hard? Was it really worth all of the strife?

"I'll come back," he said softly. "I will. I promise."

"Don't make a promise like that," I told him. "You'll regret it."

He snorted, fixing his eyes on the snow outside, but I knew. I stood, crossing over to his side of the table, and stooped over him, putting my arms around his head.

"Stop it," I said.

He shook his head. "Soup was too fucking spicy."

I smiled into the mop of his hair. He made me all right, always. Always.

ANOTHER TWENTY-THREE MONTHS LATER

13

THAT MOTHERFUCKING BUS

THIS IS HOW YOU MAKE TAMAGO. AND I'M NOT TALKING ABOUT THE cheapy, stringy omelet-type stuff you find on supermarket teriyaki bowls or cooked to gray hell and rolled into kimbap alongside pickled radish and slivers of beef. You're thinking of a close cousin, the low-effort tamagoyaki slopped together in any American kitchen. I'm talking real atsuyaki tamago, baby; a real, honest-to-God, thousand-year-old kind of work of art requiring years of patience, discipline, and the utmost, elite training. Halfway between an omelet and a savory loaf of bread. I'm getting distracted. Here's how it goes: Crack eggs, cull extraneous whites, collect in bowl; season kera-nabe with oil and heat slowly, over low flame; in mortar, pulverize equal parts sweet shrimp and fluke, and temper with flour until adequate gluten formation renders a gluelike paste, easily workable; combine with eggs; fry over same low flame with patience, compassion, fanatical, near-sociopathic adherence; flip, cut into portions, serve over rice. I'd been to a place in the city that shielded the taste of their mediocre atsuyaki tamago with a custom fry brand that burned the restaurant's logo into the crust. As a result I saw several patrons, while there, try to use their final course of omakase as a sponge to wipe their fingers.

I mean, at least they tried. In two years I haven't served tamago because I still don't fucking know how to make it. I've watched the Eater New York video on YouTube about it a hundred times but haven't yet produced a specimen adequately separating itself from a sad, runny, cold piece of scrambled egg on rice. And certainly nowhere near how Appa used to make it. The thing was a mystic art. I, a mortal, was not bound to this knowledge, and two years later, I was okay with it. I served tteok at the end of the meal, a seasonal variety I ordered from a bake shop in Leonia run entirely by old ladies disappointed in the high level of my American assimilation. People loved the colors, the sweet black sesame jam in the center. Even the Midtown banker fuckheads who came over the river to visit their families and take them out for sushi could be won over by a slice of it at the end of their meal. I didn't dare try to make it myself. I wasn't primed for disappointment like that anymore.

I was alone in the kitchen, making soup. I liked making soup for myself on Monday afternoons, the first day back after the Sunday off, the first dinner service with the cleanest cuts from the morning fish run.

Things always looked so clean on Mondays. They wouldn't be in for another hour, the two kitchen porters, the engineering major at Stevens currently seating and waiting tables. She was going back to class and cutting down to twice a week soon. James had mentioned dropping by with some résumés to cull this weekend. I'd put out dinner for the team around four, probably something with the salmon in the back of my drawer up at the bar, but was feeling something hot for myself, having skipped lunch. The soup, soondubu with shrimp and mussels, was bubbling away, red chili vapor floating up and clearing my sinuses while I watched my pot. I reached into my back pocket and found my phone, linking the speakers out in the dining room. The music filtered in through the doors sparingly.

A text came in from James.

Mailed check for January rent. Statement coming later this week. Tnx.

Noa says u want more prunes?

He picked up when I called.

"I'm at HanNam Mart."

"When have I ever asked you to buy me prunes? Am I ninety?"

"They're good for you."

"Lots of things are good for me."

"Sam likes prunes."

"Sam can have my prunes. Tell him they're on me. Wait, do you eat prunes?"

"I'm almost forty, Jack Jr., they help me shit."

I cut the stove and moved my pot out of the heat. "Do they really work?"

"Swear to God."

"If you were to get me a jar—"

"Bags. They come in bags."

I didn't want to dirty a spoon from the clean stores, so I brought along the ladle I'd used to stir and carried the pot out through the doors and to a table, securing it on top of an extra apron.

"Get me a bag."

"I told you Noa's right."

I didn't answer, taking a tentative sip of the boiling broth. "Doctor okay this morning?"

"No change," James said. "Cholesterol's down."

"That counts as a change. Good change."

James made a noise through the phone that didn't seem to connote either agreement or disagreement.

"I'll leave the prunes in your fridge. Later."

I lowered my phone, disgusted. "Later. Fuckin' boomer."

It had been snowing earlier in the day but had since faded to wet rain. I was sitting at the farthermost table, able to see through the door out onto the street. I brought the ladle to my mouth, blowing steam.

THERE WERE TWO GUYS ON what seemed like a second or third date late in the service that night. They sat at the far left end of the bar and spoke loudly enough for me to hear them at all times. The Asian one asked if we had cocktails, which we didn't. The white one wanted to know everything I planned to serve for the omakase.

"It's probably easier," I told him, "if you let me know what you don't like."

"I can't eat anything really *fishy*. You know?"

"Okay," I said without moving a single muscle in my face. "Fishy. Tuna?"

"I like tuna. I like spicy tuna."

"I can make you a roll."

"Can we get two, please?" the Asian one piped in. "We love spicy tuna."

I smiled. Behind me, our ticket machine chirped, signaling two more Grubhub orders.

"You guys on a date?"

They looked at each other funny, then nodded.

"We're finishing a date," the white one said. "Two-day date. I stayed so long we said, let's just get dinner too."

The Asian one made a cross between a laugh and a cough. I hated them. And wondered at the same time whether either had plans tonight.

"This is everything," the Asian one said to the white one. "I *love* sitting at the bar."

I put out two bowls for the juk we served to start, turning away

from them, marveling at the stamina required to make adorable conversation after marathon sex.

"Tea?" I asked them. They nodded.

"Have you been working here long?" the white one asked.

"Little over two years," I said. "My dad owned the place before me."

"That's amazing," he said. "He must be really proud of you."

I wondered how old he thought I was, given that I would've probably asked to see their IDs if they ordered sake. My stomach prick-
led a little, an aftershock of the soup. I thought of the prunes. The
white one's date had evidently picked up on what was happening,
since he'd stopped talking to me and was turned ninety degrees in
his seat to face his date full-on. I slipped away, collecting a check left
at the other end of the bar.

"JJ."

My server passed me a wooden board I used to plate sashimi
from the foremost table.

"Thanks."

"I'm really sorry," she said, "I think my mom's been calling my
phone. Would it be okay if I took it outside?"

"Go out the back," I said, nudging my head over my shoulder.
"Remember to use that stick out there to prop the door."

"You're a lifesaver."

I brought the board to the sink to rinse. Behind me, the door
clattered open.

"Give me a second," I said, peering into the kitchen, where my
porters were talking discreetly while mopping. I turned around.
"How many?"

He'd already sat at the bar, at the seat two away from the end.
His hair was long, longer, curled about his ears. He looked around at
the place and put up one finger.

The sink was still running. I reached behind me, fumbling with
the faucet, and shut it off. Juno's playlist, a new one this month,
echoed on over our heads.

I could only tell he smiled at me because of the slight divots that appeared in his beard when he did.

"I tried to make a reservation," Emil said after a long while. "Your OpenTable kept crashing."

Gradually, the sound of my breathing returned, filling the air.

"We've been hearing that," I said. "We're looking into it."

He looked a little sorry. For something, I didn't know what.

"So . . ."

"Yeah." I jolted myself further awake. "Oh, yeah. No—I mean—" I broke off, setting down the rag I'd been twisting into knots in my hand. I stepped around the bar, meeting him on his side. "Jesus . . . Hey."

He opened his arms and covered me, smelling like soap.

"What the fuck, Emil?"

"I'm sorry"—his laugh boomed in my ears—"I thought I'd surprise you. I'm sorry."

He let me go, fumbling with his coat. I nodded, the first three responses I had to this failing in my throat. I crossed over, back to my side of the bar. "Wow. You—you look good."

"Thank you," he said, "you too. I always liked this shirt you wear. Official."

"I wear one out about once a month. There's a cardboard box with a hundred others in the back."

"New sign out front," he said.

"Since last year," I told him.

"And the walls," he said.

"Painted. James did it."

"How is he?"

I had the forethought to pour his glass of water. "He's good. We're good. I don't know, we're getting older. You're . . . thirty-four."

"I'm thirty-four, yes." He nodded, smiling. "I'm happy about it."

"No you're not."

"I am," he said. "I'm out of the night shift, I make myself tea, bed by ten-thirty. Sometimes I even dream. It's a good life."

We were still for a moment. My server had returned from the kitchen and started her tour of the empty tables with a rag.

"You're . . ." I trailed off. "You're thinking . . . omakase?"

"What else?"

"I mean, we've got a deep fryer in the back now. We could do some chicken fingers for you."

"Funny," he said, "extremely funny. Do you remember the last time you served me dinner? I said—"

"Sea leech in vodka and cream," I finished for him.

"Give me your best shot," Emil said, grinning. "Add every supplement you've got in there. Black truffle, Wagyu. A thousand dollars. Swindle me."

"You're making some money now, are you?"

"Define 'some money.'"

He glanced down at his lap, shy. He watched me plate the first three pieces of sashimi for the couple, sipping water only.

"You're still out on that cliff," I said. "In the basement."

"I moved, actually," he said, "farther inland. Closer to the hospital."

"Sounds smart."

"I miss the pizza," he said.

"They've got pizza everywhere. There's pizza next door."

"I was wondering." He turned his head toward the street. "That new?"

"They give us their leftover garlic knots. Good guys, working there."

I started him out with the juk.

"How's everybody?" he asked. "How are your parents?"

"Not working anymore," I said, gesturing behind me. "I think they're going to live a lot longer for it. Juno's back at school. Fordham."

"No fucking way," Emil said, smiling. "That's incredible."

"He's happy."

"He's back here a lot?"

"Every other week, seriously," I said. "Enough already. Get back out there, have sex, do drugs, do something. He won't."

I worked him through the sashimi, a leg of snow crab, and the squid. He ate slowly, supplementing with ginger after each course.

His first nigiri was the fluke that we'd gotten in from the new vendor starting last month. Plated tight with a shiso leaf between it and the rice. I placed it in front of him. "With your fingers," I said. He did as told, closing his eyes.

"Jesus."

The couple at the other end of the bar were staring into each other's eyes and eating their neat little spicy tuna rolls. I brought over the teapot and filled a cup.

"How are you?" I asked him.

"Good. Work's good. I . . ." He trailed off. "I've got a little . . . side job."

"What's up?"

"It's the . . . it's a theater in the city. They've put on some big shows in the past. The last Mamet play. I've been reading submissions there for the past year."

I smiled at him. "You did it."

"*You* did it," he told me. "I never would've . . ."

We'd arrived at something neither of us wanted to talk about, so I spoke again.

"Anything good so far?"

"It's brutal," he said. "We get hundreds a week. Usually nobody but me reading them. The one out of fifty I'll send up, polite rejection two weeks later."

Salmon next, dotted with yuzu jam.

"Do you like it?"

"Unbelievable," he said, shaking his head. "It keeps me alive. I've seen, like, a hundred shows. We get comped tickets all over the city. Our productions too. Greg Kinnear reserved two tickets and never picked them up last week."

He paused over the salmon.

"Holy fuck."

He said this a decibel too loud, attracting the attention of the couple.

"Do you . . . ," he said. "Can I ask for seconds?"

"Are you hungry enough?"

"Probably."

I made him another. He slapped his fist down on the table, chewing. The couple paid their tab and left, holding hands. Near ten now.

"I'm glad you applied again," I said.

He nodded, pausing a moment. "It's kept me sane."

"Sane is good. Along with sleep, probably the best things for you out there."

He ate the snapper, mackerel, chu-toro, and uni, ready faster than I could make the next one. I cleaned up his area, waving my server over. "I'll close out tonight. Go home."

Emil watched me, smiling, while I ran a wet towel over the length of the bar. I brought him the tteok, pink and in the shape of a rose, another one for myself. He held out his, pinched between his two fingers, and we tapped them together, then popped them in our mouths at the same time.

"You did a great job here," he said after a while. "You must be doing okay if you can afford to fire your family."

"Business is . . . better," I said. "Not a hundred percent, but we're hoping."

He was smiling at me. "If I remember correctly, you said this whole thing was going to be 'temporary,' way back when."

"I did," I said. "And it still is."

"I don't believe you."

"Yeah, probably can't sell that story anymore," I said.

The porters had said good night and left the kitchen dark. We'd outstayed everybody tonight. Emil had been staring down at his hands for a while now.

"I owe you an apology," he said.

"For?"

He leaned backward slowly. "For the way it ended."

I'd wiped down our sides of the bar at least five times and had run out of things to do with my hands. "That wasn't your fault."

"Not entirely," he said, "but half, yeah."

He gave a sigh.

"I was embarrassed," he said. "I wanted to call, or text, to come by here even, and I tried, so many times. I just couldn't. I didn't want to face you. I was afraid of what you'd say."

He clenched his fists shut on the table.

"I'd never hurt you."

I came over to his side, sitting on the stool next to his. "You never have," I told him. "You were right. I wasn't ready. I was a mess."

"There's nothing wrong with mess," he said.

"Nothing wrong with it, but some people deserve more than mess," I said. Dim orange lights shone down above our heads. "I'm good now."

"You look like it," Emil said.

I smiled sadly. "So you just came tonight to be nice to me?"

He waited a while before speaking.

"Because I missed you."

I nodded silently. Closing time. I was afraid to touch him. It didn't seem right anymore, between us. He watched as I stood. "Want to close out with me?"

He agreed. We stacked the chairs together, closed up the kitchen and the back door. He followed me out onto the street and waited while I locked up. I turned to him, shivering slightly, on account of the wind.

"How are you getting home?"

"I walk," I said. "The van breathed its last in the summer."

Emil put his hand over his heart. "Absent friends."

"You're walking too?"

"Bus stop, two blocks down."

We had run out of things to say. His hair was being whipped about, and his coat was too thin. I thought of waiting with him for the bus, wondering if I could find something else to talk about in that time.

"Shit," he said suddenly, "I didn't even pay."

"I wouldn't have let you."

"Jack—"

"Emil," I said, putting up my hand, "you eat for free here. Always."

He seemed to know I'd made up my mind and shut himself up. We stood a few feet apart.

"Thanks for coming," I said.

"Thanks for . . . feeding me," he said.

We laughed. He opened his arms and I hugged him.

"I'll call you?" he asked. "Maybe see the family for lunch someday?"

"They'd love that."

He took a step backward, away from me.

"I'll see you around, Jack Jr."

He turned first, going down the street to the bus stop. I watched him go for a while, withstanding the cold, then went my own way. Wind whipped around my legs, biting my ankles. It was only a matter of time before it would be warm again. James and I had been thinking of putting out some tables on the sidewalk in the summer. We had room for it. Some umbrellas, maybe some planters. Might be nice. Something to look forward to, once the cold had let up. I crossed the street, continuing down.

It occurred to me that I hadn't told him that I missed him too. He'd said it the way you said something you were hoping would be reciprocated. I'd stood there and let him say it and said nothing back. I wondered if he was thinking about it now, walking down the street, farther and farther away from me.

It was a peculiar thing, to become aware of something that felt obvious, realizing that for all the time you might have spent with it, it still might have escaped you. It wasn't sad, though some might have thought it sounded sad. I didn't think so. I was never sad, or not for very long, anymore. There was too much life going on to be sad, or rather, to be sad and not to do something about it. Something like—

I turned around at the end of the block and, peering into the dark, finally saw it in the distance. Saw, just about swallowed up by the evening haze, the bus, lowering itself down on its spring wheels, opening its doors, letting Emil Cuddy climb aboard, and driving away.

"Jesus Christ." I let out an exasperated sigh. "That motherfucking bus—"

I started to run.

ACKNOWLEDGMENTS

A second book is a very strange thing. I am more familiar with the steps one must take along the awkward and unnatural path to publication. And while the second time around has had its share of challenges, I have learned to make some more space for joy. I wrote *I Leave It Up to You* partly to remind myself of that joy, in writing and in life.

To my husband, Bram McGinnis, who read this novel first: I wrote it while falling in love with you. This is yours, forever.

To Danielle Bukowski, who read this novel second: Thank you for believing in me.

To Danny Hertz, who read this novel third: Thank you for your impeccable taste and enormous vision. And for the Japan recommendations.

To Jesse Shuman, who read this novel last: Thank you for your patience, wisdom, and friendship. I'm happy to report: I am working on the next one.

To the rest of the Ballantine and Random House team—Jam Rorsoongnern, Kelly Chian, Aja Pollock, Michael Morris, Taylor Noel, Emma Thomasch, Emily Isayeff, Kara Cesare, Jennifer Hershey, Kim Hovey, and Kara Welsh—thank you for this beautiful book.

To the writers and friends who lent advance praise to this novel— Gabrielle Zevin, Bryan Washington, Crystal Hana Kim, Grant Ginder, Gina Chung, Grace D. Li, Isle McElroy, Jimin Han, Mateo Askaripour, and Rafael Frumkin—thank you for your words.

To the local sushi restaurants that fed, educated, and inspired me—Tokyo Sushi of Montgomery, NJ; the Market Fair Teriyaki Boy of Princeton, NJ; Sakura Express of Princeton, NJ; Tomo Sushi of Princeton, NJ; the Epicurean sushi bar of Georgetown University, Washington, DC; Kintaro of Washington, DC; Sushi Taro of Washington, DC; Ki Sushi (East Flatbush) of Brooklyn, NY; Hatsuhana of New York, NY; Suram (Upper West Side) of New York, NY; Mari.ne of New York, NY; and Daigo Hand Roll Bar of Brooklyn, NY: Thank you, and I'll be back.

To my One Story family—Patrick Ryan, Hannah Tinti, Maribeth Batcha, and Lena Valencia—thank you for seeing a writer in me.

To my beautiful friends—Lizzie Jones, Richa Rai, Reena Shah, Megan Kamalei Kakimoto, Madeline Garfinkle, Sam Granoff, Ben Costanza, Max Hartley, Taylor Crotty, Edward Crotty, Benny Weisman, Jane Mikus, Max Chisholm, Daniel Breland, Katherine Richardson, Danny Smith, Megan O'Brien, Danny O'Brien, Ben Germano, Ashwin Puri, Lilyan Tay, Nihir Parikh, Arielle Thomas, Josh Ben-Ami, Emily Rowe, Kristen Fedor, Jess Kelham-Hohler, and Enushé Khan: Thank you for the good times.

To my family—my brother, Jingu, my Umma and my Appa: Thank you for being my home.

ABOUT THE AUTHOR

JINWOO CHONG is the author of the novels *I Leave It Up to You* and *Flux,* a *New York Times* Editors' Choice. His short stories and other work have appeared in *The Southern Review, Guernica, The Rumpus, Literary Hub, Chicago Quarterly Review,* and *Electric Literature*. He received an MFA in fiction from Columbia University and lives in New York.

jinwoochong.com
X: @jinwoochong
Instagram: @jinwoochong